Forrest House

A novel

Mary Jane Holmes

CONTENTS

CHAPTER I

TWO LETTERS

The first, a small half-sheet, inclosed in a large thick envelope, and addressed in a childish, unformed hand to Mr. James Everard Forrest, Junior, Ellicottville, Berkshire County, Massachusetts, with a request in the lower left-hand corner for the postmaster to forward immediately; the second, a dainty little perfumed missive, with a fanciful monogram, directed in a plain round hand to J. Everard Forrest, Esq., Ellicottville, Mass., with the words "in haste" written in the corner. Both letters were in a hurry, and both found their way together to a brown-haired, brown-eyed, brown-faced young man, who sat under the shadow of the big maple tree on the Common in Ellicottville, lazily puffing his cigar and fanning himself with his Panama hat, for the thermometer was ninety in the shade, and the hour A. M. of a sultry July day. At first it was almost too much exertion to break the seals, and for a moment J. Everard Forrest, Jr., toyed with the smaller envelope of the two, and studied the handwriting.

"I may as well see what Josey wants of me in haste," he said at last, and breaking the seal, he read:

"Holburton, July 15.

"Dear Ned: You must come to-morrow on the four o'clock train. Everything has gone at sixes and sevens, for just at the very last Mrs. Murdock, who has been dying for twenty years or more, must really die, and the Murdock boys can't act, so you must take the character of the bridegroom in the play where I am to be the bride. You will have very little to say. You can learn it all in fifteen minutes, but you must come to-morrow so as to rehearse with us once at least. Now, don't you dare fail. I shall meet you at the station.

"Yours lovingly,
"Josephine Fleming.

"P. S.—Do you remember I wrote you in my last of a Dr. Matthewson, who has been in town a few days stopping at the hotel? He has consented to be the priest on condition that you are the bridegroom, so do not fail me.

Again, with love, Joe."

"And so this is my lady's great haste," the young man said, as he finished reading the letter. "She wants me for her bridegroom, and I don't know but I'm willing, so I guess I'll have to go; and now for Rossie's interesting document, which must be 'forwarded immediately.' I only wish it may prove to have money in it from the governor, for I am getting rather low."

So saying he took the other letter and examined it carefully, while a smile broke over his face as he continued:

"Upon my word, Rossie did not mean this to go astray, and has written everything out in full, even to Massachusetts and Junior. Good for her. But how crooked; why, that junior stands at an angle of several degrees above the Mr. Rossie ought to do better. She must be nearly thirteen; but she's a nice little girl, and I'll see what she says."

What she said was as follows:

"Forrest House, July 14th.
"Mr. Everard Forrest:

"Dear Sir:—Nobody knows I am writing to you, but your mother has been worse for a few days, and keeps talking about you even in her sleep. She did not say send for you, but I thought if you knew how bad she was, you would perhaps come home for a part of your vacation. It will do her so much good to see you. I am very well and your father too. So no more at present.

"Yours respectfully,
"Rosamond Hastings.

"P. S.—Miss Beatrice Belknap has come home from New York, and had the typhoid fever, and lost every speck of her beautiful hair. You don't know how funny she looks! She offered me fifty dollars for mine to make her a wig, because it curls naturally, and is just her color, but I would not sell it for the world: would you? Inclosed find ten dollars of my very own money, which I send you to come home with, thinking you might need it. Do not fail to come, will you?

"Rosamond"

Everard read this letter twice, and smoothed out the crisp ten-dollar bill, which was carefully wrapped in a separate bit of paper. It was not the first time he had received money in his sore need from the girl, for in a blank-book, which he always carried in his pocket, were several entries, as follows: "Jan. 2, from Rosamond Hastings, five dollars: March th, two dollars: June th, one dollar," and so on until the whole amount was more than twenty dollars, but never before had she sent him so large a sum as now, and there was a moisture in his eyes and his breath came heavily as he put it away in his purse, and said:

"There never was so unselfish a creature as Rossie Hastings. She is always thinking of somebody else. And I am a mean, contemptible dog to take her money as I do; but then, I honestly intend to pay her back tenfold when I have something of my own."

Thus reassuring himself, he put his purse in his pocket, and glancing again at Rossie's letter his eye fell upon Miss Belknap's name, and he laughed aloud as he said: "Poor bald Bee Belknap. She must look comical. I can imagine how it hurts her pride. Buy Rossie's hair, indeed! I should think not, when that is her only beauty, if I except her eyes, which are too large for her thin face; but that will round out in time, and Rossie may be a beauty yet, though not like Josey; no, never like Josey."

And that brought the young man back to Miss Fleming's letter, and its imperative request. Could he comply with it now? Ought he not to go at once to the sick mother, who was missing him so sadly, and who had made all the happiness he had ever known at home? Duty said yes, but inclination drew him to Holburton and the fair Josephine, with whom he believed himself to be and with whom he was, perhaps, as much in love as any young man of twenty well can be. Perhaps Rossie had been unduly alarmed; at all events, if his mother were so very sick, his father would write, of course, and on the whole he believed he should go to Holburton by the afternoon train, and then, perhaps, go home.

And so the die was cast, and the young man walked to the telegraph office and sent across the wires to Miss Josephine Fleming the three words: "I will come."

CHAPTER II

DR. MATTHEWSON

The train from Ellicottville was late that afternoon. In fact, its habit was to be late, but on this particular day it was more than usually behind time, and the one stage which Holburton boasted had waited more than half an hour at the little station of the out-of-the-way town which lies nestled among the Berkshire hills, just on the boundary line between the Empire State and Massachusetts. The day was hot even for midsummer, and the two fat, motherly matrons who sat in the depot alternately inveighed against the heat and wiped their glowing faces, while they watched and discussed the young lady who, on the platform outside, was walking up and down, seeming wholly unconscious of their espionage. But it was only seeming, for she knew perfectly well that she was an object of curiosity and criticism, and more than once she paused in her walk and turning squarely round faced the two old ladies in order to give them a better view, and let them see just how many tucks, and ruffles and puffs there were in her new dress, worn that day for the first time. And a very pretty picture Josephine Fleming made standing there in the sunshine, looking so artless and innocent, as if no thought of herself had ever entered her mind. She was a pink-and-white blonde, with masses of golden hair rippling back from her forehead, and those dreamy blue eyes of which poets sing, and which have in them a marvelous power to sway the sterner sex by that pleading, confiding expression, which makes a man very tender towards the helpless creature appealing so innocently to him for protection.

3

The two old ladies did not like Josephine, though they admitted that she was very beautiful and stylish, in her blue muslin and white chip hat with the long feather drooping low behind, too pretty by far and too much of the fine lady, they said, for a daughter of the widow Roxie Fleming, who lived in the brown house on the Common, and sewed for a living when she had no boarders from the city. And then, as the best of women will sometimes do, they picked the girl to pieces, and talked of the scandalous way she had of flirting with every man in town, of her airs and indolence, which they called laziness, and wondered if it were true that poor old Agnes, her half-sister, made the young lady's bed, and mended her clothes, and waited upon her generally as if she were a princess, and toiled, and worked, and went without herself, that Josey might be clothed in dainty apparel, unbecoming to one in her rank of life. And then they wondered next if it were true, as had been rumored, that she was engaged to that young Forrest from Amherst College, who had boarded at the brown house for a few weeks the previous summer, and been there so often since.

"A well-mannered chap as you would wish to see," one of them said, "with a civil word for high and low, and a face of which any mother might be proud; only——" and here the speaker lowered her voice, as she continued: "Only he does look a little fast, for no decent-behaved boy of twenty ought to have such a tired, fagged look as he has, and they do say there were some great carousin's at Widder Fleming's last summer, which lasted up to midnight, and wine was carried in by Agnes, and hot coffee made as late as eleven, and if you'll b'leve it"—here the voice was a whisper—"they had a pack of cards, for Miss Murdock saw them with her own eyes, and young Forrest handled them as if used to the business."

"Cards! That settles it!" was repeated by the second woman, with a shake of the head, which indicated that she knew all she cared to know of Everard Forrest, but her friend, who was evidently better posted in the gossip of the town, went on to add that "people said young Forrest was an only son, and that his father was very rich, and lived in a fine old place somewhere west or south, and had owned negroes in Kentucky before the war, and was a copperhead, and very close and proud, and kept colored help, and would not like it at all if he knew how his son was flirting with Josephine Fleming."

Then they talked of the expected entertainment at the Village Hall the following night, the proceeds of which were to go toward buying a fire-engine, which the people greatly needed. And Josephine was to figure in most everything, and they presumed she was now waiting for some chap to come on the train.

For once they were right in their conjecture. She was waiting for Everard Forrest, and when the train came in he stepped upon the platform looking so fresh, and cool, and handsome in his white linen suit that the ladies almost forgave Josephine for the gushing manner with which she greeted him, and carried him off toward home. She was so glad to see him, and her eyes looked at him so softly and tenderly, and she had so much to tell him, and was so excited with it all, and the brown house overgrown with hop-vines was so cool and pleasant, and Agnes had such a tempting

4

little supper prepared for him on the back piazza, that Everard felt supremely happy and content, and once, when nobody was looking on, kissed the blue-eyed fairy flitting so joyously around him.

"I say, Josey," he said, when the tea-things had been removed, and he was lounging in his usual lazy attitude upon the door-step and smoking his cigar, "it's a heap nicer here than down in that hot, close hall. Let's not go to the rehearsal. I'd rather stay home."

"But you can't do it. You must go," Josephine replied. "You must rehearse and learn your part, though for to-night it doesn't matter. You can go through the marriage ceremony well enough, can't you?"

"Of course I can, and can say, 'I, Everard, take thee, Josie, to be my lawful wife,' and, by Jove, I wouldn't care if it was genuine. Suppose we get a priest, and make a real thing of it. I'm willing, if you are."

There was a pretty blush on Josey's cheek as she replied, "What nonsense you are talking, and you not yet through college!" and then hurried him off to the hall, where the rehearsal was to take place.

Here an unforeseen difficulty presented itself. Dr. Matthewson was not forthcoming in his character as priest. He had gone out of town, and had not yet returned; so another took his place in the marriage scene, where Everard was the bridegroom and Josephine the bride. The play was called "The Mock Marriage," and would be very effective with the full glamour of lights, and dress, and people on the ensuing night; and Josephine declared herself satisfied with the rehearsal, and sanguine of success, especially as Dr. Matthewson appeared at the last moment apologizing for his tardiness, and assuring her of his intention to be present the next evening.

He was a tall, powerfully-built man of thirty or more, whom many would call handsome, though there was a cruel, crafty look in his eyes, and in the smile which habitually played about his mouth. Still, he was very gentlemanly in his manner, and fascinating in his conversation, for he had traveled much, and seen everything, and spoke both German and French as readily as his mother tongue. With Miss Fleming he seemed to be on the most intimate terms, though this intimacy only dated from the time when she pleaded with him so prettily and successfully to take the place of the priest in "The Mock Marriage," where John Murdock was to have officiated. At first the doctor had objected, saying gallantly that he preferred to be the bridegroom, and asking who that favored individual was to be.

"Mr. Everard Forrest, from Rothsay, Southern Ohio," Josephine replied, with a conscious blush which told much to the experienced man of the world.

"Forrest! Everard Forrest!" the doctor repeated thoughtfully, and the smile about his mouth was more perceptible. "Seems to me I have heard that name before. Where did you say he lived, and where is he now?"

Josephine replied again that Mr. Forrest's home was in Rothsay, Ohio, at a grand old place called Forrest House; that he was a student at Amherst, and was spending his summer vacation with a friend in Ellicottville.

"Yes, I understand," the doctor rejoined, adding, after a moment's pause: "I'll be the priest; but suppose I had the power to marry you in earnest; what then?"

"Oh, you wouldn't. You must not. Everard is not through college, and it would be so very dreadful—and romantic, too," the girl said, as she looked searchingly into the dark eyes meeting hers so steadily.

Up to that time Dr. Matthewson had taken but little notice of Josephine, except to remark her exceeding beauty as a golden-haired blonde. With his knowledge of the world and ready discernment he had discovered that whatever position she held in Holburton was due to her beauty and piquancy, and firm resolve to be noticed, rather than to any blood, or money, or culture. She was not a lady, he knew, the first time he saw her in the little church, and, attracted by her face, watched her through the service, while she whispered, and laughed, and passed notes to the young men in front of her. Without any respect himself for religion or the church, he despised irreverence in others, and formed a tolerably accurate estimate of Josephine and her companions. After her interview with him, however, he became greatly interested in everything pertaining to her, and by a little adroit questioning learned all there was to be known of her, and, as is usual in such cases, more too. Her mother was poor, and crafty and designing, and very ambitious for her daughter's future. That she took in sewing and kept boarders was nothing to her detriment in a village, where the people believed in honest labor, but that she traded on her daughter's charms, and brought her up in utter idleness, while Agnes, the child of her husband's first marriage, was made a very drudge and slave to the young beauty, was urged against her as a serious wrong, and, except as the keeper of a boarding-house, in which capacity she excelled, the Widow Fleming was not very highly esteemed in Holburton. All this Dr. Matthewson learned, and then he was told of young Forrest, a mere boy, two years younger than Josey, who had stopped with Mrs. Fleming a few weeks the previous summer, and for whom both Josey and the mother had, to use the landlady's words, "made a dead set," and succeeded, too, it would seem, for if they were not engaged they ought to be, though it was too bad for the boy, and somebody ought to tell his father.

Such was in substance the story told by the hostess of the Eagle to Dr. Matthewson, who smiled serenely as he heard it, and stroked his silken mustache thoughtfully, and then went down to call upon Miss Fleming, and judge for himself how well she was fitted to be the mistress of Forrest House.

When Everard came and was introduced to him after the rehearsal, there was a singular expression in the eyes which scanned the young man so curiously; but the doctor's manners were perfect, and never had Everard been treated with more deference and respect than by this handsome stranger, who called upon him at Mrs. Fleming's early in the morning, and in the course of an hour established himself on such terms of intimacy with the young man that he learned more of his family history than Josephine herself knew after an acquaintance of more than a year. Everard never could explain to himself how he was led on naturally and easily to speak of his home in Rothsay, the grand old place of which he would be heir, as he was the only child. He did not know how much his father was worth, he said, as his fortune was estimated at various sums, but it didn't do him much good, for the governor was close, and insisted upon knowing how every penny was spent. Consequently Everard, who was fast and expensive in his habits, was, as he expressed it, always hard up, and if his mother did not occasionally send him something unknown to his father he would be in desperate straits, for a fellow in college with the reputation of being rich must have money.

Here Everard thought of Rosamond and what she had sent him, but he could not speak of that to this stranger, who sat smiling so sweetly upon him, and leading him on step by step until at last Rossie's name did drop from his lips, and was quickly caught up by Dr. Matthewson.

"Rossie!" he repeated, in his low, purring tone, "Rossie! Who is she? Have you a sister?"

"Oh, no. I told you I was an only child. Rossie is Rosamond Hastings, a little girl whose mother was my mother's most intimate friend. They were school-girls together, and pledged themselves to stand by each other should either ever come to grief, as Mrs. Hastings did."

"Married unhappily, perhaps?" the doctor suggested, and Everard replied:

"Yes; married a man much older than herself, who abused her so shamefully that she left him at last, and sought refuge with my mother. Fortunately this Hastings died soon after, so she was freed from him; but she had another terror in the shape of his son, the child of a former marriage, who annoyed her dreadfully."

"How could he?" the doctor asked, and Everard replied:

"I hardly know. I believe, though, it was about some house or piece of land, of which Mrs. Hastings held the deed for Rossie, and this John thought he ought to share it, at least, and seemed to think it a fortune, when in fact it proved to be worth only two thousand dollars, which is all Rosamond has of her own."

"Perhaps he did not know how little there was, and thought it unjust for his half-sister to have all his father left, and he nothing," the doctor said, and it never once occurred to Everard to wonder how he knew that Mr. Hastings left all to his daughter, and nothing to his son.

He was wholly unsuspicious, and went on:

"Possibly; at all events he worried his stepmother into hysterics by coming there one day in winter, and demanding first the deed or will, and second his sister, whom he said his father gave to his charge. But I settled him!"

"Yes?" the doctor said, interrogatively, and Everard continued:

"Father was gone, and this wretch, who must have been in liquor, was bullying my mother, and declaring he would go to the room where Mrs. Hastings was fainting for fear of him, when I came in from riding, and just bade him begone; and when he said to me sneeringly, 'Oh, little David, what do you think you can do with the giant, you have no sling?' I hit him a cut with my riding-whip which made him wince with pain, and I followed up the blows till he left the house vowing vengeance on me for the insult offered him."

"And since then?" the doctor asked.

"Since then I have never seen him. After Mrs. Hastings died he wrote an impertinent letter to father asking the guardianship of his sister, but we had promised her mother solemnly never to let her fall into his hands or under his influence, and father wrote him such a letter as settled him; at least, we have never heard from him since, and that is eight years ago. Nor should I know him either, for it was dark, and he all muffled up."

"And have you no fear of him, that he may yet be revenged? People like him do not usually take cowhidings quietly," the doctor asked.

"No, I've no fear of him, for what can he do to me? Besides, I should not wonder if he were dead. We have never heard of him since that letter to father," was Everard's reply, and after a moment his companion continued:

"And this girl,—is she pretty and bright, and how old is she now?"

"Rossie must be thirteen," Everard said, "and the very nicest girl in the world, but as to being pretty, she is too thin for that, though she has splendid eyes, large and brilliant, and black as midnight, and what is peculiar for such eyes, her hair, which ripples all over her head, is a rich chestnut brown, with a tinge of gold upon it when seen in the sunlight. Her hair is her great beauty, and I should not be surprised if she grew to be quite a handsome woman."

"Very likely;—excuse me, Mr. Forrest," and the doctor spoke respectfully, nay, deferentially, "excuse me if I appear too familiar. We have talked together so freely that you do not seem a stranger, and friendships, you know, are not always measured by time."

Everard bowed, and, foolish boy that he was, felt flattered by this giant of a man, who went on:

"Possibly this little Rossie may some day be the daughter of the house in earnest."

"What do you mean? that my father will adopt her regularly?" Everard asked, as he lifted his clear, honest eyes inquiringly to the face of his companion, who, finding that in dealing with a frank, open nature like Everard's he must speak out plain, replied:

"I mean, perhaps you will marry her."

"I marry Rossie! Absurd! Why, I would as soon think of marrying my sister," and Everard laughed merrily at the idea.

"Such a thing is possible," returned the doctor, "though your father might object on the score of family, if that brother is such a scamp. I imagine he is rather proud; your father, I mean,—not that brother."

"Rossie's family is well enough for anything I know to the contrary," said Everard. "Father would not object to that, though he is infernally proud. He is a South Carolinian, born in Charleston, and boasts of Southern blood and Southern aristocracy, while mother is a Bostonian, of the bluest dye, and both would think the Queen of England honored to have a daughter marry their son. Nothing would put father in such a passion as for me to make what he thought a mesalliance."

"Yes, I see, and yet——"

The doctor did not finish the sentence, but looked instead down into the garden where Josephine was flitting among the flowers.

"Miss Fleming is a very beautiful girl," the doctor said, at last, and Everard responded heartily:

"Yes, the handsomest I ever saw."

"And rumor says you two are very fond of each other," was the doctor's next remark, which brought a blush like that of a young girl to Everard's cheek, but elicited no reply, for there was beginning to dawn upon his mind a suspicion that his inmost secrets were being wrung from him by this smooth-tongued stranger, who, quick to detect every fluctuation of thought and feeling in another, saw he had gone far enough, and having learned all he cared to know, he arose to go, and after a good morning to Everard and a few soft speeches to Josephine, walked away and left the pair alone.

CHAPTER III

THE MOCK MARRIAGE

The long hall, or rather ball-room, of the old Eagle tavern was crowded to its utmost capacity, for the entertainment had been talked of for a long time, and as the proceeds were to help buy a fire-engine, the whole town was interested, and the whole town was there. First on the programme came tableaux and charades, interspersed with music from the glee club, and music from the Ellicott band, and then there was a great hush of expectation and eager anticipation, for the gem of the performance was reserved for the last.

Behind the scenes, in the little anterooms where the dressing, and powdering, and masking, and jesting were all going on promiscuously, Josephine Fleming was in a state of great excitement, but hers was a face and complexion which never looked red or tired. She was, perhaps, a shade paler than her wont, and her eyes were brighter and bluer as she stood before the little two-foot glass, giving the last touches to her bridal toilet.

And never was real bride more transcendently lovely than Josephine Fleming when she stood at last ready and waiting to be called, in her fleecy tarlatan, with her long vail sweeping back from her face, and showing like a silver net upon her golden hair. And Everard, in his dark, boyish beauty, looked worthy of the bride, as he bent over her and whispered something in her ear which had reference to a future day when this they were doing in jest should be done in sober earnest. For a moment they were alone. Dr. Matthewson had managed to clear the little room, and now he came to them and said:

"I feel I shall be doing wrong to let this go any further without telling you that I have a right to make the marriage lawful, if you say so. A few years ago I was a clergyman in good and regular standing in the Methodist Episcopal Church at Clarence, in the western part of this State. I am not in regular and good standing now; the world, the flesh, and the devil, especially the latter, got the upper hand of me, but I still have the power to marry you fast and strong. You two are engaged, I hear. Suppose, for the fun of it, we make this marriage real? What do you say?"

He was looking at Everard, but he spoke to Josephine, feeling that hers would be the more ready assent of the two. She was standing with her arm linked in Everard's, and at Dr. Matthewson's words she lifted her blue eyes coyly to her lover's face, and said:

"Wouldn't that be capital, and shouldn't we steal a march on everybody?"

She waited for him to speak, but his answer did not come at once. It is true he had said something of this very nature to her only the night before, but now, when it came to him as something which might be if he chose, he started as if he had been stung, and the color faded from his lips, which quivered as he said, with an effort to smile:

"I'd like it vastly, only you see I am not through college, and I should be expelled at once. Then father never would forgive me. He'd disinherit me, sure."

"Hardly so bad as that, I think," spoke the soothing voice of the doctor, while one of Josephine's hands found its way to Everard's, which it pressed softly, as she said:

"We can keep it a secret, you know, till you are through college, and it would be such fun."

Half an hour before Everard had gone with the doctor to the bar and taken a glass of wine, which was beginning to affect his brain and cloud his better judgment, while Josephine was still looking at him with those great, dreamy, pleading eyes, which always affected him so strangely. She was very beautiful, and he loved her with all the strength of his boyish, passionate nature. So it is not strange that the thought of possessing her years sooner than he had dared to hope made his young blood stir with ecstasy, even though he knew it was wrong. He was like the bird in the toiler's snare, and he stood irresolute, trying to stammer out he hardly knew what, except that it had some reference to his father, and mother, and Rossie, for he thought of her in that hour of his temptation, and wondered how he could face her with that secret on his soul.

"They are growing impatient. Don't you hear them stamping? What are you waiting for?" came from the manager of the play, as he put his head into the room, while a prolonged and deafening call greeted their ears from the expectant audience.

"Yes, let's go," Josephine said, "and pray forget that I almost asked you to marry me and you refused. I should not have done it only it is Leap-year, you know, and I have a right; but it was all in joke, of course. I didn't mean it. Don't think I did, Everard."

Oh, how soft and beautiful were the eyes swimming in tears and lifted so pleadingly to Everard's face! It was more than mortal man could do to withstand them, and Everard went down before them body and soul. His father's bitter anger,—so sure to follow, his mother's grief and disappointment in her son, and Rossie's childish surprise were all forgotten, or, if remembered, weighed as nought compared with this lovely creature with the golden hair and eyes of blue, looking so sweetly and tenderly at him.

"I'll do it, by George!" he said, and the hot blood came surging back to his face. "It will be the richest kind of a lark. Tie as tight as you please. I am more than willing."

He was very much excited, and Josephine was trembling like a leaf. Only Dr. Matthewson was calm as he asked: "Do you really mean it, and will you stand to it?"

"Are you ever coming?" came angrily this time from the manager, who was losing all patience.

"Yes, I mean it, and will stand to it," Everard said, and so went on to his fate.

There was a cheer, followed by a deep hush, when the curtain was withdrawn, disclosing the bridal party upon the stage, fitted up to represent a modern drawing-room, with groups of gayly-dressed people standing together, and in their midst Everard and Josephine, she radiantly beautiful, with a look of exultation on her face, but a tumult of conflicting emotions in her heart, as she wondered if Dr. Matthewson had told the truth, and was authorized to marry her really, and if Everard would stand to it or repudiate the act; he, with a face white now as ashes, and a voice which was husky in its tone when, to the question: "Dost thou take this woman for thy wedded wife? Dost thou promise to love her, and cherish her, both in sickness and in health, and, forsaking all others, keep thee only unto her?" he answered: "I do," while a chill like the touch of death ran through every nerve and made him icy cold.

It was not the lark he thought it was going to be; it was like some dreadful nightmare, and he could not at all realize what he was doing or saying. Even Josephine's voice, when she too said, "I will," sounded very far away, as did Matthewson's concluding words: "According to the authority vested in me I pronounce you man and wife. What God hath joined together let no man put asunder."

How real it seemed to the breathless audience—so real that Agnes Fleming, sitting far back in the hall, in her faded muslin and old-fashioned bonnet, involuntarily rose to her feet and raised her hand with a deprecating gesture as if to forbid the bans. But her mother pulled her down to her seat, and in a low whisper bade her keep quiet.

And so the play went on, and was over at last; the crowd dispersed, and the tired actors, sleepy and cross, gathered up the paraphernalia scattered everywhere, and went to their several homes. Everard and Josephine were the last to leave, for she had so much to say, and so much to see to, that it was after twelve, and the summer moon was high in the heavens ere they started at last for home, accompanied by the young man with whom Everard was staying in Ellicottville, and who had come down to the play.

It had been arranged that young Stafford should pass the night at Mrs. Fleming's, and when the party reached the cottage they found a supper prepared for them, of which hot coffee and sherry formed a part, and under the combined effects of the two Everard's spirits began to rise, and when at last he said good-night to Josephine and went with his friend to his room, he was much like himself, and felt that it would not be a very bad state of affairs, after all, if it should prove that Josephine was really his wife. It would only be expediting matters a little, and the secret would be so romantic and unusual. Still, he was conscious of a feeling of unrest and disinclination to talk, and declared his intention of plunging into bed at once.

"Perhaps you'd better read this first," Stafford said, handing him a telegram. "It came this morning, and I brought it with me, but would not give it to you till after the play, for fear it might contain bad news."

Now young Stafford knew perfectly well the nature of the telegram, for he had been in the office when it came, and decided not to deliver it until the play was over. It was from Everard's father, and read as follows:

"To J. Everard Forrest, Jr.—Your mother is very sick. Come immediately.

J. E. Forrest."

"Oh, Stafford," and Everard's voice was like the cry of a wounded child, "why didn't you give me this before. There was a train left at five o'clock. I could have taken it, and saved——"

He did not finish the sentence, for he could not put into words the great horror of impending evil which had fallen upon him with the receipt of that telegram. Indeed, he could not define to himself the nature of his feelings. He only knew that he wished he had gone home in answer to Rossie's summons, instead of coming to Holburton. And in this he meant no disloyalty to Josephine, nor attributed any blame to her; and when, next morning, after a troubled night, in which no sleep visited his weary eyes, he met her at the breakfast-table looking as bright, and fresh, and pretty as if she too, had not kept a sleepless vigil, he experienced a delicious feeling of ownership in her, and for a few moments felt willing to defy the whole world, if by so doing he could claim her as his, then and there. He told her of the telegram, and said he must take the first train west, which left in about two hours, and Josephine's eyes instantly filled with tears, as she said:

"I am so sorry for you, and I hope your mother will recover. I have always wished to see her so much. Would you mind telling her of me, and giving my love to her?"

This was after breakfast, when they stood together under the vine-wreathed porch, each with a thought of last night's ceremony in their minds, and each loth to speak of it first. Stafford had gone to the hotel to settle his bill of the previous day and make some inquiries about the connection of the trains, and thus the family were alone when Dr. Matthewson appeared, wearing his blandest smile, and addressing

Josephine as Mrs. Forrest, and asking her how she found herself after the play.

At the sound of that name given to Josephine as if she had a right to it, a scarlet flame spread over Everard's face, and he felt the old horror and dread of the night creeping over him again. Now was the time to know the worst or the best,—whichever way he chose to put it,—and as calmly as possible under the circumstances, he turned to Dr. Matthewson and asked:

"Were you in earnest in what you said last night? Had you a right to marry us, and is Josephine my wife?"

It was the first time he had put it into words, and as if the very name of wife made her dearer to him, he wound his arm around her and waited the doctor's answer, which came promptly and decidedly.

"Most assuredly she is your lawful wife! You took her with your full consent, knowing I could marry you, and I have brought your certificate, which I suppose the lady will hold."

He handed a neatly-folded paper to Josephine, who, with Everard looking over her shoulder, read to the effect that on the evening of July th, in the Village Hall at Holburton, the Rev. John Matthewson married J. Everard Forrest, Jr. of Rothsay, Ohio, to Miss Josephine Fleming of Holburton.

"It is all right, I believe, and only needs the names of your mother and sister as witnesses to make it valid, in case the marriage is ever contested," Matthewson said, and this time he looked pitilessly at Everard, who was staring blankly at the paper in Josephine's hands, and if it had been his death-warrant he was reading he could scarcely have been paler.

Something in his manner must have communicated itself to Josephine, for in real or feigned distress she burst into tears, and laying her head on his arm, sobbed out:

"Oh, Everard, you are not sorry I am your wife! If you are, I shall wish I was dead!"

"No, no, Josey, not sorry you are my wife," he said, "I could not be that; only I am so young, and have two years more in college,—and if this thing were known I should be expelled, and father would never forgive me, or let me have a dollar again; so, you see it is a deuced scrape after all."

He was as near crying as he well could be and not actually give way, and Matthewson was regarding him with a cool, exultant expression in his cruel eyes, when Mrs. Fleming appeared, asking what it meant.

Very briefly Dr. Matthewson explained the matter to her, and laying his hand on Everard's arm said, laughingly:

"I have the honor of presenting to you your son, who, I believe, acknowledges your claim upon him."

There was a gleam of triumph in Mrs. Fleming's eyes, but she affected to be astonished and indignant that her daughter should have lent herself to an act which Mr. Forrest was perhaps already sorry for.

"You are mistaken," Everard said, and his young manhood asserted itself in Josephine's defense. "Your daughter was not more to blame than myself. We both knew what we were doing, and I am not sorry, except for the trouble in which it would involve me if it were known at once that I was married."

"It need not be known, except to ourselves," Mrs. Fleming answered, quickly. "What is done cannot be undone, but we can make the best of it, and I promise that the secret shall be kept as long as you like. Josey will remain with me as she is, and you will return to college and graduate as if last night had never been. Then, when you are in a position to claim your wife you can do so, and acknowledge it to your father."

She settled it rapidly and easily, and Everard felt his spirits rise thus to have some one think and decide for him. It was not distasteful to know that Josey was his, and he smoothed caressingly the bowed head, still resting on his arm, where Josey had laid it. It would be just like living a romance all the time, and the interviews they might occasionally have would be all the sweeter because of the secrecy. After all, it was a pretty nice lark, and he felt a great deal better, and watched Mrs. Fleming and Agnes as they signed their names to the certificate, and noticed how the latter trembled and how pale she was as, with what seemed to him a look of pity for him, she left the room and went back to her dish-washing in the kitchen.

Everard had spent some weeks in Mrs. Fleming's family as a boarder, and had visited there occasionally, but he had never noticed or thought particularly of Agnes, except, indeed, as the household drudge, who was always busy from morning till night, washing, ironing, baking, dusting, with her sleeves rolled up and her broad check apron tied around her waist. She had a limp in her left foot, and a weakness in her left arm which gave her a helpless, peculiar appearance; and the impression he had of her, if any, was that she was unfortunate in mind as well as body, fit only to minister to others as she always seemed to be doing. She had never addressed a word to him without being first spoken to, and he was greatly surprised when, after Dr. Matthewson was gone, and Mrs. Fleming and Josephine had for a moment left him alone in the room, she came to him and putting her hand on his, said in a whisper, "Did you really mean it, or was it an accident? a joke? and do you want to get out of it? because, if you do, now is the time. Say you didn't mean it! Say you won't stand it, and there surely will be some way out. I can help,—weak as I am. It is a pity, and you so young."

She was looking fixedly at him, and he saw that her eyes were soft, and dark, and sad in their expression, as if for them there was no brightness or sunshine in all the wide world,—nothing but the never-ending dish-washing in the kitchen, or serving in the parlor. But there was another expression in those sad eyes, a look of truth and honesty, which made him feel intuitively that she was a person to be trusted even to the death, and had he felt any misgivings then, he would have told her so unhesitatingly; but he had none, and he answered her:

"I do not wish to get out of it, Agnes, I am satisfied; only it must be a secret for a long, long time. Remember that, and your promise not to tell."

"Yes, I'll remember, and may God help you!" she answered, as she turned away, leaving him to wonder at her manner, which puzzled and troubled him a little. But it surely had nothing to do with Josephine, who came to him just before he left for the train, and said so charmingly and tearfully:

"I am so mortified and ashamed when I remember how eagerly I seemed to respond to Dr. Matthewson's proposition that we be married in earnest. You must have thought me so forward and bold; but, believe me, I did not mean it, or consider what I was saying; so when you are gone don't think of me as a brazen-faced creature who asked you to marry her, will you?"

What answer could he give her except to assure her that he esteemed her as everything lovely and good, and he believed that he did when at last he said good-by, and left her kissing her hand to him as she stood in the doorway under the spreading hop vine, the summer sunshine falling in flecks upon her golden hair, and her blue eyes full of tears. So he saw her last, and this was the picture he took with him as he sped away to the westward toward his home, and which helped to stifle his judgment and reason whenever they protested against what he had done, but it could not quite smother the fear and dread at his heart when he reflected what the consequences of this rash marriage would be should his father find it out.

CHAPTER IV

THE FORREST HOUSE

Just where it was located is not my purpose to tell, except that it was in the southern part of Ohio, in one of those pretty little towns which skirt the river, and that from the bluff on which it stood you could look across the water into the green fields and fertile plains of the fair State of Kentucky.

It was a large, rambling house of dark gray stone, with double piazza on the front and river side, and huge chimneys, with old-time fire-places, where cheery wood fires burned always when the wind was chill. There was the usual wide hall of the South, with doors opening front and rear, and on one side the broad oak staircase and square landing two-thirds of the way up, where stood the tall, old-fashioned clock, which had ticked there for fifty years, and struck the hour when the first Forrest, the father of the present proprietor, brought home his bride, a fair Southern girl, who drooped and pined in her Northern home until her husband took her back to her native city, Charleston, where she died when her boy was born. This boy, the father of our hero, was christened James Everard, in the grim old church, St. Michael's, and the years of his boyhood were passed in Charleston, except on the few occasions when he visited his father, who lived at Forrest House without other companionship than his horses and dogs, and the bevy of black servants he had brought from the South.

When James was nearly twenty-one his father died, and then the house was closed until the heir was married, and came to it with a sweet, pale-faced Bostonian, of rare culture and refinement, who introduced into her new home many of the fashions and comforts of New England, and made the house very attractive to the educated families in the neighborhood.

Between the lady and her husband, however, there was this point of difference;—while she would, if possible, have changed, and improved, and modernized the house, he clung to everything savoring of the past, and though liberal in his expenditures where his table, and wines, and horses, and servants were concerned, he held a tight purse-string when it came to what he called luxuries of any kind. What had been good enough for his father was good enough for him, he said, when his wife proposed new furniture for the rooms which looked so bare and cheerless. Matting and oil-cloth were better than carpets for his muddy boots and muddier dogs, while curtains and shades were nuisances and only served to keep out the light of heaven. There were blinds at all the windows, and if his wife wished for anything more she could hang up her shawl or apron when she was dressing and afraid of being seen.

He did, however, give her five hundred dollars to do with as she pleased, and with that and her exquisite taste and Yankee ingenuity, she transformed a few of the dark, musty old rooms into the coziest, prettiest apartments imaginable, and, with the exception of absolutely necessary repairs and supplies, that was the last, so far as expenditures for furniture were concerned.

As the house had been when James Everard, Jr., was born, so it was now when he was twenty years old. But what it lacked in its interior adornments was more than made up in the grounds, which covered a space of three or four acres, and were beautiful in the extreme.

Here the judge lavished his money without stint, and people came from miles around to see the place, which was at its best that warm July morning when, tired and worn with his rapid journey, Everard entered the highway gate, and walked up the road to the house, under the tall maples which formed an arch over his head.

It was very still about the house, and two or three dogs lay in the sunshine asleep on the piazza. At the sound of footsteps they awoke, and recognizing their young master, ran toward him, with a bark of welcome.

The windows of his mother's room were open, and at the bark of the dogs a girlish face was visible for an instant, then disappeared from view, and Rosamond Hastings came out to meet him, looking very fresh and sweet in her short gingham dress and white apron, with her rippling hair tied with a blue ribbon, and falling down her back.

"Oh, Mr. Everard," she cried, as she gave him her hand, "I am so glad you have come. Your mother has wanted you so much. She is a little better this morning, and asleep just now; so come in here and rest. You are tired, and worn, and pale. Are you sick?" and she looked anxiously into the handsome face, where even she saw a change, for the shadow of his secret was there, haunting every moment of his life.

"No; I'm just used up, and so hungry," he said, as he followed her into the cool family room, looking out upon the river, which she had made bright with flowers in expectation of his coming.

"Hungry, are you?" she said. "I'm so glad, for there's the fattest little chicken waiting to be broiled for you, and we have such splendid black and white raspberries. I'm going to pick them now, while you wash and brush yourself. You will find everything ready in your room, with some curtains, and tidies on the chairs. I did it myself, hoping you'd find it pleasant, and stay home all the vacation, even if your mother gets better, she is so happy to have you here. Will you go up now?"

He went to the room which had always been his,—a large, airy chamber, which, with nothing modern or expensive in it, looked cool and pretty, with its clean matting, snowy bed, fresh muslin curtains, and new blue and white tidies on the high-backed chairs, all showing Rossie's handiwork. Rossie had been in Miss Beatrice Belknap's lovely room furnished with blue, and thought it a little heaven, and tried her best to make Mr. Everard's a blue room too, though she had nothing to do it with except the tidies, and toilet set, and lambrequins made of plain white muslin bordered with strips of blue cambric. The material for this she had bought with her own allowance, at the cost of some personal sacrifice; and when it was all done, and the two large blue vases were filled with flowers and placed upon the mantel, she felt that it was almost equal to Miss Belknap's, and that Mr. Everard, as she always called him, was sure to like it. And he did like it, and breathed more freely, as if he were in a purer, more wholesome atmosphere than that of the brown house in far-off Holburton, where he had left his secret and his wife. It came to him with a sudden wrench of pain in his quiet room,—the difference between Josephine and all his early associates and surroundings. She was not like anything at the Forrest House, though she was marvelously beautiful and fair,—so much fairer than little Rossie, whose white cape bonnet he could see flitting among the bushes in the garden, where in the hot sunshine she soiled and pricked her fingers gathering berries for him. He had a photograph of Josephine, and he took it out and looked at the great blue eyes and fair, blonde face, which seemed to smile on him, and saying to himself, "She is very lovely," went down to the sitting-room, where Rossie brought him his breakfast.

It was so hot in the dining-room, she said, and Aunt Axie was so out of sorts this morning, that she was going to serve his breakfast there in the bay window, where the breeze came cool from the river. So she brought in the tray of dishes, and creamed his coffee, and sugared his berries, and carved his chicken, as if he had been a prince, and she his lawful slave.

At Mrs. Fleming's he had also been treated like a prince, but there it was lame Agnes who served, with her sleeves rolled up, and Josephine had acted the part of the fine lady, and never to his recollection had she soiled her hands with household work of any kind. How soft and white they were,—while Rossie's hands were thin and tanned from exposure to the sun, and stained and scratched, with a rag around one thumb which a cruel thorn had torn; but what deft, nimble hands they were, nevertheless, and how gladly they waited upon this tired, indolent young man, who took it as a matter of course, for had not Rossie Hastings ministered to him since she was old enough to hunt up his missing cap, and bring him the book he was reading. Now, as she flitted about, urging him to eat, she talked to him incessantly, asking if he had received her letter and its contents safely,—if it was very pleasant at Ellicottville with his friend Stafford, and if,—she did not finish that question, but her large black eyes, clear as crystal, looked anxiously at him, and he knew what she meant.

"No, Rossie," he said, laughingly, "I do not owe a dollar to anybody, except your dear little self, and that I mean to pay with compound interest; and I haven't been in a single scrape,—that is, not a very bad one, since I went back;" and a flush crept to the roots of his hair as he wondered what Rosamond would think if she knew just the scrape he was in.

And why should she not know? Why didn't he tell her, and have her help him keep the secret tormenting him so sorely? He knew he could trust her, for he had done so many a time and she had not betrayed him, but stood bravely between him and his irascible father, who, forgetting that he once was young, was sometimes hard and severe with his wayward son. Yes, he would tell Rossie, and so make a friend for Josephine, but before he had decided how to begin, Rosamond said:

"I'm so glad you are doing better, for——" here she hesitated and colored painfully, while Everard said:

"Well, go on. What is it? Do you mean the governor rides a high horse on account of my misdemeanors?"

"Yes, Mr. Everard, just that. He is dreadful when you write for more money, which he says you squander on cigars, and fast horses, and fine clothes, and girls; he actually said girls, but my,—your mother told him she knew you were not the kind of person to think of girls, and you so young; absurd!"

And Rossie pursed up her little mouth as if it were a perfectly preposterous idea for Everard Forrest to be thinking of the girls!

The young man laughed a low, musical laugh, and replied, "I don't know about that. I should say it was just in my line. There are ever so many pretty girls in Ellicottville and Holburton, and one of them is so very beautiful that I'm half tempted to run away with and marry her. What would you think of that, Rossie?"

For a moment the matter-of-fact Rossie looked at him curiously, and then replied:

"I should think you crazy, and you not through college. I believe your father would disinherit you, and serve you right, too."

"And you, Rossie; wouldn't you stand by me and help me if I got into such a muss?"

"Never!" and Rossie spoke with all the decision and dignity of thirty. "It would kill your mother, too. I sometimes think she means you for Miss Belknap; she is so handsome this summer!"

"Without her hair?" Everard asked, and Rossie replied, "Yes, without her hair. She has a wig, but does not quite like it. She means to get another."

"And she offered fifty dollars for your hair!" Everard continued, stroking with his hand the chestnut brown tresses flowing down Rossie's back.

"Yes, she did; but I could not part with my hair even to oblige her. Of course I should give it to her, not sell it, but I can't spare it."

What an unselfish child she was, Everard thought, and yet she was so unlike the golden-haired Josephine, who would make fun of such a plain, simple, unformed girl as Rosamond, and call her green and awkward and countrified; and perhaps she was all these, but she was so good, and pure, and truthful that he felt abashed before her and shrank from the earnest, truthful eyes that rested so proudly on him, lest they should read more than he cared to have them.

Outside, in the hall, there was the sound of a heavy step, and the next moment there appeared in the door a tall, heavily-built man of fifty, with iron-gray hair and keen, restless eyes, which always seemed on the alert to discover something hidden, and drag it to the light. Judge Forrest meant to be a just man, but, like many just men, when the justice is not tempered with mercy, he was harsh and hard with those who did not come up to his standard of integrity, and seldom made allowances for one's youth or inexperience, or the peculiar temptations which might have assailed them. Though looked up to as the great man of the town, he was far less popular with the people of Rothsay than his scamp of a son, with whom they thought him unnecessarily strict and close. It was well known that there was generally trouble between them and always on the money question, for Everard was a spendthrift, and scattered his dollars right and left with a reckless generosity and thoughtlessness, while the judge was the reverse, and gave out every cent not absolutely needed with an unwillingness which amounted to actual stinginess. And now he stood at the door, tall, grand-looking, and cold as an icicle, and his first greeting was:

"I thought I should track you by the tobacco smoke; they told me you were here. How do you do, sir?"

It was strange the effect that voice had upon Everard, who, from an indolent, care-for-nothing, easy-going youth was transformed into a circumspect, dignified young man, who rose at once, and, taking his father's hand, said that he was very well, had come on the morning train from Cleveland, and had started as soon as he could after receiving the telegram.

"It must have been delayed, then. You ought to have had it Wednesday morning," Judge Forrest replied: and blushing like a girl Everard said that it did reach Ellicottville Wednesday, but he was in Holburton, just over the line in New York.

"And what were you doing at Holburton?" the father asked, always suspicious of some new trick or escapade for which he would have to pay.

"I was invited there to an entertainment," Everard said, growing still redder and more confused. "You know I boarded there a few weeks last summer, and have acquaintances, so I went down the night before, and

Stafford came the next day and brought the telegram, but did not tell me till the play was over and we were in our room; then it was too late, but I took the first train in the morning. I hope my delay has not made mother worse. I am very sorry, sir."

He had made his explanation, which his father accepted without a suspicion of the chasm bridged over in silence.

"You have seen your mother, of course," was his next remark, and, still apologetically, nay, almost abjectly, for Everard was terribly afraid of his father, he replied, "She was sleeping when I came, and Rossie thought I'd better not disturb her, but have my breakfast first. I have finished now, and will go to her at once if she is awake."

He had put Rossie in the gap, knowing that she was a tower of strength between himself and his father. During the years she had been in the family Rossie had become very dear to the cold, stern judge, who was kinder and gentler to her than to any living being, except, indeed, his dying wife, to whom he was, in his way, sincerely attached.

"Yes, very right and proper that you should have your breakfast first, and not disturb her. Rossie, see if she is now awake," he said, and in his voice there was a kindliness which Everard was quick to note, and which made his pulse beat more naturally, while there suddenly woke within him an intense desire to stand well with his father, between whom and himself there had been so much variance.

For Josephine's sake he must have his father's good opinion, or he was ruined, and though it cost him a tremendous effort to do so, the moment Rosamond left the room, he said: "Father, I want to tell you now, because I think you will be glad to know, that I've come home and left no debt, however small, for you to pay. And I mean to do better. I really do, father, and quit my fast associates, and study so hard that when I am graduated you and mother will be proud of me."

The flushed, eager face, on which, young as it was, there were marks of revels and dissipation, was very handsome and winning, and the dark eyes were moist with tears as the boy finished his confession, which told visibly upon the father.

"Yes, yes, my son. I'm glad; I'm glad; but your poor mother will not be here when you graduate. She is going from us fast."

And under cover of the dying mother's name, the judge vailed his own emotions of softening toward Everard, whose heart was lighter and happier than it had been since that night when Matthewson's voice had said, "I pronounce you man and wife." And he would be a man worthy of the wife, and his mother should live to see it, and to see Josephine, too, and love her as a daughter. She was not dying; she must not die, when he needed and loved her so much, he thought, as, at a word from Rosamond, he went to the sick room where his mother lay. What a sweet, dainty little woman she was, with such a lovely expression on the exquisitely chiseled features, and how the soft brown eyes, so like the son's, brightened at the sight of her boy, who did not shrink from her as he did from his father. She knew all his faults, and that under them there was a noble, manly nature, and she loved him so much.

"Oh, Everard!" she cried, "I am so glad you have come. I feared once I should never see you again."

He had his arms around her, and was kissing her white face, which, for the moment, glowed with what seemed to be the hue of health, and so misled him into thinking her better than she was.

"Now that I have come, mother, you will be well again," he said, hanging fondly over her, and looking into the dear face which had never worn a frown for him.

"No, Everard," she said, as her wasted fingers threaded his luxuriant hair, "I shall never be well again. It's only now a matter of time; a few days or weeks at the most, and I shall be gone from here forever, to that better home, where I pray Heaven you will one day meet me. Hush, hush, my child; don't cry like that," she added, soothingly, for, struck with the expression on her white, pinched face, from which all the color had faded, and which told him the truth more forcibly than she had done, Everard had felt suddenly that his mother was going from him, and nothing in all the wide world could ever fill her place.

Laying his head upon her pillow he sobbed a few moments like a child, while the memory of all the errors of his past life, all his waywardness and folly, rushed into his mind like a mountain, crushing him with its magnitude. But he was going to do better; he had told his father so; he would tell it to his mother; and God would not let her die, but give her back to him as a kind of reward for his reformation. So he reasoned, and with the hopefulness of youth grew calm, and could listen to what his mother was saying to him. She was asking him of his visit in Ellicottville, and if he had found it pleasant there, just as Rossie had done, and he told her of the play in Holburton, but for which he should have been with her sooner, and told her of his complete reform, he called it, although it had but just begun. He had abjured forever all his wild associates; he had kept out of debt; he was going to study and win the first honors of his class; he was going to be a man worthy of such a mother. And she, the mother, listening rapturously, believed it all; that is, believed in the noble man he would one day be, though she knew there would be many a slip, many a backward step, but in the end he would conquer, and from the realms of bliss she might, perhaps, be permitted to look down and see him all she hoped him to be. Over and above all he said to her was a thought of Josephine. His mother ought to know of her, and he must tell her, but not in the first moments of meeting. He would wait till to-morrow, and then make a clean breast of it.

He wrote to Josephine that night just a few brief lines, to tell her of his safe arrival home and of his mother's illness, more serious than he feared.

"My dear little wife," he began. "It seems so funny to call you wife, and I cannot yet quite realize that you are mine, but I suppose it is true. I reached home this morning quite overcome with the long, dusty ride; found mother worse than I expected. Josie, I am afraid mother is going to die, and then what shall I do, and who will stand between me and father. I mean to tell her of you, for I think it will not be right to let her die in ignorance of what I have done. I hope you are well. Please write to me very soon. With kind regards to your mother and Agnes,

"Your loving husband,
"J. Everard Forrest."

It was not just the style of letter which young and ardent husbands usually write to their brides; nor, in fact, such as Everard had been in the habit of writing to Josephine, and the great difference struck him as he read over his rather stiff note, and mentally compared it with the gushing effusions of other times.

"By Jove," he said, "I'm afraid she will think I have fallen off amazingly, but I haven't. I'm only tired to-night. To-morrow I'll send her a regular love-letter after I have told mother;" and thus reasoning to himself, he folded the letter and directed it to—

"Miss Josephine Fleming, Holburton, N. Y."

CHAPTER V

BEATRICE BELKNAP

That afternoon Miss Beatrice Belknap drove her pretty black ponies up the avenue to the Forrest House. Miss Beatrice, or Bee, as she was familiarly called by those who knew her best, was an orphan and an heiress, and a belle and a beauty, and twenty-one, and a distant relative of Mrs. Forrest, whom she called Cousin Mary. People said she was a little fast and a little peculiar in her ways of thinking and acting, but charged it all to the French education she had received in Paris, where she had lived from the time she was six until she was eighteen, when, according to her father's will, she came into possession of her large fortune, and returning to America came to Rothsay, her old home, and brought with her all her dash and style, and originality of thought and character, and the Rothsayites received her gladly, and were very proud and fond of her, for there was about the bright girl a sweet graciousness of manner which won all hearts, even though they knew she was bored with their quiet town and humdrum manner of living, and that at their backs she laughed at their dress, and talk, and walk, and sometimes, I am sorry to say it, laughed at their prayers too, especially when good old Deacon Read or Sister Baker took the lead in the little chapel on the corner, where Bee was occasionally to be seen. Bee had no preference for any church unless it were St. Peter's, in Rome, or St. Eustace, in Paris, where the music was so fine and some of the young priests so handsome. So she went where she listed, kneeling one

Sunday in the square pew at St. John's, where her father had worshiped before her, and where she had been baptized, and the Sunday following patronizing the sect called the Nazarites, because, as she expressed it, "she liked the excitement and liked to hear them holler." And once the daring girl had "hollered" herself and had the "power," and Sister Baker had rejoiced over the new convert who, she said, "carried with her weight and measure!" but when it was whispered about that the whole was done for effect, just to see what they would say, the Nazarites gave poor Bee the go-by, and prayed for her as that wicked trifler until it came to the building of their new church, when Bee, who was a natural carpenter, and liked nothing better than lath, and plaster, and rubbish, made the cause her own, and talked, and consulted, and paced the ground and drew a plan herself, which they finally adopted, and gave them a thousand dollars besides. Then they forgave the pretty sinner, who had so much good in her after all, and Bee and Sister Rhoda Ann Baker were the very best of friends, and more than once Rhoda Ann's plain Nazarite bonnet had been seen in the little phaeton side by side with Bee's stylish Paris hat, on which the good woman scarcely dared to look lest it should move her from her serene height of plainness and humility.

In spite of her faults, Beatrice was very popular, and nowhere was she more welcome than at the Forrest House, where she was beloved by Mrs. Forrest and worshiped by Rossie as a kind of divinity, though she did not quite like all she did and said. Offers, many and varied, Beatrice had had, both at home and abroad. She might have been the wife of a senator. She might have married her music-teacher and her dancing-master. She might have been a missionary and taught the Feegee Islanders how to read. She might have been a countess in Rome, a baroness in Germany, and my lady in Edinburgh, but she had said no to them all, and felt the hardest wrench when she said it to the Feegee missionary, and for aught anybody knew, was heart-whole and fancy-free when she alighted from her phaeton at the door of Forrest House the morning after Everard's arrival. She knew he was there, and with the spirit of coquetry so much a part of herself she had made her toilet with a direct reference to this young man whom she had not seen for more than a year, and who, when joked about marrying her, had once called her old Bee Belknap, and wondered if any one supposed he would marry his grandmother.

Miss Bee had smiled sweetly on this audacious boy who called her old and a grandmother, and had laid a wager with herself that he should some day offer himself to "old Bee Belknap," and be refused! In case he didn't she would build a church in Omaha and support a missionary there five years! She was much given to building churches and supporting missionaries,—this sprightly, dashing girl of twenty-one, who flashed, and sparkled, and shone in the summer sunshine, like a diamond, as she threw her reins over the backs of her two ponies, Spitfire and Starlight, and giving each of them a loving caress bade them stand still and not whisk their tails too much even if the flies did bite them. Then, with ribbons and laces streaming from her on all sides, she went fluttering up the steps and into the broad hall where Everard met her.

Between him and herself there had been a strong friendship since the time she first came from France, and queened it over him on the strength of her foreign style and a year's seniority in age. From the very first she had been much at the Forrest House, and had played with Everard, and romped with him, and read with him, and driven with him, and rowed with him upon the river, and quarreled with him, too,—hot, fierce quarrels,—in which the girl generally had the best of it, inasmuch as her voluble French, which she hurled at him with lightning rapidity, had stunned and bewildered him; and then they had made it up, and were the best of friends, and more than one of the knowing ones in Rothsay had predicted a union some day of the Forrest and Belknap fortunes. Once, when such a possibility was hinted to Everard, who was fresh from a hot skirmish with Bee, he had, as recorded, called her old, and made mention of his grandmother, and she had sworn to be revenged, and was conscious all the time of a greater liking for the heir of Forrest House than she had felt for any man since the Feegee missionary sailed away with his Vermont school-mistress, who wore glasses, and a brown alpaca dress. Bee could have forgiven the glasses, but the brown alpaca,—never, and she pitied the missionary more than ever, thinking how he must contrast her Paris gowns, which he had said were so pretty, with that abominable brown garb of his bride.

Everard had never quite fancied the linking of his name with that of Beatrice in a matrimonial way, and it had sometimes led him to assume an indifference which he did not feel, but now, with Josephine between them as an insurmountable barrier, he could act out his real feelings of genuine liking for the gay butterfly, and he met her with an unusual degree of cordiality, which she was quick to note just as she had noted another change in him. A skillful reader of the human face, she looked in Everard's, and saw something she could not define. It was the shadow of his secret, and she could not interpret it. She only felt that he was no longer a boy, but a man, old even as his years, and that he was very glad to see her, and looked his gladness to the full. Bee Belknap was a born coquette, and would have flirted in her coffin had the thing been possible, and now, during the moment she stood in the hall with her hand in Everard's, she managed to make him understand how greatly improved she found him, how delighted she was to see him, and how inexpressibly dull and poky Rothsay was without him. She did not say all this in words, but she conveyed it to him with graceful gestures of her pretty hands, and sundry expressive shrugs of her shoulders, and Everard felt flattered and pleased, and for a few moments forgot Josephine, while he watched this brilliant creature as she flitted into the sick room, where her manner suddenly changed, and she became quiet, and gentle, and womanly, as she sat down by his mother's side, and asked how she was, and stroked and fondled the thin, pale face, and petted the wasted hands which sought hers so gladly. Bee Belknap always did sick people good, and there was not a sick bed in all Rothsay, from the loftiest dwelling to the lowest tenant house, which she did not visit, making the rich ones more hopeful and cheerful from the effect of her strong, sympathetic nature, and dazzling, and bewildering, and gratifying the poor, with whom she often left some tangible proof of her presence.

"You do me so much good; I am always better after one of your calls," Mrs. Forrest said to her; and then, when Bee arose to go, and said, "May I take Everard with me for a short drive?" she answered readily: "Yes, do. I shall be glad for him to get the air."

And so Everard found himself seated at Beatrice's side, and whirling along the road toward the village, for he wished to post his letter, and asked her to take him first to the post-office.

"What would she say if she knew?" he thought, and it seemed to him as if the letter in his pocket must burn itself through and show her the name upon it.

And then he fell to comparing the two girls with each other, and wondering why he should feel so much more natural, as if in his own atmosphere and on his good behavior, with Beatrice than he did with Josephine. Both were beautiful; both were piquant and bright, but still there was a difference. Beatrice never for a moment allowed him to forget that she was a lady and he a gentleman; never approached to anything like coarseness, and he would as soon have thought of insulting his mother as to have taken the slightest familiarity either by word or act with Bee. Josephine, on the contrary, allowed great latitude of word and action, and by her free-and-easy manner often led him into doing and saying things for which he would have blushed with shame had Beatrice, or even Rossie Hastings, been there to see and hear. Had Josephine lived in New York, or any other city, she would have added one more to that large class of people who laugh at our time-honored notions of propriety and true, pure womanhood, and on the broad platform of liberality and freedom sacrifice all that is sweetest and best in their sex. As a matter of course her influence over Everard was not good, and he had imbibed so much of the subtle poison that some of his sensibilities were blunted, and he was beginning to think that his early ideas were prudish and nonsensical. But there was something about Rosamond and Beatrice both which worked as an antidote to the poison, and as he rode along with the latter, and listened to her light, graceful badinage, in which there was nothing approaching to vulgarity, he was conscious of feeling more respect for himself than he had felt in many a day.

They had left the village now, and were out upon the smooth river road, where they came upon a young M. D. of Rothsay, who was jogging leisurely along in his high sulky, behind his old sorrel mare. Beatrice knew the doctor well, and more than once they had driven side by side amid a shower of dust, along that fine, broad road, and now, when she saw him and his sorry-looking nag, the spirit of mischief and frolic awoke within her, and she could no more refrain from some saucy remark concerning his beast and challenging him to a trial of speed than she could keep from breathing. Another moment and they were off like the wind, and to Bee's great surprise old Jenny, the sorrel mare, who, in her long-past youth had been a racer and swept the stakes at Cincinnati, and who now at the sound of battle felt her old blood rise, kept neck to neck with the fleet horses,

Spitfire and Starlight. At last old Jenny shot past them, and in her excitement Beatrice rose, and standing upright, urged her ponies on until Jenny's wind gave out, and Starlight and Spitfire were far ahead and rushing down the turnpike at a break-neck speed, which rocked the light phaeton from side to side and seemed almost to lift it from the ground. It was a decided runaway now, and people stopped to look after the mad horses and the excited but not in the least frightened girl, who, still standing upright, with her hat hanging down her back and her wig a little awry, kept them with a firm hand straight in the road, and said to the white-faced man beside her, when he, too, sprang up to take the reins: "Sit down and keep quiet. I'll see you safely through. We can surely ride as fast as they can run. I rather enjoy it."

And so she did until they came to a point where the road turned with the river, and where in the bend a little school-house stood. It was just recess, and a troop of boys came crowding out, whooping and yelling as only boys can whoop and yell, when they saw the ponies, who, really frightened now, shied suddenly, and reared high in the air. After that came chaos and darkness to Everard, and the next he knew he was lying on the grass, with his head in Bee's lap, and the blood flowing from a deep gash in his forehead, just above the left eye. This she was stanching with her handkerchief, and bathing his face with the water the boys brought her in a tin dipper from the school-house. Far off in the distance the ponies were still running, and scattered at intervals along the road were fragments of the broken phaeton, together with Bee's bonnet, and, worse than all, her wig. But Bee did not know that she had lost it, or care for her ruined phaeton. She did not know or care for anything, except that Everard Forrest was lying upon the grass as white and still as if he were really dead. But Everard was not dead, and the doctor, who soon came up with the panting, mortified Jennie, said it was only a flesh wound, from which nothing serious would result. Then Bee thought of her hair, which a boy had rescued from a playful puppy who was doing his best to tear it in pieces. The sight of her wig made Bee herself again, and with many a merry joke at her own expense, she mounted into a farmer's wagon with Everard, and bade the driver take them back to the Forrest House.

It was Rossie who met them first, her black eyes growing troubled and anxious when she saw the bandage on Everard's head. But he assured her it was nothing, while Bee laughed over the adventure, and when the judge would have censured his son, took all the blame upon herself, and then, promising to call again in the evening, went in search of her truant horses.

CHAPTER VI

MOTHER AND SON

That afternoon Mrs. Forrest seemed so much better that even her husband began to hope, when he saw the color on her cheek, and the increased brightness of her eyes. But she was not deceived. She knew the nature of her disease, and that she had not long to live. So what she would say to her son must be said without delay. Accordingly, after lunch, she bade Rossie send him to her, and then leave them alone together. Everard obeyed the summons at once, though there was a shrinking fear in his heart as he thought, "Now I must tell her of Josey," and wondered what she would say. Since his drive with Beatrice it did not seem half so easy to talk of Josephine, and that marriage ceremony was very far away, and very unreal, too. His mother was propped up on her pillows, and smiled pleasantly upon him as he took his seat beside her.

"Everard," she began, "there are so many things I must say to you about the past and the future, and I must say them now while I have the strength. Another day may be too late."

He knew to what she referred, and with a protest against it, told her she was not going to die; she must not; she must live for him, who would be nothing without her.

Very gently she soothed him into quiet, and he listened while she talked of all he had been, and all she wished him to be in the future. Faithfully, but gently, she went over with his faults, one by one, beseeching him to forsake them, and with a bursting heart he promised everything which she required, and told her again of the reform already commenced.

"God bless you, my boy, and prosper you as you keep this pledge to your dying mother, and whether you are great or not, may you be good and Christlike, and come one day to meet me where sorrow is unknown," she said to him finally; then, after a pause, she continued: "There is one subject more of which, as a woman and your mother, I must speak to you. Some day you will marry, of course——"

"Yes, mother," and Everard started violently, while the cold sweat stood in drops about his lips, but he could say no more then, and his mother continued: "I have thought many times who and what your wife would be, and have pictured her often to myself, and loved her for your sake; but I shall never see her, when she comes here I shall be gone, and so I will speak of her now, and say it is not my wish that you should wait many years before marrying. I believe in early marriages, where there is mutual love and esteem. Then you make allowance more readily for each other's habits and peculiarities. I mean no disrespect to your father, he has been kind to me, but I think he waited too long; there were too many years between us; my feelings and ideas were young, his middle-aged; better begin alike for perfect unity. And, my boy, be sure you marry a lady."

"A lady, mother?" Everard said, wondering if his mother would call Josephine a lady.

"Yes, Everard," she replied, "a lady in the true sense of the word, a person of education and refinement, and somewhere near your own rank in life. I never believed in the Maud Muller poem, never was sorry that the judge did not take the maiden for his wife. He might, perhaps, never have blushed for her, but he would have blushed for her family, and their likeness in his children's faces would have been a secret annoyance. I do not say that every mesalliance proves unhappy, but it is better to marry your equal, if you can, for a low-born person, with low-born tastes, will, of necessity, drag you down to her level."

She stopped a moment to rest, but Everard did not speak for the fierce struggle in his heart. He must tell her of Josephine, and could he say that she had no low-born tastes? Alas, he could not, when he remembered things which had dropped from her pretty lips so easily and naturally, and at which he had laughed as at something spicy and daring. His mother would call them coarse, with all her innate refinement and delicacy, and a shiver ran through him as he seemed to hear again the words "I pronounce you man and wife." They were always ringing in his ears, louder sometimes than at others, and now they were so loud as almost to drown the low voice which after a little went on:

"I do not believe in parents selecting companions for their children, but surely I may suggest. You are not obliged to follow my suggestion. I would have your choice perfectly free," she added, quickly, as she saw a look of consternation on his face, and mistook its meaning. "I have thought, and think still, that were I to choose for you, it would be Beatrice."

"Beatrice! Bee Belknap! mother," and Everard fairly gasped. "Bee Belknap is a great deal older than I am."

"Just a year, which is not much in this case. She will not grow old fast, while you will mature early; the disparity would never be thought of," Mrs. Forrest said. "Beatrice is a little wild, and full of fun and frolic, but under all that is a deep-seated principle of propriety and right, which makes her a noble and lovely character. I should be willing to trust you with her, and your father's heart is quite set on this match. I may tell you now that it has been in his mind for years, and I wish you to please him, both for his sake and yours. I hope you will think of it, Everard, and try to love Beatrice; surely it cannot be hard to do that?"

"No, mother," Everard said, "but you seem to put her out of the question entirely. Is she to have no choice in the matter, and do you think that, belle and flirt as she is, she would for a moment consider me, Ned Forrest, whom she calls a boy, and ridicules unmercifully? She would not have me, were I to ask her a thousand times."

"I think you may be wrong," Mrs. Forrest said. "It surely can't be that you love some one else?" and she looked at him searchingly.

Now was the time to speak of Josephine, if ever, and while his heart beat so loudly that he could hear it, he said, "Yes, mother, I do like some one else;—it is a young girl in Holburton, where I staid last summer. She is very beautiful. This is her picture," and he passed Josephine's photograph to his mother, who studied it carefully for two or three minutes; then turning her eyes to her son she said: "She is beautiful, so far as features and complexion are concerned, but I am greatly mistaken in you if the original of this face can satisfy you long."

"Why, mother, what fault have you to find with her? Isn't she a born lady?" Everard asked, a little scornfully, for he was warming up in Josephine's defense.

"Don't misunderstand what I mean by a lady," Mrs. Forrest said. "Birth has not all to do with it. Persons may be born of the lowliest parentage, and in the humblest shed, but still have that within them which will refine, and soften, and elevate till the nobility within asserts itself, and lifts them above their surroundings. In this case," and she glanced again at the picture, "the inborn nobility, if there were any, has had time to assert itself, and stamp its impress upon the face, and it has not done that."

"For pity's sake, mother, tell me what you see to dislike so much in Josephine!" Everard burst out, indignantly.

His mother knew he was angry, but she would not spare him, lest a great misfortune should befall him. She saw the face she looked upon was very fair, but there was that about it from which she shrank intuitively, her quick woman instinct telling her it was false as fair, and not at all the face she would have in her boy's home; so she answered him unhesitatingly:

"Shall I tell you the kind of person I fancy this girl to be, judging from her picture? Her face is one to attract young men like you, and she would try to attract you, too, and the very manner with which she would do it would be the perfection of art. There is a treacherous, designing look in these eyes, so blue and dreamy, and about the mouth there is a cruel, selfish expression which I do not like. I do not believe she can be trusted. And then, it may be a minor matter, I do not like her style of dress. A really modest girl would not have sat for her picture with so much exposure of neck and arms, and so much jewelry. Surely you must have noticed the immense chain and cross, and all the show of bracelets, and pins, and ornaments in her hair."

Everard had thought of it, but he would not acknowledge it, and his mother continued:

"The whole effect is tawdry, and, excuse me for putting it so strongly, but it reminds me of the dollar store, and the jewelry bought there. She cannot have the true instincts of a lady. Who is she, Everard, and where does she live?"

Everard was terribly hurt and intensely mortified, while something told him that his mother was not altogether wrong in her estimation of the girl, whose picture did resemble more a second-rate actress tricked out in her flashy finery than a pure, modest young girl; but he answered his mother's question, and said:

"She lives in Holburton, New York, and her name is Josephine Fleming. I boarded for three weeks last summer with her mother, Widow Roxie Fleming, as the people call her."

He spit the last out a little defiantly, feeling resolved that his mother should know all he knew about the Flemings, be it good or bad, but he was not prepared for the next remark.

"Roxie? Roxie Fleming? Is she a second wife, and is there a step daughter much older than Josephine?"

"Yes; but how did you know it, and where have you seen them?" Everard asked, eagerly, his anger giving way to his nervous dread of some development worse even than the dollar jewelry, which had hurt him cruelly.

"Years ago, when I was a young girl, we had in our family a cook, Roxie Burrows by name, competent, tidy, and faithful in the discharge of her duties, but crafty, designing and ambitious. Our butcher was a Mr. Fleming, a native of Ireland, and a very respectable man, whose little daughter used sometimes to bring us the steak for breakfast in the morning, and through whom Roxie captured the father, after the mother died. She was so sorry for the child, and mended her frocks, and made much of her till the father was won, when, it was said, the tables were turned, and little Agnes mended the frocks and darned the socks, while Roxie played the lady. I remember hearing of the birth of a daughter, but I was married about that time, and knew no more of the Flemings until a few years later, when I was visiting in Boston, and mother told me that he was dead, and Roxie had gone with the children to some place West. I am sure it must be the same woman with whom you boarded. Has she sandy hair and light gray eyes, with long yellow lashes?"

"Yes, she has; it is the same," Everard replied, with a feeling like death in his heart as he thought how impossible it was now to tell his mother that Josephine was his wife.

How impossible it was that she would ever be reconciled to the daughter of her cook and butcher, who added to her other faults the enormity of wearing dollar jewelry! And I think that last really hurt Everard the most. On such points he was very fastidious and particular, and more than once had himself thought Josey's dress too flashy, but the glamour of love was over all, and a glance of her blue eyes, or touch of her white hands always set him right again and brought him back to his allegiance. But the hands and the eyes were not there now to stand between him and what his mother had said, and he felt like crying out bitterly as he took back his photograph and listened a few moments longer, while his mother talked lovingly and kindly, telling him he must forgive her if she had seemed harsh, that it was for his good, as he would one day see. He would forget this boyish fancy in time and come to wonder at his infatuation. Forget it! with those words ever in his ears, "I pronounce you man and wife." He could not forget, and it was not quite sure that he would do so if he could. Josey's face and Josey's wiles had a power over him yet to keep him comparatively loyal. He had loved her with all the intensity of a boy's first fervent passion, which never stopped to criticise her manner, or language, or style of dress, though, now that his eyes were opened a little, it occurred to him that there might be something flashy in her appearance, and something told him that the massive chain and cross, so conspicuous on Josephine's bosom, came from that store in Pittsfield, where everything was a dollar, from an immense picture down to a set of spoons. And his mother had detected it, by what subtle intuition he could not guess; and had traced her origin back to a butcher and a cook! Well, what then? Was Josey the worse for that? Was it not America's boast that the children of butchers, and bakers, and candlestick-makers should stand in the high places and give rule? Certainly it was, and his mother herself had said it was neither birth nor blood which made the lady. It was a nobleness from within asserting itself without, and stamping its impress upon its possessor. And had Josephine this inborn refinement and nobility, or had she not? That was the point which troubled the young man as he went out from his mother's presence, and sought a little arbor in a retired part of the grounds where he would be free to think it out. With his head, which was aching terribly, bowed upon his hands, he went over all the past as connected with Josephine, detecting here and there many a word and act which, alas, went far toward proving that his mother's estimate of her was not very wrong. But how did his mother divine it? Had women some secret method of reading each other unknown to the other sex. Could Beatrice read her, too, from that photograph, and what would Bee's verdict be? He wished he knew; wished he could show it to her incidentally as the photograph of a mere acquaintance. And while he was thus thinking he heard in the distance Bee's voice, and lifting up his head he saw her coming down the long walk gayly and airily, in her pretty white muslin dress, with a bit of pink coral in her ears and in the lace bow at her throat. One could see that she was a saucy, fun-loving, frolicsome girl, with opinions of her own, which sometimes startled the staid ones who walked year by year in the same rut, but she was every whit a lady, and looked it, too, as she came rapidly toward Everard, who found himself studying and criticising her as he had never criticised a woman before. She was not like Josephine, though wherein the difference consisted he could not tell. He only knew that the load at his heart was heavier than ever, and that he almost felt that in some way he was aggrieved by this young girl, who, when she saw him, hastened her steps and was soon at his side.

"Oh, here you are," she said, "Rossie told me I should find you in the garden. I came to inquire after that broken head, for which I feel responsible. Why, Ned," she continued, calling him by the old familiar name of his boyhood, "how white you are! I am afraid it was more serious than I supposed;" and she looked anxiously into his pale, worn face.

His head was aching terribly, but he would not acknowledge it. He only said he was a little tired, that the cut on his forehead was nothing, and would soon be well; then, making Beatrice sit down beside him, he began to ask her numberless questions about the people of Rothsay, especially the young ladies. Where was Sylvia Blackmer, and where was Annie Doane, and, by the way, where was Allie Beadle, that pretty little blonde, with the great blue eyes, who used to sing in the choir.

"By Jove, she was pretty," he said, "except that her hair was a little too yellow. She looks so much like a girl east that some of the college boys rave about, only this girl, Miss Fleming, is the prettier of the two. I shouldn't wonder if I had her photograph somewhere. She had a lot taken and gave me one. Yes, here it is," he continued, after a feint of rummaging his pocket-book. "What do you think of her?" he asked, passing the picture to Beatrice, and feeling himself a monster of duplicity and deception.

Bee took the card, and looking at it a moment, said:

"Yes, she is very pretty; but you don't want anything to do with that girl. She is not like you."

It was the old story repeated, and Everard felt nettled and annoyed, but managed not to show it, as he replied:

"Who said I did want anything to do with her? But honestly, though, what do you see in her to dislike?"

"Nothing to dislike," Bee said, "I do not fancy her make-up, that's all. She looks as if she would wear cotton lace!" and having said what in her estimation was the worst thing she could say of a woman, Beatrice handed him back the picture, which he put up silently, feeling that he could not tell Beatrice of Josey.

He could not tell anybody unless it was Rossie, and he did not believe he cared to do that now, though he would like to show her the picture and hear what she had to say. Would she see dollar jewelry and cotton lace in the face he thought so divine? He meant to try her, and after Beatrice was gone he strolled off to a shaded part of the grounds, where he came upon Rossie watering a bed of fuchsias. She was not sylph-like and graceful, or clad in airy muslin, like Beatrice. She was unformed and angular, and her dress was a dark chintz, short enough to show her slender ankles, which he had once teasingly called pipe-stems, and her thick boots, which were much too large, for she would not have her feet pinched, and always wore shoes a size and a-half too big. A clean white apron, ruffled and fluted, and a white sun-bonnet, completed her costume. Josephine would have called her "homely," if she had noticed her at all, and some such idea was in Everard's mind as he approached her; but when, at the sound of his footsteps, she turned and flashed upon him from beneath the cape bonnet those great, brilliant eyes, he changed his mind, and thought: "Won't those eyes do mischief yet, when Rossie gets a little older."

She was glad to see him, and stopped watering her flowers while she inquired after his head, and if Miss Belknap found him.

"Yes, she did," he said, adding, as he sat down in a rustic chair: "Bee is handsome and no mistake."

"That's so," Rossie replied, promptly, for Bee Belknap's beauty was her hobby. "She is the handsomest girl I ever saw. Don't you think so?"

Here was his opportunity, and he hastened to seize it.

"Why, no," he said, "not the very handsomest I ever saw. I have a photograph of a girl I think prettier. Here she is." And he passed Josephine's picture toward Rossie, who set down her watering-pot, and wiping her soiled hands, took it as carefully as if it had been the picture of a goddess.

"Oh, Mr. Everard!" she cried, "she is beautiful; more so than Miss Beatrice, I do believe. Such dreamy eyes, which look at you so kind of—kind of coaxingly, somehow; and such lovely hair! Who is she, Mr. Everard?"

"Oh, she's one of the girls," Everard answered, laughingly, and experiencing a sudden revulsion of feeling in Josey's favor at Rossie's opinion of her.

Here was one who could give an unprejudiced opinion; here was a champion for Josey; and in his delight, Everard thought how, with his first spare money, he would buy Rossie a gold ring, as a reward of merit for what she had said of Josey. Her next remarks, however, dampened his ardor a little.

"She's very rich, isn't she?" Rossie asked; and he replied:

"No, not rich at all. Why do you think that?"

"Because she has such a big chain and cross, and such heavy bracelets and ear-rings, and is dressed more than Miss Belknap dresses at a grand party," Rossie said: and Everard answered her quickly:

"Rossie, you are a little thing, not much bigger than my thumb, but you have more sense than many older girls. Tell me, then, if you know, is it bad taste to be overdressed in a picture, and is it a crime, a sin, to wear bogus jewelry?"

She did not at all know at what he was aiming, and, pleased with the compliment to her wisdom, answered, with great gravity:

"Not a crime to wear flash jewelry,—no. I wore a brass ring once till it blacked my finger. I wore a glass breast-pin, too, which cost me twenty-five cents, till your mother said it was foolish, and not like a lady. But I do not think it's a crime; it's only second-classy. A great many do it, and I shouldn't wonder a bit if,"—here the little lady looked very wise, and lifted her forefinger by way of emphasis—"I shouldn't wonder a bit if this chain and cross were both shams, for now that I look at her more closely, she looks like a sham, too."

Rosamond's prospect for a ring was gone forever, and Everard's voice trembled as he took back his picture, and said:

"Thank you, Rossie, for telling me what you thought. Maybe she is a sham. Most things are in this world, I find."

Then he walked rapidly away, while Rossie stood looking after him and wondering if he was angry with her, and who the young girl was, and if he really liked her.

"I hope not," she thought, "for though she is very handsome, there is something about her which does not seem like Mr. Everard and Miss Beatrice. They ought to go together; they must; it is so suitable;" and having settled the future of Beatrice and Everard to her own satisfaction, the little girl resumed her work among the flowers, and did not see Everard again until suppertime, when he looked so pale and tired that even his father noticed it and asked if he were sick.

The cut over his eye was paining him, he said, and if they would excuse him he would retire to his room early, and should probably be all right on the morrow. The night was hot and sultry, and even the light breeze from the river seemed oppressive and laden with thunder, and for hours Everard lay awake thinking of the future, which stretched before him so drearily with that burden on his mind. How he wished that it might prove a dream, from which he should awake to find himself free once more,—free to marry Josephine if he chose, and he presumed he should, but not till his college days were over, and he could take her openly and publicly as a true man takes the woman he loves and honors. How he hated to be a sneak and a coward, and he called himself by these names many times, and loathed himself for the undefinable something creeping over him, and which made him shrink even from Josephine herself as Josephine. He said he did not care a picayune for the butcher and the cook, and he did not care for the dollar jewelry and cotton lace, though he would rather his mother and Bee had not used the opprobrious terms, but he did care for the sham of which his mother had spoken, and which even Rossie had detected. Was Josey a sham, and if so, what was his life with her to be? Alas for Everard! he was only just entering the cloud which was to overshadow him for so many wretched years. At last he fell into a troubled sleep, from which he was aroused by the noise of the storm of rain which had swept down the river and was beating against the house, but above the storm there was another sound, Rossie calling to him in tones of affright, and bidding him hasten to his mother, who was dying.

Of all which followed next Everard retained in after life but a vague consciousness. There was a confused dressing in the dark, a hurrying to his mother, whose white face turned so eagerly toward him, and whose pallid lips were pressed upon his brow as they prayed God to keep him from evil, and bring him at last to the world she was going to. There were words of love and tender parting to the stricken husband and heart-broken Rossie, who had been to her like a daughter, and whom she committed to the care of both Everard and his father, as a precious legacy left in their charge. Then, drawing Everard close to her, she whispered so low that no one else could hear:

"Forgive me if I seemed harsh in what I said of Josephine. I only meant it for your good. I may have been mistaken; I hope I was. I hope she is good, and true, and womanly, and if she is, and you love her, her birth is of no consequence, none whatever. God bless you, my child, and her, too!"

She never spoke again, and when the early summer morning looked into the room, there was only a still, motionless figure on the bed, with pale hands folded upon the bosom, and the pillow strewn with flowers, which Rosamond had put there. Rosamond thought of everything; first of the dead, then of the stern judge, who broke down entirely by the side of his lost Mary, and then of Everard, who seemed like one stunned by a heavy blow. With the constantly increasing pain in his head, blinding him even more than the tears he shed, he wrote to Josephine:

"Oh, Josey, you will be sorry for me when I tell you mother is dead. She died this morning at three o'clock, and I am heart-broken. She was all the world to me. What shall I do without my mother?"

He posted the letter himself, and then kept his room, and for the most part his bed, until the day of the funeral, when, hardly knowing what he was doing, or realizing what was passing around him, he stood by his mother's grave, saw the coffin lowered into it, heard the earth rattling down upon it, and had a strange sensation of wonder as to whom they were burying, and who he was himself. That puzzled him the most, except, indeed, the question as to where the son was, the young man from Amherst College, who drove such fast horses, and smoked so many cigars, and sometimes bet at cards. "He ought to be here seeing to this," he thought; and then, as a twinge of pain shot through his temple, he moaned faintly, and went back to the carriage, in which he was driven rapidly home.

There was a letter from Josephine in his room, which had come while he was at his mother's grave. He recognized the handwriting at once, and with a feeling as if something were clutching his throat and impeding his breath, he took it up, and opening it, read his first letter from his wife.

CHAPTER VII

JOSEPHINE

Immediately after Everard's departure she wrote to the postmaster at Clarence, making inquiries for Doctor Matthewson, and in due time received an answer addressed to the fictitious name which she had given. There had been a clergyman in town by that name, the postmaster wrote, but he had been dismissed for various misdemeanors. However, a marriage performed by him, with the knowledge and consent of the parties, would undoubtedly be binding on such parties. Latterly he had taken to the study of medicine, and assumed the title of "Doctor."

There could be no mistake, and the harrowing doubt which had so weighed on Josephine's spirits gave way as she read this answer to her letter. She was Mrs. James Everard Forrest, and she wrote the name many times on slips of paper which she tore up and threw upon the floor. Then, summoning Agnes from the kitchen, she bade her arrange her hair, for there was a concert in the Hall that night, and she was going. Always meek and submissive, Agnes obeyed, and brushed and curled the beautiful golden hair, and helped array her sister in the pretty blue muslin, and clasped about her neck and arms the heavy bracelets and chain which had been so criticised and condemned at the Forrest House. They were not quite as bright now as when the young lady first bought them in Pittsfield. Their luster was somewhat tarnished, and Josephine knew it, and felt a qualm of disgust every time she looked at them. She knew the difference between the real and the sham quite as well as Beatrice herself, and by and by, when she was established in her rightful position as Mrs. Everard Forrest, she meant to indulge to the full her fondness for dress, and make amends for the straits to which she had all her life been subjected.

"She would make old Forrest's money fly, only let her have a chance," she said to Agnes, to whom she was repeating the contents of the letter just received from Clarence.

"Then it's true, and you are his wife?" Agnes said, her voice indicative of anything but pleasure.

This Josephine was quick to detect, and she answered, sharply:

"His wife? yes. Have you any objection? One would suppose by your manner that you were sorry for Everard."

"And so I am," Agnes answered, boldly. "I don't believe he knew what he was doing. It's a pity for him, he is so young, and we so different."

"So different, Agnes? I wish you wouldn't forever harp on that string. As if I were not quite as good as a Forrest or any other aristocrat. Can't you ever forget your Irish blood? It does not follow because the poor people in Ireland and England lie down and let the nobility walk over them, that we do it in America, where it does sometimes happen that the daughter of a butcher and a cook may marry into a family above her level."

"Yes, I know all that," Agnes said. "Praised be Heaven for America, where everybody who has it in him can rise if he will; and yet, there's a difference here, just as much and more, I sometimes think, for to be somebody you must have it in you. I can't explain, but I know what I mean, and so do you."

"Yes, I do," Josephine replied, angrily. "You mean that I have not the requisite qualifications to make me acceptable at the Forrest House; that my fine lady from Boston would be greatly shocked to know that the mother of her daughter-in-law once cooked her dinner and washed her clothes."

"No, not for that,—not for birth or poverty," Agnes said, eagerly, "but because you are,—you are——"

"Well, what?" Josephine demanded, impatiently, and Agnes replied:

"You are what you are."

"And pray what am I?" Josephine retorted. "I was Miss Josephine Fleming, daughter of Mrs. Roxie Fleming, who used to work for the Bigelows of Boston till she married an Irish butcher, who was shabby enough to die and leave her to shift for herself, which she did by taking boarders. That's what I was. Now, I am Mrs. James Everard Forrest, with a long line of blue-blooded Southern ancestry, to say nothing of the bluer Bigelows of Boston. That's who I am; so please button my boots and bring me my shawl and fan; it's high time I was off."

Agnes obeyed, and buttoned the boots, and put a bit of blacking on the toe where the leather was turning red, and brought the fleecy shawl and wrapped it carefully around her sister, who looked exceedingly graceful and pretty, and bore herself like a princess as she entered the Hall and took one of the most conspicuous seats. How she wished the people could know the honor to which she had come; and when, to the question as to who she was, asked by a stranger behind her, she heard the reply, "Oh, that's Joe Fleming; her mother keeps boarders," she longed to shriek out her new name, and announce herself as Mrs. James Everard Forrest. But it was policy to keep silent, and she was content to bide her time, and anticipate what she would do in the future when her marriage was announced. Of Everard himself she thought a great deal, but she thought more of his position and wealth than she did of him. And yet she was very anxious to hear from him, and when his letter came she tore it open eagerly, while a bright flush colored her cheek when she saw the words, "My dear little wife," and her heart was very light as she read the brief letter,—so light, in fact, that it felt no throb of pity for the sick and dying mother. Josey had heard from her mother of the aristocratic Miss Bigelow, at whose grand wedding governors and senators had been present, and she shrank from this high-born woman, who might weigh her in the balance and find her sadly wanting. So she felt no sympathy with Everard's touching inquiry, "What shall I do without my mother?" He would do very well indeed, she thought, and as for herself, she would rather reign alone at Forrest House than share her kingdom with another. How she chafed and fretted that she could not begin her triumph at once, but must wait two years, at least, and be known as Josephine Fleming, who held her position in Holburton only with her pretty face and determined will. But there was no help for it, and, for the present, she must be content with the knowledge that Everard was hers, and that by and by his money would be hers also. To do her justice, however, she was just now a good deal in love with her young husband, and thought of him almost as often as of his money, though that was a very weighty consideration, and when her mother suggested that there was no reason why she should not, to a certain degree, be supported by her husband, even if she did not take his name, she indorsed the suggestion heartily, and the letter she wrote to Everard, in reply to his, contained a request for money.

The letter was as follows:

"Holburton, July—.

"Dear Everard:—I was so glad to get your letter, and oh, my darling, how sorry I am to hear of your dear mother's dangerous illness! I trust it is not as bad as you feared, and hope she may recover. I know I should love her, and I mean to try to be what I think she would wish your wife to be. I am anxious to know if you told her, and what she said.

"I have written to Clarence, as Dr. Matthewson bade me do, and find that he really was a clergyman; so there can be no mistake about the marriage, and if you do not regret it I certainly do not, only it is kind of forlorn to know you have a husband and still live apart from him, and be denied the privilege of his name. It is for the best, however, and I am content to wait your pleasure. And, now, my dear husband, don't think meanly of me, will you, and accuse me of being mercenary. You would not if you knew the straits we are driven to in order to meet our expenses. Now that I am your wife I wish to take lessons in music and French, so as to fit myself for the position I hope one day to fill in your family. You must not be ashamed of me, and you shall not, if I only have the means with which to improve my mind. If you can manage to send me fifty dollars I shall make the best possible use of it. You do not know how I hate to ask you so soon, but I feel that I must in order to carry out my plans for improvement.

"And now, my darling husband, I put both my arms around your

neck and kiss you many, many times, and ask you not to be angry with me, but write to me soon, and send the money, if possible.

"Truly, lovingly, faithfully, your wife, Joe."

"I haven't told more than three falsehoods," Josey said to herself, as she read the letter over. "I said I hoped his mother would recover, and that I knew I should love her, and that I wanted the money to pay for music and French, when, in fact, I want more a silk dress in two shades of brown. And he will send it, too. He'll manage to get it from his father or mother, and I may as well drop in at Burt's and look at the silk this afternoon, on my way to post this letter."

She did drop in at Burt's and looked at the silk, and saw another piece, more desirable every way, and fifty cents more a yard. And from looking she grew to coveting, and was sorry that she had not asked for seventy-five instead of fifty dollars, as the one would be as likely to be forthcoming as the other. Once she thought to open her letter and add a P. S. to it, but finally decided to wait and write again for the extra twenty-five. The merchant would reserve the silk for her a week or more, he said, and picturing to herself how she should look in the two shades of brown, Josey tripped off to the post-office, where she deposited the letter, which Everard found upon his table on his return from his mother's grave. It was the silk which in Josey's mind was the most desirable, but the music and the French must be had as well, and so she called upon a Mrs. Herring, who gave music lessons in the town, and proposed that she should have two lessons a week, with the use of piano, and that as compensation the lady's washing, and that of her little girl, should be done by sister Agnes, who was represented as the instigator of the plan. As the arrangement was better for the lady than for Josey, the bargain was closed at once, and Mrs. J. E. Forrest took her first lesson that very afternoon, showing such an aptitude and eagerness to learn that her teacher assured her of quick and brilliant success as a performer. The French was managed in much the same way, and paid for in plain sewing, which Josey, who was handy and neat with her needle, undertook herself, instead of putting it upon her mother or poor Agnes, who, on the Monday following, saw, with dismay, the basket piled high with extra linen, which she was to wash and iron. There was a weary sigh from the heavily-burdened woman, and then she took up this added task without a single protest, and scrubbed, and toiled, and sweat, that Josey might have the accomplishments which were to fit her to be mistress of the Forrest House.

Every day Josey passed the shop window at Burt's, and stopped to admire the silk, and at last fell into the trap laid for her by the scheming merchant, who told her that three other ladies had been looking at it with a view to purchase, and she'd better decide to take it at once if she really wanted it; so she took it, and wrote to Everard that night, asking why he did not send the fifty dollars, and asking him to increase it with twenty-five more.

CHAPTER VIII

EVERARD

He was so giddy, and sick, and faint, when he returned to the house from his mother's grave, that he had scarcely strength to reach his room, where the first object which caught his eye was Josephine's letter upon the table. Very eagerly he caught it up, and breaking the seal, began to read it, his pulse quickening and his heart beating rapidly as he thought, "She would be so sorry for me if she knew."

He was so heart-sore and wretched in his bereavement, and he wanted the sympathy of some one,—wanted to be petted, as his mother had always petted him in all his griefs, and as she would never pet him again. She was dead, and his heart went out with a great yearning after his young wife, as the proper person to comfort and soothe him now. Had she been there he would have declared her his in the face of all the world, and laying his aching head in her lap would have sobbed out his sorrow. But she was far away, and he was reading her letter, which did not give him much satisfaction from the very first. There was an eagerness to assure him that the marriage was valid, and he was glad, of course, that it was so, and could not blame her for chafing against the secrecy which they must for a time maintain; but what was this request for fifty dollars,—this hint that she had a right to ask support from him? In all his dread of the evils involved in a secret marriage he had never dreamed that she would ask him so soon for fifty dollars, when he had not five in the world, and but for Rosamond's generous forethought in sending him the ten he would have been obliged to borrow to get home. Fifty dollars! It seemed to the young man like a fabulous sum, which he could never procure. For how was he to do it? He had told his father distinctly that he was free from debt, that he did not owe a dollar, and if he should go to him now with a request for fifty dollars what would he say? It made Everard shiver just to think of confronting his stern father with that demand. The thing was impossible. "I can't do it," he said; and then, in his despair, it occurred to him that Josey had no right to make this demand upon him so soon; she might have known he could only meet it by asking his father, which was sure to bring a fearful storm about his head. It was not modest, it was not nice in her, it was not womanly; Bee would never have done it, Rossie would never have done it; but they were different—and there came back to him the remembrance of what his mother had said, and with it a great horror lest Josephine might really lack that innate refinement which marks a true lady. But he would not be disloyal to her even in thought; she was his wife, and she had a right to look to him for support when she could have nothing else. She could not take his name, she could not have his society, and he was a brute to feel annoyed because she asked him for money with which to fit herself for his wife. "She is to be commended for it," he thought. "I wish her to be accomplished when I present her to Bee, who is such a

39

splendid performer, and jabbers French like a native. Oh, if I had the money," he continued, feeling as by a revelation that Josephine would never cease her importunings until she had what she wanted.

But how should he get it? Could he work at something and earn it, or could he sell his watch, his mother's gift when he was eighteen?

"No, not that; I can't part with that," he groaned; and then he remembered his best suit of clothes, which had cost nearly a hundred dollars, and a great many hard words from his father. He could sell these in Cincinnati; he had just money enough to go there and back, and he would do it the next day, and make some excuse for taking a valise, and no one need be the wiser. That was the very best thing he could do, and comforted with this decision he crept shivering to bed just as the clock was striking the hour of eleven.

Breakfast waited a long time for him the next morning, and when she saw how impatient the judge was growing, Rosamond went to his door and knocked loudly upon it, but received no answer, except a faint sound like a moan of pain, which frightened her, and sent her at once to the judge, who went himself to his son's room. Everard was not asleep, nor did he look as if he had ever slept, with his blood-shot, wide-open eyes rolling restlessly in his head, which moved from side to side as if in great distress. He did not know his father; he did not know anybody; and said that he was not sick, when the doctor came, and he would not be blistered and he wouldn't be bled; he must get up and have his clothes,—his best ones,—and he made Rossie bring them to him and fold them up and put them in his satchel, which he kept upon his bed all during the two weeks when he lay raving with delirium and burning with fever induced by the cut on his head, and aggravated by the bleeding and blistering which he had without stint. Rossie was the nurse who staid constantly with him, and who alone could quiet him when he was determined to get up and sell his clothes. This was the burden of his talk.

"I must sell them and get the money," he would say,—but, with a singular kind of cunning common to crazy people, he never said money before his father. It was only to Rosamond that he talked of that, and once, when she sat alone with him, he said:

"Don't let the governor know, for your life."

"No, I won't; you can trust me," she replied; then, while she bathed his throbbing head, she asked: "Why do you want the money, Mr. Everard? What will you do with it?"

"Send it to Joe," he said. "Do you know Joe?"

Rossie didn't know Joe, and she innocently asked:

"Who is he?"

"Who is he?" Everard repeated: "ha, ha! that's a good joke. He,—Joe would enjoy that; he is a splendid fellow, I tell you."

"And you owe him?" Rossie asked, her heart sinking like lead at his prompt reply.

"Yes, that's it; you've hit the nail. I owe him and I must pay, and that's why I sell my clothes. I owe him money,—him,—that's capital."

He had told her that he had no debts and she believed him, and had been so glad, and thought he had broken from his old associates and habits, and was trying to do better. And it was not so at all; he had not broken off; he still had dealings with a mysterious Joe, whoever he might be. Some great hulking fellow, no doubt, who drank, and raced, and gambled, and had led Everard astray. Rossie's heart was very sad and her voice full of sorrow as she asked next:

"Was it gambling? Was it at play that you incurred this debt?"

"Yes, by George, you've hit it again!" he exclaimed, catching at the word play. "It was a play, and for fun I thought at first, but it proved to be the real thing,—a lark,—a sell,—a trap. By Jove, I b'lieve it was a trap, and they meant me to fall into it; I do, upon my word, and I fell, and now Joe must have fifty dollars from me."

"Fifty dollars!" and Rossie gasped at the enormous sum.

Where would he get it? Where could he get it? Not from his father, that was certain, and not from her, for her quarterly interest on her two thousand dollars was not due in weeks, and even if it were, it was not fifty dollars. Perhaps Miss Belknap would loan it if she were to ask her, and assume the payment herself. But in that case she must give the reason, and she would not for the world compromise Everard by so much as a breath of censure. Bee must think well of him at all costs, for Rossie's heart was quite as much set on Beatrice's being the mistress of Forrest House, some day, as the mother's had been. She could not borrow of Miss Belknap, but,—Rossie started from her chair as quickly as if she had been struck, while her hands involuntarily clutched her luxuriant hair, rippling in heavy masses down her back. She could do that for Mr. Everard, but her face was white to her lips, which quivered a little as she resumed her seat, and said:

"What is Joe's other name? Joe what?"

Everard looked at her cunningly a moment, and then replied:

"Guess!"

"I can't," she replied, "I have nothing to start from; nothing to guide me; I might guess all day, and not get it."

"Suppose you start with some kind of fruit, say pears. What varieties have we in our garden?" he said; and Rossie answered:

"There are the Seckels. Is it Joe Seckels?"

"No."

"Joe Bartlett?"

"No."

"Joe Bell?"

"No."

"Joe Vergelieu?"

"No."

"Joe Sheldon?"

"No."

"There's the Louise Bonne de Jersey. It can't be Joe Bonne de Jersey."

"No, stupid."

"Well, Flemish Beauty? It can't be that."

"How do you know? Joe is a beauty, and a Flemish one, if you change the sh into ng. No, try 'em again."

"Joe Fleming?" Rossie asked, and with an insane chuckle Everard replied:

"You bet! Rossie, you are a brick! You are a trump! You've hit it exactly,—Joe Fleming."

Rossie had in her pocket a pencil, and on a bit of newspaper wrote the name rapidly, and then asked:

"Does he live in Amherst?"

"No."

"In Ellicottville?"

"No."

"Well, then, in Holburton, where you were last summer. Didn't you board with a Fleming?"

"You are right again. He lives in Holburton," Everard replied, laughing immoderately at the idea of he as applied to Josephine.

Thus far he had answered all Rossie's questions correctly, but when she said, "Tell me, please, his right name. Is it Joel, or Joseph, or what?" the old look of cunning leaped into his eyes, and he answered her:

"No, you don't. Joe is enough for you to know. Besides, why are you questioning me so closely? What are you going to do?"

"I'm going to try and get you out of your trouble," Rossie said, and starting up in bed, Everard exclaimed:

"Get me out of the scrape! Oh, Rossie, if you only would,—if you only could!"

"I can, I will!" Rossie said, emphatically, and he continued:

"Out of every single bit of it?—the whole thing, so I'll be free again?"

"Yes," Rossie answered at random; "I think, I am sure, I will. But you must keep very quiet and not get excited, or talk. Try to sleep, and I'll fix it for you beautifully."

How hopeful she was, and the delirious man believed and trusted in her, and promised to sleep while she was gone to fix it.

"But it may take a few days, you know," she said, "so you must be patient, and wait."

He acceded to everything, and closed his eyes as she left the room and repaired to her own, where she went straight to the glass, and letting out her heavy braids of hair, suffered it to fall over her shoulders like a vail. Then Rossie studied herself, and saw a thin face, with great, wide-open, black eyes, which would look larger, more wide-open still, with all that hair gone. What a fright she would be without her hair, which was beautiful. Bee Belknap had said so, others had said so, and, if she was not mistaken, Everard had said so, too, and for his sake she'd like to keep it, though for his sake she was deciding to part with it. Maybe he did not think it pretty, after all. She wished she knew; and, yielding to a sudden impulse, she went back to his room with all her shining tresses about her, and so astonished him that he called out:

"Halloo, Lady Godiva! Are you going to ride through the town, clothed with modesty?"

Rossie was not well versed in Tennyson, and knew nothing of Lady Godiva, but she said to him:

"Mr. Everard, do you think my hair pretty?"

"Nothing extra," was his reply. "I've seen hair handsomer than that. Don't be vain, Rossie. You will never be a beauty, hair or no hair."

Her pride was hurt a little, but her mind was made up, and retiring to her room and fastening herself in, she sat down to write to Joe Fleming.

CHAPTER IX

THE RESULT

Reason said to her, "Perhaps there is no such person as Joe Fleming. Mr. Everard is crazy and does not know what he is saying;" but to this Rossie replied, "That may be, but even then there can be no harm in writing. The letter will go to the dead-letter office and no one be the wiser, and if there is a Joe, he deserves to have a piece of my mind. I shall write any way." And she did write, and this is a copy of the letter:

"Forrest House, Rothsay, Ohio,
"August 3d, 18—.

"*Mr. Fleming—Sir: I take the liberty of writing to you, because I think you ought to know how sick Mr. Everard Forrest is, and how much he is troubled about the money he owes you. He was thrown from a carriage and hurt, more than ten days ago, and his mother died that same night, and you wrote for money, and everything together made him very sick and out of his head, and that is the way I came to know about you and that gambling debt of his. I am Rosamond Hastings, a little girl who lives in the family, and Mr. Everard is like a brother to me, and I take care of him, and heard him talk of Joe and money which he had to pay, and he wanted to sell his clothes to raise it, and I found out from him that your name was Fleming, and that he owed you fifty dollars which must be paid at once.*

"*I suppose men would call it a debt of honor, but, Mr. Fleming, do you think it right to gamble and entice young men like Mr. Everard to play? I think it is very wicked, and dishonorable, and disreputable, and that you ought not to expect him to pay. Why, he cannot, for he has no money of his own, and his father would not give it to him for that, and would be so very angry that whatever comes he must never know it,— never.*

"*Now, will you give up the debt and not bother him any more? If you will, please write to him and say so. If you will not, write to me, and I shall try what I can do, for Mr. Everard must not be troubled with it.*

"Hoping you will excuse me, and that you will reform and be a better man, I am,

"Yours respectfully,
"Rosamond Hastings."

"P. S.—You are not to suppose that Mr. Everard knows I am writing, for he does not; nor are you to think that he has spoken ill of you in his delirium. On the contrary, I imagine that he likes you very much indeed, and so I am led to hope that there is much good in you, and that you will not only release him, but quit gambling yourself."

She sealed the letter, and directing it to "Mr. Joe Fleming, Esq., Holburton, Mass.," posted it herself, and then anxiously waited the answer.

Three days later, and the clerk in the post-office at Holburton said, in reply to Josey's inquiry for letters:

"There's one here for Mr. Joe Fleming; that can't be you."

"Let me see it," Josey said; and when she saw that it was from Rothsay, Ohio, she continued: "It is for me, and it is done for a joke. I will take it."

Then, hurrying home, she broke the seal and read the curious letter, amid screams of convulsive laughter, which brought both her mother and Agnes to her side.

"Look here; just listen, will you?" she said, "somebody thinks I'm a man, and a gambler, and everything bad." And she read the letter aloud, while the tears ran down her face, and she grew almost hysterical with her glee. "Did you ever know a richer joke? What a stupid thing that girl must be," she said.

But Agnes made no reply, and went quietly back to her work, while Josephine read the letter a third time, feeling a little sorry for and a little anxious about Everard. Rossie's postscript that he seemed to like her very much touched her and brought something like moisture to her eyes; but she never for a moment thought of giving up the debt. She must have the fifty dollars, for the brown silk was nearly finished, and the merchant expected his money, so she wrote to Rossie as follows:

"Holburton, August 7th, 18—.
"Miss Rosamond Hastings:—

"Your letter is received, and though I am very sorry for Mr. Forrest's illness, and agree with you that it is wrong to gamble, I must still insist upon the money, as I am in great want of it, and Mr. Forrest will tell you that my claim is a just one. I may as well add that twenty-five dollars more are due me, which I shall be glad to have you send. I have written Mr. Forrest about it, but presume he has not been able to attend to it.

"Hoping he is better, I am

"Yours truly,
"Joe Fleming."

Josephine's handwriting was large and plain, and she took great pains to make it still plainer and more masculine, and Rossie, when she received the letter, had no suspicion that it was not written by a man. Hastily breaking the seal, she read, with sinking heart, that the money must be paid, and, worse than all, that it was seventy-five instead of fifty dollars, as she had supposed. And she must raise it, and save Mr. Everard from all further trouble and anxiety. He was better now, and very quiet, and had allowed her to remove the satchel of clothes from his bed. Occasionally he spoke to her of Joe, and asked if she was sure she could help him out of the scrape.

"Yes, sure," was always the reply of the brave little girl; and she must keep her word at the sacrifice of what she held most dear, her abundant and beautiful hair.

Rossie's mind was made up, and, after lunch was over, she started for Elm Park, where Miss Belknap lived. Bee was at home, and glad to see her little friend. She was very fond of Rossie, whose quaint, old-fashioned ways amused and rested her; and she took her at once to the pretty blue chamber, which Rossie admired so much, and which seemed so in keeping with its lovely mistress. All Bee's tastes were of the most luxurious kind, and, as she had no lack of means, she gratified them to the full. The fever, which had deprived her of her hair, had hurt her pride sorely; for the wig which she was wearing until her own hair grew again was not a success, and she chafed against it, and hated herself every time she looked in the glass; and when Rosamond, who could not wait lest her courage should fail her, said, "Miss Beatrice, are you in earnest about my hair? Will you buy it now?" she answered,

"Buy it? Yes, in a moment."

"And give me seventy-five dollars?" Rossie faltered, ashamed of herself for asking this enormous sum.

But it did not at all appall Miss Belknap. Seventy-five dollars was nothing if she wished for anything, and she did want Rossie's hair. It was just the color and texture of her own, and she could have such a natural looking wig made of it.

"Yes, give you seventy-five dollars willingly;" she said. "But it seems very mean and selfish in me to take it," she continued; and Rossie, fearful lest the bargain should fall through, answered eagerly:

"Oh, no, it don't. I want the money very much indeed. I am anxious to sell it, and, if you do not buy it, I shall go to some one else. But you must not ask me why,—I can't tell that; only, it is not for myself,—it's for a friend; I don't think the hair worth seventy-five dollars, but that is what I must have, and so I asked it. Maybe if you can give me fifty, and loan me twenty-five, I can pay it when my allowance is due."

"You conscientious little chit," Bee said, laughingly, "you have not yet learned the world's creed,—take all you can get. I am willing to give you seventy-five dollars, and, even at that price, think it cheap. But you are a little girl, and will not look badly with short hair."

With her natural shrewdness and her knowledge of some of Everard's shortcomings, Bee guessed that it was for him the sacrifice was made, and, when the barber's scissors gleamed among the shining tresses, she saw that they did not cut too close and make the girl a fright. But the loss of her hair changed Rossie very much, and when she went back to the Forrest House she shrank from the eyes of the servants, and stole up to her own room, where she could inspect herself freely, and see just how she looked.

"Oh, how ugly I am, and how big my eyes are!", she said, and two hot tears rolled down her cheeks; but she resolutely dashed them away, and thought, "His mother would be so glad if she knew I was doing it for him."

And the memory of the dead woman, who had been so kind to her, helped her. For her sake she could bear almost anything, and, putting on her hat, she left the house again, going this time to the office of the family lawyer, Mr. Russell, a kind, elderly man, who was very fond of Rossie, and at once put aside his papers when she came in.

"Can I do anything for you to-day?" he asked, and she replied:

"I've come to ask you to write me just such a receipt as you would write if somebody owed you seventy-five dollars and you paid it in full. Don't ask me anything, only write it, and make it read as if the debtor didn't owe the creditor a penny after the date."

Mr. Russell looked curiously at the flushed face raised so eagerly to him, and in part guessed her secret. Like Bee, he knew of Everard's expensive habits, and suspected that this money had something to do with him. But he merely said:

"What name shall I use? The receipt will read like this: 'Received of,—blank,—seventy-five dollars,' and so forth. Now, how shall I fill the blank?"

Rossie thought a moment, and then replied:

"Will it make any difference who writes the receipt?"

"Not at all; the signature is what gives it its value."

"Then will you please give me a form,—a true one, you know,—which I can copy and send, and ought I not to register the letter to make it safe?"

She was quite a little business woman, and the old lawyer looked at her admiringly as he gave her the necessary directions, suggesting that a draft or post-office order would be better than to send the money. But Rossie did not care for so much publicity as she fancied drafts and post-office orders would involve. She preferred to send the bills, a fifty, a twenty, and a five, directly to Joe, and she did so that very afternoon, for, as good luck would have it, Beatrice asked her to drive to an adjoining town, where she registered and posted her letter, and felt as if a weight were lifted from her mind. She had no suspicion of Joe's playing her false. He would, of course, return the receipt, and Mr. Everard would be free, and her heart was almost as light as her head when she returned home and went to Everard's room. That poor shorn head, how it stared at her in the glass, and how she tried to brush up the short, wavy hair, and make the most of it. But do the best she could, she presented rather a forlorn appearance when she went in to Everard, and asked him how he was.

He had missed her very much that day, and greeted her with a bright smile, so much like himself, that she exclaimed, joyfully:

"Oh, Mr. Everard, you are better; you are almost well!"

He was better, but his mind was still unsettled, and running upon the scrape from which Rossie was to extricate him, and he said to her:

"Have you fixed it yet? Is it all right?"

"Yes, all right," she answered; and he continued:

"Every single bit right? Am I cut loose from the whole thing?"

She thought he was, and soothed him into quiet until he suddenly noticed her head, and exclaimed:

"Halloa, what have you been doing? Where's your hair? Have you taken it off and laid it in the drawer as mother used to do? I thought yours was a different sort from that; not store hair, but genuine. I say, Rossie, you look like a guy."

She knew he was not responsible for what he said, but it hurt her all the same, and tears sprang to her eyes as she answered him:

"My hair was very heavy and very warm this hot, sultry weather. I am sorry you do not like my looks. It will grow again in time."

That was Rossie's one comfort. Her hair would grow again, and she met bravely the exclamations of her girl friends and of the servants, who asked her numberless questions. But she kept her own counsel, and waited impatiently for the assurance that the money had gone in safety to Holburton. It came at last, on the very day when Everard began to seem like himself, and spoke to those about him rationally and naturally. His reason had returned, and his first question to Rossie was to ask if any letters had come to him during his illness, and his second, to interrogate her with regard to her hair, and why she had cut it off. She told him the old story of its being heavy and warm, and then hastened to bring his letters, of which she had taken charge. She was certain that some of them were from Joe Fleming, though the handwriting was much finer than that which had come to her in that morning's mail. Joe had sent back the receipt without a word of comment, but Rossie did not care for that; she only felt that Everard was free, and she had the receipt in her pocket, and her face was almost pretty in her bright eagerness and gladness as she came to his bedside and handed him his letters. Three were from college chums, and three from Josephine. These he opened first, beginning with the one bearing the oldest date. She had not then heard of his mother's death, and she wrote for more money,—twenty-five dollars more, which were absolutely needed. Seventy-five in all it was now, and the perspiration started from every pore and stood thickly on Everard's forehead and about his lips, as, with an involuntary moan, he dropped the letter from his nerveless hand and turned his eyes toward Rossie, not with a thought that she could help him, only with a feeling that he would tell her, and ask her what to do, and if it were not better to leave college at once, acknowledge his marriage, and hire out as a day laborer, if nothing better offered.

She saw the hunted, hopeless expression in his eyes, and guessed the cause of it. In hers there was a great gladness shining, as she said:

"I am almost certain that letter is from Mr. Joe Fleming, and I have one from him, too, or rather, a receipt in full for the gambling debt!" and taking the receipt from her pocket, she handed it to Everard, and watched him while he read it.

There it was in black and white, an acknowledgment of seventy-five dollars, and a receipt in full of all Everard Forrest's indebtedness to Joe

Fleming up to that date. What did it mean? What could it mean? Everard asked, while through his mind there flitted a vague remembrance of something about Joe, and money, and the scrape from which Rossie was to extricate him.

"Rossie, tell me, what do you know of Joe? What does it mean?" he asked, and then Rossie told him how he had raved about a Joe, to whom he said he owed money, and how once, when he seemed a little rational, she had questioned him, and found out that the man was Joe Fleming, who lived in Holburton, and to whom he owed fifty dollars which he could not pay.

"You had your best clothes in your valise on the bed, and were going to sell them to get it," Rossie said, "and I felt so sorry for you that I wrote to Mr. Fleming myself, and told him what I thought about such debts, and how sick and crazy you were, and your mother just dead, and you no way to pay, and asked him to give up the debt."

"Yes, yes," Everard gasped, while his face grew white as ashes; and still he could not forbear a smile at the mistake with regard to Joe's sex, a mistake of which he was very glad, however. "Yes," he continued, "you wrote all this, and what was the reply?"

"Just what you might expect from the bad, unprincipled, grasping man," Rossie said, energetically, shaking her shorn head. "I told him it was wrong to gamble and tempt you to play, and told him how sick you were, and how angry your father would be, and added that, if after all this, he still insisted upon the money, he was not to trouble you, but write directly to me, and he was mean enough to do it. He said he was sorry you were sick, but he must have the money, and that you owed him seventy-five, and you would tell me he had a right to ask it."

"Yes," Everard said again, but the yes was like a groan, and every muscle of his face twitched painfully, "yes. He wrote this to you, and you raised the money; but how?"

Rosamond hesitated a moment, and then replied:

"Do you remember I told you that Miss Belknap once offered to buy my hair?"

"Oh, Rossie!" Everard exclaimed, as the truth flashed upon him, making the plain face of that heroic little girl seem like the face of an angel,—"oh, Rossie, you sold your beautiful hair for me, a scamp, a sneak, a coward! Oh, why did you humiliate me so, and make me hate and loathe myself?" and in his great weakness and utter shame Everard covered his face with his hands and sobbed like a child.

Rosamond was crying, too,—was shedding bitter tears of disappointment that she had made the great sacrifice for nothing except to displease Mr. Everard.

"Forgive me," she said at last, "I thought you would like it. I did not want you to sell your clothes,—did not want your father to know. I meant to do right. I am sorry you are angry."

"Angry!" and in the eyes which looked at Rossie there was anything but anger. "I am not angry except with myself; only I am so mortified, so ashamed. I think you the dearest, most unselfish person in the world. Who else would have done what you have?"

"Oh, ever so many," Rossie said, "if they were sorry for you and loved you; for, Mr. Everard, I am so sorry, and I love you a heap, and then,—and then, I did it some because I thought your mother would like it if she knew."

Rosamond's lip quivered as she said this, and there was such a pitiful look in her soft eyes that Everard raised himself in bed, and drawing her toward him, took the thin little face between his hands and kissed it tenderly, while his tears flowed afresh at the mention of his dead mother, who had been so much to him.

"Rossie," he said, "what can I ever do to show you how much I appreciate all you have done for, and all you are to me?"

The girl hesitated a moment, and then said:

"If you will promise never to have anything to do with Joe Fleming, I shall be so happy, for I am sure he is a bad man, and leads you into mischief. Will you promise not to go near Joe Fleming again?"

Everard groaned as he answered her:

"You do not know what you ask. I cannot break with Joe Fleming. I,— oh, Rossie, I am a coward, a fool, and I wish I were dead,—I do, upon my word! But there is one thing I can promise you, and I will. I pledge myself solemnly, from this day forth, never to touch a card of any kind in the way of gambling, never to touch a drop of spirits, or a cigar, or a fast horse, or to bet, or do anything of which you would not approve."

"I am so glad," Rossie said, "and to make it quite sure, suppose you sign something just as they do the pledge to keep from drinking."

He did not quite know what she meant, but he answered, unhesitatingly:

"I'll sign anything you choose to bring me."

"I'm going to write it now," Rossie said, and the next moment she left the room, and Everard was free to finish his letters alone.

Taking the second one from Josephine, he read that she was sorry to hear of his affliction, and wished she could comfort him, and that it must be a consolation for him to know that his mother was in heaven, where he would one day meet her if he was a good man.

This attempt at piety disgusted Everard, who knew how little Josephine cared for anything sacred, and how prone she was to ridicule what she called pious people.

Immediately following this mention of his mother, she said she was missing and longing for him so much, and hoped he would write at once, and send her the money for which she was obliged to ask him. Then she added the following:

"I find myself in rather a peculiar position. So long as I am known as Miss Fleming, I shall of course be subject to the attentions of gentlemen, and what am I to do? Shall I go on as usual,—discreetly, of course,—and receive whatever attentions are paid to me, never allowing any one to get so far as an offer? I ask you this because I wish to please you, and because, since my marriage, it seems as if so many men were inclined to be polite to me. Even old Captain Sparks, the millionaire, has asked me to ride after his fast horses; and as there was no reason which I could give him why I should not, I went, and he acted as silly as an old fool well can act. Tell me your wishes in the matter, and they shall be to me commands."

For an instant Everard felt indignant at Captain Sparks for presuming to ride with and say silly things to Josephine, but when he reflected a moment he knew that to the captain there was no reason why he should not do so. Josephine was to him a young, marriageable maiden, and rumor said that the old man was looking for a fourth wife, and as he would, of course, look only at the young girls, it was natural for him to single out Josephine as an object of favor.

"Josey must, of course, hold her place as an unmarried person," he thought, "but oh! the horror of this deception. I'd give worlds to undo the work of that night."

He thought so more than ever when he read the third and last letter, in which, after expressing her sorrow and concern for his sickness, she told him of her correspondence with Rosamond, and which, as it gives a still clearer insight into the young lady's character, we give, in part, to the reader:

"Dear Everard:—What do you suppose has happened? Why, I laughed until I nearly split my sides, and I almost scream every time I think of the funny letter I got from Rosamond Hastings, the little girl who lives with you, and who actually thinks I am a man, a bad, good for nothing, gambling, swearing man, who leads you into all sorts of scrapes, and to whom you owe money. It seems she gathered this when you were crazy, and took it upon herself to write to Mr. Joe Fleming;— that's what she called me,—and lecture him soundly on his badness. You ought to hear her once; but I'll keep the letter and show you. She wished me to give up the debt, which she took for granted was a gambling one, but said if I would not I must write to her and not trouble you. Now, I suppose it would have been generous and nice in me to say I did not care for the money, but you see I did; I must have it to pay my bills; and so I wrote to her and said you would tell her my claim was a just one, if she asked you about it. In due time she sent me seventy-five dollars, though how she raised it I am sure I cannot guess, unless she coaxed it from your father, and I hardly think she did that, as she seemed in great fear lest he should know that you owed Joe Fleming! She is a good business woman,—for, accompanying the money was a receipt, correctly drawn up, and declaring you discharged in full from all indebtedness to me. I wonder what the child would have done if I had not returned it, and just for the mischief of it I thought once I wouldn't, for a while at least, and see what she would do. But Agnes made such a fuss that I thought better of it, and shall send the receipt in the same mail which takes this to you. By the way, you've no idea how much Agnes has you and your interests at heart. I believe, upon my word, she thinks you did a dreadful thing to marry me as you did, and she says her prayers in your behalf, to my certain knowledge, three or four times a day. Verily, it ought to make your calling and election sure.

"Dr. Matthewson was in town yesterday, and inquired particularly for you. I told him of your mother's death, and that I had written to Clarence as he bade me do, and made inquiries about him, and had not received a very good report of his character as a clergyman. He took it good-humoredly, and said that the Gospel didn't agree with him very well. I like the doctor immensely, he is so amusing and friendly. I hope you will not care because I told him of Rosamond's mistake, and showed him her letter. How he did roar! Why, he actually laid down on the grass, and rolled and kicked, and would not believe me till I showed him the letter. He left town this morning, saying he should be here again in the fall, and would like to board with mother.

"How I hate this life,—planning how to get your bread and butter,—and how glad I shall be when I am out of it; but I mean to be patient and bear it, knowing what happiness there is in the future for me. When shall I see you, I wonder? Will you not come as soon as you are able to travel and spend the remainder of your vacation with me? You will at least stop here on the way to Amherst, and for that time I live.

"Lovingly yours, Joe."

It would be impossible to describe the nature of Everard's feelings as he read this letter, which seemed to him coarse, and selfish, and heartless in the extreme. Couldn't Josephine, understand such a character as Rossie's, or appreciate the noble thing she had done? Could she only see in it a pretext for laughing till "she split her sides," and was it a nice thing in her to tell Dr. Matthewson of the letter, and even show it to him, making him roll on the grass, and roar and kick in her presence? Had she no delicacy or refinement, to allow such a thing? Would any man dare do that with Bee or even Rossie, child though she was? Was Josey devoid of that womanly dignity which puts a man always on his best behavior? He feared she was, he said sadly to himself, as he recalled the free and easy manner he had always assumed with her. How many times had he sat with his feet higher than his head, and smoked directly in her face, or stretching himself full length upon the grass while she sat beside him, laid his head in her lap and talked such slang as he would blush to have Rossie hear; and she had laughed, and jested, and allowed it all, or at the most reproved him by asking if he were not ashamed of himself. Josey was not modest and womanly, like his mother, and Bee, and Rosamond. She was not like them at all, and for a moment there swept over the young man such a feeling of revulsion and disgust that his whole being rose up against the position in which he was placed, and from his inmost soul he cried out, "I cannot have it so!"

He had sown the wind, and he was beginning to reap the whirlwind; and it was a very nervous, feverish patient which Rossie found when she came back to him, bringing the paper he was to sign, and which was to keep him straight. She called it a pledge, and it read:

"I hereby solemnly promise never to drink a drop of liquor, never to smoke a pipe or cigar, never to race with fast horses, never to play cards or any other game for money, never to bet, and to have just as little to do with Joe Fleming as I possibly can.

"Signed by me, at the Forrest House, this —— day of August, 18—."

"There!" Rossie said, as she read it to him, and offered him the pen; "you'll sign that and then be very safe."

"Rossie," he said vehemently, "I wish to Heaven I could honorably subscribe to the whole of it, but I cannot. I must erase the part about Joe Fleming. I cannot explain to you why, but I must keep my acquaintance with Joe, but I'll promise not to be influenced in that direction any more. Will that do?"

"Yes, but I did so hope you would break with him entirely. I know he makes you bad. You told me when you came home you had no debts, and I believed you, and yet you owed this man seventy-five dollars, and I was so sorry to find you did not tell me true."

Rossie's eyes were full of tears as she said this, for losing faith in Everard had hurt her sorely, but he hastened to reassure her.

"Rossie," he said, "I did not know of this debt then. It has come up since. What I told you was told in good faith. Bad as I am, I would not tell a deliberate lie, and you must believe me."

She did believe him, and watched him as he put his pen through the sentence, "have just as little to do with Joe Fleming as I possibly can," and then signed his name to the paper.

"There!" he said, as he handed it to her with a sickly effort to smile. "Keep it, Rossie, and if I break that pledge, may I never succeed in anything I undertake so long as I live; and now bathe my head with the coldest ice-water in the house, for it feels as if there was a bass drum in it."

He was very restless and nervous, and did not improve as fast as the doctor had said he would, if once his reason returned. Indeed, for a few days he did not seem to improve at all, and Beatrice and Rosamond both nursed him tenderly, and pitied him so much when they saw him lying so weak and still, with his eyes shut, and the great tears rolling down his face.

"It's for his mother," Rossie whispered to her companion, and her own tears gathered as she remembered the sweet woman whose grave was so fresh in the church-yard.

But it was not altogether for the dead mother that Everard's tears were shed. It was rather from remorse and sorrow for the deed he would have given so much to undo; for he was conscious of an intense desire to be free from the chain which bound him. Not free from Josephine, he tried to make himself believe, for if that were so he would indeed be the most wretched of men, but free from his marriage vow, made so rashly. How was it that he was tempted to do it? he asked himself, as he went over in his mind with the events of that night. He was always more or less intoxicated with Josephine's beauty when he was with her, and he remembered how she had bewitched and bewildered him with the touch of her soft hands, and sight of her bare arms and neck. She had challenged him to the act, and Dr. Matthewson had given him the wine, which he knew now must have clouded his reason and judgment, and so he was left to his fate. And a terrible one it seemed, as, in his weakness and languor, he looked at it in all its aspects, and saw no brightness in it. Even Josephine's beauty seemed fading into nothing, though he tried so hard to keep his hold on that, for he must hold to something,—must retain his love for her or go mad. But she was so unlike Beatrice, so unlike Rosamond, so unlike what his mother had been, and they were his standards for all that was noble, and pure, and sweet in womankind. Josey was selfish and unrefined; he could not put it in any milder form when he remembered the past as connected with her, and remembered how she had ridiculed little Rossie Hastings, whose letter she had shown to Dr. Matthewson. How plainly he could see that scene, when the doctor rolled upon the grass and roared and kicked, and Josephine laughed with him at the generous, unselfish child who, to save him, had sacrificed her only beauty. And Josephine was his wife, and he must not cease to respect her one iota, for that was his only chance for happiness, and he struggled so hard to keep her in his heart and love that it is not strange the great drops of sweat stood thickly on his brow, or that the hot tears at intervals rolled down his cheeks.

It was Rossie who brushed them away, Rossie who wiped the sweat from his face, and whispered to him once:

"Don't cry, Mr. Everard. Your mother is so happy where she has gone, and I don't believe she has lost all care for you either, she loved you so much when she was here."

Then Everard broke down entirely, and holding Rossie's little, brown, tanned hands in his, said to her:

"It isn't that, though Heaven knows how much I loved my mother, and how sorry I am she is dead; but there are troubles worse than death, and I am in one now, and the future looks so dark and the burden so heavy to carry."

"Can I help you bear it?" Rossie asked, softly, with a great pity in her heart for this young man who had given way like a child.

"No, Rossie, nobody can help me,—nobody," he said; and after a moment Rossie asked timidly: "Is it Joe Fleming again?"

"Yes, Rossie, Joe Fleming again;" and Everard could scarcely restrain a smile, even in his grief, at this queer mistake of Rossie's.

In her mind Joe Fleming was a dreadful man, through whom Mr. Everard had come to grief, and she ventured at last to speak of him to Beatrice as somebody of whom Everard had talked when he was crazy, and who had led him into a great trouble of some kind.

"And that's what ails him now, and keeps him so weak and low, and makes him cry like a girl," she said.

And then Beatrice resolved to help the sick youth, if possible, and that afternoon when she sat alone with him for a few moments, she said to him:

"Everard, I am quite sure that something is troubling you, something which retards your recovery. I do not ask to know what it is, but if money can lighten it let me help you, please. I have so much more than I know what to do with. Let me lend you some, do."

"Oh, Bee," Everard cried, "don't talk to me that way; you will kill me, you and Rossie together; and you can't help me. Nobody can. It is past all help."

She did not at all know what he meant, but with her knowledge of what money could do, she felt sure it could help, and so she said:

"Not so bad as that, I am sure. You have probably been led astray by some designing person, but there is always a backward path, you know, and you will take it sure; and if you should want money, as you may, will you ask me for it, Everard? Will you let me give it to you, as if I were your sister?"

He did not know; he could not tell what he might do in sore need, for he felt intuitively that the call on him for money, commenced so soon, would increase with every year; so he thanked her for her kind offer, which, he said, he would consider, should the time ever come when he wanted help.

For ten days more Everard kept his room, and then arose suddenly one morning and said that he was able to go back to college, where he ought to have been two weeks ago, for he was getting far behind his class, and would have to study hard to overtake and keep up with it as he meant to do. Nothing could restrain him; go he must, and go he did, early one morning in September, before the people of Rothsay were astir. He had held a short conference with Rosamond, and bidden her tell the postmaster to forward to Amherst any letters which might come to him, and on no account let them go to the Forrest House. And Rossie had promised to comply with all his wishes, and pressed upon him a twenty-dollar bill which she made him take, because, as she said, she did not need it a bit, and should just squander it for peanuts, and worsteds, and things which would do her no good. It was a part of her quarterly interest, and she could do what she liked with it, and so Everard took it, and felt humiliated, and hated himself, especially as he knew just where the money would go. A letter from Josephine had come to him, asking for more funds, with which to replenish her wardrobe for the autumn. They had no boarders now except Dr. Matthewson, who was occasionally in town for a day or two and stopped with them, and Mrs. Fleming did not get as much sewing as usual, and so Josey was compelled to come to her husband for money, though sorely against her will, for she feared she must seem mercenary to him, and she hoped he would forgive her and love her just the same.

It was this letter which had determined him to return to Amherst without delay. On his way thither, he should stop in Holburton over a train, and tell Josephine how impossible it was for him to supply her demands until in a position to help himself.

"If father would only give me something more than my actual needs," he thought; and, strangely enough, his father did.

Possibly the memory of the dead mother pleaded for her boy, and prompted the judge to give his son at parting a fifty-dollar bill over and above what he knew was needed for board and tuition.

"Make it go as far as you can; it ought to last you the whole year," he said, and Everard's spirits sank like lead as he foresaw the increasing drain there would be on him, and felt how impossible it would be to ask his father for more.

There was still his best suit of clothes; and a little diamond pin and a ring Rossie had given him, and his books, which he could sell, and perhaps he could find something to do after study hours which would bring him money. He might write for the magazines or illustrate stories; he had a natural taste for drawing, and could dash off a sketch from nature in a very few minutes. He could do something, he assured himself, and his heart was a little lighter, when he at last said good-by to Rossie and his father, and started northward for college and Josephine.

CHAPTER X

HUSBAND AND WIFE

He had sent no word of his coming, for he did not know just when he should reach Holburton. His strength might fail him, and he be obliged to stop for the night on the road. But he kept up wonderfully, and arrived at Holburton on the same train which had taken him there from Ellicottville on that memorable day which he would gladly have stricken out. There was no one at the little station except the ticket agent, who, being new to the place, scarcely noticed him as he crossed the platform and passed down the street toward the brown house on the common. There had been a storm of wind and rain the previous day, and the hop vine, which in the summer grew over the door, was torn down and lay upon the ground. A part of the fence, too, was nearly down, and a shutter hung by one hinge and swayed to and fro in the autumn wind. Taken as a whole, the house presented rather a forlorn appearance, and he found himself wondering how he had ever thought it so attractive. And still he felt his blood stir quickly at the thought of meeting Josephine again, and he half looked to see her come flying out to meet him as she had sometimes done. But only the cat, who was chasing a grasshopper through the uncut grass, came to welcome him by purring and rubbing herself against his legs as he went up the walk.

Agnes let him in,—the same sun-bonnet on her head he had seen so many times, her sleeves rolled up, and her wide apron smelling of the suds she had come from.

At sight of him she uttered an exclamation of surprise, and for a moment her tired face lighted up with something like pleasure; then that expression faded and was succeeded by an anxious, startled look, as she glanced nervously down the road as if expecting some one to whom she would give warning. Mrs. Fleming was in Boston, seeing to some mortgage on the house, and Josey had gone to ride, she said, as she led the way into the little parlor, which, even to Everard's not very critical eye, presented an appearance of neglect unusual in Mrs. Fleming's household. Evidently it had not been cared for that day, for the chairs were moved from their places, two standing close together, just where their last occupants had left them. There were crumbs of cake on the carpet, and two empty wineglasses on the table, with a fly or two crawling lazily on the inside and sipping the few red drops left there.

As Agnes opened the window and brushed up the crumbs, she said she was intending to right up the room before Josephine came home, then, bidding Everard make himself as comfortable as possible, she left him alone, and went back to her work in the kitchen.

Taking a chair near the window, where he could command a view of the street, the young man sat waiting for Josephine, until he heard at last a loud, long laugh, which was almost a shriek, and, looking through the shutters of the open window, he saw first a cloud of dust, and then a low buggy coming rapidly across the common, in the direction of the house. In the buggy sat Captain Sparks, the millionaire, whose penchant for young and pretty girls was well known throughout the entire county. Short, fat and grizzly, he sat with folded arms, smiling complacently upon the fair blonde, who, in her brown silk dress of two shades, with a long white lace scarf twisted round her hat and flying far behind, held the reins of the high-mettled horse, and was driving furiously. In his surprise and indignation, Everard failed to note how beautiful she was, with the flush of excitement on her cheeks and the sparkle in her eye; he only thought she was his wife, and that Captain Sparks lifted her very tenderly to the ground, and held her by the shoulders a moment, while he said something which made her turn her head coquettishly on one side, as she drew back from him, and said:

"You mean old thing! You ought to be ashamed!"

Everard had heard this form of expression many times. Indeed, it was her favorite method of reproof for liberties of speech or manner, and meant nothing at all. Everard knew it did not, and Captain Sparks knew it did not, and held her hand the tighter; but she drew it away at last, and ran gayly up the walk, throwing him a kiss from the tips of her daintily-gloved hand. Then she entered the side door, and Everard heard her say to Agnes, who was hurrying to meet her and announce his arrival:

"Upon my word, if you are not in that old wash-dud yet! I'll bet you haven't touched the parlor, and the captain is coming at eight o'clock. Wha-a-t?" and her voice fell suddenly, as Agnes said something to her in a tone too low for Everard to hear.

That it concerned him and his presence there he was sure, and he was not greatly surprised when the next instant the door opened swiftly, and Josephine rushed headlong into his arms. He opened them involuntarily to withstand the shock, rather than to receive her; but the result was the same,—she laid her golden head on his bosom and sobbed like a child. Josey could feign a cry admirably when she chose to do so, and now she trembled and shook, and made it seem so real that Everard forgot everything except that she was very fair and undeniably glad to see him. Very gently he soothed her, and made her lift her head, that he might look into her face, and hated himself for thinking that for such a thunder-gust as she had treated him to her eyes were not very red, nor her cheeks very wet. But she was so happy, and so glad he had come, and so sorry she was not there to receive him.

"That old fool, Captain Sparks, had recently taken to haunting her with attentions, and as the easiest way to be rid of him, she had consented for once to ride with him, and had taken the occasion to tell him it could not be repeated. But then it was rare fun to drive his fast horse,—she was so fond of driving, and Blucher was so fleet and spirited, and had brought them up to the house in such style. Did Everard see them,—and what did he think?"

"Yes, I saw you, and thought you were enjoying it hugely," Everard said; and Josey detected something in his tone which made her suspect that he did not quite like the captain's manner of lifting her from the carriage. But she was equal to the emergency, and made fun of the old man, and called him a love-sick muff, and took him off to the life, and then, in a grieved, martyred kind of way, said, "it was rather hard for her to know just what to do, situated as she was, married, and yet not married, in fact. She would not for the world do anything to displease Everard, but must she decline all attention and make a nun of herself, and how soon could she let her marriage be known?"

"Not yet, Josey," Everard said, explaining to her rapidly how much worse the matter was for them now his mother was dead.

She might, and would, have helped them when the crisis came, but now there was no one to stand between him and his father, who was sure to take some desperate step if he knew of the rash marriage before his son was through college.

"We must wait, Josey, two years, sure," he said; and, because she could not help herself, Josephine assented, very sweetly, though with something of an injured air, and managed next to speak of money, and asked if he hated her for being such a leech.

"You mustn't, for I couldn't help it," she said, and she leaned on his arm, and buttoned and unbuttoned his coat, and caressed him generally, as she continued: "Maybe you didn't know how poor the bride was, or you would not have taken her. Mother is in Boston now about some mortgage on the house, and it takes so much to live decently, and my lessons cost frightfully; but you are glad to have me improve, dearest?"

Of course he was glad, he said, but he had no means of getting money except from his father, and if she knew to what humiliation he was subjected when he asked for funds, she would spare him all she could. By and by, when he had money of his own, there should be no stint, but now she must be economical, he told her; and then she spoke of Rosamond, and asked who and what that queer little old-fashioned thing could be.

"Such a lecture as she gave Mr. Joe Fleming for gambling, and leading you wrong generally. Why, I laugh till I cry every time I think of it," Josey said, proving the truth of what she asserted by laughing heartily.

But the laugh grated on Everard, as in some way an affront to Rossie, and he shrank from saying much of her, except to tell who she was, and how she came to be living at the Forrest House.

"And was it her own money she sent me, or where did she get it? Has she the open sesame to your father's purse? If so, you had better apply to her, when in need," Josey said; and in a sudden spasm of fear lest in some way Rossie should become a victim of the greed he was beginning dimly to comprehend, he told the story of the hair, but withheld the name of Beatrice, from a feeling that he would rather Josephine should not know of his acquaintance with her.

"What do you think of a girl who could do so generous a thing as that for a great lout like me?" he asked, and Josephine replied, "I think she was a little goose! Catch me parting with my hair; though I am glad she did it, as it relieved you, and was of great benefit to Joe Fleming!"

She laughed lightly, but Everard was disgusted and indignant at her utter want of appreciation of the sacrifice which few girls would have made. She saw the shadow on his face, and, suspecting the cause, changed her tactics, and became greatly interested in Rosamond, and said that she must be a generous, self-denying little thing, and she wished Everard would allow her to write to her in her own proper character as his wife. But to this he would not consent. He was not deceived by this change in her manner. He knew Josey had expressed her real sentiments at first, and there was in his heart a constantly increasing sense of disappointment and loss of something, he scarcely knew what. Nor could all Josephine's wiles and witcheries lift the shadows from his face, and make him feel just as he used to do when he sat alone in the little parlor with her at his side. She was very charming in her brown silk, which fitted her admirably, and Beatrice herself could not have been softer, and sweeter, and gentler than she tried to be; but there was something lacking, and though Everard put his arm around her slender waist, and her golden head was pillowed on his shoulder, his heart beat with heavy throbs of pain as he spoke of her last letter to him, in which she had asked for more money. It had been his intention to give her all he had, and bid her make it last the year, but he changed his mind suddenly, and handed her only twenty dollars, and told her it was by mere chance that he was fortunate enough to have so much to give her, and that he hoped she would do the best she could with it; for, though he would gladly give her ten times the amount, if he could, the thing was impossible.

She thanked him graciously, and said she meant to be very economical, only things did cost so much, and as Mrs. Forrest, she felt that she must dress better than Josephine Fleming had done. If he said so she would take in sewing, or even washing, if he liked,—anything to show him she really meant to please him. He vetoed the washing and the sewing, of course, and then, as he heard the rattling of dishes in the adjoining room, he hastened to say that he was to leave on the half-past seven train, so as to reach Amherst that night. There was a passionate protest, and a pretty, pouting declaration that he did not care for her any more, and then she allowed herself to be comforted, and felt really relieved when she remembered Captain Sparks and his engagement for eight o'clock. There were waffles for supper,—Everard's favorites,—and Josephine sat by him and buttered them for him, and made his tea, and helped him to peaches and cream, and between times studied the face which baffled and puzzled her so, with its new expression, born of remorse and harrowing unrest. She had married a boy whom she thought to mold so easily, but she found him now a man, for whom she felt a little awe and fear, and there was something of real timidity and shyness in her manner when at last she said good-by to him, and watched him through the darkness as he went rapidly from her to the train which was to take him on his way to Amherst.

CHAPTER XI

AFTER TWO YEARS

It is not my intention to linger over the incidents of the next two years, or more than glance at the Forrest House, where Rosamond Hastings laughed, and played, and romped, gaining each day health, and strength, and girlish beauty, but retaining always the same straightforward, generous, self-denying, truthful character which made her a favorite with every one. To Everard she was literally a good angel, and never was a son watched more carefully by an anxious mother than she watched and guarded him. She wrote him letters of advice and sage counsel such as a grandmother of seventy might have written, and which frequently had in them some word of warning against bad associates in general, and Joe Fleming in particular. She knew he had not broken with Joe altogether, for he told her so, and more than once in his sore need he had taken the money she never failed to send him when her quarterly allowance was paid. But for the rest, he was manfully keeping to the pledge which she had drawn for him to sign. Only once in all the two years had he ventured to ask his father for more money than that close-dealing man chose to give him, and the storm of anger which that request had evoked determined him never to repeat the act. He sent his father's letter to Josephine, that she, too, might understand how difficult it was for him to supply her constantly increasing wants, and for a time the effect was good; but an inordinate fondness for dress was one of Josey's weaknesses, and having once indulged it to a certain extent she could not readily deny herself, especially as she felt she had a right to a part, at least, of the Forrest money. So she wrote to Everard again and again, sometimes for five dollars, sometimes for ten, or twenty, and when she found that sooner or later it came she ventured to ask for more, and at last demanded fifty dollars, which she needed for furs, as her old ones were worn-out. Then Everard sold the little diamond pin his mother had given him, and parted with it almost without a pang, he was getting so accustomed to these things. He had long before parted with his best suit of clothes, and from the most exquisitely dressed young man in college he was fast becoming the plainest, and was getting the reputation of penuriousness in everything. His first-class boarding-house was exchanged for a third-rate club, where the poorest young men lived; he wrote articles for the magazines and sold them for whatever he could get, and once, when the janitor was sick for a week, he took his place, and earned a few dollars with which to swell the amount he found it necessary to keep on hand for the woman who sported a handsomer wardrobe than the greatest lady in Holburton.

Of course the world must have some explanation for this, or the girl's reputation be ruined forever. And Josey made the explanation, and said a distant relative of her father's had died in Ireland, and left her a few pounds to do with as she liked. And in this story there was a semblance of truth, for a maiden aunt, who for years had lived in Portrush, on the northern coast of Ireland, and taken lodgers during the summer season, did die and leave to her grand-nieces in America the sum of fifty pounds, which was ostensibly divided between Agnes and Josephine, though the latter had the greater share, and immediately appeared on the street in an expensive velvet sack, which attracted much attention and elicited a great many remarks from those who were watching the career of the young girl. She was not popular, for with her fine dress she had also put on all sorts of airs, and her manner was haughty and offensive in the extreme, while her flirtations with gentlemen were so marked as to make her notorious as a heartless and unprincipled coquette. Captain Sparks had laid himself and his immense fortune at her feet, only, of course, to be refused; but she had told him no so sweetly, with tears in her liquid blue eyes, that he was not more than half convinced that she meant it, and dangled still in her train of hangers-on. Dr. Matthewson, too, was there frequently, and people had good reasons for thinking him the favored one, judging from the familiar relations in which they seemed to stand to each other. Once in a great while Everard himself went over to Holburton, but he never stopped more than a few hours at the most, and was seldom seen in the street with Josephine, who was supposed to have lost her hold on him,—and so in fact she had; all his fancied love for her was dead, and her beauty never moved him now, or made his pulses quicken one whit faster than their wont. She was his wife, and he accepted the fact, and resolved to make the best of it, but the future held nothing bright in store for him. On the contrary, he shrank from it with a kind of nervous terror, and felt no throb of joy when his college days drew near their close, and he knew that he stood first in his class, and should graduate with every possible honor. He had worked hard for that, but it was more to please Beatrice and Rosamond than for any good to himself that he had studied early and late, and made himself what he was. They were coming on from Rothsay with his father, to see him graduated, and hear his valedictory, for that honor was awarded him, and he had engaged rooms for them at a private house where he knew they would be more comfortable than at the hotel. Rossie was all eagerness and excitement, and wrote frequently to Everard, telling him once that if Joe Fleming was there not to let him know who she was, but to be sure to point him out to her, as she had a great desire to see a real gambler and blackleg. She had recently applied this last term to Joe Fleming, and Everard smiled when he read the letter, but felt a great pang of fear lest Josephine should thrust herself upon the notice of his father and Beatrice. He had given her no hint that her presence would be agreeable to him, but he knew she did not need it, and was not at all disappointed when he received a note from her saying that she was coming down to see him graduate, but should not trouble him more than she could help, as a friend who lived about a mile from town had asked her to spend a few days with her, and be present at the exercises. She should, of course, expect him to call and pay her any little attention which he consistently could.

It was long since Josephine had attempted anything like love-making with Everard, for she felt that he understood her perfectly now, and had no respect whatever for her. He had found her a sham, just as Rossie had said she was, and had accepted his fate with a bitterness and remorse such as few men of his age had ever experienced. He did not believe in her at all, and whenever he was with her, and met the soft, pleading glance of the eyes which had once so fascinated and bewitched him, he only felt indignant and disgusted, for he knew how false it all was, and that the eyes which looked so beseechingly up to him would the next hour rest as lovingly upon Dr. Matthewson, or Captain Sparks, or any other man whom she deemed worthy of her notice. Once, when he was in Holburton, he accidentally discovered that the washing and ironing, with which Agnes seemed always busy, were done to pay the music bills and sundry other expenses, for which he had sent the money, and in his surprise he asked a few leading questions and learned more than he had dreamed of. As the worm will turn when trodden upon, so Agnes, who chanced to be smarting under some fresh indignity imposed upon her, turned upon her tyrant and told many things which, for Everard's peace of mind, would have been better unsaid, for she dwelt mostly upon Josey's free-and-easy manner with the gentlemen who came to the house to call, or chanced to be boarding there.

"I don't mean she does anything bad," she said, "anything you could sue for if you wanted to, but she just makes eyes at them, and leads them on, and gets them all dangling on her string, and wants to be their sister, and all that sort of stuff, and when the fools offer themselves, as some of them do, she rises up on her tiptoes and wonders how they could presume to do such a thing, as she had never meant to encourage them,—she was simply their friend; and, if you'll believe it, they mostly stick to her just the same, and the sister business goes on, and she a married woman! I'm sorry for you, Mr. Forrest!"

And oh, how sorry he was for himself, and how after this revelation he shrank from the gay butterfly which flitted around him so gracefully, and treated him to the eyes of which Agnes had spoken so significantly. And still there was no open rupture between the two, no words of recrimination or reproach on either side. He was always courteous and polite, though cold as the polar sea; while she was sweetness itself, and only the expression of her face told occasionally that she fully realized the situation, and knew just how she stood with him. But he was her husband, and as such would one day be known to the world, and she was far prouder of him now in his character as a man than she had been when she took him, a boy; and she meant to see him on the stage in Amherst, and compel him to pay her some attention which should mark her as an object of preference. She knew he did not wish to have her there, but she did not care for that, and wrote to him her intention to be present at the Commencement, and her wish that he should pay her some attention.

The old, weary, hopeless look, which had become habitual to his face, deepened in intensity as Everard read the note, and then began to calculate the chances of a meeting between his friends and Josey. He was very morbid about this secret, which he had kept so long that it seemed to him now that he never could divulge it, even if sure that his father's bitter anger would not follow. And he did not wish Beatrice and Rossie to see his wife, if he could help it, and perhaps he could. There would be a great crowd in the church; they could not see her there; and, as Mrs. Everts lived more than a mile from town, they might not meet her at all, unless at the reception given by the president, and to this Josey would hardly be invited. So he breathed a little more freely, and completed his arrangements for his family, and wrote a line to Josey, saying he would call upon her at Mrs. Everts' when she came, but should be so very busy that he could not be with her a great deal.

To Rosamond he wrote quite differently, and told her how glad he was that she was coming, and how much he hoped she would enjoy the trip, and that there was the coziest, prettiest room imaginable waiting for her in one of the pleasantest houses in town. And Rossie was crazy with delight and anticipation, and scarcely slept a wink the night before they started. And still she was very bright, and fresh, and pretty, in her suit of Holland linen, and never was journey more enjoyed than she enjoyed hers, seeing everything, and appreciating everything, and declaring that she was not a whit tired when at last they reached Amherst, and found Everard waiting for them.

CHAPTER XII

COMMENCEMENT

It was nearly a year since they had seen Everard, and Bee and Rossie were struck at once with the great change in his personal appearance, while even the judge noticed how thin and pale he was, but attributed it naturally to hard study. Fresh air and exercise at home would soon make that all right, he thought, and so dismissed it from his mind. But Beatrice and Rosamond both saw more than the thin face, which had grown so pale and troubled. They saw that Everard's hat was the same worn the year before when he was at home; saw that his pants were shining about the knees, and his coat shining and worn about the sleeves, while his boots were carefully patched. Once he had been the best and most fashionably-dressed young man in college, but he was far from that now, though he was scrupulously neat and clean, and looked every whit a gentleman as he walked with the young ladies down the shaded street, and tried to seem natural, and answer gayly to Beatrice's light badinage and Rossie's quaint remarks. But it was uphill business, for how could he be happy when he knew that Josey would soon be watching for him, and expecting him to pass a part of the evening, at least, with her? What if she should take it into her head to come to town and hunt him up, and find him there with his friends? What could he say or do, and what would they think of her? It made him faint and sick just to imagine Beatrice weighing Josephine as she would weigh her, and discovering more than the enormity of cotton lace and dollar jewelry, while Rossie,—he could not define to himself why he shrank so nervously from having her clear, honest eyes scan Josephine Fleming, as he knew they would do.

After tea was over, Everard took his father through the town and introduced him to some of the professors, and then, as the twilight began to fall, asked to be excused a short time, as he had an engagement to call upon a friend; so his father returned alone to his lodgings, and Everard started on a rapid walk toward Mrs. Everts'. He did not know the lady personally, but he knew where she lived, and was soon at her gate, where he paused a moment in some surprise at the sounds of talking and laughter which greeted his ears. The parlor was lighted up, and through the open windows he caught a glimpse of Josephine, fair and lovely, in pure white, with only a bit of honeysuckle at her throat and in her hair, which fell like a golden shower upon her neck, and gave her a very youthful appearance. Gathered around her were four young men, juniors and sophomores, each striving for the preference, and each saying some soft thing to her, at which she laughed so prettily and coquettishly that their zeal and admiration were increased tenfold.

"How did these puppies know her?" Everard asked himself, as he leaned against the gate; then he remembered having heard that one of them had spent a little time in Holburton, and probably he was in the habit of going there occasionally, and had taken the others with him.

At all events she seemed to know them well, and they were in the full tide of flattery and mirth when his ring broke the spell, and he was ushered into the parlor.

"Oh, I am so glad to see you!" Josey exclaimed, coming gracefully forward, and giving him both her hands, an act which was noted by the juniors and sophomores, and mentally resented.

What business had that grave, dignified Forrest there, and why should Miss Fleming greet him so cordially, and where did she know him anyway? They had heard he was very wealthy, and that he once was very fast and wild, but something had changed him entirely, and transformed him into a sober, reticent, and, as they believed, very proud and stingy young man, whose perfectly correct behavior was a living rebuke to themselves. He was not popular with their set, and they showed it in their faces, and pulled at their cravats, and fingered the bouquets in their button-holes, and stood round awkwardly, while he talked with Josey, and asked her of her journey, and her mother and Agnes, and answered her questions about the exercises the next day, and the best place for her to sit.

"Oh, we will arrange that; we will see that you have a good seat," the juniors and sophomores echoed in chorus; and with a slight sneer, perceptible to Josey, on his face, Everard said to her: "I do not see that there is any chance for me to offer you any attention, you seem so well provided for."

Josey bit her lip with vexation, for though she was delighted to have so many admirers at her side, she would far rather have been cared for particularly by this husband, of whom she was beginning to be a good deal afraid. He was so greatly changed that she could not understand him at all, or guess what was passing in his mind, and when at last he rose to go she said to him almost beseechingly:

"I hope I shall see you to-morrow."

"Possibly, though I shall be very busy," was his reply; and just then one of the juniors said to him:

"By the way, Forrest, who is that fine-looking, elderly gentleman I saw with you this evening? Your father?"

"Yes, my father," Everard replied, feeling a desire to throttle the young man, and glancing involuntarily at Josephine, over whom a curious change had come.

The was a blood-red spot on her cheeks, and an unnatural glitter in her eyes, as she said to the quartette around her:

"Excuse me a moment. I have just thought of something which I particularly wish to say to Mr. Forrest."

The next moment she stood in the hall with him, and was saying to him rapidly and excitedly: "Your father is here, and you did not tell me. I don't like it. I wish to see him,—wish him to see me, and you must introduce me at the reception. I intend to be there."

"Very well," was all Everard said, but he felt as if a band of iron was drawn around his heart as he went back to Beatrice and Rossie, who were waiting for him, and who noticed at once the worried look upon his face, and wondered a little at it.

Had anything happened to disquiet him, that he should seem so absent-minded and disturbed? Rossie was the first to reach a solution of the mystery, and when at his request Beatrice seated herself at the piano and began to play, she stole up to him, and whispered very low, "Have you seen Joe Fleming to-night?"

"Yes," was his reply, and Rossie's wise little nod said plainly, "I guessed as much."

In her mind every trouble or perplexity which came to Everard had something to do with the mysterious Joe Fleming, though in what way she could not guess. She only knew that it was so, and she felt an increased desire to see this bete noir of Mr. Everard's.

"And perhaps I shall have a chance to-morrow night at the reception. It will be just like his impudence to be there," she thought, when at last she laid her tired head upon her pillow.

Rossie was very pale and haggard when she came down to breakfast the next morning. She was accustomed to the headache, and knew that one was coming on, but she fought the pain back bravely, for she could not miss the valedictory.

It was comparatively early when she and Beatrice entered the church, which, even at that hour, was densely packed. But good seats were found for them, and Rossie sat all through the exercises and listened breathlessly to Mr. Everard's oration, and threw him a bouquet, and wondered who the beautiful lady was who stood up on tiptoe to cheer him, and who seemed so desirous that her bouquet of pansies and rose geraniums should reach him in safety. Beatrice did not see the lady, but she saw the bouquet of pansies which fell at Everard's feet, where he seemed disposed to let it lie, until a boy picked it up and handed it to him. It was very pretty, and the pansies showed well against the background of green, but Beatrice little guessed how faint and sick the young man felt as he held them with the flowers Rossie had thrown. These he had picked up himself, and smiled pleasantly upon the young girl, whose pride and satisfaction shone in her brilliant eyes, and whose face was almost as white as the dress she wore. For Rossie was growing sick very fast, and when the exercises were over she could not even wait to speak to Everard, but hurried with Beatrice to her room, where she went directly to bed.

The reception was given up, but Rossie saw Everard a moment and told him how proud she was of him, and how fine she thought his valedictory.

Everard's spirits were much lighter now than they had been in the morning, but when he remembered what had lightened them, he felt himself a very brute and monster, for it was nothing less than the sight of Rossie's pale, sick face, and the knowing that she would not attend the reception, or Beatrice either, for the latter insisted upon staying with the little girl, and said she was only too glad to do so, for she did not care for the people she should meet, and would much rather remain at home with Rossie.

CHAPTER XIII

THE RECEPTION

It was a rather stupid affair, with a great many more gentlemen than ladies. Indeed, there were but very few of the latter present, and these mostly the wives and daughters of the professors, with any guests who chanced to be visiting them, so that when Josephine entered the room in her flowing robes of white, with her beautiful hair falling down her back, she created a great sensation. How she obtained an invitation to the reception it would be difficult to tell, but obtained it she had, and had spent hours over her dress, which was a master-piece of grace and girlish simplicity. It was white tarlatan, which fitted her perfectly, and left bare just enough of her neck and arms to be becoming. Clusters of pansies looped up the overdress, and formed her shoulder-knots, while a bunch of the same flowers, mingled with sweet mignonette, was fastened at her throat, and around her neck was a delicate chain of gold from which was suspended a turquoise locket, set with a few small pearls. Everything about her, though not costly, was in perfect taste, and she looked so charming, so fresh and lovely, when she entered the hot parlor, accompanied by one of the seniors, who was her escort, that the guests held their breath for a moment to look at her; then the gentlemen who knew her,—and there were a dozen or more of them,—pressed eagerly forward, each ambitious to pay her some attention.

Everard was standing by his father and the president when she came in, and at sight of her, smiling sweetly and bearing herself so royally, he felt for an instant a thrill of something like pride in her. But when he remembered that this beauty, and grace, and sweetness was all there was of the woman; that her manner was studied, even to the smile on her lips and the expression of her eyes, he turned from her with a feeling of disgust, but glanced nervously at his father to see what effect she would have upon him. Judge Forrest saw her, and stopped a moment in the midst of something he was saying to the president to look at her; then, moved by one of those unaccountable prejudices which one sometimes takes against a stranger without knowing why, he turned his back and resumed his interrupted conversation, and so he did not see young Allen, her attendant, when he presented her to Everard as one whom she had never met.

There was a comical gleam in Josey's eyes, and Everard's face was scarlet as he said,

"I have the pleasure of knowing Miss Fleming, I believe."

Seeing an opening in the crowd, Allen tried to pass on; but Josey had no intention of leaving that locality, and, as soon as she could, she disengaged herself from him, and standing close to Everard, said, in a low tone:

"Present me to your father."

He had no alternative but to obey, and in a few moments Josey's great

66

blue eyes were looking up coyly and deferentially at the stern old judge, and, a few moments later, her arm was linked in his, and he was leading her toward an open window, where it was cooler, and the crowd was not so great. She had complained that it was warm and close, and asked the judge if he would mind taking her near the conservatory, where it must be more comfortable.

And so the judge gave her his arm and piloted her to the window, where she got between him and the people and compelled him to stand and listen, while she talked in her most flattering strain, telling him how glad she was to meet him, she had heard so much of him from his son, who sometimes visited at her mother's, and how much he was like what she had fancied him to be from Everard's description, only so much more youthful looking.

If there was anything the judge detested it was for an old man to look younger than his years. It was in some sense a living lie, he thought, and he abominated anything like deception. So when Josephine spoke of his youthful appearance, he answered gruffly, "I am sixty, and look every day of it. If I thought I didn't, I'd proclaim it aloud, for I hate deception of every kind."

"Yes, I should know you did, and there we agree perfectly," Josephine replied, and she leaned a little more heavily upon his arm and made what Agnes called her eyes at him, and asked him to hold her fan while she buttoned her glove, and asked him about Charleston as it was before the war, and wished that she could have seen it in its glory.

"Do you know," and she spoke very low and looked straight up into his face, "it is very naughty in me, I admit, but at heart I believe I'm a bit of a rebel, and though, of course, I was very young when the war broke out, and didn't quite know what it was about, I secretly sympathized with you Southerners, and held a little jubilee by myself when I heard of a Southern victory. Do you think me a traitor?" and she smiled sweetly into the face which never relaxed a muscle, but was cold and frigid as ice.

Judge Forrest was, to his heart's core, a Southerner, and had sympathized with his people during the rebellion, because they were his people; but had he been born North he would have been just as strong a Federal as he was a Confederate, so, instead of thinking more highly of Miss Josey for her rebel sentiments, he thought the less of her, and answered rebukingly, "Young woman, I do not quite believe you know all the word traitor implies; if you did, you wouldn't voluntarily apply it to yourself."

"No, perhaps not. I'm a foolish, silly girl, I know," Josey answered him humbly, while great tears swam in her blue eyes, but produced no effect upon the judge.

Indeed, he scarcely saw them, he was so intent upon ridding himself of this piece of affectation and vulgarity, as he mentally pronounced her, and it was all in vain that she practiced upon him the little coquetries which she was wont to play off on other men with more or less success. He did not care for her innocence, nor her pretty pretense of ignorance of the world, nor timidity nor shyness, nor love of books and poetry, nor admiration of himself, for she tried all these, one after another, and felt herself growing angry with this man who stood so unmoved before her and seemed only anxious to get away. She had made no impression on him whatever, at least no good impression, and she knew it, and resolved upon one final effort. He might be reached through his son, and so she mentioned Everard, and complimented his oration, and told how high he stood in the estimation of the professors, and what an exemplary young man he was, and ended by saying, "You must be very proud of him, are you not?"

Here was a direct question, but the judge did not answer it. There was beginning to dawn upon him a suspicion that this girl, whose flippant manner he so much disliked, was more interested in his son than in himself, and if so, possibly, his son was interested in her. At all events he meant to know the extent of their acquaintance, and instead of answering her question, he asked:

"Have you known my son long?"

Josey thought the truth would answer better than equivocation, and she told him that Everard had boarded with her mother a few weeks three years ago.

"You remember," she said, "he spent his long vacation East, and a part of it in Holburton, where we live. Perhaps you may have heard him speak of my mother. She knew your wife well, and was at your wedding, though you would not remember her, of course, among so many strangers."

The judge did not remember her, nor could he recall the name as one which he had ever heard, but he did not think of doubting Josey's word, and never suspected that, though her mother had been present at his bridal, it was as a former servant in the Bigelow family; he only knew that if she had been the most intimate friend of his wife, he did not like her daughter, and he greeted with rapture the young man who at last appeared and took her off his hands. Her attempt at familiarity with him had failed, and she felt intensely chagrined, and mortified, and disappointed, for she began to understand how difficult it would be for Everard to confess his marriage, and to fear the consequences if he did. A tolerably skillful reader of human nature, she saw what kind of man Judge Forrest was, and felt that Everard had not misrepresented him. She saw, too, that he had conceived a dislike to herself, and for the first time began to dread the result should he know that she was his daughter-in-law. Disinheritance of Everard might follow, and then farewell to her dream of wealth, and luxury, and position. It is true the latter would be hers to a certain extent, for the wife of Everard Forrest would always take precedence of Josephine Fleming, but Josey liked what money would bring her better than position, and perhaps it would be well to keep quiet a while longer, provided her rapidly increasing wants were supplied. In this conclusion she was greatly strengthened when, the morning following the reception, Everard came for a few moments to see her and escort her to the train, for she was to leave that morning for home.

Between Everard and his father there had been a little conversation concerning Miss Josey, and not very complimentary to her either.

"Who was that bold, brazen-faced girl you introduced to me?" the judge had asked, and Everard replied:

"Do you mean that blonde in white? That is Miss Fleming from Holburton. She is called very beautiful."

"Umph! looks well enough, for that matter, but I do not like her. She is quite too forward, and familiar, and affected. There's nothing real about her, but her brass and vulgarity. And you boarded there, it seems, and knew her well?" the judge said, testily, and Everard stammered out that he did board with Mrs. Fleming, and had found Josephine a very agreeable young lady.

He must say so much in defense of the girl who was his wife, but it seemed to vex his father, who began to lose his temper, and said he should think very little of a young man who could find anything agreeable in that girl!

"Why, she's no modesty or womanly delicacy at all, or she would not try to attract as she does with her eyes, and her hands, and her fan, and her naked arms, and the Lord only knows what. You are no son of mine if you can find pleasure in the society of such women as she represents. Why, she is as unlike Beatrice and Rossie as darkness is unlike daylight."

This was the judge's verdict, and Everard felt his chain cutting deeper and deeper as he thought how impossible it was for him to acknowledge the marriage now. He did not sleep at all that night, and the morning found him pale, and haggard, and spiritless, as he walked down the road in the direction of Mrs. Everts'. Josey was waiting for him and ready for the train. She had not told any of her numerous admirers that she expected to leave that morning, as she wished to see Everard alone. She was neither pale, nor fagged, nor tired-looking, though she, too, had passed a sleepless night, but her complexion was just as soft, and creamy, and smooth, and her eyes just as bright and melting as she welcomed her husband, and laying her hand on his, said to him: "You are going with your father, I suppose. How long before I can come too?"

There was a sudden lifting of his hand to his head as if he had been struck, and Everard staggered a little back from her, as he replied:

"Come to Forrest House? I don't know. I am afraid that will never be while father lives."

"Yes, I saw he took a great dislike to me, and probably he has been airing his opinion of me to you," she said, tartly; then, as Everard did not speak, she continued: "Tell me what he said of me."

"Why should he say anything of you to me? He knows nothing," Everard asked, and Josephine replied:

"I don't know why. I only know he has; so, out with it. I insist upon knowing the worst. What did he say?"

There was a hard ring in her voice, which Agnes knew well, but which Everard had never heard before, and a look in her eyes before which he quailed; and after a moment, during which she twice repeated:

"Tell me what he said," he answered her:

"I would rather not, for I have no wish to wound you unnecessarily, and what father said was not complimentary."

"I know that. I knew he hated me, but I insist upon knowing just what he said and all he said," Josie cried passionately, for she, who seldom lost her temper except with Agnes, was beginning to lose it now.

"If you will insist I must tell you, I suppose," Everard said, "but remember that father's prejudices are sometimes unfounded."

He meant to soften it to her as much as possible, but he told her the truth, and Josie was conscious of a keener pang of mortification than she had ever felt before. She had meant to win the judge, just as she won all men when she tried, but she had failed utterly. He disliked and despised her, and if he knew she was his son's wife he might go to any length to be rid of her, even to the attempting a divorce. Once, when sorely pressed, Agnes had suggested that idea as something which might occur to Everard, and said:

"You know that under the circumstances he could get one easily."

Josephine knew that he could, too, but she had faith in Everard. He would not bring this publicity upon himself and her; but his father was quite another sort of person. She was afraid of him, and of what he might do if roused to action as a knowledge of the marriage would rouse him. He must not know of it at present, and though she had intended to make Everard acknowledge her as soon as he was graduated and settled at home she changed her mind suddenly, and was almost as anxious to keep the secret as Everard himself.

"I am greatly obliged to your father for his opinion of me," she said, when she could command herself to speak. "He is the first man I ever failed to please when I really tried to do so, and I did try hard to make an impression, but it was all a waste of words; he is drier and stiffer than an old powder-horn. I don't like your father, Everard, and I am free to say so, though, of course, I mean no blame to you. I am glad I have met him, for I understand the situation perfectly, and know just how you shrink from letting him know our secret. I hoped that you would take me home as soon as you were settled at your law studies in your father's office, but I am convinced that to announce your marriage with me at present would be disastrous to your future; so we must wait still longer, hoping that something will turn up."

She spoke very cheerfully, and her hand was on Everard's, and her eyes were wearing their sweetest expression as she added:

"But you will write to me often, won't you, and try to love me again as you did before that night, which I wish had never been for your sake, because I know you are sorry."

He did not say he was not; he did not say anything, but the shadow lifted from his face, and his heart gave a great bound when he heard from her own lips that she should not urge her claim upon him at once. He had feared this with such fear as a freed slave has of a return to his chains, and now that he was to have a little longer respite, he felt so happy and grateful withal that when she said to him:

"I wish you'd kiss me once for the sake of the old time;" he stooped and kissed her twice, and let her golden head rest against his bosom, where she laid it for a moment, but he felt no throb of love for this woman who was his wife. That was dead, and he could not rekindle it, but he could be kind to her, and do his duty to her, and he talked with her of his future, and said he meant to go to work at something at once, and hoped to become a regular contributor to a magazine which paid well, and he seemed so bright and cheerful that Josey flattered herself that she had touched him again. Nothing could have been farther from the truth, though he was very polite to her and went with her to the station, where she was immediately surrounded by a bevy of students who were there also to take the train, and who, in their eagerness to serve her, left Everard far in the background.

The fact that young Forrest, who, from the fastest, wildest young man in college had become the soberest, most reserved, and, as they fancied, most aristocratic member of his class, had attended Miss Fleming to the train, did not in the least lessen her in the estimation of the students who gathered round her so thickly. Indeed, it increased her importance, and she knew it, and felt a great pride in the tall, handsome, dignified man who stood and saw one take her satchel, another her shawl, and another her umbrella, while he who alone had a right to render her these attentions looked on silently. Whatever he thought he gave no sign, and his face was just as grave as ever when at last he said good-by, and walked away.

"Did you come up here to see that girl off?" was said close to his ear, in a voice and tone he knew so well, just as he left the depot, and turning suddenly, he saw his father, with an unmistakable look of displeasure on his face.

The judge was taking his morning stroll, and had sauntered to the station just in time to see the long curls he remembered so well float out of the car window, and to see the fluttering of the handkerchief Josephine was waving at his son.

"Yes, father, I came to see her off. There was no one else to do it, and I know her so well; her mother was very kind to me."

"Umph! I've no doubt of it. Such people always are kind to young men like you," the judge said, contemptuously; "but I won't have it; I tell you, I won't! That girl is just as full of tricks as she can hold, and is never so happy as when she has twenty or more fools dangling after her. She will marry the one with the most money, of course, but it must not be you; remember that. I believe I'd turn you out of doors."

Just then they met one of the professors, and that changed the conversation, which did not particularly tend to raise Everard's spirits, as he went to the house where Beatrice and Rosamond were stopping. Still, he felt a great burden gone when he remembered that of her own free will Josephine had decided that their secret must be kept for a while longer, and something of his own self came back to him as he thought of months, if not a whole year of freedom, with Beatrice and Rossie, at the old home in Rothsay.

CHAPTER XIV

TWO MONTHS

Of the every-day lives of the three young people, Beatrice, Everard, and Rosamond, I wish to say a few words before hurrying on to the tragedy which cast so dark a shadow over them all. But there was no sign of the storm now in the rose-tinted sky, and Everard never forgot that bright summer and autumn which followed his return from college,—when he was so happy in the society of Beatrice and Rossie. It is true he never forgot that he was bound fast, with no hope of ever being free, but here in Rothsay, miles and miles away from the chain which bound him, it did not hurt so much or seem quite so hard to bear.

Josephine was not very troublesome; in fact, she had only written to him twice, and then she did not ask for money, and seemed quite as anxious as himself that their secret should be kept from his father until some way was found to reconcile him to it. Possibly her reticence on the subject of money arose from the fact that he sent her fifty dollars in his first letter written after his return to Rothsay. This large sum he had got together by the most rigid economy in his own expenses, and by the interest on a few shares of railroad stock which a relative had left to him as her godson. This stock for a time had been good for nothing, but recently it had risen in value, so that a dividend had been declared, and Everard had sent the first proceeds to Josephine; but his boyish love was dead, and he did not try to resuscitate it, or build another love where that had been; he was content with the present as it was. His father, who was very kind to him, and seemed trying to make amends for his former severity and harshness, had said he was not to enter the office to study until October. Looking in his boy's face, he had seen something which he mistook for weariness, and too close application to books, and he said, "You do not seem quite well. Your mother's family were not strong; so rest till October. Have a good time with Rossie and Bee, and you will be better fitted to bone down to work when the time for it comes."

This was a great deal for Judge Forrest to say, but he felt very indulgent toward his son, who had graduated with so much honor, and who seemed to be wholly upright and steady; and in a fit of wonderful generosity he went so far as to present him with a fine mustang, as a fitting match to Beatrice's fleet riding-horse. This was just what Everard wanted, and he and Miss Belknap rode miles and miles together over the fine roads and through the beautiful country in the vicinity of Rothsay. Rosamond sometimes accompanied them, but she was not fond of riding, and old Bobtail, the gray mare, sent her up so high, and seemed so out of place beside Bee's shining black pony, and Everard's white-faced mustang, that she preferred remaining at home; and so the two were left to themselves, and people talked knowingly of what was sure to be, and hinted it to Rosamond, who never contradicted them, but by her manner gave credence to the story. She believed implicitly that Beatrice was coming to be mistress of the Forrest House, and was very happy in the prospect, for next to Mr. Everard she liked Bee Belknap better than any person in the world. Many were the castles she built of the time when Everard should bring his bride home. Since Mrs. Forrest's death so many rooms had been shut up, and the house had seemed so lonely and almost dreary, especially in the winter, but with Bee there all would be changed, and Rossie even indulged in the hope that possibly the furniture in her own little room might be replaced by better, or at least added to. The judge, too, watched matters with an immense amount of satisfaction. Years ago he had settled it that Everard would marry Bee, and he was sure of it now. That girl with the yellow hair, as he always called Josephine to himself, was not anything to his son, as he had once feared she might be. Everard could never stoop to her; Everard would marry Bee, and it might as well take place at once; there was no need to wait, and just as soon as his son was established in the office he meant to speak to him, and if it were not already settled it should be, and Christmas was the time fixed in his own mind as a fitting season for the bridal festivities. He would fill the house with guests all through the holidays, and when they were gone the young couple might journey as far as Washington, or even Florida, if they liked. Then in the spring Bee could fit up the south side of the house as expensively as she chose, and Rossie should have the large corner room next his own on the north side, thus leaving the newly-married pair as much to themselves as possible.

And so the wires were being laid, and Everard stepped over and around them all unconsciously, and took the goods the gods provided for him, whether in the shape of Beatrice, or Rosamond, or his father's uniform kindness toward him; and the September days went by, and October came, and found him a student at last in his father's office, where he bent every energy to mastering the law and gaining his profession. There were no more long rides with Beatrice, and his mustang chafed and fretted and grew unmanageable for want of exercise. There were no more strolls in the leafy woods with Rossie, who gathered the nuts, and ferns and grasses alone, and rarely had Everard's society except at meal-time, when she managed to post him with regard to all the details of her quiet, every-day life. She was reading Chateaubriand's "Atala" in French, and found it rather stupid; or she was learning a new piece of music she knew he would like; or old Blue had six new kittens in his trunk up in the garret, and she wished him to go and see them.

Everard was always interested in what interested Rosamond, and on no one did his glance rest so kindly as on this little old-fashioned girl, in whom there seemed to be no guile; but he had no leisure time to give her. It was his plan to get his profession as soon as possible, and then, taking Josephine, go to some new place in the far West, where he could grow up with the town, and perhaps be comparatively independent and happy. But his future had been ordered otherwise, and suddenly, without a note of warning, his house of cards came down, and buried him in its ruins.

CHAPTER XV

THE HOUSE OF CARDS BEGINS TO FALL

Everard had been in his father's office five weeks or more, when, on a rainy morning early in November, just as he was settling himself to his books, and congratulating himself upon the luxury of a quiet day, his father came in, and after looking over the paper, and poking the fire vigorously, seated himself opposite his son, and began:

"Everard, put down your book; I want to talk with you."

"Yes, sir," Everard replied, closing the book and facing his father with an unaccountable dread that something unpleasant was coming.

"It's never my way to beat round the bush," the judge began; "I come to the point at once, and so I want to know if you and Bee have settled it yet?"

"Settled what?" Everard asked; and his father replied:

"Don't be a fool and put on girlish airs. Marrying is as much a matter of business as anything else, and we may discuss it just the same. You don't suppose me in my dotage, that I have not seen what is in everybody's mouth,—your devotion to Beatrice and her readiness to receive it; wait till I'm through," he continued, authoritatively, as he saw Everard about to speak. "I like the girl; have always liked her, though she is a wild, saucy thing, but that will correct itself in time. Your mother believed in her fully, and she knew what was in women. She hoped you would marry Bee some day, and what I wish to say is this: you may think you must wait till you get your profession, but there is no need of that at all. You are twenty-two. You have matured wonderfully the last two years, and I may say improved, too; time was when I could hardly speak peaceably of you for the scrapes you were eternally getting into, but you dropped all that after your poor mother died. I was proud of you at Commencement. I am proud of you now, and I want you to marry at once. The house needs a mistress, and I have fixed upon Christmas as the proper time for the wedding, so if you have not settled it with Bee, do so at once."

"But, father," Everard gasped, with a face as white as snow, "it is impossible that I should marry Beatrice. I have never for a moment considered such a thing."

"The deuce you haven't," the judge exclaimed, beginning to get angry. "Pray, let me ask you why you have been racing and chasing after her ever since you came home, if you never considered the thing, as you say? Others have considered it, if you have not. Everybody thinks you are to marry her, and, by George, I won't have her compromised. No, I won't! She could sue you for breach of promise, and recover, too, with all this dancing, and prancing, and scurripping round the country. If you have not thought of it, you must think of it now. You surely like the girl."

He stopped to take breath, and Everard answered him:

"Yes, father, I like her very much, but not in that way,—not as a wife, and I never can. It is impossible."

"Why impossible? What do you mean?" the judge said, loudly and angrily. "Is there somebody else? Is it that yellow-haired hussy who made those eyes at me, because, if it is, by Jove, you are no son of mine, and you may as well understand it first as last. I'll never sanction that, never! Why don't you answer me, and not stare at me so like an idiot? Do you like that white-livered woman better than Beatrice? Do you think her a fitter wife for you and companion for Rosamond?"

Everard had opened his lips to tell the truth, but what his father said of Josephine sealed them tight; but he answered his father's last questions, and said:

"No, I do not think her a fitter companion for Rossie than Beatrice, and I do not like her better."

"Then what in thunder is in the way?" the judge asked, slightly appeased. "Have you any fears of Bee's saying no? I can assure you there. I know she won't. I am as certain of it as that I am living now."

Suddenly there shot across Everard's mind a way of escape from the difficulty, a chance for a longer respite, and he said:

"If I were to ask Bee to marry me and she refused would you be satisfied?"

"With you? Yes, but, I tell you she won't refuse. And don't you ask her unless you intend to stick to it like a man," the judge replied, as he rose to end the conference.

"I shall ask her, and to-night," was Everard's low-spoken answer, which reached his father's ears, and sent him home in a better frame of mind.

He was very gracious to Everard at dinner, and paid him the compliment of consulting him on some business matter, but Everard was too much pre-occupied to heed what he was saying, and declining the dessert excused himself from the table, and went to his own room.

Never since his ill-starred marriage had he felt so troubled and perplexed as now, when the fruit of his wrong-doing was staring him so broadly in the face. That his father would never leave him in peace until he proposed to Beatrice, he knew, and unless he confessed everything and threw himself upon his mercy, there was but one course left him to pursue,—tell Beatrice the whole story, without the slightest prevarication, and then go through the farce of offering himself to her, who must, of course, refuse. This refusal he could report to his father, who would not blame him, and so a longer probation would come to himself.

In his excitement he did not stop to consider what a cowardly thing it was to throw the responsibility upon a girl, and make her bear the burden for him. To do him justice, however, he did not for a moment suppose Beatrice cared for him as his father believed she did, or he would never have gone to insult her with an offer she could not accept.

He knew she was beautiful and sweet, and all that was lovely and desirable in womanhood, but she was not for him. She, nor any one like her, could ever be his wife. He had made that impossible; had by his own act put such as she far out of his reach. But when he reached Elm Park and saw her, so graceful and lady-like, and heard the well-bred tones of her voice, and remembered how pure and good she was, there did come to him the thought that if there was no Josephine in the way, he might in time have come to say in earnest to this true, spotless girl what now was but a cruel jest, if she cared for him,—which she did not in the way his father believed she did;—he was her friend, her brother. The Feejee missionary, whose name she saw so often in the papers, and who had recently been removed to a more eligible field, had never been quite forgotten, though there was nothing left to her now of him except a faded pond-lily, given the day she told him no, and with his kiss, the first and last, upon her forehead, sent him away to the girl among the Vermont hills, with the glasses and the brown alpaca dress. She had no suspicion of the nature of his errand, and was surprised when, as if anxious to have it off his mind, he began, impulsively:

"Beatrice, I have come to say something serious to you to-night, and I want you to stop jesting and be as much in earnest as I am, for I,—I am terribly in earnest for once in my life. Bee,—I,—I feel as if I were going to be hung and do the deed myself."

But his face was white as marble, and his voice shook as he continued:

"I am going to tell you something,—going to ask you something,—going to ask you to be my wife, but you must refuse."

It was an odd way of putting it, and not at all what Everard had intended to do. He meant to tell her first and offer himself afterward as a mere form, but in his agitation and excitement he had just reversed it,—had told her he was there to ask her to marry him, and she must tell him no! and a look of scorn sprang to her eyes as she drew back from him and said, "You presume much on my good nature, when you tell me in one instant that you propose asking me to be your wife, and next that I must refuse you if you do. What reason have you to think I would accept you, pray?"

He knew she was indignant, and justly so, and he answered her with such a pleading pathos in his voice as disarmed her at once of her wrath.

"Don't be angry with me, Bee. I have commenced all wrong. I believe my mind is not quite straight. I did not come to insult you. I came because I must come. I want you for a friend, such as I have not in all the world. I want your advice and sympathy. I want,—oh, I am the most wretched person living!"

And he seated himself upon the sofa, and sat with his face buried in his hands, while Beatrice stood looking at him a moment; then, going forward she laid her hand softly on his head, and said, "What is it, Everard? What is it you wish to tell me?"

Without looking up he answered her:

"Oh, Bee, I wish I were dead! Sit down beside me and listen to all I have to tell."

She sat down beside him, and listened intently to the story Everard told her in full, concealing nothing where he was concerned, but shielding Josephine as far as was possible. Rosamond's noble sacrifice of her hair was explained, and her mistake about Joe Fleming, who in her imagination still existed somewhere in whiskers and tall boots, and was the evil genius of Everard's life. Here Beatrice laughed merrily once, then questioned Everard rapidly with regard to every particular of his marriage, and the family, and the girl. Where was she now and what was she like?

"You have seen the picture, Bee," he said. "I showed it to you that day I broke my head, two years ago, and you said she looked as if she might wear cotton lace, while mother, to whom I showed it, too, hinted at dollar jewelry, and Rossie said she looked as if she were a sham."

Here Everard laughed himself, but there was more of bitterness than mirth in it, and Beatrice laughed, too, as she said:

"That was rather hard;—cotton lace, dollar jewelry, and a sham, though, after all, Rossie's criticism was really of the most consequence, if true; perhaps it is not. Have you her picture now?"

He passed it to her, and with a shrewd woman's intuition, quickened by actual knowledge, Beatrice felt that it was true, and her first womanly instinct was to help and comfort this man who had brought his secret to her.

"Ned," she said to him, and the name, now so seldom used, took her back to the days when she first came from France and played and quarreled with him. It made her altogether his sister, and as such she spoke. "Ned, I am so sorry for you; sorrier than I can express, and I want to help you some way, and I think it must be through Josephine. She is your wife, and by your own showing you were quite as much in fault as she."

"Yes, quite," and Everard shivered a little, for he guessed what was coming.

"Well, then," Beatrice went on, "ought you not to make the best of it? You took her for better or worse, knowing what you were doing. You loved her then. Can you not do so again? Is it not your duty to try?"

"Oh, Bee, you do not know, you do not understand. She is not like you, nor Rossie, nor mother."

"Well, try to make her like us, then," Beatrice replied. "If her surroundings are not such as please you, remove her from them at once. Recognize her as your wife. Bring her home to Forrest House and I will stand her friend to the death."

Everard knew that Bee meant what she said, and that her influence was worth more than that of the whole town, and if he could have felt any love or even desire for Josephine, it would have seemed easy to acknowledge his marriage, with Bee's hopeful words in his ear and Bee's strong nature to back him, but he did not. He had no love, no desire for her; he was happier away from her, happier to live his present life with Beatrice and Rossie; and, besides that, he could not bring her home; his father would never permit it, and would probably turn him from the door if he knew of the alliance. This Bee did not know, but he told her of the great aversion his father had conceived for the girl whom he stigmatized as the yellow-haired hussy from Massachusetts, "and after that, do you think I can tell him?" he asked.

"It will be hard, I know," Beatrice replied, "but it seems your only course, if he insists upon your marrying me."

"But if I tell him you refused me, it may make a difference, and things can go on as they are until I get my profession," Everard pleaded, with a shrinking which he knew was cowardly from all which the telling his father might involve.

"Even then you are but putting off the evil day, and a thing concealed grows worse as time goes on," Bee said. "You must confess it some time, and why not do it now. At the most your father can but turn you from his door, and if he does that take your wife and go somewhere else. You are young, and the world is all before you, and if there is any true womanhood in Josephine, it will assert itself when she knows all you have lost for her. She will grow to your standard. She has a sweet, childish face, and must have a loving, affectionate nature. Give her a chance, Everard, to show what she is."

This giving her a chance was just what Everard dreaded the most. So long as his life with Josephine was in the future, he could be tolerably content, and even happy, but when it looked him square in the face, as something which must be met, he shrank from meeting it.

"Oh, I cannot do that, at least, not yet," he said. "It will hamper me so in my studies. I cannot tell father, and bear the storm sure to follow. Josephine must stay where she is till I see what I can do."

"But is that best for her?" Beatrice asked. "What sort of a woman is her mother? She may be a lady, and still be very poor. What is she, Everard?"

He had refrained from speaking of Josephine's antecedents to Beatrice. He would rather she should not know all he knew of the family. It would be kinder to Josephine to spare her so much; but when Beatrice appealed to him with regard to the mother, he told just who Mrs. Fleming was.

Bee Belknap was a born aristocrat, and some of the bluest blood of Boston was in her veins. Indeed, she traced her pedigree back to Miles Standish on her father's side, while her mother came straight down from a Scottish earl, who married the rector's daughter. She was proud of her birth, and the training she had received at home and abroad had tended to increase this pride, and it was hard for her to understand just how people like Roxie Fleming could stand on the same social platform with herself. She knew they did, but she rebelled against it, and for a moment Josephine's cause was in danger of being lost so far as she was concerned. She had thought of her as probably the daughter of some poor, but highly respectable farmer, or mechanic, whose mother took boarders, as many women do to make a little money, and whose daughters, perhaps, stitched shoes or made bonnets, as New England girls often do, but now that she knew the truth she stood for a moment aghast, and then, her strong, sensible nature asserted itself and whispered to her, "a man's a man for a' that." Josephine was no more to blame for the accident of her birth than was she, Beatrice Belknap, to be praised for hers. "I'll stand by her all the same," she said to herself, but she did not urge quite so strenuously upon Everard the necessity of telling his father at once, for she felt sure the irascible judge would leave no stone unturned to ascertain who his daughter-in-law was, and that the ascertaining would result even worse than Everard feared.

"It may be better to keep silent a little longer," she said, and meanwhile she'd turn the matter over in her own mind and see what she could do to help him.

"But in order to have any peace at home I must tell father that you refused me," Everard said, "and I have not yet gone through the farce of offering myself, or you of refusing the offer."

Then, with the ghost of a smile on his face he arose, and standing before Beatrice, continued: "Bee, will you marry me?"

"No, Everard, I will not," was Bee's reply, as she, too, rose, and looked at him, with eyes in which the hot tears gathered swiftly, while there came to her suddenly a feeling that she had lost something which had been very dear to her, and that her intercourse with Everard could never again be just what it had been. It is true, she had never seriously thought of him as her future husband, but she knew that others had thought it, and with his words, "Bee, will you marry me?" it came to her with a great shock that possibly, under other circumstances, she might have answered yes. But all that was over now. He had put a bar between them, and by neither word nor look must she tempt him to cross it; so, brushing her tears away with a quick, impatient gesture, and forcing a merry laugh, which sounded not unlike a hysterical sob, she said, "What children we are, Everard."

Yes, they were children in one sense, and in another the man and woman was strong within them, and Everard saw something in the girl's eyes which startled him, and made his heart throb quickly as he, too, thought "it might have been." But with the instincts of a noble, true man he forced the new-born feeling down, and taking both her hands in his held them while he said:

"You must forgive me, Bee, for seeming to insult you with words which were a mere farce. You have been my friend,—the best I ever had,—and your friendship and society are very dear to me, who never knew a sister's love. Can I keep them still after showing you just the craven coward and sneak I am?"

"Yes, Everard, you may trust me. I will always be your friend, and your wife's friend as well," Beatrice replied, and then Everard went away, and she was left alone to think of the story she had heard, and to realize more and more all she had lost in losing Everard. The boy, whom she had teased, and ridiculed, and tormented, and who had likened her to his grandmother, had become so necessary to her in his fresh young manhood, that it was hard to give him up; but Bee was equal to the emergency, and with a little laugh she said:

"On the whole I am glad there is one man whom I cannot get upon my string, as Aunt Rachel would say; but that this man should be the boy who I once vowed should offer himself to me and be refused, or I would build a church in Omaha, is mortifying to my pride. He has offered and been refused, and so the church obligation is null and void. But I must do something as a memorial of this foolishness, which I never dreamed of until to-night. I wonder if Sister Rhoda Baker don't want something for her church by this time. I'll go and see to-morrow, and take her mother to ride. It's an age since I gave her an airing, and my purple velvet will contrast beautifully with her quilted hood and black shawl."

Bee Belknap was a queer compound, and when, next morning, the distant relative who lived with her as chaperon, and whom she called Aunt Rachel, said to her: "What was that Forrest here for so late? I thought he'd never go," she answered, readily:

"He was here to ask me to marry him, and I refused him flat."

"You refused him! Are you crazy, Beatrice?" Aunt Rachel exclaimed, putting down her coffee-cup and staring blankly at the young girl, who replied:

"Yes. Have you any objections?"

"Objections! Beatrice Belknap! I thought this was sure. See if you don't go through the woods and take up with a crooked stick at last. Do you know how old you are?"

"Yes, auntie. I am twenty-three; just eleven months and fifteen days older than Everard, and in seven years more I shall be thirty, and an old maid. After that, tortures cannot wring my age from me. Honestly, though, Everard was not badly hurt. He will recover in time, and maybe marry,—well, marry Rossie; who knows?"

"Marry Rossie! That child,—homely as a hedge fence!" was the indignant reply of Aunt Rachel, who was not always choice in her selection of language.

"Rosamond is fifteen, and growing pretty every day," Beatrice retorted, always ready to defend her pet. "She has magnificent eyes and hair, and the sweetest voice I ever heard. Her complexion is clearing up, her face and figure rounding out, and she will yet be a beauty, and cast me in the shade, with my crows-feet and wrinkles; see if she does not; but I cannot afford to quarrel any longer; I am going to take Widow Ricketts out to ride, so good-by, auntie, and don't be sorry that I am not to leave you yet. You and I will have many years together, I hope."

She kissed her aunt, and went gayly from the room, singing as she went. An hour later and she was whirling along the smooth river road, with the quilted hood and black shawl of Widow Ricketts, who, unused to such fast driving, held on to the side of the little phaeton, sweating like rain with fear, and feeling very glad when at last she was set down safe and sound at her daughter's door without a broken neck.

Rhoda's church was wanting a new furnace, and Bee's check for fifty dollars made the heart of the good Nazarite woman very warm and tender toward the girl who had once pretended to have the "power," just for the fun of the thing! On reaching home Bee found a note from Everard, which had been left by a boy from the village, during her absence, and which ran as follows:

"Dear Bee:—After leaving you last night, I went to father, who was waiting for me, and goaded me into telling him everything there was to tell of Josephine. Of course, he turned me out of doors immediately, and said I was no longer his son. I might sleep in my room during the night,

but in the morning I must be off. But I did not sleep there. I couldn't, with his dreadful language in my ears. If I had been guilty of murder, he could not have talked worse to me than he did, or called me viler names. So I packed a few things in my valise, and staid in the carriage-house till it was light. Now, I am writing this to you, and shall have some boy to deliver it, as I take the first train South. I have given up law, and shall find something in Cincinnati or Louisville which will bring me ready money. If you should wish to communicate with me, direct to the Spencer House. I shall get my mail there a while, as I know the clerk. Don't tell Rossie of Josephine. I'd rather she should not know. God bless her and you, my best friends in all the world. And so, good-by. I've sown the wind, and am reaping the whirlwind with a vengeance.

J. E. Forrest."

CHAPTER XVI

THE HOUSE OF CARDS GOES DOWN

It was past eleven when Everard left Elm Park after his interview with Beatrice, and nearly half-past when he reached home, expecting to find the house dark, and the family in bed. But as he walked slowly up the avenue, he saw a light in his father's room, and the figure of a man walking back and forth, as if impatient of something.

"Can it be he is waiting for me?" he thought, and a sigh escaped him as he felt how unequal he was to a conflict with his father that night.

Entering the hall as noiselessly as possible he groped his way up stairs to the broad landing, when the darkness was suddenly broken by a flood of light which poured from Rossie's room, and Rossie herself appeared in the door, holding her gray flannel dressing-gown together with one hand, and with the other shedding her hair back from her face, which looked tired and sleepy, as she said: "Oh, I'm so glad you've come. Your father wants to see you, and asked me to sit up and tell you when you came. Good-night!" and she stepped back into her room, while he passed slowly down the hall, and she saw him knock at his father's room at the far end of the passage.

"Well, my son, so you've come at last," the judge said to him, but there was no anger in his voice, only a slight tone of irritation that he had been kept up so late. "You have been to see Bee, I take it, and, from the length of time you staid, conclude that you settled the little matter we were talking about this morning."

"Yes, father, we settled it," Everard said, but his voice was not the voice of a hopeful, happy lover, and his father looked suspiciously at him as he continued:

"With what result?"

"Beatrice refused me;" and Everard's voice was still lower and more hopeless.

"Refused you! 'Tis false! You never asked her!" the judge exclaimed, growing angry at once.

"Father!" and now Everard looked straight in his sire's face, "do you mean to say I lie, and I your son and mother's?"

The judge knew that in times past Everard had been guilty of almost everything a fast young man ever is guilty of, but he had never detected him in a falsehood, and he was obliged to answer him now:

"No, not exactly lie, though I don't understand why she should refuse you. If I know anything about girls she is not averse to you, and here you come and tell me that she refused you flat. There's some trick somewhere; something I do not understand. Beatrice likes you well enough to marry you, and you know it. Why then did she refuse you, unless you made a bungle of the whole thing, and showed her you were not more than half in earnest, as upon my soul I believe you are not; but you shall be. I've had my mind on that marriage for years, and I will not easily give it up. Do you hear or care for what I am saying?" he asked, in a voice growing each instant louder and more excited.

"Yes, father," Everard answered wearily, with the air of one who did not really comprehend. "I hear,—I care,—but I am so tired to-night. Let me off, won't you, till another time, when I can talk with you better and tell you all I feel."

"No, I won't let you off," the judge replied. "I intend to know why you are so indifferent to Bee. Is it, as I have suspected, that yellow-haired woman? Because if it is, by the lord Harry, you will be sorry! She shall never come here; never! The bold-faced, vulgar thing!"

"Father!" and Everard roused himself at last, "you must not speak so of Josephine. I will not listen to it."

That was the speech which fired the train, and the judge grew purple with rage as he demanded by what right his son forbade him to speak as he pleased of Josephine.

"What is she to you?" he asked, and with white, quivering lips Everard answered back:

"She is my wife!"

The words were spoken almost in a whisper, but they echoed like thunder through the room, and seemed to repeat themselves over and over again during the moment of utter silence which ensued. Everard had told his secret, and felt better already, as if the worst was over; while his father stood motionless and dumb, glaring upon him with a baleful light in his eyes, which boded no good to the sorely-pressed young man, who was the first to speak.

"Let me tell you all about it," he said, "and then you may kill me if you choose; it does not matter much."

"Yes, tell me;" his father said, hoarsely; and without lifting up his bowed head, or raising his voice, which was strangely sad and low, Everard told his story,—every word of it, even to Josephine's parentage and Rossie's generous conduct in his behalf.

Of Josephine herself he said as little as possible, and did not by the slightest word hint at his growing aversion for her. That would not help matters now. She was his wife, and he called her so two or three times, and did not see how at the mention of that name his father ground his teeth together and clutched at his cravat as if to tear it off, and give himself more room to breathe.

"I have told you everything now, father," Everard said in conclusion, "everything there is to tell, except that since that night I have not committed a single act of which I am not willing you should know. I have tried to do my best, as I promised mother I would the last time I talked with her. She believed in me then; she would forgive me if she were here, and for her sake I ask you to forgive me too. I am so sorry,—sorrier than you can possibly be. Will you forgive me for mother's sake?"

He had made his plea and waited for the answer. He knew how ungovernable his father's temper was at times, but it was so long since he had met it in its worst form that he was wholly unprepared for the terrible burst of passion to which his father gave vent. He had listened quietly to his son's story, without comment or interruption, but his anger had grown stronger and fiercer with each detail, so that even the mention of his dead wife had no power to move him now. On the contrary, it exasperated him the more, and, at Everard's appeal for pardon, the storm burst and he began in a voice of such withering scorn and contempt that Everard looked wonderingly at the old man, who shook with rage and whose face was livid in spots. There was nothing to be hoped for from him, and Everard bowed his head again, while the tempest raged on.

"Forgive you for your mother's sake! Dastard! How dare you cringe and creep behind her name, when you have disgraced her in her coffin? Forgive you? Never! So long as I have sense and reason left!"

This was the preface to what followed, for, taking up the case as a lawyer takes up the case of the criminal whom it is his duty to prosecute, the judge went through it step by step, speaking first of the puling weakness which would allow one to fall into the damnable trap set for him by a crafty, designing woman, then of the base hypocrisy, the living lie of years, the systematic deception, the mean cowardice, the sneaking, contemptible spirit which would even take money from a child to squander on that yellow-haired Jezebel, the insult to Beatrice, asking her to marry him just for a farce, and lastly, the audacity in thinking such enormities could be forgiven.

Everard did not think they could by the time his case was summed up. He did not think of much of anything, he was so benumbed and bewildered, and his father's voice sounded like some great roaring river very far away.

"Forgive you!" it said again, with all the concentrated bitterness of hatred. "Forgive you! Never, so long as I live, will I forgive or own you for my son, or in any way recognize that jade as your wife. From this time on you are none of mine. I disown you. I cast you off, forever. You may sleep here to-night, but in the morning you leave, and go back to your darling and her high-born family, but you'll never cross my threshold again while I am living. Do you hear, or are you a stone, a clod, that you sit there so quietly?"

His son's demeanor exasperated him, and he would have been better pleased had Everard fought him inch by inch, and given him back scorn for scorn. But this Everard could not do; he was too completely crushed to offer a word in his own defense. Only at the last, when he heard himself disowned, he roused and said, "Do you mean it, father? Mean to turn me from your house?"

"Mean it? Yes; don't you understand plain language when you hear it?" thundered the judge.

"Yes, father, I understand, and I will go," Everard said, rising slowly, as if it were painful to move; then, half staggering to the door, he stopped a moment and added, "I deserve a great deal, father, but not all you have given me. You have been too hard with me, and you will be sorry for it some day. Good-by; I am going."

"Go, then, and never come back," came like a savage growl from the infuriated man, and those were the last words which, ever passed between the father and the son.

"Good-by, father, I am going."

"Go, then, and never come back."

They sounded through the stillness of the night, and Everard shivered, as he went through the long, dark hall and up the stairs, where the old clock was striking one, and where the light from Rossie's door again shone into the gloom, and Rossie's face looked out, pale and scared this time, for she had heard the judge's angry voice, and knew a dreadful battle was in progress. So she wrapped a shawl about her and waited till it was over, and she heard Everard coming up the stairs. Then she went to him, for something told the motherly child that he was in need of comfort and sympathy, and such crumbs as she could give she would. But she was not prepared for the cowed, humiliated look of utter hopelessness, and not knowing what she was doing, she drew him into her room, and making him sit down, she took his icy hands and rubbed and chafed them, while she said, "What is it, Mr. Everard? Tell me all about it. I heard your father's voice so loud and angry that it frightened me, and I sat up to wait for you and tell you how sorry I am. What is it?"

Her sympathy was very sweet to Everard, and touched him so closely that for a moment he was unable to speak; then he said:

"I cannot tell you, Rossie, what it is; only that it is something which dates far back, before mother died, and father has just found it out, and has turned me from his door."

"Oh, Mr. Everard, you must have misunderstood him; he did not mean that. You are mistaken," Rossie cried, in great distress; and Everard replied:

"When a man calls his son a sneak, a coward, a clod, a villain, a scoundrel, a scamp, a hypocrite, a liar, there can be no misunderstanding the language, or what it means; and father called me all these names, and more, and said things I never can forget. I deserve a great deal, but not all this. Oh, if I had died years and years ago!"

His chin quivered and his voice trembled as he talked, while Rossie's tears flowed like rain as she stood, not holding his hands now, but gently stroking the hair of the head bowed down so low with its load of grief and shame.

"Mr. Everard," she said at last, "has this trouble anything to do with Joe Fleming?"

"Yes, everything!" Everard answered, bitterly; and Rossie continued:

"Oh, I am so sorry! I hoped you had broken with him forever. You have been so good and nice, and kept that pledge so beautifully! How could you have anything to do with Joe?"

"I tell you it dates far back,—a hundred years ago, it seems to me. I got into an awful scrape, from which I cannot extricate myself," Everard said, and Rossie continued:

"I see, you did something which Joe knows about, and so has you in his power, and you have just told your father."

"Yes, that is it, very nearly," Everard replied.

"I wish you'd tell me what it is. I 'most know I could help you; at all events, I could speak to your father; he is always kind to me, and will listen to reason, I think," Rossie said; and then Everard looked up quickly, and spoke decidedly:

"Rossie, you must not speak to father for me. I will not have it. He has taunted me enough with 'hanging on to the apron-strings of a little girl;' that's what he said, referring to my having taken money from you; for you see I told him everything, even to the hair you sold, and I think that made him more furious than all the rest. It was a dastardly thing in me, and there must be no repetition. You must not interfere by so much as a word; remember that when I am gone, for I am going to Cincinnati first, and if I find nothing to do there, I shall go on to Louisville, and possibly farther South. I shall write to you as soon as I know what I am going to do,— perhaps before; and, Rossie, among all the pleasant memories of my old home, the very sweetest will be the memory of the little girl who always in my sorest need lightened, if she could not remove, the burden. Hush, Rossie; don't cry so for me. I am not worth it," he said, as she burst into a passionate fit of weeping.

He had risen now and was bending over her and holding her hands in his, and when he saw her sobbing thus he wound his arm around her, and drawing her close to him, tried to quiet and comfort her.

"Don't, Rossie, don't; you unman me entirely, to see you give way so; I'd rather remember you as the brave little woman who always controlled herself."

Down over Rossie's shoulders her unbound hair was falling, and lifting up one of the wavy tresses, Everard continued, "I shall be gone in the morning, Rossie, and I want to take with me a lock of this hair. It will be a constant reminder of the sacrifice you once made for me, and keep me from temptation. May I have it, Rossie?"

She would have given him her head had he asked for it, and the lock was soon severed from the rest and laid in his hand. Holding it to the light he said, "Look how long, and bright, and even it is. You have beautiful hair, Rossie."

He meant to divert her mind, but her heart was very sore, and her face tear-stained and wet as she tied the hair with a bit of ribbon, and placing it in a paper, handed it to him.

"Thank you, Rossie," he said; "no man ever had a dearer sister than I, and if I am ever anything, it will be wholly owing to your influence and Bee's."

At the mention of Bee's name Rossie looked quickly up, struck with a sudden idea.

"Oh, Mr. Everard," she said, "how can you go away and leave Miss Beatrice? and I thought you and she would some time be married, and we should all be so happy."

"That can never be," Everard replied; "Beatrice will not have me; I cannot have her. We settled that to-night, but are the best of friends, and I esteem her as one of the noblest girls I ever knew. You may tell her so if she ever speaks of me after I am gone; tell her that with you she represents to me all that is purest and sweetest in womanhood; and now, Rossie, I must say good-by. It is almost two o'clock."

He took her upturned face between both his hands and held it a moment, while he looked earnestly into the clear, bright eyes which met his without a shadow of consciousness, except the consciousness that he was going away, and this was his farewell. Then he stooped and kissed her forehead and said, "God bless you, Rosamond; be a daughter to my father. You are all the child he has now."

An hour later and Rosamond had cried herself to sleep, and did not hear Everard's cautious footsteps, as, with his satchel in his hand, he stole down the stairs and out to the carriage-house, where he passed the few remaining hours of the November night, feeling that he was indeed an outcast and a wanderer.

CHAPTER XVII

THE NEXT DAY

How much or how soundly the judge slept after that stormy interview with his son, or whether there came to him any twinges of regret for all the bitter things he had said, none ever knew. He prided himself upon seldom changing his mind, when once it was made up; and so, perhaps, his temper was still at a boiling pitch when promptly at his usual hour he descended to the breakfast-room, and bade John bring in the coffee and eggs. His face was very red, and his eyes were blood-shot and watery, and his hands, which held the morning paper, trembled so, that John glanced curiously at him as he brought in the breakfast and arranged it upon the table.

"Where's Miss Rosamond and my son? Are they not ready?" the judge asked a little irritably, for he required every one to be prompt where he was concerned.

His questions were partly answered by the appearance of Rosamond, who looked as fresh and bright as usual, as she took her seat at the table and began to pour the coffee. She had slept soundly, and did not feel the effects of last night's excitement, except in a little tremor of fear and anxiety with regard to Everard. Whatever happened, she was not to interfere or plead for him. He had said so expressly, and she must obey, and as she looked furtively at the inflamed face opposite her, she felt for the first time in her life a great fear of the man, who, as Everard did not appear, said angrily, "Go to my son's room and see what is keeping him; and tell him I sent you," he added, as if that message would necessarily hasten the laggard young man.

Then Rossie dropped her spoon and sat shaking in her chair until the servant came swiftly back, with wonder and alarm upon his face, saying that his young master was not there and his bed had not been slept in.

"Not there! and his bed not slept in! What does it mean? Where is he, then?" the judge asked, in a voice that made Rossie tremble even more than the announcement that Everard was gone.

"I dunno, mass'r, where he can be. I know he's not thar, an' I disremember seen' him since he went out last night after dinner. Maybe he didn't come back."

"Blockhead, he did come back, and he's here now, most likely. I'll see for myself," said the judge, as he started for his son's room, followed by Rossie and John, the latter of whom said:

"Very well, mass'r, you see for yourself; he gone sure, an' left the bed as Axie fix it for him, an' lemme see, yes, shoo nuff, his big satchel gone wid him, and his odder suit. I shouldn't wonder if he's gone away," the loquacious negro continued, as he investigated the closet and room.

"You black hound," roared the infuriated judge, "why should he run away? What had he to run from? Leave the chamber instantly, before I kick you down stairs, for giving your opinion."

"Yes, mass'r, I's gwine," was John's reply as he disappeared from the scene, leaving the judge and Rossie alone.

The latter was white as a sheet, and leaned against the mantel, for she knew now that Everard was really gone. Her paleness and agitation escaped the judge's attention, for just then he picked up from the dressing-table the few lines that Everard had left for him, and which read as follows:

"Father:—You have always said your yea was yea, and your nay nay, and I know you meant it when you bade me leave your house and never come back again; so I have taken you at your word, and when you read this I shall be many miles away from Rothsay. After what you said

to me I cannot even pass the night under this roof, and shall stay in the carriage-house until time to take the train. I am sorry for all that has passed, very sorry, and wish I could undo my part of it, but cannot, and so it is better for me to go. Good-by, father.

Your son, Everard."

Notwithstanding the judge's favorite assertion that his yea was yea, and his nay nay, it is very possible that if Everard had not taken him so promptly at his word,—if he had staid and gone to breakfast as usual and about his daily avocations, his father would have cooled down gradually, and come in time to look the matter over soberly and make the best of it. But Everard had gone, and the irascible old man broke forth afresh into invectives against him, denouncing him as a dog, to sleep in carriage-houses, and then run away as if there was anything to run from.

"I'll never forgive him," he said to Rossie, who had stood silently by, appalled at the storm of passion such as she had never seen before, until at last, forgetful of Everard's charge not to interfere, she roused in his defense.

"Yes, you will forgive him," she said. "You must. He is your son, and though I don't know what he has done to make you so angry, I am sure it is not sufficient for you to treat him so, and you will send for him to come back. I know where he's gone. He came and told me he was going, though I did not think it would be till this morning, when I hoped you might make it up."

"And so he asked you to intercede for him as you have been in the habit of doing, and maybe told you the nice thing he had done?" the judge said, forgetting her assertion that she did not know.

"No, sir. Oh, no," Rossie cried. "He did not ask me to intercede; he said, on the contrary, that I was on no account to mention him, and he did not tell me what it was about, except that it happened long ago; and he is so sorry and has tried to be good since. You know he was trying, Judge Forrest, and you will forgive him, won't you?"

"By the lord Harry, no! and you would not ask it if you knew the disgrace he has brought upon me. I'll fix him!" was the judge's angry reply, as he broke away from her, and striding down the stairs took his hat from the hall-stand, and hurried to his office.

Great was the consternation among the servants in the Forrest household when it was known that Mr. Everard had left the house, and gone no one knew whither, and many were the whispered surmises as to the cause of his going.

"Some row between him and old mass'r," John said, and his solution of the mystery was taken as the correct one, the negroes all siding with Mr. Everard, who was very popular with them.

Old Axie, the cook, ventured to question Rosamond a little; but Rossie kept her own counsel, and, returning to her room, was crying herself sick, when a message came that Beatrice was asking for her. Immediately after reading Everard's note, Beatrice had driven over to the Forrest House, where she was admitted at once to Rossie's room, and heard all that Rossie knew of the events of the previous night.

"Oh, Miss Beatrice," Rossie said, "why did you refuse him? He told me about it, and I 'most know if you had said yes it would all have been so different."

Bee's face was scarlet as she replied:

"He told you that, and nothing more?"

"Yes, he said something about wouldn't and couldn't,—I don't know what, for it is all confused to me. I thought you liked him and he liked you. He said he did, and he bade me tell you that you were the purest and sweetest woman in the world, and the best, or something like that, and I think you ought to marry him, I do," and Rossie looked reproachfully at poor Bee, who was very pale, and whose voice was sad and low as she said:

"Rossie, I could not marry Everard if I wished to. There is an insuperable barrier, and if he did not explain, I must not. Did he give you any hint as to the cause of his quarrel with his father?"

"No," Rossie replied, "only that it dated far back, and had something to do with Joe Fleming. I wish Joe was in Guinea; he is always doing harm to Mr. Everard."

Beatrice could not forbear a smile at this ludicrous mistake of sex, and for a moment was tempted to tell the girl the truth; but remembering that Everard had said Rossie was not to know, she held her peace, and Rossie was left in ignorance of Joe's real identity.

After leaving the Forrest House Beatrice drove past the judge's office, with a faint hope that she might see him, and perhaps be of some service to Everard by speaking for him, should the opportunity occur. It was years since the judge, who once stood high in his profession, had done much business, and his office was occupied by Mr. Russell, his legal adviser; but he was frequently there, and as Bee drove down the street she saw him standing outside the door, glancing up and down as if looking for some one. Something in his attitude or manner induced her to rein her ponies up to the curbstone, where she could speak to him.

"Good morning, Judge Forrest," she said, as naturally as if in her heart she did not think him a monster of cruelty. "Were you waiting for me?"

"No, not exactly," and a faint smile appeared on the dark face. "I was looking for Parker, but maybe you'll do as well if you choose to step in and witness my will."

"Your will!" Bee replied, and all the blood in her body seemed surging into her face as she felt intuitively that a will made just now would be disastrous to Everard. "Have you never made your will before?" she asked, and he replied:

"Never; but it's high time I did. Yes, high time!" and he shook his head defiantly at something invisible. "Can you go in as well as not?" he continued; and, summoning all her courage for the conflict, Beatrice said to him:

"I am willing to go in, but not to witness any will which is in any way adverse to Everard."

"Who said it was adverse to him, the dog? Do you know how he has disgraced me? but yes, you do; he said he told you all, and insulted you with an offer, and now he has run away as a crowning feat. If you can forgive him, I can't;" and the judge trembled from head to foot as he talked of his son to Beatrice, who came bravely to the rescue, and standing nobly for Everard, tried to bring his father to reason, and make him say he would forgive his son and endure the wife because she was his wife.

But she might as well have given her words to the winds, for any effect they had. The judge was past all reason, and only grew more and more angry as he talked of the disgrace which Everard's marriage had brought upon his name. Finding that what she said was of no avail in the judge's present mood, Beatrice bade him good morning and drove away, resolving to see him again as soon as his temper had cooled, and try what she could do by way of a reconciliation.

The next morning breakfast was much later than usual at Elm Park, for Beatrice had slept but little, and she was still in bed when her maid brought a message to her from Rosamond to the effect that she must come at once to the Forrest House, as the judge had been smitten suddenly with apoplexy, and was lying in a half unconscious condition, nearly resembling death. Terrified beyond measure, Beatrice dressed herself hurriedly, and was soon on her way to the house, where she found matters even worse than she feared.

CHAPTER XVIII

THE SHADOW OF DEATH

Breakfast at the Forrest House had been late that morning, for the judge, who was usually so prompt, did not make his appearance, and Rosamond waited for him until the clock struck eight. Then, as the minute-hand crept on and he still did not come down, she went to the door of his room and knocked, but there came no answer, though she thought she heard a faint sound like the moan of some one in pain. Knocking still louder, with her ear to the keyhole, she called, "Judge Forrest, are you awake? Do you hear me? Do you know how late it is?"

This time there was an effort to reply, and without waiting for anything further, Rosamond went unhesitatingly into the room. The shutters were closed and the heavy curtains drawn, but even in the darkness Rossie could discern the white, unnatural face upon the pillow, and the eyes which met hers so appealingly as the judge tried in vain to speak, for the blue lips gave forth only an unmeaning sound, which might have meant anything. There was a loud call for help, and in a moment the room was full of the terrified servants, who ran over and against each other in their frantic haste to execute Miss Rossie's orders, given so rapidly.

"Open the shutters and windows wide and let in the air, and bring some camphor, and hartshorn, and ice-water, quick, and somebody go for the doctor and Miss Belknap as soon as they can, and don't make such a noise with your crying, it's only a,—a,—a fit of some kind; he will soon be better," Rossie said, with a forced calmness, as she bent over the helpless man and rubbed and chafed the hands which, the moment she let go of them, fell with a thud upon the bed-clothes, where they lay helpless, nerveless, dead, as it were, to all action or feeling; and while she rubbed and worked over him and asked him questions he could not answer, his eyes followed her constantly, as if with some wish the dumb lips could not express.

The doctor was soon there, but a glance at his patient convinced him that his services were of no avail, except to make the sufferer a little more comfortable. It was partly apoplexy, partly paralysis, induced by some great excitement or over-work, he said to Rosamond, whom he questioned closely as to the judge's appearance the previous night. He had come home about four o'clock, Rosamond said, and eaten a very hearty dinner, and drank more wine than usual. She noticed, too, that his face was very red, and that he smoked a long time after dinner before he came into the parlor where she was getting her lessons. He had asked her to play some old-fashioned tunes, which he liked best, he said, because they took him back to the time when he was a boy at home in Carolina. Then he told her of his home and his mother, and talked of his dead wife, and said he hoped Forrest House would one day have a mistress as sweet and good as she was. When at last he said good-night, he kissed her forehead and said, "My child; you are all I have left me now. Heaven bless you!" then he went up stairs, and Rossie knew nothing more till she found him in the morning.

There was no hope; it was merely a matter of a few days at most, the doctor said; and then he asked where Everard was, saying, he ought to be sent for. This was to Beatrice and Rossie both, after the former had arrived and before she had seen the judge. The two girls exchanged glances, and Beatrice was the first to speak.

"Everard left home for Cincinnati early yesterday morning," she said, "but I know his address, and will telegraph at once."

"Very well," the doctor replied, looking curiously at her, for he had heard a flying rumor of something wrong at the Forrest House, which had driven the heir away.

Accordingly, a telegram was sent to the Spencer House, Cincinnati, to the effect that Judge Forrest was dangerously ill, and Everard must come immediately.

"Not here, and has not been here," was the answer telegraphed back; and then a message went to the Galt House, in Louisville, where Everard always stopped, but that too elicited the answer "Not here."

Where was he, then,—the outcast son,—when his father lay dying, with that white, scared, troubled look upon his face, and that vain effort to speak and let his wishes be known. Dead his body was already, so far as power to move was concerned, but the mind was apparently unimpaired, and expressed itself in the agonized expression of his face, and the entreating, beseeching, pleading look of the dim eyes which followed Rosamond so constantly and seemed trying to communicate with her.

"There is something he wants," Rossie said to Beatrice, who shared her vigils, "and if I could only guess what it was;" then, suddenly starting up, she hurried to his side, and taking the poor, palsied hand in hers rubbed and caressed it pityingly, and smoothing his thin hair, said to him, "Judge Forrest, you want something, and I can't guess what it is, unless,—unless—;" she hesitated a moment, for as yet Everard's name had not been mentioned in his hearing, and she did not know what the effect might be; but the eyes, fastened so eagerly upon her, seemed challenging her to go on, and at last she said,—"unless it is Mr. Everard. Has it anything to do with him?"

Oh, how hard the lips tried to articulate, but they only quivered convulsively and gave forth a little moaning sound, but in the lighting up of the eager eyes, which grew larger and brighter, Rossie thought she read the answer, and emboldened by it went on to say that they had telegraphed to Cincinnati and Louisville both, and had that morning dispatched a message to Memphis and New Orleans.

"We shall surely find him somewhere," she continued, "and he will come at once. I do not think he was angry with you when he went away, he spoke so kindly of you."

Again the lips tried to speak, but could not; only the eyes fastened themselves wistfully upon Rosamond, following her wherever she went, and as if by some subtle magnetism bringing her back to the bedside, where she stayed almost constantly. How those wide-open, never-sleeping eyes haunted and troubled her and made her at last almost afraid to stay alone with them, and meet their constant gaze! Beatrice had been taken sick, and was unable to come to the Forrest House, and the judge seemed so much more quiet when Rossie was sitting where he could look her straight in the face, that the man hired to nurse him staid mostly in the adjoining room, and Rossie kept her vigils alone, wearying herself with the constantly recurring question as to what it was the sick man wished to tell her. Something, sure, and something important, too,—for as the days went on, and there came no tidings of his son, the eyes grew larger, and seemed at times about to leap from their sockets, to escape the horror and remorse so plainly written in them. What was it he wished to say? What was it troubling the old man so, and forcing out the great drops of sweat about his lips and forehead, and making his face a wonder to look upon? Rosamond felt sometimes as if she should go mad herself sitting by him, with those wild eyes watching her so intently that if she moved away for a moment they called her back by their strange power, and compelled her not only to sit down again by them, but to look straight into their depths, where the unspeakable trouble lay struggling to free itself.

"Judge Forrest," Rossie said to him the fifth day after his attack, "you wish to tell me something and you cannot, but perhaps I can guess by mentioning ever so many things. I'll try, and if you mean no look straight at me as you are looking now; if you mean yes, turn your eyes to the window, or shut them, as you choose. Do you understand me?"

There was the shadow of a smile on the wan face, and the heavy eyelids closed, in token that he did comprehend. Rossie knew the judge was dying, that at the most only a few days more were his, and ought not some one to tell him? Was it right to let that fierce, turbulent spirit launch out upon the great sea of eternity unwarned?

"Oh, if I was only good, I might help him, perhaps," she thought; "at any rate he ought to know, and maybe it would make him kinder toward Everard," for it was of him she meant to speak, through this novel channel of communication between herself and the sick man.

She must have the father's forgiveness with which to comfort the son, and with death staring him in the face he would not withhold it; so she said to him:

"You are very sick, Judge Forrest; you know that, don't you?"

The eyes went slowly to the window and back again, while she continued in her plain, outspoken way:

"Do you think I ought to tell you if you are going to die?"

There was a momentary spasm of terror on the face, a look such as a child has when shrinking from the rod, and then the eyes went to the window and back to Rossie, who said:

"We hope for the best, but the case is very bad, and if you do not see Mr. Everard again shall I tell him you forgive him, and were sorry?"

Quick as lightning the affirmative answer agreed upon between them was given, and in great delight Rossie exclaimed, "I am so glad, for that is what you have tried so hard to tell me. You wish me to say this to Mr. Everard, and I will. Is that all?"

This time the eyes did not move, but looked into hers with such an earnest, beseeching expression, that she knew there was more to come. Question after question followed, but the eyes never left her face, and she could see the pupils dilate and the color deepen in them, as they seemed burning themselves into hers.

"What is it? What can it be?" she asked, despairingly. "Does it concern Mr. Everard in any way?"

"Yes," was the eye answer quickly given, and then Rosamond guessed everything she could think of, the possible and impossible, but the bright eyes kept their steady gaze upon her until, thinking of Joe Fleming, she asked, "Is somebody else concerned in it?"

"Yes," was the response, and not willing to introduce Joe too soon, Rossie said: "Is it the servants?"

"No."

"Is it Beatrice?"

"No."

"Is it I?"

She had no thought it was, and was astonished when the eyes went over to the window in token that it was.

"Is it something that I can do?" she asked, and the eyes seemed to leap from her face to the window.

"And shall I some time know what it is?"

Again the emphatic "yes," while the sweat ran like rain down his face.

"Then, Judge Forrest," and Rossie put on her wisest, oldest air, "you may be certain I'll do it, for I promise you solemnly that if anything comes to light which you left undone, and which I can do, I'll do it, sure."

The eyes fairly danced now, and there was no mistaking the joy shining in them, while the lips moved as if in blessing upon the girl, who took the helpless hand and found there was a slight pressure of the limp, lifeless fingers which clung to hers.

"Is that all? have you made me understand?" she asked, and he answered yes, and this time his eyes did not come back to her face, but closed wearily, and in a few moments he was sleeping quietly, as he had not done before since his illness.

The sleep did him good, and he was far less restless after he awoke, and there was a more natural look in his face, but nothing could prolong his life, which hung upon a thread, and might go out at any time. There was no more following Rossie with his eyes, though he wanted her with him constantly, and seemed happier when she was sitting by him and ministering to his comfort. Sometimes he seemed to be in a deep reverie, with his eyes fixed on vacancy, and the great sweat-drops standing thickly on his face from the intensity of his thought. Of what was he thinking as he lay there so helpless? of the wasted years which he could not now reclaim? of sins committed and unforgiven in the days which lay behind him? of the wife who had died in that room and on that very bed? of the son to whom he had been so harsh and unforgiving, and who was not there now to cheer the dreary sick room? And did the unknown future loom up darkly before him and fill his soul with horror and dread of the world so near to him that he could almost see the boundary line which divides it from us?

Once, when Rossie said to him, "Shall I read you something from the Bible?" he answered her with the affirmative sign, and taking her own little Bible, which her mother once used, she opened it at the first chapter of Isaiah, and her eyes chancing to fall upon the th verse, she commenced reading in a clear, sweet voice, which seemed to linger over the words, "Come now and let us reason together, saith the Lord; though your sins be as scarlet they shall be white as snow; though they be red like crimson, they shall be as wool." There were spasms of pain distorting the pinched features on the pillow, as the judge listened to those blessed words of promise and hope for even the worst of sinners. Scarlet sins and crimson sins all to be forgiven, and what were his but these?

"I do believe he's concerned in his mind," Rossie thought, as she looked at him; and bending close to him she whispered, amid her own tears, "Shall I say the Lord's Prayer now?"

She knew he meant yes, and kneeling by his bedside, with her face on his hands, she said the prayer he could not join in audibly, though she was sure he prayed in his heart; and she wished so much for some one older, and wiser, and better than herself, to see and talk to him.

"Shall I send for the minister or for Mrs. Baker?" she asked, feeling in that hour that there was something in the Nazarite woman, fanatical though she might be, which would answer to the sore need.

But the judge wished neither the clergyman nor Mrs. Baker, then; he would rather that pure young girl should read to and pray with him, and he made her understand it, and every day from that time on until the end came, she sat by him and read, and said the simple prayers of her childhood, and his as well,—prayers which took him back to his boyhood and his mother's knee, and made him sob sometimes like a little child, as he tried so often to repeat the one word "forgive." Gradually there came a more peaceful expression upon his face; his eyes lost that look of terror and dread, and the muscles about his mouth ceased to twitch so painfully, but of the change within,—if real change there had been,—he could not speak; that power was gone forever, and he lay, dead in limb as a stone, waiting for the end.

Once Rossie said to him, "Do you feel better, Judge Forrest, about dying. I mean, are you afraid now?"

He looked her steadily in the face and she was sure his quivering lips said no to her last question. That was the day he died, and the day when news was received from Everard. He had returned to Louisville from a journey to Alabama, had found the telegrams, and was hastening home as fast as possible. Beatrice was better, and able to be again at the Forrest House, but it was Rossie who took to the dying man the message from his son. He was lying perfectly quiet, every limb and muscle composed, and a look of calm restfulness on his face, which lighted suddenly when Rossie said to him, "We have heard from Mr. Everard; he is on his way home; he will be here to-night. You are very glad," she continued, as she saw the unmistakable joy in his face. "Maybe you will be able to make him understand what it was you wished to have done, but if you cannot and I ever find it out, depend upon it I will do it, sure. You can trust me."

She looked like one to be trusted, the brave, unselfish little girl, on whom the dying eyes were fixed, so that Rossie's was the last face they ever saw before they closed forever on the things of this world, and entered upon the realities of the next. Everard was not there, for the train was behind time, and when at last the Forrest House carriage came rapidly up the avenue, bringing the son who ten days ago had been cast out from his home and bidden never to enter it again, there were knots of crape upon the bell-knobs, and in the chamber above a sheeted figure lay, scarcely more quiet and still than when bound in the relentless bands of paralysis, but with death upon the white face, which in its last sleep looked so calm and peaceful.

CHAPTER XIX

THE JUDGE'S WILL

It was Rosamond who met Everard as he came into the house, and taking his hands in hers, held them in token of sympathy, but said no word by way of condolence, or of the dead father either. She merely asked him of his journey and the delay of the train, and if he was not cold and hungry, and saw that his supper was served him by a bright, cheerful fire, and made him in all respects as comfortable as she could, while the servants vied with each other in their attentions to him, for was he not now their master, the rightful heir of all the Forrest property. Whether Everard experienced any sense of freedom and heirship, or not, I cannot tell, or what he felt when at last he stood by his dead father, and looked upon the face which, when he saw it last, had been distorted with passion and hatred of himself. How placid and even sweet it was in its expression now,—so sweet that Everard stooped down, kissing the cold forehead, and whispered softly: "I am so sorry, father, that I ever made you angry with me;" then, he replaced the covering and went out from the silent room. In the hall he met Rossie, who, seeing the trace of weeping on his face, thought to comfort him by repeating the message left him by his father.

"Would you mind my telling you all about his sickness; can you bear to hear it?" she asked, and he replied:

"Yes, tell me about it,—from the very first."

So they sat down together, and in her quaint, straightforward way Rossie told the story of the last ten days, softening as much as possible the judge's anger when he found his son had taken him at his word and gone, and dwelling the most upon the change which came over him while lying so helpless and weak. She told of the method of communication she managed to establish, and which had been suggested to her by reading Monte Cristo, and then continued:

"He seemed so glad when I told him we had sent for you, and so sorry that we could not find you, and his eyes kept following me all the time as if there was something he wanted to say and couldn't, and at last I found out what it was. If he never saw you again, he wished me to tell you that he forgave you everything; that was it, I know, and he was so happy and quiet after it, though he wanted you to come so much."

Here Rossie paused, and thought of that mysterious thing which had seemed to trouble him the most, and which she was pledged to do when she found out what it was.

"I wonder if I ought to tell him that now," she thought, and finally concluded that she would not until something definite came to her knowledge of which she could speak.

The next morning Beatrice came over, with a great pity in her heart for Everard, and a great fear as well, when she remembered the angry man who had asked her to witness his will. Had he carried out his purpose and left behind him a paper which would work mischief to his son, or had he thought better of it, and destroyed it, perhaps, or left it unwitnessed? She could not guess. She could only hope for the best, so far as the will was concerned; but there was a heavier trouble in store for the young man than loss of property,—the acknowledging his marriage and bringing home his wife, for he would do that now, of course. There was no other way, and Beatrice resolved at once to stand bravely by Mrs. J. E. Forrest when she should arrive.

Then came the funeral,—a grand affair, with a score of carriages, a multitude of friends, and crowds of people, who came to go over the house and through the grounds more than for any respect they had for the man who lay in his costly coffin, unmindful of the curious ones who looked at him and speculated upon the nature of the trouble which had driven his only son from home. Everybody knew there had been trouble, and each one put his or her construction on it, and all exonerated Everard from more blame than naturally would attach to the acts of a young man like him, as opposed to the ideas of a man like his father.

Beatrice went with Everard and Rossie to the grave, and then back to the house, which in their absence had been cleansed from the atmosphere of death. The windows and doors had been opened to admit the fresh, pure air blowing up from the river; then they were closed again and wood fires kindled on the hearth, and the table arranged in the dining-room, and one of Aunt Axie's best dinners was waiting for such of the friends as chose to stay.

Between Beatrice and Lawyer Russell there had been a private talk concerning the will which so much troubled Bee, and the lawyer had inclined to the belief that there was none of recent date, or he should have known it. He would look, however, he said, as he had a key to the judge's private desk in the office. He had looked, and to his surprise had found a will, which must have been made the very day before the judge's sickness, and during his own absence from the office. This he communicated to Beatrice, and with her remained at the Forrest House to dinner for the purpose of making the fact known to Everard as soon as possible. As for Everard, he had not thought of a will, or indeed of anything, except in a confused, general kind of way, that he was, of course, his father's natural heir, and that now Josephine must come there as his wife, and from that he shrank with a feeling amounting to actual pain; and he was not a little surprised when, after dinner was over, and they had returned to the long parlor, Lawyer Russell, as the old and particular friend of the family, said to him, "I found in looking over your father's papers a will, and as it was inclosed in an envelope directed to me, I took charge of it, and have it with me now. Shall I read it aloud, or give it to you?"

"A will!" Everard said, and a deep flush spread itself over his face as if he dimly felt the coming blow which was to strike him with such force. "Did father leave a will? I never supposed he made one. Read it aloud, of course. These are all my friends," and he glanced at the clergyman and his wife, and Beatrice and Rossie, the only people present.

The two girls were sitting side by side on a low sofa, and opposite them was Everard, looking very pale and nervous as he bent forward a little to listen to the will. It was made the day before the judge's illness, and was duly drawn up and witnessed by Parker and Merritt, the two students in the office, and after mentioning a few thousands which were to be given to different individuals and charities, the judge went on: "the remainder of my estate, both real and personal, I give, bequeath, and devise to the girl, Rosamond Hastings, and——"

Lawyer Russell got no further, for there was a low cry from Rossie as she sprang to her feet, and crossed swiftly to Everard's side. He, too, had risen, and with clasped hands was gazing fixedly at the lawyer, like one listening to his death-warrant.

"What did he say, Mr. Everard, about me? What does it mean?" Rossie asked, laying both hands on Everard's arm, and drawing his attention to herself.

"It means that my father disinherited me, and made you his heir," Everard answered her, a little bitterly, while she continued:

"It is not so. It does not read that way. There is some mistake;" and before the lawyer was aware of her intention she snatched the paper from him, and ran her eye with lightning rapidity over what was written on it, comprehending as she read that what she had heard was true.

Everard was disinherited, and she was the heiress of all the Forrest estate. Her first impulse was to tear the paper in pieces, but Everard caught her hands as she was in the act of rending it asunder, and said:

"Rossie, you must not do that. The will will stand just as my father meant it should."

Rossie's face was a study as she lifted it toward Everard, pale as death, with a firm, set look about the mouth, and an expression in her large black eyes such as the Cenci's might have worn when upon the rack.

"Oh, Mr. Everard," she said, "you must always hate me, though I'll never let it stand. I did not know it. I never dreamed of such a thing. I shall never touch it, never. Don't hate me, Mr. Everard. Oh, Beatrice, help me,— somebody help me. I believe I am going to die."

But she was only fainting, and Everard took her in his arms and carried her to an open window in the adjoining room, and giving her to the care of Beatrice, waited to see the color come back to her face and motion to her eyelids; then he returned to the parlor, where Lawyer Russell was examining the document which had done so much harm and made the memory of the dead man odious.

"Everard, this is a very strange affair; a most inexplicable thing," the lawyer said. "I cannot understand it, or believe he really meant it. I do not wish to pry into your affairs, but as an old friend of the family, may I ask if you know of any reason, however slight, why he should do this?"

"Yes," Everard answered promptly, "there is a reason; a good one, many would say; and that I was rightly punished. The will is just; I have no fault to find with it. I shall not try to dispute it. The will must stand."

He spoke proudly and decidedly, with the air of one whose mind was made up, and who did not wish to continue the conversation, and who would not be made an object of pity or sympathy by any one. But when

Lawyer Russell was gone, and Beatrice came to him as he sat alone by the dying fire, and putting her hand on his bowed head, said to him:

"I am so sorry, and wish I could help you some way," he broke down a little, and his voice shook as he replied:

"Thank you, Bee. I know you do, and your friendship and sympathy are very dear to me now, for you know everything, and I can talk to you as to no one else. Father must have been very angry, and his anger reaches up out of his grave and holds me with a savage grip, but I do not blame him much, and, Bee, don't think there is no sweet with the bitter, for that is not so. It is true I like money as well as any one, and I do not say that I had not to some degree anticipated what it would bring me, but, Bee, with that feeling was another, a shrinking from what would be my plain duty, if I were master here. You know what I mean."

"You would bring your wife home," Bee answered, and he continued:

"Yes, that would have to be done, and,—Heaven forgive me if I am wrong,—but I almost believe I would rather be poor and work for her,—she living in Holburton,—than be rich and live with her here. And then, if I must be supplanted, I am so glad it is by Rossie. She takes it hard, poor child; how was she when you left her?"

"Over the faint, but crying bitterly, and she bade me tell you to come to her," Beatrice replied, and Everard went to Rossie's room, where she was lying on the couch, her eyes swollen with weeping, and her face very pale.

She was taking it hard,—her sudden accession to riches, and when she saw Everard she began sobbing afresh as if her heart would break.

"Please go away," she said to Beatrice, "I want to see him alone."

Beatrice complied, and the moment she was gone Rosamond began to tell Everard how impossible it was that she should ever touch the money left her in a fit of anger.

"It is not mine," she said. "I have no shadow of right to it, and you must take it just the same as if that will had never been. Say you will, or I believe I shall go mad."

But Everard was as immovable as a rock, and answered her:

"Do you for a moment think my pride, if nothing else, would allow me to touch what was willed away from me? Never, Rossie. I would rather starve; but I shall not do that. I am young and strong, and the world is before me, and I am willing to work at whatever I find to do, and shall do so, too, and make far more of a man, I dare say, than if I had all this money. I am naturally indolent and extravagant, and very likely should fall into my old expensive habits, and I don't want to do that. I am so glad you are the heiress; so glad to have you mistress here in the old home. You will make a dear little lady of Forrest House."

He spoke almost playfully, hoping thus to soothe and quiet her, for she was violently agitated, and shook like a leaf; but nothing he said had any effect upon her. Only one thing could help her now. She felt that she had unwittingly been the means of wronging Everard, and she never could rest until the wrong was righted, and his own given back to him.

"I'll never be the lady of Forrest House," she said, energetically. "I shall give it back to you, whether you will take it or not. It is not mine."

"Yes, Rossie, it is yours. He knew what he was doing; he meant you to have it," Everard said; and starting suddenly, as the remembrance of something flashed upon her, Rossie shed back her hair from her spotted, tear-stained face, and exclaimed, with a ring of joy in her voice:

"He might have meant it at first, when he was very angry, but he repented of it and tried to make amends. I see it now. I know what he meant,—the something which concerned you, and which I was to do. I promised solemnly I would,—it will be a dreadful lie if I don't; but you will let me when you hear,—when you know how he took it back."

She was very much excited, and her eyes shone like stars as she stood before Everard, who looked at her curiously, with a thought that her mind might really be unsettled.

"Sit down, Rossie, and compose yourself," he said, trying to draw her back to the couch; but she would not sit down, and she went on rapidly:

"I told you how I managed to talk with your father, and to find out that he wanted to forgive you, but I did not tell you the rest. I thought I'd wait till it came to me what I was to do, and it has come. I know now just what he meant. He was not quiet after the forgiveness, as I thought he'd be, but his eyes followed me everywhere, and said as plain as eyes could say, 'There is something more;' so I began to question him again, and found it was about you and another person. That person was myself, and I was to do something when I found out what it was. I said, 'Is it something I am to do for Mr. Everard?' and his eyes went to the window; then I asked, 'Shall I some day know what it is?' and he answered 'Yes.' Then I said, 'I'll surely, surely do it,' and the poor, helpless face laughed up at me, he was so pleased and happy. After that he was very quiet. So you know he meant me to give the money back, and you will not refuse me now?"

For a moment Everard could not speak. As Rossie talked, the great tears had gathered slowly and dropped upon his face. He could see so vividly the scene which she described,—the dim, eager eyes of his dead father trying to communicate with the anxious, excited little girl, who had, perhaps, interpreted their meaning aright. There could be but little doubt that his father, when his passion cooled down, was sorry for the rash act, and Everard was deeply moved by it, and for a little space of time felt uncertain how to act, but when he remembered who must share his fortune with him, and all his father had said of her, he grew hard and decided again, and said to Rosamond:

"I am glad you told me this, Rossie. It makes it easier to bear, feeling that possibly father was sorry, and wished to make reparation, but that does not change the facts, nor the will. He gave everything to you, and you cannot give it to me now, if you would. You are not of age, you see."

"Do you mean," Rosamond asked, "that even if you would take the money, I cannot give it back till I am twenty-one?"

"Not lawfully, no," Everard replied; and Rossie exclaimed, almost angrily:

"I can; I will. I know there is some way, and I'll find it out. I will not have it so, and I think you are mean to be so proud and stiff."

She was losing all patience with Everard for what she deemed his obduracy; her head was aching dreadfully, and after this outburst she sank down again upon the couch, and burying her face in the pillow told him to go away and not come again till he could do as she wished him to do. It was not often that Rosamond was thus moved, and Everard smiled in spite of himself at her wrath, but went out and left her alone as she desired.

CHAPTER XX

THE HEIRESS

She looked like anything but an heiress the next morning when she came down to breakfast, with her swollen face and red eyes, which had scarcely been for a moment closed in sleep. Everard was far brighter and fresher. He had accepted the situation, and was resolved to make the best of it, and though the memory of his father's bitter anger rested heavily on his heart, it was softened materially by what Rosamond had told him, and, contrary to his expectations, he had slept soundly and quietly, and though very pale and worn, seemed much like himself when he met Rossie in the breakfast-room. Not a word was said on the subject uppermost in both their minds; he carved, sitting in his father's old place, and she poured the coffee with a shaking hand, and Bee did most of the talking, and was so bright and merry that when at last she said good-by and went to her own home, Rossie's face was not half so sorry-looking, or her heart so heavy and sad, though she was just as decided with regard to the money.

She had not yet talked with Lawyer Russell, in whom she had the utmost confidence. He surely would know some way out of the trouble,—some way by which she could give Everard his own; and she sent for him to come to the house, as she would not for the world appear in the streets with this disgrace upon her,—for Rossie felt it a disgrace,—of having supplanted Everard; and she told the lawyer so when he came, and assuring him of her unalterable determination never to touch a dollar of the Forrest money, asked if there was not some way by which she could rid herself of the burden and give it back to Everard. She told him what had occurred between herself and the judge, and asked if he did not think it had reference to the will. The lawyer was certain it had, and asked if Everard knew this fact. Yes, Rossie had told him, and though he seemed glad in one way to know his father had any regrets for the rash act, he still adhered to his resolve to abide by the will.

"But he cannot; he shall not; he must take the money. I give it to him;

it is not mine, and I will not have it," she said, impetuously, demanding that he should fix it some way.

Mr. Russell had seen Everard for a few moments that morning, and heard from him of his firm resolve not to enter into any arrangement whereby he could be benefited by his father's fortune.

"Father cast me off," he said, "and no arguments can shake my purpose. Rossie is the heiress, and she must take what is thrust upon her; but make it as easy as you can for the child; let her choose her own guardian, and I trust she will choose you. I know you will be trustworthy."

All this the lawyer repeated to Rossie, and then, as she still persisted in giving back, as she expressed it, he explained to her how impossible it was for her to do it until she reached her majority, even if Everard would take it.

"You are a minor yet," he said; "are what we call an infant. You must have a guardian, and I propose that you take Everard, and he may also be appointed administrator of the estate; he will then be entitled to a certain amount of money as his legitimate fees, and so get some of it."

Exactly what the office of guardian and administrator was, Rosamond did not know, but she grasped one idea, and said:

"You mean that whoever is administrator will be paid, and if Mr. Everard is that he will get some money which belongs to him already; that is it, is it not? Now, I want him to have it all; if I cannot give it to him till I am twenty-one, I shall do it then, so sure as I live to see that day, and, meanwhile, you must contrive some way for him to use it just the same. You can, I know. I am quite resolved."

She had risen as she talked and stood before him, her cheeks flushed, her eyes unnaturally bright, and her head thrown back, so that she seemed taller than she really was. Lawyer Russell had always liked Rossie very much, and since that little business matter touching the receipt, he had felt increased respect and admiration for her, for he was certain she had helped Everard out of some one of the many scrapes he used in those days to be in. Looking at her now he thought what a fine-looking girl she was growing to be, and started suddenly as he saw a way out of the difficulty, but such a way that he hesitated a moment before suggesting it. Taking off his glasses, and wiping them with his handkerchief, he coughed two or three times and then said:

"How old are you, Rossie?"

"Fifteen last June," was her reply, and he continued:

"Then you are almost fifteen and a half, and pretty well grown. Yes, it might do; there have been queerer things than that."

"Queerer things than what?" Rossie asked, and he replied:

"Than what I am going to suggest. There is a way by which Everard can use that money if he will."

"What is it? Tell me," she exclaimed, her face all aglow with excitement.

"He could marry you, and then what was yours might be his."

The lawyer had thrown the bombshell and waited for the explosion, but there was none. Rossie's face was just as bright and eager, and showed not the slightest consciousness or shrinking back from a proposition which would have covered some girls with blushes and confusion. But Rossie was a simple-hearted girl, who, never having associated much with companions of her own age, had never had her mind filled with lovers and matrimony, and when the lawyer proposed her marrying Everard she looked upon it purely as a business transaction,—a means of giving him his own; love had nothing to do with it, nor did it for a moment occur to her that there would be anything out of the way in such an act. She should not live with him, of course; that would be impossible. She should simply marry him, and then leave him to the enjoyment of her fortune, and her first question to the lawyer was:

"Do you think he would have me?"

The old man took his glasses off again and looked at her, wondering much what stuff she was made of. Whatever it was he was sure she was as modest, and pure, and innocent as a new-born child, and he answered her:

"I've no doubt of it. I would if I were in his place."

"And if he does, he can live right along here as if there had been no will?" was her next question; and the lawyer replied:

"Yes, just as if there had been no will;" then, remembering he had an engagement with a client and that it was already past the hour, he arose to go, and Rosamond was left alone.

It was not her nature to put off anything she had to do, and feeling that she should never rest until something definite was settled, she inquired at once where Everard was, and finding that he was in his father's room, started thither immediately. He was sitting in his father's chair by the table, arranging and sorting some papers and letters, but he arose when she came in and asked what he could do for her.

"I have been talking with Lawyer Russell," she said, "trying to fix it some way, and he says I cannot give it to you till I am twenty-one; then I can do as I please, but it is so long to wait,—five years and a-half. I am most fifteen and a-half now. (This in parenthesis, as if to convince him of her mature age, preparatory to what was to follow.) I want you to have the money so much, for it is yours, no matter what the law may say. I do not like the law, and there is but one way out of it,—the trouble, I mean. Lawyer Russell says if you marry me, you can use the money just the same. Will you, Mr. Everard? I am fifteen and a-half."

This she reiterated to strengthen her cause, looking him straight in the face all the time, without the slightest change of color or sign of self-consciousness.

Had she proposed in serious earnestness to murder him Everard could not have been more startled, or stared at her more fixedly than he did, as if to see what manner of girl this was, asking him to marry her as coolly and in as matter-of-fact a way as she would have asked the most ordinary favor. Was she crazy? Had the trouble about the will actually affected her brain! He thought so, and said to her very gently, as he would have spoken to a child or a lunatic:

"You are talking wildly, Rossie. You do not understand what you are saying. You are tired and excited. You must rest, and never on any account let any one know what you have said to me."

"I do know what I am saying, and I am neither tired nor excited," Rossie answered. "Lawyer Russell said that was the only way you could use the money before I was twenty-one."

"And did he send you here to say that to me?" Everard asked, and she replied:

"No, he only suggested it as a means, because I would have him think of something. I came myself."

He saw she was in earnest; saw, too, that she did not at all comprehend what she was doing, or the position in which she was placing herself if it should be known. In her utter simplicity and lack of worldly wisdom, she might talk of this thing to others and put herself in a wrong light before the world, and however painful the task, he must enlighten her.

"Rossie," he began, "you do not at all know what you have done, or how the act might be construed, by women, especially, if they knew it. Girls do not usually ask men to marry them; they wait to be asked."

Slowly, as the shadow of some gigantic mountain creeps across the valley, there was dawning on Rossie's mind a perception of the construction which might be put upon her words, and the blood-red flame suffused her face and neck, and spread to her finger-tips, as she said, vehemently: "You mistake me, Mr. Everard, I did not mean it as you might marry Miss Beatrice, or somebody you loved. I did not mean anything except a way out. I was not going to live here at all; only marry you so you could have the money, and then I go away and do for myself. That's what I meant. You know I do not love you in a marrying way, and that I'm not the brazen-faced thing to tell you so if I did. If I thought you could believe that of me, I should drop dead at your feet, and I almost wish that I could now, for very shame of what I have done."

As she talked there had come to Rossie more and more the great impropriety and seeming immodesty of what, in all innocence of purpose she had done, and the knowledge almost crushed her to the earth, making her cover her burning face with her hands, and transforming her at once from a child into a woman, with all a sensitive woman's power to feel and suffer. She did not wait for him to speak, but went on rapidly:

"You cannot despise me more than I despise myself, for I see it now just as you do, and I must have been an idiot, or crazy. You will loathe me always, of course, and I cannot blame you; but remember. I did not mean it for love, or think to stay with you. I do not love you that way; such a thing would be impossible, and I would not marry you now for a thousand times the money."

She had used her last and heaviest weapon, and without a glance at him turned to go from the room, but he would not suffer her to leave him thus. Over him, too, as she talked, a curious change had come, for he saw the transformation taking place and knew he was losing the sweet, old-fashioned, guileless-child, who had been so dear to him. She was leaving him, forever, and in her place there stood a full-fledged woman, rife with a woman's instincts, quivering with passion, and burning with resentment and anger, that he had not at once understood her meaning just as she understood it. How her words,—"I do not love you that way; such a thing is impossible; and I would not marry you now for a thousand times the money," rang through his ears, and burned themselves into his memory to be recalled afterward, with such bitter pain as he had never known. He did not quite like this impetuous assertion of the impossibility of loving him. It grated upon him with a sense of something lost. He must stand well with Rossie, though her love that way, as she expressed it, was something he had never dreamed of as possible.

"Rossie," be said, putting out his arm to detain her, "you must not go from me feeling as you do now. You have done nothing for which you need to blush, because you had no bad intent, and the motive is what exalts or condemns the act. Sit here by me. I wish to talk with you."

He made her sit down beside him upon the sofa, and tried to take her hand, but she drew it swiftly away, with a quick, imperative gesture. He would never hold her hand again, just as he had held the little brown, sunburned hands so many times. She was a woman now, with all her woman's armor bristling about her, and as such he must treat with her. It was a novel situation in which he found himself, trying to choose words with which to address little Rossie Hastings, and for a moment he hesitated how to begin. Of her strange offer to himself he did not mean to speak, for there had been enough said on that subject. It is true he had neither accepted nor refused, but that was not necessary, for she had withdrawn her proposition with such fiery energy as would have made an allusion to it impossible, if he had been free and not averse to the plan. He was not free, and as for the plan, it struck him as both laughable and ridiculous, but he would not for the world wound the sensitive girl beside him more than she had wounded herself, and so when at last he began to talk with her it was simply to go again over the whole ground, and show her how impossible it was for him to take the money or for her to give it to him. He appreciated her kind intentions; they were just like her, and he held her as the dearest sister a brother ever had; but she must keep what was her own, and he should make his fortune as many a man had done before him, and probably rise higher eventually than if he had money to help him rise. He had not yet quite decided what he should do, but that he should leave Rothsay was probable. He should, however, stay long enough to see that her affairs were in a way to be smoothly managed, and to see her fairly installed in the Forrest House with some respectable elderly lady as her companion and protector. Lawyer Russell would, of course, be her guardian, and the administrator of the estate. She could not be in better hands; and however far away he might be, he should never lose his interest in her or cease to be her friend.

"Meanwhile," he said, with an effort to smile, "I shall be glad if you will allow me to make your house my home until my arrangements are completed. I am not so proud that I will not accept that hospitality at your hands."

I do not think that Rosamond quite comprehended his last words. She only knew that he would not hurry away from the Forrest House, and she looked up eagerly, and said:

"I am so glad, and I hope you will not hate me, or ever believe I meant the foolish thing I said,—in that way."

"No, Rossie," he answered her, "I am far from hating you, and how can I think you meant that way when you have repeatedly declared that you would not marry me now for a thousand times the money?"

"No, now nor ever!" Rosamond exclaimed, energetically; and he replied:

"Yes, I know; men generally understand when a girl tells them she has no love or liking for them."

There was something peculiar in his voice, as if what she said hurt him a little, and Rossie detected it, and in her eagerness to set him right involuntarily laid her hand on his arm, and flashing upon him her brilliant, beautiful eyes, in which the tears were shining, said to him:

"Oh, Mr. Everard, you must not mistake what I mean. I do like you, and shall for ever and ever; but not in a marrying way, and I am so sorry I have come between you and your inheritance. You have made me see that I cannot now help myself, but when I am twenty-one, if I live so long, so help me Heaven, I'll give you back every dollar. You will remember that, and knowing it may help you to bear the years of poverty which must intervene."

Again the long, silken lashes were lifted, and the dark, bright eyes looked into his with a look which sent a strange, sweet thrill through every nerve of the young man's body. Rosamond had come up before him in an entirely new character, and he was vaguely conscious of a different interest in her now from what he had felt before. It was not love; it was not a desire of possession. He did not know what it was; he only knew that his future life suddenly looked drearier than ever to him if it must be lived away from her and her influence. She had risen to her feet as she was speaking, and he rose also, and went with her to the door, and let her out, and watched her as she disappeared down the stairs, and then went back to his task of sorting papers, with the germ of a new feeling stirring ever so lightly in his heart,—a sense of something which might have made life very sweet, and a sense as well of bitter loss.

Full of shame and mortification at what she had done, Rossie resolved to go at once to Elm Park and confess the whole to Beatrice, whom she found at home. She was thinking of the Forrest House and the confusion caused by the foolish will of an angry old man, when Rossie was announced, and, sitting down at her feet, plunged into the very midst of her trouble by saying:

"Oh, Miss Beatrice, I have come to tell you something which makes me wish I was dead. What do you suppose I have done?"

"I am sure I cannot guess," Beatrice replied, and Rossie continued, "I asked Mr. Everard to marry me,—actually to marry me!"

"Wha-at!" and Beatrice was more astonished than she had ever been in her life. "Asked Everard Forrest to marry you! Are you crazy, or a——"

She did not finish the sentence, for Rossie did it for her, and said,

"Yes, both crazy and a fool, I verily believe!"

"But how did it happen? What put such an idea into your head?"

Briefly and rapidly Rosamond repeated what had passed between herself and Lawyer Russell, who had asked how old she was, and on learning her age had suggested her marrying the young man and thus giving him back the inheritance.

"And you went and did it, you little goose," Beatrice said, laughing until the tears ran down her cheeks; but when she saw how distressed Rosamond was she controlled her merriment, and listened while Rossie went on:

"Yes, I was a simpleton not to know any better, but I never meant him to marry me as he would marry you or some one he loved; that had nothing to do with it at all. And I was going right away from Forrest House to take care of myself. I knew I could find something to do, as nurse, or waitress, or ladies' maid, if nothing more; and I meant to go just as soon as the ceremony was over and leave him all the money, and never, never come back to be in the way."

"And you told him this, and what did he say?" Beatrice asked, her mirth all swept away before the great unselfishness of this simple-hearted girl, who went on:

"I did not tell him all that at first. I asked him to marry me, just as I would have asked him to give me a glass of water, and with as little thought of shame, but the shame came afterward when I saw what I had done. I can't explain how it came,—the new sense of things,—I think he looked it into me, and I felt in an instant as if I had been blind and was suddenly restored to sight. It was as if I had been walking unclothed in my sleep, fearlessly, shamelessly, because asleep, and had suddenly been roused to consciousness and saw a crowd of people staring and jeering at me. Oh, it was so awful! and I felt like tearing my hair and shrieking aloud, and I said so many things to make him believe I did not mean it for love or to live with him."

"And what did he say to the offer? Did he accept or refuse?" Beatrice asked, and Rosamond replied:

"I do not think he did either. I was so ashamed when it came to me, and talked so fast to make him know that I would not marry him for a thousand times the money, and did not love him, and never could."

"I'll venture to say he was not especially delighted with such assertions; men are not generally," Beatrice said, laughingly, but Rosamond did not comprehend her meaning, or if she did, she did not pay any heed to it, but went rapidly on with her story, growing more and more excited as she talked, and finishing with a passionate burst of tears, which awakened all Bee's sympathy, and made her try to comfort the sobbing girl, who seemed so bowed down with shame and remorse.

Her head was aching dreadfully, and there began to steal over her such a faint, sick feeling, that she offered no remonstrance when Bee proposed that she spend the night at Elm Park, and sent word to that effect to the Forrest House.

The message brought Everard at once, anxious about Rosamond, whom he wished to see. But she declined; her head was aching too hard to see any one, she said, especially Everard, who must despise her always.

Everard had certainly lost the child Rossie; and the world had never seemed so dreary to him as that night in Bee's boudoir, when he fairly and squarely faced the future and decided what to do, or rather, Bee decided for him; and with a feeling of death in his heart he concurred in her opinion, and said he would go at once to Josephine, and telling her of his father's death and will, ask her to help him build up a home where they might be happy. He was not to show her how he shrank back and shivered even while taking her for his wife. He was to put the most hopeful construction on everything, and see how much good there was in Josie.

"And I am sure she will not disappoint you," Beatrice said, infusing some of her own bright hopefulness into Everard's mind, so that he did not feel quite so discouraged when he said good-night to her, telling her that he should start on the next morning's train for Holburton, but asking her not to tell Rossie of Josephine until she heard from him.

CHAPTER XXI

A MIDNIGHT RIDE

It was after midnight when Everard reached Albany, the second day after he left Rothsay. There the train divided, the New York passengers going one way, and the Boston passengers another. Everard was among the latter, and as several people left the car where he was, he felicitated himself upon having an entire seat for the remainder of his journey, and had settled himself for a sleep, with his soft traveling hat drawn over his eyes, and his valise under his head, when the door opened and a party of young people entered, talking and laughing, and discussing a concert which they had that evening attended. As there was plenty of room Everard did not move, but lay listening to their talk and jokes until another party of two came hurrying in just as the train was moving. The gentleman was tall, fine-looking, and exceedingly attentive to the lady, a fair blonde, whom he lifted in his arms upon the platform, and set down inside the door, saying as he did so:

"There, madam, I did get you here in time, though I almost broke my neck to do it; that last ice you took came near being our ruin."

"Ice, indeed! Better say that last glass you took," the lady retorted, with a loud, boisterous laugh, which made Everard shiver from head to foot, for he recognized Josephine's voice, and knew it was his wife who took the unoccupied seat in front of him, gasping and panting as if wholly out of breath.

"Almost dead," she declared herself to be, whereupon her companion, who was Dr. Matthewson, fanned her furiously with his hat, laughing and jesting, and attracting the attention of everybody in the car.

For an instant Everard half rose to his feet, with an impulse to make himself known, but something held him back, and resuming his reclining attitude, with his hat over his eyes in such a manner that he could see without being himself seen, he prepared to watch the unsuspecting couple in front of him, and their flirtation, for it seemed to be that in sober earnest.

Josey was all life and fun, and could scarcely keep still a moment, but turned, and twisted, and tossed her head, and coquetted with the doctor, who, with his arm on the seat behind her, and half encircling her, bent over her, and looked into her beaming face in the most lover-like manner.

Just then the door at the other end of the car opened, and the conductor appeared with his lantern and demand for tickets.

"I shall have to pay extra," Matthewson said. "You ate so long that I did not have time to get my tickets."

"Nonsense," Josey answered, in a voice she evidently did not mean to have heard, but which nevertheless reached Everard's ear, opened wide to receive it, "Nonsense! This one," nodding towards the conductor, "never charges me anything; we have lots of fun together. I'll pass you; put up your money and see how I'll manage it."

And when the conductor reached their seat and stopped before it and threw the light of his lantern in Josey's face, he bowed very blandly, but glanced suspiciously at her companion, who was making a feint of getting out his purse.

"My brother," Josey said, with a mischievous twinkle in her blue eyes; and with an expressive "all right," the conductor passed on and took the ticket held up to him by the man whose face he could not see, and at whom Josephine now for the first time glanced.

But she saw nothing familiar in the outstretched form, and never dreamed who it was lying there so near to her and watching all she did. So many had left at Albany and so few taken their places that not more than half the seats were occupied, and those in the immediate vicinity of Josey and the doctor were quite vacant, so the young lady felt perfectly free to act out her real nature without restraint; and she did act it to the full, laughing, and flirting, and jesting, and jumping just as Everard had seen her do many a time, and thought it charming and delightful. Now it was simply revolting and immodest, and he glared at her from under his hat, with no feeling of jealousy in his heart, but disgusted and sorry beyond all power of description that she was his wife. Rossie had stood boldly up before him and asked him to marry her, but in her innocent face there was no look like this on Josey's,—this look of recklessness and passion which showed so plainly even in the dimness of the car. At last something which the doctor said, and which Everard could not understand, elicited from her the exclamation:

"Aren't you ashamed of yourself, and I a married woman?"

"The more's the pity," the doctor replied, with an expression on his face which, had Everard cared for or even respected the woman before him, would have prompted him to knock the rascal down. "The more's the pity,—for me, at least. I've called myself a fool a thousand times for having cut off my nose to spite my face."

"What do you mean?" Josey asked, and he replied:

"Oh, nothing; only, can't you get a divorce? I don't believe he cares two cents for you."

"I know he don't," and Josey shrugged her shoulders significantly; "but so long as he keeps me in money I can stand it."

"And does he do that pretty well nowadays?"

"Yes, so-so; he is awfully afraid of his father, though, and I do not blame him. Such an old curmudgeon. I saw him last summer."

"You did? Where?"

"Why, at Amherst; at Commencement. I went to the president's reception, and made Everard introduce me, and tried my best to captivate the old muff, but it was of no use; he took a dreadful dislike to me, and expressed himself freely to his son, who reported to me——"

"The mean coward to do that," the doctor exclaimed, and Josephine replied, "No, not mean at all. I made him tell me just what his father said. I gave him no peace till he did, for I wanted the truth, so as to know how far to press my claim to recognition; and I made up my mind that my best plan was to keep quiet a while, and let matters adjust themselves. Maybe the old man will die; he looked apoplectic, as if he might go off in some of his fits of temper, and then won't I make the money fly, for no power on earth shall keep me from the Forrest House then."

"And you'll ride over everybody, I dare say," the doctor suggested, and she answered him, "You bet your head on that," the slang dropping from her pretty lips as easily and naturally as if they were accustomed to it, as indeed they were.

"Is Everard greatly improved?" was the next question, and Josephine replied, "Some would think so, perhaps, but I look upon him as a perfect milksop. I don't believe I could fall in love with him now. Why, he is just as quiet and solemn as a graveyard; never laughs, nor jokes, nor smokes, nor anything; he is fine-looking, though, and I expect to be very proud of him when I am really his wife."

"Which you never shall be, so help me Heaven!" was Everard's mental ejaculation, as he ground his teeth together.

He had made up his mind, and neither Bee nor any one else could change it. That woman, coquetting so heartlessly with another man, and talking thus of him, should never even be asked to share his poverty, as he had intended doing. He would never voluntarily go into her presence again. He would return to Rothsay, tell his story to Bee and see what he could do to help Rossie, and then go to work like a dog for money with which to keep the woman quiet. And when the day came, as come it must, that his secret was known, there should be a separation, for live with her a single hour he would not. This was his decision, and he only waited for the train to stop in order to escape from her hateful presence. But it was an express and went speeding on, while the two in front of him kept up their conversation, which turned at last on Rosamond, the doctor asking "if she still lived at the Forrest House."

Josephine supposed so, though she had heard nothing of her lately, and Dr. Matthewson asked next what disposition she intended to make of her when she was mistress of Forrest House.

"That depends," Josephine replied, with her favorite shrug; "if there is nothing objectionable in her she can stay; if she proves troublesome, she will go."

Oh, how Everard longed to shriek out that the girl who, if she proved troublesome, was to go from Forrest House, was the mistress there, with a right to dictate as to who would go or stay; but that would be to betray himself; so he kept quiet, while Josey, growing tired and sleepy, began to nod her golden head, which drooped lower and lower, until it rested on the shoulder of Dr. Matthewson, whose arm encircled the sleeping girl and adjusted the shawl about her, for it was growing cold and damp in the car.

Just then they stopped at a way station, and, taking his valise, Everard left the train, which after a moment went whirling on, leaving him standing on the platform alone in the November darkness.

There was a little hotel near by, where he passed a few hours, until the train, bound for Albany, came along, and carried him swiftly back in the direction of home and Rossie, of whom he thought many times, seeing her as she looked standing before him with that sweet pleading expression on her face, and that musical ring in her voice, as she asked to be his wife. How her eyes haunted him,—those brilliant black eyes, so full of truth, and womanly softness and delicacy. He could see them now as they had confronted him, fearlessly, innocently, at first, but changing in their expression as the sense of what she had done began to dawn upon her, bringing the blushes of shame to her tear-stained face.

"Dear little Rossie!" he thought; "if I were free, I believe I'd say yes,— not for the money, but for all she will be when she gets older." And then there crept over him again that undefinable sense of something lost which he had felt when Rossie said to him, "I would not marry you now for a thousand times the money."

He was growing greatly interested in Rossie, and found himself very impatient during the last few hours of his journey. What had been done in his absence, he wondered, and was she more reconciled to the fortune which had been thrust upon her, and how would she receive him, and how would she look? She was not handsome, he knew, and yet her face was very, very sweet; her eyes were beautiful, and so was the wavy, nut-brown hair, which she wore so becomingly in her neck,—and at the thought of her hair there came a great lump in Everard's throat as he remembered the sacrifice the unselfish girl had made for him two years before.

"In all the world there is no one like little Rossie," he said to himself, and felt his heart beat faster with a thrill of anticipation as the train neared Rothsay and stopped at last at the station.

Taking his valise, which was not heavy, he started at once for the Forrest House, which he reached just as it was growing dark, and the gas was lighted in the dining-room.

CHAPTER XXII

THE NEW LIFE AT ROTHSAY

His first impulse was to ring like any stranger at a door not his own, but thinking to himself, "I will not wound her unnecessarily," he walked into the hall, and, depositing his satchel and hat upon the rack, went to the dining-room, the door of which was ajar, so that the first object which met his view as he entered was Rossie, standing under the chandelier, but so transformed from what she was when he last saw her, that he stood for an instant wondering what she had done; for, instead of a child in short frock and white aprons, with loose flowing hair, he saw a young woman in a long black dress, with her hair twisted into a large, flat coil, and fastened with a comb.

The morning after Everard's departure Rossie had gone with Beatrice to order a black dress, which she insisted should be made long. "I am through with short clothes now," she said to Beatrice. "I feel so old since I did that shameful thing, that for me to dress like a child would be as absurd as for you to do it. I am not a child. I am at least a hundred years old, and you know, it would never do for an heiress to be dressed like a little girl. How could I discuss business with my lawyer in short clothes and bibs," and she laughed hysterically as she tried to force back her tears.

She had become convinced that for a few years she must submit to be the nominal owner at least of the Forrest property, and she had made up her mind to certain things from which she could not be turned. One was long dresses, and she carried her point, and gave orders concerning some minor details with a quiet determination which astonished Bee, who had hitherto found her the most pliable and yielding of girls. The dress had been sent home on the very afternoon of Everard's arrival, and without a thought of his coming, Rossie shut herself in her room, and began the work of transformation, first by twisting up her flowing hair, which added, she thought, at least two years to her appearance, though she did not quite like the effect, it was so unlike herself. But the long dress was a success, and she liked the sound of the trailing skirt on the carpet, and looked at herself in the glass more than she had ever done before in her life at one time, and felt quite satisfied with the tout ensemble when she at last went down to the dining-room, where she was standing when Everard came in.

She had been very lonely during his absence, and she was wondering where he had gone, and when he would return, when the door in the hall opened, and he was there before her.

For a moment she stood regarding him just as he was studying her; then, forgetting everything in her joy at seeing him again, she went forward to meet him, and giving him both her hands, while a beautiful flush dyed her cheeks, said to him:

"I am so glad you have come back; it was so lonesome here, and I was just thinking about you."

112

Her greeting was so much more cordial than Everard had expected that it made him very happy, and he kept her hands in his until she drew them away with a sudden wrench, and stepping back from him, put on the dignity she had for a moment dropped. But the action became her and her long dress, and Everard looked closely and admiringly at her, puzzled to know just what it was which had changed her so much. He guessed that she was thinking of that scene in his father's room, but he meant to ignore it altogether, and, if possible, put her on her old familiar footing with himself; so, looking at her from head to foot, he said:

"What is it, Rossie? What have you done to yourself? Pieced down your gown, or what, that you seem so much taller and grander every way,—quite like Bee, in fact? Yes, you have got on a train, sure as guns, and your hair up in a comb; that part I don't like; the other change is rather becoming, but I'd rather see you so;" and playfully pulling the comb from her head, he let the wavy hair fall in masses upon her neck and shoulders. "There, that's better; it gives me little Rossie again, and I do not wish to lose my sister."

He was trying to reassure her, and she knew it, and was very grateful to him for the kindness, and said, laughingly, that she put up her hair because she thought it suited the long dresses which she meant to wear now that she was a woman of business, but if he liked it in her neck it should be worn so; and then she asked him of his journey, and if he was not tired and hungry.

"Tired? No; but cold as a frog and hungry as a bear. What have we for dinner?" And he turned to inspect the little round table laid for one. "Nothing but toast and tea. Why, that would starve a cat. Did you dine in the middle of the day?"

Rosamond colored painfully as she answered:

"I had lunch, as usual. I was not hungry. I am never hungry now, and just have tea at night."

"Rossie," and Everard laid both hands on her shoulders and looked her squarely in her eyes, "Rossie, are you practicing economy, so as not to use the money you think belongs to me?"

He divined her motive, for it was the fear of using the Forrest money needlessly which was beginning to rule her life, and had prompted her to omit the usual dinner, the most expensive meal of the day, and have, instead, plain bread and butter, or toast and tea; and Everard read the truth in her tell-tale face, and said:

"That will never do, and will displease me very much; I wish you to live as you ought, and if it is on my account you are trying the bread and water system, I am here now and hungry as a fish, so you can indulge for once and order on everything there is."

There was not much, but a slice of cold ham was found, and some cheese, and jam and pickles, and Axie made a delicious cup of coffee, and brought more bread and butter, and offered to bake him a hoe cake if he would wait, but he was too nearly starved to wait for hoe cakes, he said, and he took his father's place at the table, and was conscious of a great degree of comfort in and satisfaction with his surroundings, especially with the sight of the young girl who sat opposite to him and poured his coffee, and once or twice laughed heartily at some of his funny remarks. He seemed in excellent spirits, and though much of it was forced for Rossie's sake, he really was happier than he had been since his father's death. His future, so far as Josephine was concerned, was settled. He should never attempt to live with her now.

All the evening he sat with Rossie, and piled the wood upon the fire until the flames leaped merrily up the chimney, and infused a genial warmth through the large room. And Rosamond enjoyed it thoroughly because it was done for him. She would never have added a single superfluous chip for herself, lest it should diminish what was one day to go back to him; but for Everard she would almost have burned the house itself and felt she was doing her duty.

The next morning he spent with Beatrice, to whom he told the story of the midnight ride from Albany.

"After seeing and hearing what I did, I cannot ask her to live with me lest she should consent," he said, and Beatrice could not say a word in Josephine's defense, but asked what he proposed to do. Was he going away, or would he remain in Rothsay? A few days ago Everard would have answered promptly, "No, anywhere but here, in the place so full of unpleasant memories;" but now matters had somehow changed. That coming home the previous night, that bright fire on the hearth, and more than all, the sweet young face on which the firelight shone, and the eyes which had looked so modestly at him had made him loth to leave Rothsay and go away from the shadowy firelight and the young girl with the new character and the long dress. He might have left the child Rossie in the hands of Beatrice and Lawyer Russell, knowing she would be well cared for, but to leave Miss Hastings was quite another thing, and when Bee questioned him of his intentions, he hesitated a moment and was glad when, in her usual impetuous, helpful way, she said:

"Let me advise you before you decide. I saw Lawyer Russell in your absence, and had a long talk with him, and he thinks the best thing you can do is to stay in the office where you are and accept the guardianship of Rossie and the administration of the estate. That will bring you money which you certainly can have no scruples in taking, as it will be honestly earned and must go to some one. You can still go on with your study of law and write your essays and reviews, and so have plenty of means to satisfy Josephine, if money will do it. I do not suppose you will live at the Forrest House, that might not be best; but you will be in the village near by and can have a general oversight of Rossie herself as well as her affairs. What do you think of my plan?"

The idea of remaining in Rothsay and having an oversight of Rosamond was not distasteful to the young man, and when he left Beatrice he went directly to his father's office, where he found Lawyer Russell, who made the same suggestion with regard to the guardianship and administration of the estate which Beatrice had done. Of course it was necessary that Rosamond herself should be seen, and the two men went to the Forrest House to consult with her on the subject.

They found her more than willing, and in due time Everard was regularly installed as guardian to Rosamond and administrator of the estate. And then began a conflict with the girl, who manifested a decision of character and dignity of manner with which Everard found it difficult to cope. She insisted upon knowing exactly how much the Forrest property was estimated at, where the money was invested, and when interest on each investment was due. This she wrote down in a book of her own, and then she made an estimate of the annual expenses of the household as it was at present conducted.

"Don't you think that a great deal?" she asked.

"Father did not find it too much, and he was as close about expenditures as one need to be," Everard replied; and Rosamond continued:

"Yes, but I propose to reduce everything."

"What do you mean, Rossie?" Everard asked, greatly puzzled to understand this girl, who seemed so self-possessed and assured in her long dress, to which he charged everything new or startling in her conduct.

Rosamond hesitated a moment, and then replied:

"You have convinced me against my will that I am at present the lawful heir of your father's property; I have tried hard not to accept that as a fact, but I am compelled to do so. You say that I am really and truly the mistress of Forrest House, and don't mistresses of houses do as they like about the arrangement of matters in the house?" Everard said, "Generally, yes," and Rossie went on.

"Well, then, this is what I mean to do. First, I shall keep a strict account of the income and a strict account of the outgo, so far as that outgo is for me personally. You know I have two thousand dollars of my own, and I shall use that first, and by the time that is gone I hope to be able to take care of myself. I am going to have some nice, middle-aged lady in the house as companion and teacher, and shall study hard, so that in a year or two at most I shall be able to go out as governess or teacher in some school. My mind is quite made up. There are some things I cannot do, and there are some things I can, and this is one of them. I shall have the teacher and get an education, and meanwhile shall live as economically as possible; and I wish you to sell the horses and carriage, too; I shall never use them, and horses cost so much to keep. I like to walk, and have good strong feet and ankles,—great big ones, you used to say," and she tried to smile, but there was a tear on her long eyelashes as she referred to a past which had been so pleasant and free from care. "A part of the land is a park," she went on, "and does not need much attention except to pick up and prune, and cut the grass occasionally. Uncle Abel told me so. I have talked with him ever so much, and he says if I give him three dollars more a month he can do all there is to be done in the grounds, if he does not have the horses to look after, so I shall keep him, and his little grandson, Jim, to do errands and wait on the table and door, and Aunt Axie to work in the house, and send the rest away."

"Why, Rosamond," Everard said, staring at her in amazement, "you don't know what you are talking about; Aunt Axie cannot do all the work."

"Nor will she," Rossie said; "I am going to shut up most of the house, and only use two rooms up stairs, one for myself and one for the teacher, and the dining-room down stairs, and little sitting-room off for any calls I may have. I can take care of my own room and the teacher's, too, if she likes."

She had settled everything, and it only remained for Everard, as her guardian, to acquiesce in her wishes when he found that nothing which he could say had power to change her mind. She had developed great decision of character, and so clear a head for business in all its details, that Everard told her, laughingly, that it would be impossible for him to cheat her in so much as a penny without being detected. He was intensely interested in this queer girl, as he styled her to himself, and so far as was consistent with her good, did everything she asked, proving himself the most indulgent of guardians and faithful of administrators. Together with Beatrice he inquired for and found, in Cincinnati, a Mrs. Markham, a lady, and the widow of an English curate, who seemed exactly fitted for the situation at Forrest House as Rossie's teacher and companion. All Rossie's wishes with regard to reducing the expenditures of the household were carried out, with one exception. Everard insisted that she should keep one of the horses, which she could drive, and the light covered carriage which had been Mrs. Forrest's. To this Rossie consented, but sent away three of the negroes, and shut up all the rooms not absolutely essential to her own and Mrs. Markham's comfort. In this way she would save both fuel and lights, and the wear of furniture, she said, and to save for Everard had become a sort of mania with her. And when he saw he could not move her, Everard humored her whims and suffered her in most things to have her way. He had a cheap, quiet boarding-house in town, where he was made very comfortable by his landlady, who felt a little proud of having Judge Forrest's son in her family, even if he were disowned and poor. Blood was better than money, and lasted longer, she said, and as Everard had the bluest of blood, she made much of him, and petted him as he had never been petted in his life. And so, under very favorable auspices, began the new life of the two persons with whom this story has most to do.

So far as Rossie was concerned it bade fair to be very successful. Mrs. Markham was both mother and friend to the young girl, in whom she was greatly interested. A thorough scholar herself, she had a marvelous power of imparting her information to others, and Rossie gave herself to study now with an eagerness and avidity which astonished her teacher, and made her sometimes try to hold her back, lest her health should fail from too close application. But Rossie seemed to grow stronger, and fresher, and rounder every day, notwithstanding that all her old habits of life were changed.

Every day Beatrice came to the Forrest House, evincing almost as much interest in Rosamond's education as Mrs. Markham herself, and giving her a great deal of instruction with regard to her French accent and music. Every Sunday Everard dined with her, and called upon her week days when business required that he should do so; and he looked forward to these visits with the eagerness of a schoolboy going home. In some respects Everard was very happy, or, at least, content, during the first months of the new life. He was honorably earning a very fair livelihood, and at the same time advancing with his profession. No young man in town was more popular than himself, for the people attached no blame to him for his father's singular will, which they thought unjustifiable. There was, of course, always present with him a dread of the day which must come when his secret would be known,—but Holburton was an out-of-the-way place, where his friends never visited, and it might be months or even years before Josephine heard of his father's death, and until that time he meant to be as happy as he could. Josephine did not trouble him often with letters which he felt obliged to answer. He took care to supply her frequently with money, which he sent in the form of drafts, without any other message, and she seemed satisfied. He had sold his horse, his stock was yielding him something regularly now, and with the percentage due him for his services as administrator, he was doing very well, and would have been quite content but for that undefinable sense of loss ever present, with him. He had lost the child Rossie, and he wanted her back again, with the short gingham dress and white apron, and cape bonnet, and big boots, and little tanned hands; wanted the girl whom he had teased, and petted, and domineered over at will; who used to romp the livelong day with the dogs and cats, and teach even the colts and calves to run and race with her; who used to chew gum, and burst the buttons off her dress, and eat green apples and plums, and cry with the stomach-ache. All these incidents of the past as connected with Rossie came back to him so vividly, that he often said to himself:

"What has become of the child Rossie?"

She had been such a rest, such a comfort to him, and in one sense she was a comfort now, at least she was a study, an excitement and a puzzle to him, and he always found himself looking forward to the visits which he made her with an immense amount of interest. Every Sunday he dined with her, and walked with her to church in the evening, and sat in his father's pew, and walked back with her and Mrs. Markham to the house after service was over, and said good-night at the door, and wondered vaguely if women like Mrs. Markham always went to church, if they never had a headache, or a cold, and were compelled to stay at home. Occasionally, too, he went to the Forrest House on business, asking only for Rosamond; but Mrs. Markham always appeared first, coming in as if by accident, and seating herself, with the shawl she was knitting, far off by the window, just where she could see what was done at the other end of the room. After a little Rosamond would appear, in her long black gown, which trailed over the carpet as she walked, and exasperated Everard with the sound of its trailing, for to that he charged the metamorphosis in Rossie. It was the cause of everything, and had changed her into the quiet, dignified Miss Hastings, to whom it was impossible to speak as he used to speak to Rossie.

One day as he was looking from his office window he saw Mrs. Markham going by for the long walk she was accustomed to take daily. He had seen her pass that way frequently with Rosamond at her side, but

Rossie was not with her now; and though Everard had been at the Forrest House the night before, he suddenly remembered a little matter of business which made it very necessary for him to go again, and was soon walking rapidly up the long avenue to his old home. Aunt Axie let him in, and went for Rossie, who came to him at once,—evincing some surprise at seeing him again so soon, and asking, rather abruptly, if there was more business.

"Yes," and he blushed guiltily, and felt half vexed with her for standing up so straight and dignified, with her hands holding to the back of a chair, while he explained that the Ludlow mortgage would be due in a few days, and asked if she would like to have it renewed, as it could be, or have the money paid and invested somewhere else at a higher rate? He had forgotten to mention it the previous night, he said, and as she had expressed a wish to know just how the moneys were invested, he thought best to come again and consult her.

Rossie did not care in the least; she would leave it entirely to him, she said, and then waited, apparently for him to go. But Everard was in no haste, and passing her a chair he said:

"Sit down, Rossie. I am not going just yet. Now that I have you to myself for a few moments, I wish to ask how long this state of things is to go on?"

She did not know at all what he meant, and looked at him wonderingly as she took the proffered chair and said, "What state of things? What do you mean?"

"I mean the high and mighty air you have put on toward me. Why, you are so cold and dignified that one can't touch you with a ten-foot pole, and this ought not to be. I have a right to expect something different from you, Rossie. I dare say I can guess in part what is the matter. You are always thinking of that day you came to me in father's room and said what you did. But for Heaven's sake, forget it. I have never thought of it as a thing of which you need feel ashamed. You had tried every way to give me the money, and when that idea was suggested you seized upon it without a thought of harm, and generously offered to marry me and then run away, and so reinstate me in my rights."

Rossie's face was scarlet, but she did not speak, and he continued:

"It was a noble, unselfish act, and just like you, and I don't think a whit the less of you for it. I know you did not mean it that way, as you assured me so vehemently. I am your brother. You have known me as such ever since you can remember anything here, and my little sister was very dear to me, and I miss her so much now that I have lost her."

"Lost her, Mr. Everard! Lost me! No, you haven't," Rosamond said, her eyes filling with tears, which shone like stars, as Everard went on:

"Yes, I have. I lost her when you put on those long dresses and began to meet me in such a formal way, with that prim, old duenna always present, as if she was afraid I was going to eat you up. Mrs. Markham is very nice, no doubt, but I don't like that in her. It may be English propriety, but it is not American. I'm not going to hurt you, and I want sometimes to see you here alone and talk freely and cozily, as we used to talk,—about your cats, if you like, I don't care what, if it brings you back to me, for you don't know how I long for the child whom I used to tease so much."

He stopped talking, and Rossie was almost beautiful, with the bright color in her cheeks and the soft light in her eyes, which were full of tears, as she said, impulsively, "You shall have the child Rossie again, Mr. Everard. I am glad you have told me what you have. It will make it so much easier now to see you. I was always thinking of that, and feeling that you were thinking of it, too, and I am happy to know you are not. I don't wish to be stiff and distant with you, and you may come as often as you choose, and Mrs. Markham need not always be present,—that was as much my idea as hers; but the long dress I must wear now; it suits me better than the short clothes which showed my feet so much. You know how you used to tease me." She was beginning to seem like herself again, and Everard enjoyed himself so well that he staid until Mrs. Markham returned, and when at last he left, it was with a feeling that he liked the graceful, dignified young girl almost as well as he had once liked the child Rossie.

CHAPTER XXIII

BEE'S FAMILY

A few days after Everard's interview with Rossie, Beatrice went to New York, where she spent the winter, returning home early in April, and bringing with her a dark-eyed, dark-haired, elfish-looking little girl, whom she called Trixey, and whose real name was Beatrice Belknap Morton. She was the daughter of a missionary to the Feejee Islands, who had brought his invalid wife home to America, hoping the air of the Vermont hills might restore life and health to her worn-out, wasted frame. Bee did not know of his return, and saw him first at a missionary meeting which she attended with the friend at whose house she was stopping.

"The Rev. Theodore Morton will now tell us something of his labors among the Feejees," the presiding clergyman said, and Bee, who was sitting far back near the door, rose involuntarily to her feet in order to see more distinctly the man who was just rising to address the audience, and who stood before them, tall, erect, and perfectly self-possessed, as if addressing a crowded New York house had been the business of his life.

Was it her Theo, whom she had sent from her to the woman in Vermont, more willing than herself to share his toils and privations in a heathen land. That Theo had been spare and thin, with light beard and sandy hair; this man was broad-shouldered, with well-developed physique, and the hair, which lay in curls around his massive brow, was a rich chestnut brown, as was the heavy beard upon his cheek. It could not be

Theo, she though, as she sank back into her seat; but the moment she heard the deep, musical tones of the voice which had once a power to thrill her, she knew that it was he, and listened breathlessly while he told of his work in those islands of the sea, and by his burning eloquence and powers of speech stirred up his hearers to greater interest in the cause. He loved his work because it was his Master's, and loved the poor, benighted heathen, and he only came home because of the sick wife and little ones, who needed change of scene and air.

Where was his wife, Bee wondered, and when the meeting was over she drove to the house of a clergyman who she knew kept a kind of missionary hotel, and from him learned the address of the Rev. Theodore Morton. It was not at an uptown hotel, but at a second-rate boarding-house on Eighth street, where rooms and board were cheap, and there, on the third floor back, she found Mrs. Theodore Morton, the school-mistress from Vermont, who had so offended her taste with spectacles and a brown alpaca dress. The landlady had bidden her go directly to the room, where she knocked at the door, and then stood listening to a sweet, childish voice singing a lullaby to a baby. Again she knocked, and this time the voice said "Come in," and she went in, and found a little girl of five years old, with black hair and eyes, and a dark, saucy, piquant face, seated in a low rocking-chair, and holding in her short, fat arms a pale, sickly baby of four months or thereabouts, which she was trying to hush to sleep. Near her, in an arm-chair, sat a round, rosy-cheeked little girl, who might have been three years old, though her height indicated a child much younger than that. On the bed, with her face to the wall, and apparently asleep, lay a woman, emaciated and thin, with streaks of gray in the long, black hair floating in masses over the pillow. Bee thought she must have made a mistake, but something in the blue eyes of the chubby girl in the chair arrested her attention, and she said to the elf with the baby in her arms:

"Is Mrs. Morton here,—Mrs. Theodore Morton?"

"Yes, that's ma,—on the bed. She's sick; she's always sick. Tum in, but don't make a noise, 'cause I'se tryin' to rock baby brother to seep, like a good 'ittle dirl."

"An' I's dood, too," chirped the dumpling in the high chair. "I've climbed up here to det out of the way, an' not wake mamma an' make her head ache, an' papa's goin' to bring me some tandy, he is, when he tums from the meetin'."

There was no mistaking that blue-eyed, fair-haired child for other than Theodore Morton's, and Beatrice stooped down and kissed her round, rosy cheek, and asked:

"What is your name, little one?"

"Mamie,—Mamie Morton; but dey calls me Bunchie, 'cause I's so fat, an' I's mamma's darlin', and was tree 'ears old next week," was the reply; and then Bee turned to the elf, and laying her hand on the jet-black hair, said:

"And your name is what?"

"Trixey everybody calls me but papa, who sometimes says Bee; but that ain't my very name. It's ever so long, with many B's in it," was the reply, and Bee's heart gave a great bound, as she said:

"Is it Beatrice?"

"Yes, an' more too, Beatrice sometin'."

"Beatrice Belknap, perhaps," guessed the lady, and the child replied:

"That's it, but how did you know?" and the great eyes, so very black and inquisitive, looked wonderingly at Bee, who answered:

"I am Beatrice Belknap, the lady for whom you were named, and I've come to see you. I used to know your father. Is he well?"

"Papa? Yes, he's very well, but mamma," and the child put on a very wise and confidential look as she added in a whisper, "mamma's shiffless all the time."

Bee could not repress a smile at this quaint form of speech, and she asked:

"And do you take care of baby? Is there no nurse?"

"We had Leah over home," Trixey said, "but she couldn't come with us, 'cause we're so poor, an' papa has no money."

"But he buyed me some yed soos," Bunchie said, sticking up her little feet, encased in a new pair of red morocco shoes, the first she had ever had or probably seen.

How Beatrice's heart yearned over these little ones who had known only poverty, and how she longed to lavish upon them a part of her superfluous wealth. There was a stir on the bed; the sleeper was waking, and a faint voice called:

"Trixey, are you here?"

"Yes, mamma. I've rocked brother to seep," Trixey said, starting up, but holding fast to the baby as a cat holds to its kitten. "There's a lady here, mamma, comed to see us," the child continued, and then Mrs. Morton roused quickly, and turning on her side fixed her great sunken eyes inquiringly on Beatrice, who stepped forward, and with that winning sweetness and grace so natural to her, said:

"I doubt if you remember me, Mrs. Morton, as you only saw me once, and that for a few moments, before the Guide sailed from here six years ago. I am an old friend of your husband's. I met him in Paris first and many times after in America. Perhaps you have heard him speak of Miss Beatrice Belknap?"

"Yes, Trixey was named for you. It was kind in you to call," Mrs. Morton said, and now she sat upon the side of the bed and began to bind up her long black hair, which had fallen in her neck.

"Let me do that," Bee said, as she saw how the exertion of raising her arms made the invalid cough; and drawing off her gloves, her white hands, on which so many costly jewels were shining, were soon arranging and twisting the long hair which, though mixed with gray, was very glossy and luxuriant. "You have nice hair, and so much of it," she said, and Mrs. Morton replied:

"Yes, it is very heavy even yet, and is all I have left of my youth, though I am not so very old, only thirty; but the life of a missionary's wife is not conducive to the retaining of one's good looks."

"Was it so very dreadful?" Bee asked, a little curious about the life which might have been her own.

"Not dreadful, but hard; that is, it was very hard on me, who was never strong, though I seemed so to strangers. I could not endure much, and was sick all the way out, so sick that I used to wish I might die and be buried in the sea. Then Trixey came so soon, and the care of her, and the food, and the climate, and the manner of living there, and the terrible homesickness! Oh, I was so homesick, at first, that I should surely have died, if Theo had not been so good. He was always kind, and tried to spare me every way."

"Yes, I am sure he did," Bee said; feeling at the same time a kind of pity for Theo, who, for six years, had spared and been kind to this woman, after having known and loved her, Beatrice Belknap.

There was a great difference between these two women; one, bright, gay, sparkling, full of life and health, with wealth showing itself in every part of her elegant dress, from the India shawl which she had thrown across the chair, to the sable muff which had fallen on the floor; the other, sick, tired, disheartened, old before her time; and, alas, habited in the same brown alpaca in which she had sailed away, and which had been so obnoxious to Beatrice. The material had been the best of the kind, and after various turnings and fixings, had been made at last into a kind of wrapper, which was trimmed with a part of another old brown dress of a different shade. Nothing could be more unbecoming to that thin, sallow face, and those dark, hollow eyes, than that dress, and never was contrast greater between two women than that revealed by the mirror which hung just opposite the bed where Mrs. Morton was sitting, with Beatrice standing by her. Both looked in it together, and met each other's eyes, and must have thought of the same thing, for Mrs. Morton at once changed her seat where she could not see herself, and as the hair was put up Beatrice also sat down, and, without seeming to do so, inspected very minutely the woman who was Theodore Morton's wife.

She was well educated,—and she was well born, too, being the daughter, and granddaughter, and great-granddaughter of clergymen, while on her mother's side she came from merchants and lawyers, and very far back boasted a lieutenant-governor. But she lacked that softness, and delicacy, and refinement of manner which was Bee's great charm. She had angles and points, and was painfully frank and outspoken, and never practiced a deception in her life, or kept back anything she thought she ought to say, or flinched from any duty. In short, she was New England to the back-bone, and showed it in everything. Vermont, or rather the little town of Bronson, where she was born, was placarded all over her, just as Paris and New York were written all over Bee, and she rejoiced in it and was proud of her birthplace. Beatrice's presence there was evidently a trouble and an embarrassment. When Theodore Morton went to her and asked her to be his wife he had told her frankly that he had loved another and been refused, and she had accepted him, and asked no question about her rival. On board the ship in the harbor she had been so occupied with her own personal friends who were there to say good-by, that, though introduced to Miss Belknap, she had paid no attention to her, or noticed her in any way. When her first child was born, ten months after her marriage, she had wished to name it Sarah, for her mother, but her husband said to her: "I would like to call it Beatrice Belknap, if you do not mind."

She did mind, for she knew now that Beatrice Belknap was her husband's first choice, but she held it every wife's duty to obey her husband so far as it was right, and as there was nothing wrong in this proposition she consented without a word, and the baby was named for Beatrice, but familiarly called Trixey, as that pet name suited her better. Of the Beatrice over the sea Theodore never spoke, and his wife never questioned him, and so she knew nothing of her until she woke from sleep and found her there in all her fresh beauty and bright plumage, which seemed so out of place in that humble room. Of course she was embarrassed and confused, but she would not apologize, except as she spoke of the life of privation they had led in that heathen land.

"And yet there was much to make me happy," she said. "I knew we were doing God's work,—which somebody must do,—and when some poor creatures blessed us for coming to tell them the story of Jesus, I was so glad that I had gone to them, and my trials seemed as nothing. And then, there was Theo, always the same good, true husband to me." She said this a little defiantly, as if to assure Beatrice that the heart, which once might have beaten for her, was now wholly loyal to another.

And Bee accepted it sweetly, but had her own opinion on the subject still.

"Yes, the Mr. Morton I used to know could never be anything but kind to one he loved well enough to make his wife," she said; and then, by way of turning the conversation from Theodore to something else, she asked: "Were you sick all the time you were there?"

"Yes, most of the time. My children were born so fast,—four in five years. I lost a noble boy between Mamie and baby Eddie; that almost killed me, and I've never been the same since. There is consumption in our family far back, and I fear I have inherited it. My cough is terrible at times, but I hope much from Vermont air and Vermont nursing. Oh, I have longed so for the old home at the foot of the mountain, for some water from the well, for mother, and to lie on her bed as I used to when I was a child, and had the sick-headache."

Her eyes filled with tears as she said this, and she leaned wearily back in her chair, while Bee involuntarily laid her soft, warm hand upon the thin, wasted one where the wedding-ring sat so loosely. Just then the door opened and Theodore Morton came in, the same Beatrice had heard at the missionary meeting, the same with whom she had strolled through the Kentucky woods and on the shore of Quinsigamond Pond. He knew her at once, but nothing in his face or voice betrayed any consciousness of the past, if he felt it. He met her naturally and cordially, said he was very glad to see her, that it was kind in her to find them out, and then passed on to his sick wife, on whose head he laid his hand caressingly, asking if it ached as hard as ever, or if she was feeling a little better.

"You look better certainly," he said, regarding her curiously, not knowing that the improvement was owing to the artistic way in which

Beatrice had knotted up the heavy hair, which showed at the sides and added apparent breadth to the thin, narrow face.

What a noble-looking man he was, and how well he appeared, as if he had associated with kings and queens instead of the poor heathen, and what a change his presence made in that dingy back room, which, with him in it, had at once an atmosphere of home and domestic happiness. He had been there but a few moments at the most, but in that time he had smoothed his wife's hair, and called her Mollie, the pet name she liked, and made her smile, had tossed Bunchie in the air and stuffed her fat hands with candy, had kissed little Trixey, and given her a new picture-book, and taken the baby from her and was walking with it up and down the room to hush its wailing cry. And between times he talked to Beatrice, naturally and easily, asking for the people he used to know in Rothsay, and if she was living there now; then, stopping suddenly, he said:

"I beg your pardon for taking it for granted you were Miss Belknap still. Are you married? You used to be a sad flirt."

He said the last playfully, and the two looked at each other an instant, and their eyes dropped suddenly as if alarmed at what they saw.

"I am Bee Belknap still, and as great a flirt as ever," Bee replied; and then the Rev. Theo did a most remarkable thing; he turned to his wife, and said:

"Mollie, dear, do you know I was once foolish enough to ask this gay bird to go with me to the Feegees, and she had the good sense to refuse. Wouldn't she have cut a fine figure out there with all her finery and fashion?"

"Yes, I know," Mollie said faintly, while Bee rejoined, laughingly: "You ought to be very thankful that I preferred fashion to Feegees; such a life as I should have led you."

"You would have died," Mollie rejoined, and the conversation on that subject ceased.

Theo had set things right for them all by his plain and playful allusion to the past, which, from that allusion, would be supposed to have no part in his present life, and to have left no mark upon him. He seemed very happy with his children, and very kind to his wife, who was a different creature with his strong, mesmeric influence near her.

"I believe she'd be passably good-looking if she were decently dressed. She has good hair, not bad features, and rather fine eyes; but where are the glasses, she surely wore them away?" Beatrice thought, and at last she ventured to say: "Excuse me, Mrs. Morton, but did you not wear glasses on shipboard six years ago?"

"Yes," was the reply, "my eyes were weak from over-study, trying to master the language, and I was obliged to wear glasses for a time. I laid them off after Trixey was born. Theo never liked me in them."

As the short March afternoon was wearing to a close Beatrice soon rose to go, after first asking how long the Mortons intended to remain in the city.

"We have written to mother to know if she can receive us," Mrs. Morton said, "and shall go as soon as we get her answer. I am afraid we shall crowd and worry her too much, for the house is small, and she and father are old and poor, and may not want us all."

"Never mind, Mollie," Theo said, "don't kill the bear till you see it;" then, turning to Beatrice, he added, not complaining, but laughingly, "Mollie has a great way of borrowing trouble, while I wait till it comes."

"It's my poor health; my nerves; I can't help it," the invalid said, with a quiver in her voice and about her lips.

"Of course you can't, Mollie," and again the broad, warm hand was placed upon Mollie's head by way of reassurance.

Theo went with Bee to her carriage, and handed her in, and told her to come again, and said he would call on her, and was not one whit more demonstrative when alone with her than he was up in that back room with his nervous wife looking on. But Bee did not quite believe he was perfectly happy. How could he be with Mollie.

And yet she was very sorry for Mollie, who, she was sure, was a much better woman than herself, and the next day, which was very fine, she drove again to No.—— Eighth street, and invited the sick woman to ride.

"The coupé is close, and I brought an extra shawl to keep you nice and warm," she said, as she threw over Mrs. Morton's shoulders her second-best India shawl, which covered up the black delaine, trimmed with half-worn silk, which Mollie wore.

It was her best, Bee knew, for little Trix had said, exultingly, "Ma's got on her bestest down to day."

"Yes, my best, and almost my all," Mrs. Morton said, "but I have money for a new one; some English ladies give it me, and told me to get a black silk. I've never had one in my life: would you mind going with me somewhere and helping me pick it out: you are a so much better judge of silk than I am?"

Bee flinched a little inwardly as she looked at the dowdy woman, in her queer, old-fashioned bonnet, and thought of the fashionable ladies, her friends, who were sure to be shopping at this hour, and who always spied her out and pounced upon her. But she shut her teeth together hard, bade the coachman drive to Arnold's, resolved to beard the elegant man at the silk counter, who was always so obsequious to Miss Belknap, the heiress and belle. Everybody was out that day, and Bee met at least half a dozen friends before she reached the silk counter, where she found her man, bland, attentive, and eager to serve her.

"Black silk," she said, and he showed her at once samples varying in price from eight to ten dollars a yard.

"Oh, dear, no! something cheaper, much cheaper," Mrs. Morton gasped; and then the clerk knew that the faded, countrified-looking woman whom he had not at all considered as belonging to Miss Belknap, was the real customer, and his face changed its expression at once as he put back his high-priced silks with an injured air, and said: "You will find what you want farther down. We have nothing cheap here."

"I think you have," Beatrice said to him. "Show me something at four dollars a yard."

"Certainly," and again the clerk was all smiles and attention, and began to exhibit his goods, while Mrs. Morton whispered nervously, "But, Miss Belknap, you don't understand. I've only forty dollars; I cannot afford it."

"I can," Beatrice replied. "I have more money than I can spend. Let me give you the dress. I'll take it as a great favor, and you can use the forty dollars for something else."

There were tears in Mrs. Morton's eyes, and her face was very white, as she said:

"No, no; that's too much from you, a stranger. Theo would not like it."

"I'll make it right with Theo. I'm not a stranger to him," Bee answered, and so the silk was bought, and velvet to trim it with, and then they moved to another part of the store for something for the children, and met a whole regiment of ladies, Mrs. Gen. Stuckup with Mrs. Sniffe, who were delighted to see Bee, but looked askance at her companion, wondering if it was some poor relation of whom they had never heard, and commiserating Bee, who must feel so mortified.

She was not mortified one whit now, though she had been at the start, but she despised herself thoroughly for it and was very attentive to her companion, and when Mrs. Sniffe, who was frightfully envious of her, and never failed to sting her if she could do it, asked her in an aside, with a roll of her eyes; "Who is that frump of a woman, and how came she fastened to you?" she answered, readily, "It is Mrs. Theodore Morton, wife of a returned missionary, whose name you must have seen if you ever read the papers. He is very highly esteemed by the board as a Christian and a gentleman. Some connection of Gov. Morton, of Massachusetts, I believe."

"Oh, yes, and you are doing missionary work in your own way, I see. It's quite like you," Mrs. Sniffe said, as she passed on to the laces and left Bee and Mrs. Morton to themselves.

"That woman made fun of me and called me a frump," Mrs. Morton falteringly said, with a quivering lip, but fire in her eye, as she looked after the retreating bundle of velvet, and silk, and ostrich feathers.

"Never mind. You don't care for her. They say she used to work in the factory at Lowell, and married a man old enough to be her father, but he had a million, and died, and left it to her, and now she is Mrs. Sniffe, and leads a certain class of simpletons," Bee replied, and so Mrs. Morton was reconciled to Mrs. Sniffe's snub, and more than reconciled to her husband's first love when she saw how kind and generous she was, spending her money so freely, and doing it all as if it were a great favor to herself rather than an act of charity to the poor woman, who returned to her boarding-house laden with more dry-goods for herself and children than she had seen during the entire period of her married life.

It was two days before Beatrice went again to her family on Eighth street, and then she found Mrs. Morton alone, and very much depressed, on account of a letter that morning received from her father.

As she gave Beatrice the letter to read, I will give it to my readers. It was as follows:

"My Beloved Daughter:—Many thanks be to God for having brought you safely to America, and given us to believe that we shall see your face

again and that of the little ones, our grandchildren. I cannot tell you how glad we are, your mother, and myself, and Aunt Nancy, too, though I think she dreads the litter and the grease-spots the children are sure to make, her life has been so quiet, you know. For myself, I long to see the bairns and hear their young voices. It will make me young again, though the years are bearing me down now so fast. Sixty-eight is nigh on to three score and ten, our allotted time.

"And now about your coming here for the summer. Of course you are welcome as the blossoms of May, but I should be keeping back something if I did not tell you just the situation of things in the old parsonage. Your mother is down with nervous prostration, and has been for months, and as she is very weak I occupy a separate room from hers. Your Aunt Nancy has another, and that only leaves your own old room for you and Theodore and the three children. Of course, I don't count that place over the woodshed, where we can have a bed for a girl or a boy. You cannot have three children in your room even when your husband is away, it is so small, and Nancy would as soon have a woodchuck in with her as a child; so at first it was a question how to dispose of you. But Providence provided, as He always does. Your mother and I made it a subject of prayer, asking in our blind way that God would incline Nancy either to change rooms, or to have a little cot set up in hers, and feeling confident He would hear the prayer of faith. He did hear and answer, but in His own way, which was not ours. He did not soften your Aunt Nancy, but he sent your cousin Julia to us to say that she would gladly take one of the little girls for a while. You know she is rich and has no children, and it will be a nice home for the child, and Nancy says, 'Let her have the one that will be likely to fill our house the fullest and make the most to do,' whatever that may be.

"And now, having stated the case as it is, we shall be glad to see you any day, only on Nancy's account you may as well let us know, as everything will have to be scoured with soap and sand. I hear her now at the kitchen table, which somebody has spilt a drop of milk on.

"Your mother joins me in love, and prays for you.

"Affectionately your father,
"Cyrus Brown."

"What a nice letter, and what a good old man he must be," Beatrice said, as she finished reading.

"Yes," Mrs. Morton answered, hesitatingly; "it is nice, and he is good, and mother, too; but the idea of losing one of the children is dreadful to me. There is always some thorn in my rose. I have thought so much of going back to the old house under the apple trees, and having my little ones with me; and now you see what he says,—one must go to Cousin Julia Hayden."

In Mrs. Morton's roses there would always be thorns, fancied or real, but Bee did not tell her so; she merely asked: "Who is Mrs. Hayden? Is she fond of children? Will she be kind to them?"

"She is my cousin on mother's side," Mrs. Morton said. "She is the great woman of Bronson, and the richest, and lives in the grandest house. She never had any children of her own, and I do not think her very fond of them. She would be kind in a certain way, but very exacting. She does not understand them. She used to teach school, and was very strict, indeed. She could not make allowances for the difference between herself and little folks. She is Aunt Nancy's own niece."

"And who is Aunt Nancy?" Bee asked, and Mrs. Morton replied, "Mother's old maid sister, Nancy Phillips, who has always lived with us. She is the neatest, most particular person you ever saw; and because she is strong and willing, and mother is feeble, she has run the house so long that she thinks it is her own, and orders father as if he were a dog. But she has many excellent traits, and they could not live without her. She was always kind to me, and I'd rather trust my children with her than with Cousin Julia Hayden. It is very hard, and makes me so nervous."

"Yes, I can fancy it all," Bee said; and then, recurring to the letter, she added: "You are to give up the one which will fill the house the fullest and make the most noise. Now, which is that?"

Instantly the eyes of both went over to the window, where Trixey was combing and brushing Bunchie's hair, pulling and snarling it awfully, and talking all the time as fast as her tongue could fly. Yes, there was no mistake. Little Trix would fill the house the fullest and make the greatest to do, and Mrs. Hayden would never understand her, or make allowance for her busy, active ways; and Beatrice wanted her for herself, and said at last to Mrs. Morton: "Will you let me have Trixey, for as long a time as Mrs. Hayden would keep her? I know I can make her happy. You can trust her with me."

Mrs. Morton was sure of that. During the few days she had known Miss Belknap she had received from her too many kindnesses to think of her as other than a friend, and one to be trusted. At first, she had looked a little suspiciously upon the elegant woman who had been Theo's first choice, and who was so unlike herself, and she had more than once thought, "How could he have chosen me after knowing her?" She did not say "love me," for she had been morally sure that when she became Theodore Morton's wife there was not much love on his side at least. She had loved him for years, and been picked out for his wife since she was a little girl. His father and grandfather had been clergymen, and he had been her father's pupil when the Rev. Mr. Brown taught a small school for boys, by way of ekeing out his salary. Theo had said then he meant to be a missionary, and she had said she meant to be one, too, and wise ones predicted that they might go together. But the young man wandered very far away from quiet Bronson, and its staid, old-fashioned people, and went to Europe, and fell in with Bee Belknap, and forgot the plain, angular Mary Brown, in the home under the apple trees, who had mended his clothes, and studied Latin and Greek, and talked enthusiastically of a missionary's life as the happiest and best a man could choose. He had never quite believed it possible that a bright, gay creature like Bee, with hundreds of thousands at her command, would go with him to those islands in the far-off Pacific, but he nevertheless asked her the question, and her answer, given tearfully and sadly, and rather as a refusal of the Feejees than of himself, scattered the sweetest dream of his life, and with a new-made grave in his heart he went back to Bronson on a matter of business he had with Mr. Brown. That he should take a wife with him seemed a necessity, and as Mary was ready, and more than willing, and he cared little now who it was, so that she was good and true and pure, he married her with no love in his heart for her, only a great respect, and a registered vow that she should receive from him everything but love, and if it were possible, should never feel the absence of that. And she had not, for he had kept his vow religiously, and only when he gave the name to Trixey had she experienced a little prick of jealousy, and felt curious with regard to the original Beatrice. If he did not choose to tell her of the lady she would not ask, and so knew nothing till she met her in New York, and was dazzled and bewildered, and troubled, and a very little annoyed at first, and finally won by the sparkling, brilliant woman who had done so much for her, and who now stood offering to take Trixey off her hands and save her from Mrs. Hayden. She knew she could trust her, and that Trix would be safe with her, but she shrank from parting with the helpful, motherly child, who did so much for her and the baby, and she hesitated in her answer, and said at last she would see what Theodore would say.

Theodore approved the plan heartily, if Trixey must go somewhere to be out of the sick grandmother's and Aunt Nancy's way. But now there arose trouble in an unexpected quarter. Trixey herself demurred. She loved the pretty lady, and was interested to hear about the dolls and dresses, and the cats and kittens, and pretty little tea-set and table, and wash-tub, and flat-iron, which should all be hers in that new home in Ohio. The wash-tub, and flat-iron, and tea-set made her waver a little, till she glanced at Bunchie, when, with quivering lip, she said:

"What good to have ever so many sings, and Bunchie not with me to see me use the flat-iron and was-tub, and sit at the other end of the table when I makes the tea?"

This was the ground she took. Bunchie would not be there to share her happiness, and she did not swerve from it until her father appealed to her sense of right, and told her the real reason why she should go. Grandpa's house was very small, and he was poor. Grandma was sick, and Aunt Nancy could not have so many children round.

"But I could help her lots. I'd rock baby brudder to seep, and wipe the dishes ever so many times, and be so good and still as Bunchie," pleaded the little girl; but she was persuaded at last to go because it was right, and God would love her if she did, and take care of Bunchie and baby brother, and in the summer she should come and see them in the old home; and so it was quite settled that Trixey was to go with Beatrice, who felt more and more the wisdom of the decision when that very afternoon she met Mrs. Hayden herself in Mrs. Morton's room, and had an opportunity of judging what manner of person she was, and what Trixey's chance for happiness would have been with her.

She was a tall, large, finely-formed woman, with great black eyes, bushy eyebrows, and a growth of hair about her wide mouth which gave her a more masculine appearance even than did her figure and size. She spoke loudly and decidedly, as one used to her own way, as well as to dictate the way of others. Her dress was very rich and showy, but not New-Yorkey a bit, Bee decided, after a rapid survey of the lady, who scrutinized her as closely, and decided that she was New-Yorkey, and wondered who her dressmaker was. To faded, plain Mrs. Morton she was very patronizing and frank, and told her that what she wanted was fresh air, and cold baths, and oatmeal to bring her up again, while her mother, who had been sick so long, needed effort and energy. She could get up if she only thought so. Nervous prostration was not a disease; it was a fancy, which, if indulged in, would end in one's being bed-ridden.

"I've made it a rule to guard against nervousness in every form, and what is the result? I have never been sick a day in my life, and have no idea how it feels to have the headache, or the toothache, or the backache, or, in fact, any ache, and that is the way it should be."

She looked the woman never to have an ache or pain, or if she had, to strangle it at once, and Beatrice shrank from her involuntarily as from an Amazon, while poor, sick Mrs. Morton colored scarlet, and roused in defense of her own ailments, which Mrs. Hayden seemed to think she could help.

"Just because you've never been sick, Julia," she said, "you cannot understand it in others, but you go out a missionary once, and have four children in six years, and be as poor as poor can be, and you might know something of aches and pains, and have some weaknesses which cold baths and oatmeal could not cure."

"I would not go out as a missionary, and I would not have the four children in six years; so you see it is not a supposable case," Mrs. Hayden retorted, and then Bee hated her, and was doubly glad that little Trix was not to fall into her hands.

Mrs. Hayden herself was not sorry. She had made the offer from a sense of duty, for she was high up in everything of that kind, and performed her duties rigidly, from dieting her husband, a weak, feeble man, on oatmeal and pearl barley, to telling her neighbors their faults, and how they could amend them. She did not like children, and it had cost her something to make up her mind to have one in her house; but she had made the offer, and meant to stand by it if it should be accepted. Finding it convenient just then to visit New York, she had called upon her poor relations to learn the result of her offer, and when told what it was she expressed no regret, but asked many question about Miss Belknap, who seemed to her to be crazy to think of taking Trixey. Suddenly there flashed upon her the recollection of a rumor heard years ago, and, in her usual brusque way, she asked:

"Is she the girl to whom Theo was once engaged, and who jilted him?"

"They never were engaged, but he liked her," Mrs. Morton answered faintly, while a throb of neuralgic pain shot through her head, and a bright red spot burned on her cheeks.

She was far more a lady, in her brown alpaca dressing-gown, than was this blunt women in her velvet and silk; and so Beatrice thought when she came in immediately after her identity with Theo's first love had been proved. Mrs. Hayden never acknowledged any person her superior, but she saw at a glance that Miss Belknap was somebody, and an important somebody, too, and thought to stamp herself as somebody, by talking of her house, and grounds, and servants, and the watering-places she frequented, and the people she had met. She was now stopping on Madison avenue with Mrs. Sniffe, who was Mr. Hayden's cousin; probably Miss Belknap knew Mrs. Sniffe, or at least had heard of her. She attended Dr. Adams' church, and was quite a leader there.

"Do you know her?" she asked squarely; and Bee replied:

"Yes, I have some acquaintance with Mrs. Sniffe. I meet her occasionally at parties."

Something in the tone made Mrs. Hayden look suspiciously at Beatrice, as she wondered whether it was Mrs. Sniffe who was only to be met at general parties, or Miss Belknap herself; while Mrs. Morton felt emboldened to say:

"Mrs. Sniffe,—that's the woman we met at Arnold's who called me a frump. Maybe she forgets that she once worked in the factory at Lowell."

She had fired her heavy gun, and felt better for it, inasmuch as she had hit the enemy, who reddened, as she replied:

"I believe she was there for a short time, but honest labor does not hurt a person in this country."

Then she talked of Mrs. Sniffe's grandeur and style, until Bee was tired of it and arose to go, promising to call next day and decide when to take Trixey. Mrs. Hayden followed her into the hall, and, begging her pardon, asked who made the dress she was wearing.

"Mademoiselle Verwest made it and sent it to me. Her address is No.——, Rue St. Honoré, Paris," Bee replied.

And, somewhat discomfited, Mrs. Hayden bowed her thanks, and returned to her cousin, whom she badgered about her weak nerves, and want of energy, until the poor woman burst into an uncontrollable fit of weeping, and cried herself sick.

Beatrice found her in bed next day, and as the little room seemed so close and full of children, she carried Trixey away with her to her friend's house, and for a day or two devoted herself wholly to the child, who was kept in such a state of surprise and bewilderment that she did not once cry for the mother down on Eighth street. Beatrice bought her a doll nearly as large as herself, and bought her a kitchen, with wash-tub and stove, and a China tea-set and table, and beautiful dresses for herself, and then whisked her off to the train before she had time to recover from the excitement of so many wonderful things. Mr. Morton was at the depot, but Trixey did not see him. It was thought better that she should not, so he looked his farewell from a distance, but said good-by to Beatrice, and held her hand closely pressed in his own, as he said:

"God bless you, Bee, for all you have done for us. We never can forget it. Good-by. You will, of course, write to Mollie as soon as you get home."

"Yes, certainly," Beatrice said, hating herself because the name Mollie as spoken by Theo grated on her nerves, and seemed in some way a wrong to herself.

Bee knew such feelings were foolish, and as often as they rose within her, she took Trix in her lap and kissed her, and talked to her of the mother they were leaving so far behind, and whose eyes looked at her through the child's, save that Trixey's were larger, and more weird in their expression.

It was late in the afternoon when they reached Rothsay, and were driven to Elm Park. Bee had telegraphed to Aunt Rachel that she was coming with a little girl, so everything was in readiness for them, and Trixey was made much of, and talked to and looked at, until she began to nod in her chair, and was taken up to bed.

That evening Everard came up to Elm Park with Rosamond. They had just heard of Bee's return, and hastened at once to see her. Everard was looking about the same as when Beatrice saw him last, except that he was perhaps a little thinner. He was working pretty hard, he said, and earning some money, but his dress did not indicate anything like reckless expenditure upon himself, and Beatrice felt sure that Josephine was drawing heavily upon him.

He was now quite at home at the Forrest House, and was there nearly every evening, and Beatrice felt something like a throb of fear when she saw his eyes resting upon Rossie, as if loth to leave the fresh young face, which had grown so bright and attractive during the last few months. She was growing very pretty, and her figure looked graceful and womanly when at last she arose to go, and stood while Everard folded her shawl around her, drawing it close up about her neck so as to shield her throat, which was a little sore. Something in that shawl adjustment and the length of time it took sent another thrill through Bee's nerves, and the moment they were gone she went to her room, where Trixey lay sleeping, and bending over the child, wondered if in all lives things got as terribly mixed as they were in hers and Everard's.

CHAPTER XXIV

IN THE SUMMER

Trixey did not thrive well in her new home, though everything which human ingenuity could devise was done to make her happy and contented. But in spite of everything Trixey could not quite overcome her homesickness. Many times a day she disappeared from sight and was gone a long time, and when she came back there was a mysterious redness about her eyes, which she said, by way of explanation, were "kind of sore, she dessed. Maybe she had got some dust in 'em."

This went on for weeks, until at last, in a fit of remorse lest she had been guilty of a lie, the conscientious child burst out:

"'Tain't dust, 'tain't sore that makes 'em red; it's wantin' to see papa, and mamma, and Bunchie, and baby brudder. Was it a lie, and is I a naughty dirl to make breve it was dust?"

Then Bee felt that it would be wrong to keep her any longer, and wrote to Mrs. Morton to that effect.

Mrs. Morton and Bunchie were still in Bronson, but Theo was supplying a vacant pulpit in Boston, and only saw his wife once in two or three weeks. There was room in the parsonage now for homesick Trixey, for the sickly baby had died suddenly with cholera infantum, and the same letter which carried the news to Beatrice asked that Trixey might be sent to Vermont.

"Send her by express," Mrs. Morton wrote, "or will you bring her yourself? We shall be so glad to see you, though we cannot offer you a bed here, we are so full, but there is a good country hotel near us, and Cousin Julia Hayden, whom you met in New York, wishes me to say that she will be very glad to entertain you at her own house. I hope you will come, for though our acquaintance is so recent, you seem to me like a friend of years, and I feel that the sight of you may do me good, now that my heart is so sore with the loss of my baby."

"I'll go," Bee said, as she finished reading the letter, deciding all the more readily on account of a little incident which had occurred the night before, and which filled her with alarm for both Everard and Rosamond.

They had walked together to Elm Park, and sat with her for an hour or more on the piazza, where the full moon was shining brightly. This time there had been no shawl to adjust, for the early June night was warm and balmy, but there was a slight dampness in the air, and Everard's solicitude lest Rosamond should take cold or contract a sore throat was noticeable in the extreme. Two or three times he pulled the fleecy cloud of Berlin wool about her neck, and asked if she were quite comfortable, and once he let his hand rest on her shoulder for some minutes, while he sat looking at her with an expression on his face which Josephine might have resented had she seen it. And Bee, with her strong sense of right and wrong, resented it for her, or rather for Rosamond, whom she would not see sacrificed without a protest. So when they arose to go home, she led Everard away from Rossie, and when sure she could not be heard, said to him, earnestly:

"Pardon me, Everard, but you are altogether too solicitous about Rosamond's health. Let her take care of herself. She is capable of doing it, and, remember, there are bounds you must not pass, or suffer her to approach. It would be very cruel to her."

"Yes, I know," he answered, coloring deeply as he spoke. "You need not fear for Rossie. She is my sister, nothing more; and even if I were disposed to make her something else, do you suppose I can ever forget the past?"

He spoke bitterly, and showed plainly how gladly he would free himself, if possible, from the bond which held him, and which was growing daily more and more hateful to him.

As far as she could see them in the moonlight Beatrice watched Everard and Rossie as they walked slowly down the avenue which led to the street, and when they were out of sight she said to herself: "He ought to acknowledge his marriage, and he must, even if he does not take his wife, which might be the better thing to do. There must be good in her,—something to build upon, if under the right influence, with somebody to encourage and stimulate her to do her best. I wish I knew her,—wish I dared face her in her own home, and judge what kind of person she is."

This was Bee's thought the night before she read Mrs. Morton's letter inviting her to Bronson, and when she read it the thought resolved itself into a fixed purpose, the first step of which was to take Trixey to her mother. Poor little Trixey, who turned so white, but did not at first shed a tear, when told of her baby brother's death. Half an hour later, however, Beatrice found her in the garden, with her face in the grass, sobbing as if her heart would break for the dead brother, of whom she said to Bee, "I wouldn't feel so bad to have him with Jesus, only I shaked him once hard, when he was so cross and heavy, and I was so tired, and he wouldn't go to sleep. I'se so sorry. Will God let me go to Heaven some day and see him, and tell him I'se sorry?"

As well as she could, Beatrice comforted and reassured the weeping child, whose conscientiousness and sweet faith and trust in God were leading her into ways she had only known in theory, but which were beginning to be very pleasant to her feet, as she learned each day some new lesson from the trusting child.

It was near the latter part of June, the season of roses, and pinks, and water lilies in New England, when she at last took Trixey to the old brown house under the shadow of the apple trees, where the mountain air was filled with perfume from the flowers blossoming on the borders by the door, and where Bunchie played in the soft summer sunshine under the snow-ball tree by the well. It was such a plain, but pleasant old house, with the rafters overhead showing in the kitchen, and the great box-like beams in the corners of the room,—for the old house claimed to have seen a hundred years, and to have heard the guns of the Revolution. But it was very cheerful and home-like, and neat as soap and sand and Aunt Nancy's hands could make it. Aunt Nancy was the first to welcome Miss Belknap, looking a little askance at her style and manners, and wondering how they could ever entertain so fine a lady even for a few hours. Mrs. Morton was sick with a headache, and Mrs. Brown was still down with nervous prostration, having stoutly resisted all Mrs. Julia Hayden's advice about making an effort, and hints which sometimes amounted to assertions that she could get up if she liked, and would diet on oatmeal and barley. In her last letter to Mrs. Morton, Beatrice had declined Mrs. Hayden's offer, and said she should feel more independent at the hotel for the short time she should remain in Bronson, but within half an hour after her arrival at the parsonage, Mrs. Hayden was there also, in her handsome carriage, drawn by her shining black horses, and driven by a shining black coachman, in gloves and brass buttons, and she insisted so hard upon Beatrice stopping with her, that the latter finally accepted the invitation, but said she would remain for the day where she was and see if she could not be of some comfort and help to Mrs. Morton, who seemed better from the moment she came and laid her soft hands on her head.

"Nothing can help her or her mother, either, unless they make an effort," Mrs. Hayden said, with a toss of her head, and a flash of her black eyes. "Spleeny and notional both of them as they can be; call it nervous, if you like; what's nervousness but fidgets? I was never nervous; but if I'd give up every time the weather changes, or I felt a little weak, I might have prostration, too. There's Harry, my husband, would have died long ago if I had not kept him up just by my own energy and will. I make him sleep with the windows open, and he takes a cold bath every morning at six o'clock, and eats oatmeal for his breakfast, with a cup of hot water instead of coffee or tea."

"And does he thrive on that diet? Is he well and strong?" Bee asked, and Mrs. Hayden replied:

"Well and strong? No: he could not be that in the nature of things, he comes from a sickly stock; but he keeps about, which is better than lying in bed and moping all the time."

How strong and full of life Mrs. Hayden was, and so unsympathetic that Beatrice did not wonder Mrs. Morton shivered and shrank away even from the touch of her large, powerful hands.

"I am sometimes wicked enough to wish she might be sick herself, or at least nervous, so as to know how it feels," Mrs. Morton said, after her cousin had gone. "She thinks I can do as she does, and the thing is impossible. My health is destroyed, and I sometimes fear I shall never be well again."

She had failed since Beatrice saw her, and her eyes looked so large and glassy as she lay upon the pillow, and her cough was so constant and irritating, that to talk of effort and oatmeal to her seemed preposterous and cruel. What she needed was rest, and nursing, and care, and change of thought and occupation, and these she could not have in their fullest extent at the parsonage, with poverty and a sick mother, and bustling, irritable Aunt Nancy to act as counter influences. She must be taken entirely away, and amused, and nursed, and petted, and Beatrice began to see the first step of that vague plan formed in Rothsay, and which she meant to carry out.

For a day or two she staid in Bronson, sleeping and eating in Mrs. Hayden's grand house, and feeling all her sympathies enlisted for shriveled-up Mr. Hayden, who in the morning came shivering to the table from his cold bath, and swallowed his oatmeal and hot water dutifully, but with an expression on his thin, sallow face which showed how his stomach rebelled against it and craved the juicy steak and fragrant coffee with which his blooming wife regaled herself, because she was strong and could bear it. Once Bee ventured to suggest that steak and beef-tea might be a more nutritious diet even for a dyspeptic than oatmeal and barley, varied with dry toast and baked apples; but Mrs. Hayden knew. She had read up on stomachs, and nerves, and digestion, and knew every symptom of dyspepsia, and its cause, and what it needed, and how a person ought to feel; and her husband submitted quietly, and said, "Julie was right," and grew thinner, and paler, and weaker every day with cold baths and starvation; but he kept the respect of his wife because he tried to be well, and that was a great thing to do, for in his estimation she was a wonderful woman, and represented the wisdom of the world.

On the third day Beatrice left Bronson, to look, she said, for some quiet, pleasant nook, where she could spend a few weeks during the hot weather. She found such a place in Holburton, whither she came one warm July afternoon, when the town was at its best. It was not an unheard-of thing for city people to pass a few weeks in Holburton during the hot weather, and no one was surprised when Miss Belknap registered her name on the hotel books, and said she was looking for some quiet and reasonable boarding-house for an invalid with two children. Several were recommended to her, and with the list in her hand she started out to reconnoiter.

Mrs. Roxie Fleming was the fourth name on her paper, but she went there first, and was pleased with the place at once, because it looked so cool and inviting under the wealth of hop vines which covered one side of it.

The day was warm, and Mrs. Fleming, in her clean purple calico gown, sat sewing on the door-steps, while a woman with a deep pasteboard bonnet on her head, concealing her face from view, was sweeping the grass in the back yard. But she turned as she heard the gate open, and seeing Beatrice, came forward until she saw her mother; then she withdrew, leaving Mrs. Fleming to confer with the stranger.

She had rooms to let, she said; did the lady wish them for herself? and she looked curiously at Beatrice, who was so different from the boarders who usually came to her, for her rooms were low and scantily furnished, and not at all like the apartments city people desired.

Miss Belknap wanted board for herself and a friend with two children; two sleeping-rooms and a parlor would do nicely for them all, and she was willing to pay whatever it was worth.

Mrs. Fleming readily guessed that money was no consideration with the lady, and as it was of much importance to her, she decided to ask the highest possible price at first, and then fall if necessary. After a moment, during which she seemed to be thinking, she said:

"I don't know but I can accommodate you with three rooms, though I do not often rent an extra parlor, and if I do so now my daughter Josephine must give up the room she occupies when she is here."

"Then she is not at home?" Beatrice said, feeling that she must know that fact before she engaged board, where the only attraction was Josephine who, she found, had only gone for a week or so to Oak Bluffs, with a party of friends, and was expected daily.

The price named for the three rooms, though high for Holburton, did not seem unreasonable to Beatrice, and the bargain was closed with the understanding that Beatrice was to take immediate possession.

"It will be a change for Mrs. Morton; a relief to Aunt Nancy; a possible benefit to Everard, and an amusement to me," Beatrice thought, as she hurried back to Bronson, where she found the Rev. Theodore himself, handsomer, more elegant in appearance, because better dressed, than when she saw him last, and very glad to see her, as an old friend who was kind to his wife and children.

To the Holburton plan he listened approvingly. It would do Mollie good, he said, for two sick people in one house were quite too many for the comfort of either. But Mollie demurred; she could not sleep in new places unless everything were right, and she presumed there were swarms of crickets and tree-toads, and possibly bull-frogs, there among the mountains, to make the night hideous.

It would be impossible to portray the scorn and disgust which blazed in the black eyes of Mrs. Julia Hayden, who was present, when Mollie uttered her protest against Holburton.

"Crickets, and tree-toads, and bull-frogs, indeed! She'd like to see the bull-frog which could keep her awake, even if it sat on her pillow and croaked in her ear; it was all nonsense, such fidgets. Just use your will and a little common sense, and you will sleep through everything."

This was Mrs. Hayden's theory, which made Mollie cry and Beatrice angry, and Theodore laugh. He had to stand between them all, and keep them from quarreling, and he did it admirably, and smoothed everything so nicely, and made the trip to Holburton seem so desirable, that Mollie began to want to go, especially as he assured her he could well afford it, as the church in Boston paid him liberally, and had just given him a hundred dollars to do with as he liked. Beatrice had intended to meet the expenses herself, but could not press the matter without hurting more than she did good. It was just possible that Mrs. Hayden might follow them with her husband, if good rooms and board could be found for her, for she had taken a great liking to Miss Belknap, who stood even higher in her estimation than Mrs. Sniffe, and whose acquaintance she readily saw would do her more real good in a social point of view. So it was finally arranged that Mollie and the children should go to Holburton for the summer, and word to that effect was forwarded to Mrs. Fleming, with instructions to have the rooms in readiness by the middle of July.

CHAPTER XXV

MRS. FLEMING'S BOARDERS

It was a lovely summer day when the party arrived at Holburton and were driven to the brown house on the common, where they found everything in readiness for them, and Mrs. Fleming and Agnes waiting to receive them. Josephine was not visible, for she had resolutely set her face against them.

She did not want a lot of women in the house any way, she said; they were a nuisance, and made as much again trouble as men. They were never satisfied with their board, were always in the kitchen washing out their pocket-handkerchiefs, heating flat-irons and making a muss generally. For her part, she liked to be free to do as she liked without the fear of being torn into shoestrings by some meddling, jealous old woman. If they must have boarders, take gentlemen; there were plenty who would be glad to come. She would rather have clerks, or even mechanics, than the fine lady they described and a sick woman with her brats, and blue as a whetstone undoubtedly, inasmuch as she was a missionary's wife. She'd be wanting family prayers and a blessing at the table, and be horrified to know there were two packs of cards in the house, and that they were used, too!

This was Josephine's opinion, but her mother had her way in spite of it, and went on with her preparations, while Josephine sulked, and declared her intention of avoiding them entirely, and never, in any way, coming in contact with them. Still, there was a consolation in the fact that the small room she was compelled to take was down stairs, and so far removed from the boarders that they would not know how late she was out on the street with admirers, of which she had several, or how long they staid with her after she came in. Josephine liked the kind of life she was leading at present. No lady in town dressed better than she did, and though she knew that people commented upon it, and wondered where she got the money, and hinted at things which no real modest woman would like to have laid to her charge, she did not care, so long as she knew it was all right, and that some day everything would be explained, and she stand acquitted before the world, which criticised her unmercifully, but because there was no tangible proof against her, noticed her just the same as if there were no breath of suspicion attaching to her name. She would be noticed, and if she saw signs of rebellion in any quarter she fought it down inch by inch and rode triumphantly over the opinions of those who tried to slight her. No young lady in town could boast as many admirers as she, and she managed to keep them at her side even after they found there was no hope. Old Captain Sparks, the millionaire, had long known this, and yet, as the moth flutters around the candle, so he hovered around the young beauty, accepting the position of father instead of brother, and from time to time presenting his daughter with costly presents, which she accepted so sweetly and prettily because she knew it would hurt him if she refused. To the other lovers she was sister and friend, and she gave them a great deal of good advice, and made them believe they were much safer with her than they would be elsewhere.

Only Dr. Matthewson knew her thoroughly, and him she never tried to deceive. And still, the doctor was more absolutely under her influence than any of the train who visited her constantly. But just now he was away on business, he called it, though Josephine knew that the business was gambling, that being his only means of livelihood. A fortunate play, or series of plays, had put a large sum of money into his hands, and he had gone on a sailing vessel to the West Indies, thinking to visit England before returning to America. Josephine was a little ennuyeed without the doctor, whom she preferred to any man living. And yet, could she have had him by giving up Everard she would not have done it, for though she had no love for her husband, she had a fancy for the money and position he could give her by and by, and for which she was patiently waiting. Had her life been less pleasant and exciting, or had Everard sent her less money, she might have rebelled against it, and taken steps which would have resulted in her learning the state of affairs at the Forrest House. But as it was she was content to wait and enjoy herself in her own way, which was to dress and flirt, and come and go at her pleasure, and be waited on at home as if she were some princess of the blood.

And this was about the state of affairs when Beatrice reached the Fleming house with Mrs. Morton, who, contrary to her expectations, was pleased at once.

"I do believe I shall rest here and get well again, everything is so comfortable," she said, as she lay down upon the chintz-covered lounge for a few moments before taking the cup of tea which was brought to her by Agnes, who, in her clean calico dress, with her dark hair combed smoothly back, and a sad but peaceful expression on her white, tired face, enlisted Beatrice's sympathies at once, for she saw from her manner that she was a mere household drudge, and resolved to stand her friend whatever might come.

Agnes was very fond of children, and when she had arranged the tray for Mrs. Morton, she turned to the little ones and tried to coax them to her side. Bunchie came at once, but Trixey held aloof, and, with her hands behind her, watched the woman curiously, and it would seem without a very complimentary verdict in her favor. Trixey was fond of bright, gay colors and elegant apparel. Beatrice's style suited her better than this faded, spiritless woman, whom she, nevertheless, regarded very intently, and at last startled with the question:

"How did you look when you were new?"

"Oh, Trixey!" Mrs. Morton and Beatrice both exclaimed, in a breath, fearing lest Agnes' feelings should be hurt, but she only laughed a hearty, merry laugh, which changed her face completely, and made it almost young and pretty, as she said:

"I don't know how I looked, it was so very long ago; but I love little girls like you, and my old black hands have made them so many pies and cakes, and paper dollies, and they shall make some for you, if you'll let me kiss you."

Trixey was won by this, and when Agnes went back to the kitchen she was followed by both the children, who were intent upon the little cakes she had made that morning in expectation of their coming.

Josephine had watched the arrival of the ladies through the half-closed shutters, deciding that Mrs. Morton was a dowdy country woman, and that Miss Belknap was very elegant even in her plain traveling dress, and that, perhaps, she was somebody whom it would be policy to cultivate. But she would not present herself that afternoon; she was tired, and wished to keep herself fresh for evening, when she expected a call from a young man from Albany, whose mother had taken rooms at the hotel for the summer, and whom she had met at a picnic the day before.

The next day was Sunday, and though breakfast was served later than usual, Josephine was later still, and the meal was nearly half over when she entered the room, attired in a blue cambric gown, with gold pendants in her ears, and a bit of honeysuckle at her throat. There was a very sweet, apologetic expression on her face as she went up to her mother and kissed her good morning, saying, coaxingly:

"Late again, as usual, mamma, but you must excuse me. I was so sleepy;" then, with a graceful recognition of the strangers, she took her seat at the table by the side of Trixey, whom she patted on the head, saying: "And how is the little girl, this morning?"

Mrs. Fleming was accustomed to all manner of moods and freaks in her daughter, but the kissing was something new, and surprised her a little, especially as there were no gentlemen present to witness the pretty, childish scene. She passed it off, however, naturally enough, and introducing her daughter to the ladies went on serving the breakfast. Agnes waited upon the table, and so there was no kiss for her, only a gracious nod and a "good morning, sister," as if this was their first meeting, when, in fact, Agnes had been in and out of Josephine's room three or four times, carrying hot water, and towels, and soap. But Agnes was accustomed to such things and made no sign, except as a slight flush passed across her pale face, which was unobserved by Beatrice, who was giving all her attention to the young beauty, sipping her coffee so leisurely, and saying pretty things to Trixey.

How beautiful she was, with those great dreamy blue eyes, those delicately chiseled features, and that dazzling complexion, which Bee thought at first must be artificial, it was so pure, and white, and smooth. But she was mistaken, for Josephine's complexion had never known powder or paste, or wash of any kind. It was very brilliant and fresh, and she looked so young, and innocent, and child-like that Beatrice found it hard to believe there was aught of guile or deceit in her. Everard must have become morbidly sensitive to any faults she might have, and Bee's thoughts were at once busy with what she meant to do for this estranged couple. There must be much of good in her. Surely that face and those eyes, which looked so confidingly at you, could not cover a bad heart. Weak, and vain, and faulty she might be, but not bad; not treacherous and unwomanly, as Everard believed, and Beatrice was so glad she had come there to see and judge for herself. Every action was perfectly lady-like, every movement graceful, while the voice was soft and low, and well-bred in its tone; and during the few moments they talked together after breakfast, Beatrice felt herself fascinated as she had never been before by any human being. As she was tired, and had a slight headache, she did not go to church that morning, but saw Josephine leave the house, and watched her out of sight with feelings of wonder and perplexity. Could this be the woman whom Everard regarded with so much disgust? the Joe Fleming whom she had thought so detestable? Nor was her wonder at all diminished when, that afternoon, she found Josephine in the garden, seated under a tree with Bunchie in her lap and Trixey at her side, listening intently while she told them the story of Moses in the bulrushes. They had heard it before, but it gained new power and interest when told in Josephine's dramatic way, and they hung on every word, and when it was done begged her for another. Surely, here was more of the angel than the fiend, and Beatrice, too, sat down, charmed in spite of herself with the girl she had expected to despise.

"She must be good, and Everard is surely mistaken," she thought, and her admiration was at its height when Josephine finished her stories and began to talk to her. Mrs. Fleming had received an impression that Miss Belknap was from New York, and Josephine began to question her of that city, asking if she had always lived there.

"I was born there," Beatrice replied, "but I was educated in Paris, and my home is really in Rothsay, a little town in southern Ohio."

At the mention of Rothsay Josephine started, and there was an increase of color in her face, but otherwise she was very calm, and her voice was perfectly natural as she repeated the word Rothsay, evidently trying to recall something connected with that place. At last she succeeded, and said, "Rothsay—Rothsay, in Ohio. Why, that is where Mr. Forrest lives. Mr. J. Everard Forrest, Jr. He boarded with mamma two or three years ago. He was in college at Amherst. Probably you know him," and the blue eyes looked very innocently at Beatrice, who, warned by the perfect acting to be cautious and guarded, replied, "Oh, yes, I know Everard Forrest. His mother was a distant relative of mine. She is dead. Did you know?"

"I think I heard so. Everard was very fond of his mother," Josephine said; then, after a pause she added, "Judge Forrest is very wealthy, and very aristocratic, isn't he?"

"He was always called so, and the Forrest property is said to be immense," Beatrice replied, quieting her conscience with the fact that, so far as the judge was concerned, she had put him in the past tense, and spoken of what he was once rather than of what he was at present, but Josephine paid no attention to tenses, and had no suspicion whatever of the truth.

She was really a good deal startled and shaken, mentally, notwithstanding the calmness of her demeanor. Here was a person from Rothsay who knew Everard Forrest, and who might be of great service to her in the future, and it behooved her to be on her best behavior.

"Is Everard married yet?" she asked after a moment.

"Married?" Beatrice repeated, and she felt the color rising in her face. "Why, he has not his profession yet, but is studying very hard in his father's office."

"Ah, yes, I remember, he intended to be a lawyer. I liked him very much, he was so pleasant and gentlemanly," Josephine said, and there was a drooping of the heavy lashes over her blue eyes, as if with regret for the past, when she knew and liked Everard Forrest.

"But is there no one to whom he is particularly attentive?" she asked. "He used to be very fond of the girls, and there most be some one in Rothsay suitable for him, or is his father so proud that he would object to everybody?"

Beatrice knew perfectly well what Josephine meant, and answered that she had heard the judge was very particular, and would resent a marriage which he thought beneath his son, "but if the woman was good, and true, and pure, and did her best, I think it would all be well in time," she added, as an encouragement to this girl in whom she was trying to believe; and Josephine continued:

"He used to speak of a little girl, Rosamond, I think, was the name. She must be well grown by this time. Is she there now?"

"You mean Rossie Hastings, his adopted sister. Yes, she is there still, and a very nice, womanly little thing. She is sixteen, I believe, though she seems to me younger," Beatrice said, and the impression left on Josephine's mind of Rossie was of a child, in whom Everard could not be greatly interested except in a brotherly way.

She had made all the inquiries she cared to make just then, lest she should excite suspicion in Beatrice, and was meditating a retreat, when the sound of rapid wheels reached them, and a moment after a tall, slender young man, not over twenty, came down the walk flourishing his little cane and showing plainly the half-fledged boy, who was beginning to feel all the independence and superiority of a man. Bowing very low to Beatrice, to whom he was introduced as Mr. Gerard from Albany, he told Josephine he had come to ask her to drive after his fast horse. "You were at church all the morning, and deserve a little recreation," he said, as he saw signs of refusal in Josey, who, sure that Miss Belknap would not accept a like invitation felt that she, too, must refuse; so she said very sweetly and a little reprovingly:

"Thank you, Mr. Gerard, but I do not often ride on Sunday. Some other day I shall be happy to go with you, for I dote on fast horses, but now you must excuse me."

Young Gerard was surprised, for he had not expected to find conscientious scruples in the girl who the previous night, had played euchre with him until half-past eleven, and then stood another half hour at the gate, laughing and flirting with him, though she had met him but once before.

He was not accustomed to be thwarted, and he showed that he was annoyed, and answered loftily:

"Certainly, do as you think best. If you won't ride with me, I must find somebody who will. I wish you good-afternoon, ladies."

Touching his hat very politely he walked away; but Josephine could not let him go in this mood. He was her latest conquest, and she arose and followed him, and walked with him to the gate, and said to him apologetically:

"I want to go awfully, but it will never do with a missionary's family in the house."

"Bother take the missionaries," he said. "I wanted to show you how fast Dido can trot."

"Yes, I know; but there are other days than Sunday, and there are lots of girls aching to go with you to-day," Josephine said, as she fastened a little more securely the bouquet in his button-hole, and let her hands rest longer on his coat-sleeve than was necessary.

"But I shan't take 'em. I shall wait for you," he answered, quite soothed and mollified.

Then he bade her good-by, and drove off, while Josephine returned to Beatrice and said, laughingly:

"What bores boys of a certain age are, and how they always fasten upon a girl older than themselves! This Gerard cannot be over twenty. He reminds me a little in his dress of Everard Forrest when he first came here, so fastidious and elegant, as if he had just stepped from a bandbox."

"He is very different from that now," Beatrice replied, rousing up at once in Everard's defense. "Of course he can never look like anything but a gentleman, but he wears his coats and boots and hats until they are positively shabby. It would almost seem as if he were hoarding up money for some particular purpose, he is so careful about expense. He neither smokes, nor chews, nor drinks, and it is said of him that he has not a single bad habit; his wife, should he ever have one, ought to be very proud of him."

Beatrice was very eloquent and earnest in her praises of Everard, and watched closely the effect on Josephine. There certainly was a different, expression on her face as she listened to this high encomium on her husband, whose economies she well knew were practiced for her, and there was something like a throb of gratitude or affection in her heart when she heard that the money she had supposed was given him by his father was earned or saved by himself, that she might be daintily clothed.

"I am delighted with this good account of him, and so will mamma be," she said; "he must have changed so much, for he was very extravagant and reckless when we knew him, but I liked him exceedingly."

Again there was the sound of wheels stopping before the gate, and excusing herself, Josephine hurried away to meet the second gallant who had come to take her to ride. Of course she could not go, and so the young man staid with her, and Walter Gerard drove back that way, and seeing her in the parlor tied his horse to the fence and came sauntering in with the air of one sure of a welcome.

Josephine did not appear at the tea-table, but Beatrice saw Agnes taking a tray into the parlor, and knew the trio were served in there, and felt greatly shocked and disgusted when she heard the clock strike twelve before the sound of suppressed voices and laughter ceased in the parlor, and the two buggies were driven rapidly away.

CHAPTER XXVI

JOSEPHINE'S CONFIDENCE

The next day Josephine wrote Everard the first real letter she had sent him for many weeks. Heretofore she had merely acknowledged his drafts made payable to her mother, but now she filled an entire sheet, and called him her dear husband, and told him of Miss Belknap's presence in the house, and what she had said of his habits and strict economy.

"I know it is all for me," she wrote, "and I felt like crying when she was talking about you. I am so glad she told me, for it has made me resolve to be worthy of you and the position I am one day to fill as your wife. When will that be, Everard? Must we wait forever? Sometimes I get desperate, and am tempted to start at once for Rothsay, and, facing your father, tell him the truth, and brave the storm which I suppose would follow. But then I know you would be angry at such a proceeding, and so I give it up, and go on waiting patiently, for I do wish to please you, and am glad this Miss Belknap is here, as I am sure of her friendship when the time of trial comes. She is very sweet and lovely, and I wonder you did not prefer her to your unworthy but loving Josey."

Beatrice also wrote to Everard that day, and told him where she was, and why, and said of Josephine, "there must be good in her, or she could not seem so sweet, and amiable, and affectionate. A little vain she may be, and fond of attention, and why not? She cannot look in the glass and not know how beautiful she is. And her voice is so soft, and low, and musical, and her manners so lady-like. You see I am more than half in love with her, and I am quite disposed to advise a recognition on your part of her claim upon you. Of course I shall not betray you. That is not my business here. I came to see what this girl is, whose life is joined with yours. I find her quite up to the average of women, and think it your safer course to acknowledge her, and not leave her subject to the temptations which must necessarily beset a pretty woman like her, in the shape of admiration and attention from every marriageable man in town. It is your safer way, Everard, for remember there is a bar between you and any other face which may look to you inexpressibly fair and sweet, and all the sweeter and fairer because possession is impossible."

These letters reached Everard the same evening, and he found them in his office on his return from the Forrest House, where he had sat with Rossie an hour on the piazza, with the moonlight falling on her face and softening the brilliancy of her great black eyes. How beautiful those eyes were to him now, and how modestly and confidingly they looked up occasionally in his face, and drooped beneath the long lashes which rested on the fair cheeks. She was so sweet and loving, this pure, fresh young girl; and her face and eyes haunted Everard all the way down the avenue and the long street to his office, where he found his letters,—one from Beatrice, one from Josephine, and this last he saw first, recoiling from it as from a serpent's touch, and remembering with a bitter pain the face seen in the moonlight, and the pressure of the hand he had held in his at parting. Then he took Bee's letter, and turned it over, and saw it was postmarked at Holburton, and with a start of fear and apprehension tore it open and read it eagerly.

"But I shall never do it," he said, as he read Bee's advice with regard to recognizing Josephine. "The goodness is not there; and so Bee will discover if she stops there long enough."

Then, as he finished her letter, he felt as if all the blood in his body were rushing to his head, for he guessed what she meant by "that other face, so inexpressibly fair and sweet." It was Rossie's, and he ground his teeth together as he thought of the bar which made it sinful for him to look too often upon that face, fast budding into rare beauty, lest he should find it too sweet and fair for his own peace of mind. And then he told himself that Rosamond was only his sister; his ward, in whom he must necessarily have an unusual interest. Beatrice was too fastidious, and did not trust enough to his good sense. He was not in love with Rosamond, nor in danger of becoming so.

Thus the young man reasoned, while he tore Josey's letter into shreds, which he tossed into the waste-basket. He did not believe in her or intend to answer it, for whenever he thought of her now it was as he saw her last, at midnight in the car, sleeping on Dr. Matthewson's arm. He wrote to Beatrice, however, within a few days, expressing his surprise at what she had done,—and telling her that any interference between Josephine and himself was useless, and that if she staid long in Holburton she would probably change her mind with regard to the young lady.

And in this he was right, for before his letter reached Holburton, Beatrice and Mrs. Morton both had learned that the voice, so soft and flute-like and well-bred when it addressed themselves, had another ring when alone in the kitchen with Agnes, who drudged from morning till night, that the unusually large household might be kept up. There were more boarders now in the house, for Mrs. Julia Hayden and husband had come to Holburton, hoping a change would benefit Mr. Hayden, who liked the quiet, pleasant town, and the pure air from the hills, which was not quite so bracing as that which blew down from the mountains around Bronson. The Haydens occupied the parlor below, greatly to the annoyance of Miss Josey, who was thus compelled to receive her numerous calls either in the dining-room or on the back piazza, or on the horse-block near the gate.

It was not unusual for Josey to receive three admirers at a time, and she managed so admirably that she kept them all amiable and civil, though each hated the other cordially, and wondered why he would persist in coming where he was not wanted. Night after night Mrs. Morton and Mr. Hayden were kept awake till after midnight by the low hum of voices and occasional bursts of suppressed laughter which came from the vicinity of the horse-block, and when Mrs. Morton complained of it in the presence of Josephine, that young lady was very sorry, and presumed it was some of the hired girls in town, who had a great way of hanging over gates with their lovers, and sitting upon horse-blocks into all hours of the night.

But Mrs. Julia was not deceived. Her great black eyes read the girl aright, and when she saw a female figure steal cautiously up the walk into the house, and heard the footsteps of two or three individuals going down the road, she guessed who the "hired girls" were, and Josephine suspected that she did, and removed her trysting-place from the horse-block to the rear of the garden, where she was out of ear-shot of the "old muffs," as she styled Mrs. Morton and Mrs. Hayden. And here she received her friends, as she called them,—and laughed, and flirted, and played with them, but was very careful not to overstep certain bounds of propriety, and thus give Everard an excuse on which to base an action for divorce, should he ever bring himself to consider such an act, which she doubted. He was too proud for that, and would rather live with and dislike her, than repudiate her openly, and bring a stain upon the Forrest name. It was impossible for her to understand his real feelings toward her. Indifferent he was, of course, and sorry, no doubt, for the tie which bound them; but she was so thoroughly convinced of her own charms and power to fascinate, that she had little fear of winning him back to something like allegiance when she once had him under her influence again. He could not resist her; no man could, except the old judge; and secure in this belief she went on her way, while Beatrice watched her narrowly, and began at last to believe there was no real good in her.

"The most shameless flirt I ever saw, with claws like a cat," Mrs. Hayden said of her,—"why, she has actually tried her power on Harry, and asked him so insinuatingly and pityingly if he really thought oatmeal agreed with him as well as a juicy steak or mutton-chop."

Bee laughed merrily at the idea of Josey's casting her eyes upon poor, shriveled, dyspeptic Harry Hayden, whom, to do her justice, she did pity, for the cold baths he was compelled to take every morning, and the rigid diet on which he was kept. That he lacked brain force, as his wife asserted, she did not doubt, or he would never have submitted as meekly as he did, with the stereotyped phrase, "Julie knows best," but she pitied him just the same, and occasionally conveyed to him on the sly hot cups of beef-tea or mutton-broth, and once coaxed him to drink lager-beer, but Mrs. Julia found it out by the culprit's breath, and disliked Josey worse than ever.

It was now five weeks since Beatrice first came to Holburton, and as Mrs. Morton did not seem to improve, she was thinking of finding another place for her, when Josephine came to her one morning as she was sitting alone with her work, and, taking a seat beside her, began to talk of herself and the life she was leading.

"I am of no use to any one," she said, "for both mother and Agnes are afraid I shall soil my hands or burn my face. I am tired of this kind of life. I want to see the world and have larger experiences; and fortunately I have an opportunity to do so. When I was at the sea-side I met a widow-lady, a Mrs. Arnold, who is rich and an invalid. She was kind enough to pretend to like me, and I think she did, for I have received a letter from her, asking me to go as a companion with her to Europe, she defraying all the expenses, of course, and leaving me nothing to do but to make myself agreeable to her, and enjoy what I see. Now, would you go or not?"

"I think I would," Beatrice replied, for it seemed to her as if this going to Europe would somehow be the severing link between Everard and Josephine. Something would happen to bring on the crisis which must come sooner or later.

"I would go, most certainly," she said again, and then she asked some questions concerning Mrs. Arnold, whose letter Josey showed to her. Evidently she was not a woman of great discernment or culture, but she was sincere in her wish to take Josephine abroad, and disposed to be very generous with her.

"She will be gone a year at least, and possibly two, and I can see so much in that time, I am quite dizzy with anticipation," Josephine said, while Beatrice entered heart and soul into the project, which was soon known to the entire household. That night young Gerard from Albany called on Josephine as usual, and hearing of the proposed trip to Europe offered himself to her, and cried like a baby when she gave him her final "no," and made him understand that she meant it. But she held his hand in hers, and there was one of her tears on his boyish face when at last he said good-night and walked away, somewhat soothed and comforted with the thought that he was to be her friend of friends, the one held as the dearest and best in her memory when she was far over the sea.

The news of the intended journey made Everard wild with delight, for, with the ocean between them, he felt that he should almost be free again; and he sent her a hundred dollars, and told her he hoped she would enjoy herself, and then, intoxicated with what seemed to him like his freedom, went up to see Rosamond, and staid with her until the clock was striking ten, and Mrs. Markham came into the room to break up the tete-a-tete.

It was the last day of August that the Nova Zembla sailed out of the harbor of Boston with Josephine on board, her fair hands waving kisses and adieux to the two men on the shore, watching her so intently,—young Gerard and old Captain Sparks, who had followed her to the very last, each vieing with the other in the size and cost of the bouquets, which filled one entire half of a table in the dining saloon, and stamped as somebody the beautiful girl who paraded them rather ostentatiously before her fellow-passengers.

For two days they adorned the table at which she sat, and filled the saloon with perfume, and were examined and talked about, and she was pointed out as that young lady who had so many large and elegant bouquets; and then, the third day out, when their beauty and perfume were gone, they were thrown overboard by the cabin-boy, and a great wave came and carried them far out to sea, while Josey lay in her berth limp, wretched and helpless, with no thought of flowers, or Gerard, or Captain Sparks, but with a feeling of genuine longing for the mother and Agnes, whose care and ministrations she missed so much in her miserable condition.

147

CHAPTER XXVII

EVENTS OF ONE YEAR AT
THE FORREST HOUSE

It was near the last of October when Bee returned to Rothsay, where Everard greeted her gladly as one who could understand, and sympathize with him. It had come to him at last like a shock that he loved Rosamond Hastings as he had never loved Josephine, even in the days of his wildest infatuation; and far different from that first feverish, unhealthy passion of his boyhood was this mightier love of his maturer manhood, which threatened at last to master him so completely that he determined at last to go away from Rothsay for a month, and, amid the wilds of California and the rocky dells of Oregon try to forget the girl whom to love was sin.

To Beatrice he confessed everything, and rebelled hotly against the bar which kept him from his love.

He had thought of divorce, he said. He could easily obtain one under the circumstances, but he was sure Rossie would never believe in any divorce which was not sanctioned by the Bible. He had assumed a case similar to his own, which he pretended was pending in the court, and warmly espousing the husband's cause, had asked Rosamond if she did not think it perfectly right for the man to marry again.

And she had answered decidedly:

"I should despise him and the woman who married him. I abominate these divorces so easily obtained. It is wicked, and God will never forgive it."

After this there was nothing for Everard to do but to take up his burden and carry it away with him to the Far West, hoping to leave it there. But he did not, and he came back to Rothsay to find Rossie sweeter, fairer than ever, and so unfeignedly glad to see him that for an hour he gave himself up to the happiness of the moment, and defying both right and wrong, said things which deepened the bloom on Rossie's cheeks, and brought to her eyes that new light which is so beautiful in its dawning, and which no one can mistake who is skilled in its signs.

He did not tell her he loved her; but he told her how he had missed her, and how she alone had brought him back sooner than he meant to come. And with a shyness which sat so prettily on her, and a drooping of the eyelids, she listened to him, and though she said but little the mischief was done, and never again would her eyes meet his as frankly and readily as before. Something in the tone of his voice and the unwonted tenderness of his manner kindled a fire in that young heart which many waters could not extinguish, and to Rossie it came with a thrill, half fearful, half ecstatic, that she loved Everard Forrest, not as a sister loves a brother or friend loves friend, but as a true, good woman loves the one who to her is the only man in all the world. But could she have followed him back to his room she would scarcely have known the white-faced, haggard man whom the dawn found with his head resting upon the table, where it had lain most of the night, while he fought the demon trying so hard to conquer him. He must not love Rosamond Hastings; he must not let her love him; and to prevent it he must tell her the whole truth, and this was what he was trying to make up his mind to do.

Possibly his resolution to confess the whole to Rosamond was in a measure prompted by a sudden fear which had come upon him lest the knowledge of his marriage should reach her through some other channel. On his return from Oregon, and before he went to the Forrest House, he had found several letters which had come during his absence, and which had not been forwarded. One was from Josephine, who was still abroad and perfectly happy, if her word was to be believed. She had found Mrs. Arnold everything that was kind, and generous, and considerate; had made many delightful acquaintances; had learned to speak both German and French, and had come across Dr. Matthewson, who was at the same hotel with herself, the Victoria, in Dresden.

This letter did not particularly affect Everard either way. Dresden was very far off, and Josephine might remain abroad another year, and into that time so much happiness might be crowded that he would take the good offered him, and not cross the river of difficulty until he fairly reached it. But on his return from the Forrest House he found two more letters on his desk, one postmarked at Dresden, the other at Holburton, and this he opened first. It was from Agnes, and had been sometime on the road, and told him that Mrs. Fleming had died suddenly, after an illness of two days only, and Agnes was left alone. There was still a mortgage on the house, she said, and after that was paid, and the few debts they were owing, there would be but little left for her, and this little she must, of course, divide with Josephine. She offered no complaint, nor asked for any help. She said she could take care of herself, either as housekeeper, cook, or nurse, and, on the whole, she seemed to be in a very resigned and cheerful state of mind for a person left so entirely alone. The other letter proved to be from a Cincinnati acquaintance, with whom he had once been at school, and who had recently married and gone abroad, and was in Dresden, at the Victoria Hotel, where, he said, there were many pleasant Americans, both from Boston and New York, and Everard felt morally sure that the pleasant people from Boston were Mrs. Arnold and Josephine. And his friend, Phil Evarts, was just the man to be attracted by Josey, even if he had a hundred wives, and Josephine was sure to meet him more than half-way, and find out first that he was from Cincinnati, and then that he had been in Rothsay, and knew Judge Forrest's family, and then,—a cold sweat broke out all over Everard's face as he thought, what then? while something whispered to him, "Then you will reap the fruit of the deception practiced so long, and you deserve it, too."

Everard knew he deserved it, but when one is reaping the whirlwind, I do not think it is any comfort to know that he has sowed the wind, or this harvest would never have been. It certainly did not help Everard, but rather added to the torments he endured as he thought of Josephine, enraged and infuriated, swooping down upon him, bristling all over with injured innocence, and making for herself a strong party, as she was sure to do. But worse than all would be the utter loss of Rossie, for she would be lost to him forever, and possibly turn against him for his duplicity, and that he could not bear.

"I'll tell her to-morrow, so help me Heaven!" he said, as he laid his throbbing head upon his writing-table and tried to think how he should commence, and what she would say.

He knew how she would look,—not scornfully and angrily upon him,—but so sorry, so disappointed, and that would hurt him worse than her contempt. How fair and sweet she seemed to him, as he went over all the past as connected with her, remembering, first, the quaint, old-fashioned child he had teased so unmercifully, and of whom he had made a very slave; then the girl of fifteen, whose honest eyes had looked straight into his without a shadow of shame or consciousness, as she asked to be his wife; and, lastly, the Rossie of to-day, the Rossie of long dresses and pure womanhood, who was so dear to him that to have had her for his own for one short, blessed year he felt that he would give the rest of his life. But that could not be. She could never be his, even were he free from the hated tie, as he could be so easily. In her single-heartedness and truth she would never recognize as valid any separation save that which death might make, and this he dared not wish for, lest to his other sins that of murder should be added. He must tell her, and she would forgive him, even while she banished him from her presence; but after she knew it, whose opinion was worth more to him than that of the whole world, he could bear whatever else might come. But how could he tell her? Verbally? and so see the surprise, and disappointment, and pain which would succeed each other so rapidly in those clear, innocent eyes which faithfully mirrored what she felt. He knew there would be pain, for as he loved her so he felt that she cared or could care for him, if only it were right for her to do so, and selfish as he was, it hurt him cruelly that she must suffer through his fault. But it must be, and, at last, concluding that he never could sit face to face with her while he confessed his secret, he decided to write it out and send it to her, and then wait a few days before going to see the effect. He made this resolve just as the autumnal morning shone full into his room, and he heard across the common the bell from his boarding-house summoning him to breakfast. But he could not eat, and after a vain effort at swallowing a little coffee, he went back to his office, where, to his utter amazement and discomfiture, he found Rosamond herself seated in his chair and smiling brightly upon him as he came in.

When he was with her the night before she had forgotten to speak to him of a certain matter of business which must be attended to that day, and immediately after breakfast, which was always early at the Forrest House, she had walked down to the office, and telling the boy in attendance that he need not wait until Mr. Forrest's return, she sent him to his breakfast, and was there alone when Everard came in.

"Oh, Rossie, Rossie," he gasped, as if the sight of her unnerved him entirely, "why did you come here this morning?"

She did not tell him why she came, for she forgot her errand entirely, in her alarm at his white, haggard face, and the strangeness of his manner.

"Oh, Mr. Everard!" she cried, for she called him "Mr. Everard" still, as she had done when a child. "You are sick. What is the matter? Sit down and let me do something for you. Are you faint, or what is it?" and, talking to him all the time, she made him sit down in the chair she vacated, and brought him some water, which he refused, and then, standing beside him, laid her soft, cool hand upon his forehead, and asked if the pain was there.

At the touch of those hands Everard felt that he was losing all his self-command. Except as he had held them a moment in his own when he met her, or said good-by, he had not felt those dainty fingers on his flesh since the weeks of his sickness after his mother's death, when Rossie had been his nurse, and smoothed his aching brow as she was doing now. Then her hands had a strange power to soothe and quiet him, but now they made him wild. He could not bear it, and, pushing her almost rudely from him, he exclaimed: "Don't, Rossie! I can't bear that you should touch me."

There were tears in Rossie's eyes at being so repulsed, and for an instant her cheeks grew scarlet with resentment, but before she could speak, overcome by an impulse he could not resist, Everard gathered her swiftly in his arms, and, kissing her passionately, said:

"Forgive me, Rossie. I did not mean to be rude, but why did you come here this morning to tempt me. I was going to write and tell you what I ought to have told you long ago, and the sight of you makes me such a coward. Rossie, my darling; I will call you so once, though it's wrong, it's wicked,—remember that. I am not what I seem. I have deceived you all these years since father died, and before, too,—long before. You cannot guess what a wretch I am."

It was a long time since Rossie had thought of Joe Fleming, with whom she believed Everard had broken altogether; but she remembered him now, and, at once attributing Everard's trouble to that source, she said, in her old, child-like way:

"It's Joe Fleming again, Mr. Everard, and I hoped you were done with him forever."

She was very pale, and her eyes had a startled look, for the sudden caress and the words "my darling," had shaken her nerves, and roused in her a tumult of joy and dread of she scarcely knew what; but she looked steadily at Everard, who answered her bitterly:

"Yes, it is Joe Fleming,—always Joe Fleming,—and I am going to tell you about it; but, Rossie, you must promise not to hate me, or I never can tell you. Bee knows and does not hate me. Do you promise, Rossie?"

"Yes, I promise, and I'll help you if I can," Rossie said, without the slightest suspicion of the nature of the trouble.

She never suspected anything. The shrewd, far-seeing ones, who scent evil from afar, would say of her that she was neither deep nor quick, and possibly she was not. Wholly guileless herself, she never looked for wrong until it was thrust in her face, and so was easily deceived by what seemed to be good. She certainly suspected no evil in Everard, and was anxious to hear the story which he would have told her had it not been for an interruption in the shape of Lawyer Russell, who came suddenly into the office, bringing with him a stranger who wished to consult with both the old lawyer and the young. That, of course, broke up the conference, and Rosamond was compelled to retire, thinking more of the hot kiss which she could still feel upon her forehead, and the words "my darling," as spoken by Everard, than of the story he had to tell.

And all that day she flitted about the house, warbling snatches of song, and occasionally repeating to herself "my darling," as Everard had said it to her. If indeed she were his darling, then nothing should separate them from each other. She did not care for his past misdeeds,—or for Joe Fleming. That was in the past. She believed in Everard as he was now, and loved him, too. She acknowledged that to herself, and her face burned with blushes as she did so. And, looking back over the past, she could not remember a time when she did not love him, or rather worship him, as the one hero in the world worthy of her worship. And now?—Rossie could not give expression to what she felt now, or analyze the great happiness dawning upon her, with the belief that as she loved Everard Forrest, so was she loved in return. She was very beautiful with this new light shining over her face, and very beautiful without it. It was now two years since she went unabashed to Everard and asked to be his wife. Then she was fifteen and a-half, and a mere child, so far as knowledge of the world was concerned, and in some respects she was a child still, though she was seventeen and had budded into a most lovely type of womanhood. Her features were not as regular as Bee's, nor her complexion as soft and waxen; but it was very fresh and bright and clear, and there was something inexpressibly sweet and attractive in her face and the expression of her eyes, while her rippling hair was wound in masses about her well-shaped head, adding somewhat to her apparent height and giving her a more womanly appearance than when she wore it loosely in her neck. If Rossie thought herself pretty, it was never apparent in her manner. Indeed, she never seemed to think of herself at all, though, as the day of which I am writing drew to a close, she did spend more time than usual at her toilet, and when it was finished felt tolerably satisfied with the image reflected by her mirror, and was sure that Everard would be suited, too. He would come that night, of course. There was nothing else for him to do after the events of the morning.

But Everard did not come, and about noon of the next day she received a few lines from him saying that a business matter, of which Lawyer Russell and the stranger with him were the harbingers, would take him for a week or more, to southern Indiana. He had not time to say good-by in person, but he would write to her from Dighton, and he hoped to find her well on his return.

That was all. Not an allusion to the confession he was going to make,—not a sign that he had held her for a moment in his arms and kissed her passionately, while he called her his darling. He was going away on business and would write to her. Nothing could be briefer or more informal, though he called her his dear Rossie. And Rossie, whose faith was not easily shaken, felt that she was dear to him even though he disappointed her. She would hold to that while he was absent, and though her face was not quite as bright and joyous as the night before, there was upon it an expression of happiness and content which made watchful Mrs. Markham think that, as she expressed it to herself, "something had happened."

CHAPTER XXVIII

SOMETHING DOES HAPPEN

It had rained all day in Dresden,—a steady, persistent rain, which kept the guests of the Hotel Victoria in-doors, and made them so tired, and uncomfortable, and restless that by night every shadow of reserve was swept away, and they were ready to talk to any one who would answer them in their own tongue. Conspicuous among the guests assembled in the parlor was Miss Fleming,—"Miss Josephine Fleming, Boston, U. S. A.," she was registered, and she passed for one of those Bostonians who, whether deservedly or not, get the reputation abroad of being very exclusive, and proud, and unapproachable. Just now this character suited Josephine, for she found that she was more talked about when she was reserved and dignified than when she was forward and flippant; so, though they had been at the Victoria some weeks, she had made but few acquaintances, and these among the English and the most aristocratic of the Americans. And Josephine had never been so beautiful as she was now. And she had the satisfaction of knowing that she was always the most attractive woman in every company, and the one most sought after. Of her poverty she made no secret, and did not try to conceal the fact that she was Mrs. Arnold's companion. But she had seen better days, of course, before papa died and left his affairs so involved that they lost everything, and mamma was compelled to take a few boarders to eke out their income.

This was her story, which took well when told by herself, with sweet pathos in her voice and a drooping of her long lashes over her lovely blue eyes. Every one of her acquaintances of any account in America had been stepping-stones in Europe, where she met people who knew the Gerards, and John Hayden, and Miss Belknap, who was her very heaviest card, the one she played most frequently, and with the best success. The New Yorkers all knew Beatrice, and were inclined to be very gracious to her friend. Occasionally she had come across some graduate from Amherst, whom she had met before, but never till the rainy day with which this chapter opens had she seen any one from the vicinity of Rothsay, or who knew her husband personally. She was in the habit of looking over the list of arrivals, and had seen the names of "Mr. and Mrs. Philip Evarts, Cincinnati, U. S. A.," and had readily singled out the new-comers at table d'hote, divining at once that the lady was a bride; but no words had passed between them until the evening of the rainy day; then Josephine entered the parlor faultlessly gotten up, and looking very sweet and lovely in her dark-blue silk and velvet jacket, with her golden hair caught up with an ivory comb. Nothing could be prettier than she was, and Phil Evarts, who, as Everard had said, was just the man to be attracted by such a woman as Josephine, and whose wife was sick with a headache in her room, managed to get near the beauty, who took a seat apart from the others, and met his advance with a swift glance of her dreamy eyes, which made his heart beat faster than a man's heart ought to beat when his wife is up stairs with the headache.

It was her business to speak first, and she said, very modestly:

"Excuse me, sir, but do you know if there has been a mail since lunch?"

"I don't," he replied, "but I will inquire. I am just going to the office. What name shall I ask for?"

She told him, and during the few minutes he was gone he found out who Miss Fleming from Boston was, and all about her that the English-speaking clerk knew. But there was no letter for her, for which he was very sorry. She was sorry, too; she did so want to hear from home and sister. She did not say mamma, for she knew her mother was dead, and had known it for a week, and kept it to herself until she could decide whether to wear black or not, and so shut herself out from any amusements they might have in Paris, where they were going next.

Naturally the two began to talk of America, and when Mr. Evarts spoke of Cincinnati as his home, she said:

"I have a friend who was once at school there. Everard Forrest, of Rothsay, do you know him?"

She had no idea that he did, and was astonished at the vehemence with which he responded:

"Ned Forrest, of Rothsay! Of course I know him. We were at school together. He's the best fellow in the world. And he is your friend, too?"

"Yes," Josey answered, beginning at once to calculate how much knowledge of Everard she would confess to. "I knew him when he was in college at Amherst. We lived in Holburton then, a little town over the line in New York, and he was sometimes there, but I have not seen him for a long time. I hope he is well."

"He was the last time I saw him, which was three or four months ago, perhaps more," Mr. Evarts replied. "He was in the city for a day, and I saw him just a moment. He is working like a dog; sticks to his business like a burr, which is so different from what I thought he'd do, and he so rich, too."

"Is he?" Josephine asked; and Evarts replied:

"Why, yes; his father must have been worth half a million, at least, and Ned got the whole, I suppose. There are no other heirs, unless something was given to that girl who lived in the family. Rosamond Hastings was the name, I think."

"Is his father dead?" Josephine asked; and in her voice there was a sharp ring which even stupid Phil Evarts detected and wondered at.

"Dead? Yes," he replied. "He has been dead I should say nearly, if not quite, two years."

Josephine was for a moment speechless. Never in her life had she received so great a shock. That Judge Forrest should have been dead two years and she in ignorance of it seemed impossible, and her first feeling after she began to rally a little was one of incredulity, and she asked:

"Are you not mistaken?"

"No, I'm not," Mr. Evarts replied. "I saw Everard in Covington a few weeks after his father's death, and talked to him of the sickness, which was apoplexy or something of that sort. Anyway, it was sudden, and Ned looked as if he hadn't a friend in the world. I did not suppose he cared so much for his father, who, I always thought, was a cross old tyrant. I used to visit at Forrest House occasionally years ago, when we were boys, but have not been there since the judge's death. Ned does not often come to Cincinnati, and as I have been gone most of the time for the last two years, I have heard but little of him."

"How long, did you say, has his father been dead?" Josephine asked; and Mr. Evarts replied:

"It must be two years in November, or thereabouts."

"And this Rosamond Hastings who lives there, how old is she, and is he going to marry her?" Josephine asked next; while Evarts thought to himself:

"Jealous, I do believe," but he answered her:

"Miss Hastings must be seventeen or eighteen, and when I saw her, five or six years ago, was not so very handsome."

"Yes, thank you," Josey said, and as she just then saw Mrs. Arnold coming into the salon, she bowed to her new acquaintance, and walked away, with such a tumult in her bosom as she had never before experienced.

It would take her a little time to recover herself and decide what to do. She must have leisure for reflection; and she took it that night in her room, and sat up the entire night thinking over the events of the last two years, as connected with Everard, and coming at last to the conclusion that he was a scoundrel, whom it was her duty as well as pleasure to punish by going to America at once and claiming him as her husband.

In the first days of her sudden bereavement, Agnes' kind heart had gone out with a great yearning for her young sister, to whom she had at once written of their mutual loss, saying how lonely she was, and how she hoped they would henceforth be more to each other than they ever had been. And Josephine had been touched and softened, and had written very kindly to Agnes, and had cried several times in secret for the dead mother she would never see again, but whose death she did not then see fit to announce to Mrs. Arnold; but she would do so now, and make it a pretext for going home at once. Nothing should keep her from wreaking swift vengeance on the man who had deliberately deceived her for two years, and who, she had no doubt, was faithless to her in feeling, if not in act. Of course there was a woman concerned in the matter, and that woman was probably Rossie Hastings, who, Mr. Evarts said, was still living at the

Forrest House, whither she meant to go in her own person as Mrs. J. E. Forrest, and so rout the enemy, and establish her own claims as a much-injured wife. She did not mean to be violent or harsh, only grieved, and hurt, and forgiving, and she had no doubt that in time she should be the most popular woman in Rothsay, not even excepting Beatrice, whose silence with regard to the judge's death she could not understand, inasmuch as she could have had no reason for keeping it a secret.

It may seem strange that as a friend of Everard's Phil Evarts had not heard of the judge's will, but for the last two or three years he had led a wandering kind of life, and spent most of his time in Rio Janeiro, and as Everard had never spoken of his affairs on the few occasions they had met since the judge's death, he was in total ignorance of the manner in which the judge had disposed of his property. Had he known it, and told Josephine, she might have acted differently, and hesitated a little before she gave up a situation of perfect ease and comparative luxury for the sake of a husband whom she did not love, and who had nothing for her support except his own earnings. But she did not know this, and she was eager to confront him and the jade, as she stigmatized Rosamond, and she packed some of her clothes that night that she might start at once.

Fortunately for her plans the next morning's mail from Paris brought her another letter from Agnes, who thought she might be anxious to know what she had decided to do, for the present, at least, until they could consult together. But Josephine cared very little what Agnes did. She was going to the Forrest House, and she was glad that Dr. Matthewson, who had been with her for a time at the hotel, had started for Italy only a few days before. He might have opposed her plan, and she knew from experience that it was hard to resist the influence he had over her. Utterly reckless and unprincipled, he seemed really to like this woman, whom he thoroughly understood, and in whose nature he recognized something which responded to his own. Two or three times he had talked openly to her of a divorce, and had hinted at a glorious life in Italy or wherever she chose to go. But Josephine was too shrewd to consider that for a moment. Dr. Matthewson lived only by his wits, or to put it in plainer terms, by gambling and speculation and intrigue. To-day he was rich, indulging in every possible luxury and extravagance, and to-morrow he was poor and unable to pay even his board; and much as she liked him she had no fancy to share his style of living. She preferred rather to be the hated wife of Everard Forrest and the mistress of his house; so she took Agnes's letter to Mrs. Arnold, and with a great show of feeling told her her mother was dead, and her sister Aggie left all alone, and wanting her so badly that she felt it her imperative duty to start at once for America.

"I am sorry, of course, to leave you," she said, "but you have so many acquaintances now, and your health is so much better, that you will do very nicely without me, I am sure, and I have long felt that my position was merely a sinecure. I am only an unnecessary expense."

Mrs. Arnold knew that to some extent this was true. Josephine was rather an expensive luxury, and she had more than once seen in her signs of selfishness and duplicity which shocked and displeased her. But the girl had been uniformly kind and attentive to her, and she was loth to part with her, and tried to persuade her to wait till spring. But Josephine was determined, and seeing this Mrs. Arnold ceased to oppose her, and generously gave her two hundred dollars for her expenses home; and Josephine took it, and smiled sweetly through her tears, and kissed her friend gushingly, and then hurried away to complete her preparations.

The next day she left Dresden for Paris, where she staid a week, while she selected a most becoming wardrobe in black, and was delighted to see what a pretty, appealing woman she was in her mourning, and how fair and pure her skin showed through her long crape vail, and how blue and pathetic her eyes looked, especially when she managed to bring a tear into them.

Of course she was noticed, and commented upon, and admired on shipboard, and when it was known why she was going home alone, and why she was in such deep mourning, she had everybody's sympathies, and was much sought after and petted.

She was certainly a very fair picture to contemplate, and the male portion of her fellow travelers indulged in that pastime often, and anticipated her every movement, and vied with each other in taking her chair to the most sheltered and comfortable place, and adjusting her wraps, and drawing her shawl a little closer around her neck, and helping her below whenever she was at all dizzy, as she frequently was; and when at last the Ville de Paris came into port, and she stood on shore, frightened, bewildered, and so much afraid of those dreadful custom-house officers, though she had nothing dutiable except a Madonna bought for mamma before she knew she was dead, at least ten gentlemen stood by her, reassuring her and promising to see her through, and succeeding so well that not one of her four big trunks was molested, and the captain himself helped her into the carriage which was to take her to the Harlem depot. With all the gallantry of a Frenchman he saw her comfortably adjusted, and squeezing her hand a little, lifted his hat politely, and wishing her bon voyage, left her to drive away toward the new life which was to be so different from the old.

CHAPTER XXIX

MRS. J. E. FORREST

Everard had been gone nearly two weeks instead of one, and Rosamond had not heard from him except through Mr. Russell, who told her that the business, which had reference to sundry infringements on patents and some missing deeds, was occupying him longer than he had supposed it would, as it required much research and a good deal of travel; "but he ought to be home now, very soon," he said to her one rainy morning in November, when he came to see her on business and found her sick in her room with a sore throat and severe cold. Rossie had been very lonely with both Everard and Beatrice away,—for the latter had been in New York since September, and at last accounts was on her way to Florida with Mollie Morton, who wished to try the effect of a milder climate than Vermont, and as Mr. Morton could not leave his church in Boston, which had now become a permanency, Bee had consented to accompany her, so Rossie was alone, and in a measure defenseless, on the afternoon when Mrs. Markham announced that the hack which ran to and from the depot had turned into the avenue and was coming to the house, and that it contained two ladies and at least three trunks, if not four.

"Ladies and trunks coming here?" Rossie exclaimed, starting up in bed and trying to listen to the voices, which were soon heard speaking together at the side door, where the hack had stopped.

But she could distinguish nothing, and Mrs. Markham went to ascertain who the strangers were. Half-way down the stairs she met old Aunt Axie, who held in her hand a black-bordered card on which was engraved the name, "Mrs. J. E. Forrest."

"The young lady done gin me this to fotch to Miss Hastings," Axie said, as she handed the card to Mrs. Markham, who twice repeated the name "Mrs. J. E. Forrest."

"Who can she be? Had the judge any near relatives?" she asked Axie, who replied:

"Not's I knows on. I never hearn tell of any J. E. Forrests, but Mars'r Everard."

"Where is the lady?" was Mrs. Markham's next question, and Axie replied:

"In the 'ception room, kind of shivrin' and shakin' as if she war cold. I reckon she's come to stay a spell, case the four big trunks is all in a pile in de side entry, and she acts as ef she think she belong here, for she ask sharp like, 'Ain't thar no fire you can take me to? I'm chilled through.'

"'Thar's a fire in Miss Rossie's room,' I said, 'but she's sick.'

"'Miss who?' she said, sharper still. 'Is it Miss Hastings you mean? Take her my card and say I'd like to see her if possible,' and that's every blessed thing I know 'bout 'em, only the old one looks queer and scart like, and nothin' in the house for dinner but a bit of bacon," and having told all she knew of the visitors, Axie went on her way to report the same to Rosamond, and confer with her about the dinner and the rooms the guests were to occupy, while Mrs. Markham went down to the reception-room to meet Mrs. J. E. Forrest.

Josephine had greatly surprised her sister by walking in upon her unannounced one morning a few days previously, and had still further astonished her by saying that Judge Forrest was dead, and that she had come home in order to go at once to Rothsay and her husband. She laid great stress on that word, and gave Agnes to understand that he had written to her of his father's death, and that it was at his request she had crossed the sea to join him.

"But won't he come here for you? Seems to me that would have a better look," Agnes said, and her sister replied:

"He is quite too busy to waste his time that way, for we can go alone; he knows I am accustomed to traveling. We will start at once, I am so anxious to be there. We can shut up the house for the present, until matters are adjusted, when you or I can come back and see to the things."

Could Agnes have had her choice she would have preferred remaining where she was, for she dreaded change of any kind. But go she must, for her presence would add weight and respectability to Josephine, who was very kind to her, and made the leaving Holburton as easy as possible. To a few of her old friends Josephine told the secret of her marriage, showing her certificate, and saying, now her father-in-law was dead there was nothing in the way of publishing the marriage to the world, and that she was going to her husband.

Of course all Holburton was excited, some believing the story, others discrediting it, but all remembering the play and the mock marriage which had seemed so solemn and real. But Josephine was not popular, and few if any regrets were sent after her when she started for the Forrest House, which she reached on the chill November day, when everything was looking its very worst.

Even the grounds had a bare, gray look, but they were very spacious and large, and Josephine felt a throb of pride as she rode up the avenue, looking eagerly out at the great, square, old-fashioned building, which, though massive, and stately, and pretentious, was not quite what she had expected to find. There was about it a shut-up, deserted air, which made her ask the hackman if there was any one at home, or why the blinds were all closed except in the wing.

The hackman was a negro who had once been in Judge Forrest's employ, and he replied:

"Miss Rossie's dar whar you see de shutters open, but de rest she keep closed sense old marster died."

There was something like a flash of indignation in Josephine's eyes as she thought how soon she would change the administration of the household, and make Miss Rossie know her place.

They had reached the side entrance by this time, and Josephine waited in her seat an instant in the hope that her truant lord might come himself to see who his visitors were. In that case she meant to be forgiving, and put her arms around his neck, and kiss him, and whisper in his ear: "I know everything, but I come in peace, not in war. Let us be friends, and do you leave the explanation to me."

She had decided upon this plan since leaving Holburton, for the nearer she drew to Rothsay the more she began to dread and fear the man who she knew had outlived all love and respect for her. But only Aunt Axie's broad, black face looked out into the rain, and beamed a smile on Luke, the driver, who was a distant relative.

Springing lightly from the carriage Josey ran up the steps into the hall, where she stood while Agnes joined her, and Luke deposited the heavy trunks and claimed his customary fee, and a little more on the plea of "so many big boxes to tote."

But Josephine refused him sharply, and then followed Aunt Axie into the cold reception-room, where no fire had been made that day, for Rossie had never abandoned her determination to use as little as possible of the Forrest money, and nothing superfluous was expended either in fuel, or eatables, or dress. So far as her own income,—a matter of one hundred and forty dollars or thereabouts,—was concerned, she was very generous and free; but when it came to Everard's money, as she called it, her economies were almost painful at times, and wrung many a remonstrance from old Axie, the cook.

With a shiver and a quick, curious glance around the cheerless room, Josephine turned to Aunt Axie and said:

"Is Mr. Forrest at home,—Mr. Everard Forrest?"

"No, miss. He done went away quite a spell ago, but Miss Rossie's 'spectin' him every day. He don't live here, though, when he's home; he stay mostly in de town."

Josephine did not understand her, and continued:

"He will come here, I suppose, as soon as he returns?"

"Yes, miss, he's sure to do dat," and Axie nodded knowingly.

Of course, she had no suspicion who this lady was, walking about the room and examining the furniture with a critical and not favorable eye, and asking, at last, if there was no fire where she could warm herself after her cold ride?

On being told there was a fire in Miss Rossie's room, she took from her purse one of the cards she had had engraved in Paris, and bidding Axie take it to Miss Hastings, sat down to await the result. To Agnes she said, in something of her old, dictatorial tone:

"Pray, don't look so nervous and frightened, as if we were a pair of burglars. It is my husband's house, and I have a right here."

"Yes, I know," faltered Agnes; "but it looks as if they did not expect you,—as if he did not know you were coming, or he would have been home, and it's all so dreary; I wish I was back in Holburton," and poor, homesick Agnes began to cry softly.

But Josephine bade her keep quiet.

"You let me do the talking," she said. "You need not speak, or if you have to you must assent to what you hear me say, even if it is not all quite true."

Josephine had expected Rosamond herself, and had taken a very pretty attitude, and even laid off her hat so as to show her golden hair, which, in the dampness, was one mass of waves and curls and little rings about her forehead. She meant to astonish and dazzle the girl whom she suspected as her rival, and who she imagined to be plain and unprepossessing, and when she heard a step outside she drew herself up a little, but had no intention of rising. She should assert her superiority at once, and sit while she received Miss Hastings rather than be received by her. How then was she disappointed and chagrined when, instead of Rossie, there appeared on the threshold a middle-aged woman, who showed that she was every whit a lady, and whose manner, as she bowed to the blonde beauty, brought her to her feet immediately.

"Mrs. Forrest?" Mrs. Markham said, interrogatively, consulting the card she held, and then glancing at Josephine, who answered her:

"Yes, Mrs. J. E. Forrest. My husband, it seems, is not here to receive me and explain matters, for which I am very sorry."

Even then Mrs. Markham had no suspicion of the truth. The husband referred to was, of course, some distant relative, who was to have been there in advance of his wife, and she replied:

"No, there has been no gentleman here, but that does not matter, except as it may be awkward for you. Miss Hastings will make you very welcome, though she is sick to-day and in bed. Your husband is a relative of Mr. Everard Forrest, I presume."

"A relative! My husband is Mr. Everard Forrest," Josephine said. "We were married four years ago last summer, and at his request, I have kept it a secret ever since. But my sister," and she nodded toward Agnes, "saw me married, and I have my marriage certificate in my bag. Agnes, give me my satchel, please," and she turned again to Agnes, who knew now that they were there unexpected and unknown, and her face was very white as she brought the satchel for Josephine to open.

Mrs. Markham was confounded and incredulous, and she showed it in her face as she dropped into a chair and stared wonderingly at her visitor, who, from a little box fastened with lock and key, abstracted a paper which she handed her to read.

"I know just how I must seem to you," Josephine said. "You think me an adventuress, an impostor, but I am neither. I am Everard Forrest's lawful wife, as this certificate will show you."

Mrs. Markham did not reply, for she was reading that, at Holburton, New York, on the evening of the th of July, —, Mr. James E. Forrest, of Rothsay, Ohio, was united in matrimony to Miss Josephine Fleming, by the Rev. Mr. Matthewson. There could be no mistake apparently, unless this paper was a forgery and the woman a lunatic, and still Mrs. Markham could not believe it. She had a great respect and liking for Everard, and held him as a model young man, who would never stoop to deception like this, and then,—there was Rossie! and the kind-hearted woman felt a pang of pity and a throb of indignation as she thought how Rossie had been wronged and duped if this thing were true, and this woman confronting her so calmly and unflinchingly were really Everard's wife.

"I cannot believe it. I will not believe it," she thought; and as composedly as it was possible for her to do, she said:

"This is a strange story you tell me, and if it is true it bears very heavily against Mr. Forrest, who has never been suspected of being a married man."

"I knew it; I guessed as much. Oh, Josey, why did you come before he sent for you? Let's go away. You are not wanted here!" Agnes exclaimed, as she came swiftly to her sister's side and laid her hand on her arm.

But Josephine shook it off fiercely, and in a tone she knew so well how to assume, said commandingly, as if speaking to a child:

"Mind your business, Agnes, and let me attend to my own affairs. I have kept quiet long enough; four years of neglect would try the patience of any woman, and if he does not choose to recognize me as his wife I shall compel him to do so. You saw me married; you know I am telling the truth. Speak, Agnes, did you not see me married to Everard Forrest?"

"Yes, I did, may God forgive me," was Agnes' meek reply, but still Mrs. Markham could not believe her, and was silent while Josephine went on:

"I do not wish for any scene, or talk, or excitement. I am Everard Forrest's wife, and I wish only to be known as such. I hoped to find him here, for then it would be his duty to explain, not mine. Do I understand he is not in town, or not at home? Possibly he is in his office, in which case I will seek him there."

"He is not in town," Mrs. Markham said; "he went to Indiana on business more than a week ago, and has not yet returned. He does not live here when he is at home; he boards in the village. Miss Hastings lives here; this is her house; perhaps you do not know that Judge Forrest died, and—"

"Yes, I do," Josephine interrupted her, beginning to get irritated and lose her self-command as she saw that she was not believed, "I do know Judge Forrest is dead, and has been for two years or more; but I learned it accidentally, and as he was the only obstacle in the way of my recognition as Everard's wife, I came at once, as I had a right, to my husband's house."

"But this is not his house," Mrs. Markham replied. "It belongs to Miss Hastings. Everything belongs to her. Judge Forrest left it to her by will. Didn't you know that?"

"No, I did not," Josephine answered, and for a moment she turned deathly white as she saw the ground slipping from under her feet. "Left everything to Miss Hastings and disinherited his son! Why was that?" she asked.

"I don't know why he did it," Mrs. Markham replied, "I know only that he did, and it is strange Mr. Forrest did not write that to you, as you must, of course, have been in correspondence with him."

She spoke sarcastically, and Josephine knew she was looked upon with distrust, notwithstanding the certificate, which she had thought would silence all doubt; and that, added to what she had heard of the disposition of the Forrest property, provoked her to wrath, and her eyes, usually so dreamy and blue, emitted sparks of anger, and seemed to turn a kind of whitish gray as she burst out:

"My correspondence with my husband has not been very frequent or full. I told you I did not hear from him of his father's death; he never hinted at such a thing, and how was I to know that he was disinherited? If I had it might have made a difference, and I should have thought twice before crossing the sea and giving up a life I enjoyed, for the sake of coming here to find myself suspected as an impostor, which, under the circumstances, is natural perhaps, and to find also that my husband is a pauper, and the home I had confidently expected would one day be mine given to a stranger."

Josephine was almost crying when she finished this imprudent speech, in which she betrayed that all she really cared for was the home and the money which she had expected to find. Mrs. Markham saw this, and it did not tend to increase her respect for the lady, though she did pity her, if, as she affirmed, she were really Everard's wife, for with her knowledge of human nature, she guessed that if there really had been a marriage it was a hasty thing, repented of almost as soon as done, by Everard at least. But she did not know what to say until Josephine, who had recovered herself, continued: "I should like to see Miss Hastings, if possible, and apologize for my intrusion into her house, and then I will go to the hotel and await my husband's return;" then she answered quickly; "Miss Hastings, I am sure, will say you are welcome to remain here as long as you like, but I do not think she will see you to-day, and if you will excuse me, I will go to her now, as she must be anxious to know who her visitors are."

With this Mrs. Markham arose, and bowing to Josephine left the room, and went directly to Rosamond.

CHAPTER XXX

HOW ROSSIE BORE THE NEWS

She did not bear it well at all, although she was in some degree prepared for it by the card which Axie brought her.

"Mrs. J. E. Forrest,—Mrs. J. E. Forrest," she repeated as she examined the card, while something undefinable, like the shadow of coming evil, began to stir her heart. "Who can she be, and where did she come from? You say she has a maid?"

"Yes, or suffin' like dat,—a quar-lookin' woman, who has a lame hand. I noticed the way she slung the lady's satchel over it, and it hung slimpsey like."

"How does the lady look, and what did she say? Tell me everything," Rosamond said; and Axie, who began to have a suspicion that the lady was not altogether welcome, replied:

"She done squabble fust thing wid the driver, who ax more for fetchin' and liftin' her four big trunks, an' she hold up her gown and walk as ef the groun' wasn't good enough for her, an' she looked round de room kind o' sniffin' like, wid her nose turned up a bit as she axed me was thar no fire. But my, she be very hansom' and no mistake. All in black, with such nice skin and pretty eyes, wid dem great long lashes, like Miss Beatrice."

Rossie could deny herself everything, but she was never indifferent to the comfort of others, and though she could not help feeling that this woman, who called herself Mrs. J. E. Forrest, would in some way work her harm, she could understand just how cold and cheerless the house must seem to her on that rainy day; and she ordered Axie to build fires in both the rooms below, as well as in the chamber where Everard occasionally spent a night, and which was the only guest-room she kept in order. There was also a consultation on the important subject of dinner, and then Rossie was left alone for a few moments to puzzle her brain as to who this woman could be, and wonder why her heart should feel so like lead, and her pulse beat so rapidly. She did not have long to wait for a solution of the mystery before Mrs. Markham came in, showing at once that she was agitated and distressed.

"What is it, Mrs. Markham? Is she any relation to Mr. Everard?" Rossie asked eagerly.

It would be wrong to keep her in suspense a moment longer than was necessary, and going up to her, Mrs. Markham replied:

"She says she is Everard's wife; and I have seen the certificate. They were married more than four years ago, before his mother died, and she,— oh, Rossie, my child, my child, don't give way like that; it may—it must be false," she added, in alarm, as she saw the death-like pallor which spread over Rossie's face, and the look of bitter pain and horror which leaped into her eyes, while the quivering lips whispered:

"Everard's wife? No, no, no!"

"Don't, Rossie,—don't!" Mrs. Markham said again, as she passed her arm around the girl, whose head drooped upon her shoulder, in a hopeless kind of way, and who said: "You saw the certificate? What was the name? Was it——"

"Fleming,—Josephine Fleming, of Holburton," Mrs. Markham replied, and with a shiver Rossie drew herself away from Mrs. Markham's arms, and turning her face to the wall, said: "Yes, I know. I understand it all. She is his wife. She is Joe Fleming."

After that she neither spoke nor moved, and when Mrs. Markham, alarmed at her silence, bent down to look at her, she found that she had fainted. The shock had proved too great for Rossie, whose mind, at the mention of Josephine Fleming, had with lightning rapidity gathered all the tangled threads of the past, and comprehended what had been so mysterious at times in Everard's behavior. He was married,—hastily, no doubt, but still married; and Joe Fleming was his wife, and he had never told her, but suffered her to believe that he loved her, just as she knew now that she loved him. It was a bitter humiliation, and for an instant there gathered round her so thick a horror and blackness that she fancied herself dying; but it was only a faint, and she lay so white and rigid that Mrs. Markham summoned Aunt Axie from the dining-room, where she was making preparations for kindling a fire in the grate.

"Be quiet," Mrs. Markham said to her as she came up the stairs. "Miss Rossie has fainted, but don't let those people know it; and bring me some hot water for her feet, quick."

Axie obeyed, wondering to herself why her young mistress should faint, when she never knew her to do such a thing before, and with her ready wit connecting it in some way with the strangers whom Mrs. Markham had designated as "those people," and whom the old negress directly set down as "no 'count folks."

It was some time before Rossie came back to consciousness, and when she did her first words were:

"Where is she? Where is Everard's wife? Don't let her come in here; I could not bear it now."

"Everard's wife! Mars'r Everard's wife!" Axie repeated, tossing her turbaned head and rolling up her eyes in astonishment. "In de deah Lord's name, what do de chile mean? Dat ain't Mars'r Everard's wife?" and she turned to Mrs. Markham, who, now that Rossie had betrayed what she would have kept until Everard came to confirm or deny the tale, replied:

"She says she is; but we must wait until Mr. Forrest comes before we admit it. So don't go talking outside."

"Catch me talkin'," was Axie's rejoinder. "It's a lie. Mars'r Everard hain't got no wife. I should of knowed it if he had. Don't you b'lieve it, honey," and she laid her hard black hand caressingly on the head of the girl whom she had long since singled out as Everard's future wife, watching shrewdly the growing intimacy between the two young people, and knowing better than they did just when the so-called brother merged into the lover, and she would not for a moment believe in another wife, and a secret one at that. "No, honey," she continued, "don't you b'lieve it. Mars'r Everard hain't got no wife, and never will have, but you."

"Yes, Aunt Axie," Rossie said, "this woman tells the truth. She is his wife, and Everard ought to come home. We must telegraph at once. He is in Dighton still."

Mrs. Markham accordingly wrote on a slip of paper:

"To J. E. Forrest, Dighton:—Come immediately.

"S. Markham."

And Axie's granddaughter Lois, who lived in the house, was commissioned to take it to the office. A fire had been kindled by this time in the chamber Josephine was to occupy, and she was there with Agnes, and had rung for warm water, which Lois took up to her before going on her errand. As the child was leaving the room Josephine said to her: "Is there a paper published in town?"

"Yes'm, the Rothsay Star" was the reply.

"When does it come out?" was the next question, and Lois said:

"Saturday,—to-morrow."

"Very well. I wish you to take a notice to the office of the Star for me to-night, and I will give you a quarter."

Twenty-five cents seemed a fortune to the little negro girl, who was greatly impressed with the beauty of the lady, and who replied:

"Yes, miss, I'll do 'em. I's gwine to the village directly with a telegraph to Mars'r Everard, and I'll take yourn same time."

So, when, a little later, she started for the telegraph office, she bore with her to the Rothsay Star the following:

"Married.—In Holburton, N. Y., July , —, by the Rev. John Matthewson, James Everard Forrest, of Rothsay, Ohio, and Miss Josephine Fleming, of Holburton."

CHAPTER XXXI

MRS. FORREST'S POLICY

When Aunt Axie was called so suddenly by Mrs. Markham, she was kindling the fire in the dining-room, which adjoined the room where Josephine sat shivering with cold, and feeling like anything but a happy wife just come to her husband's ancestral halls. Tired with her rapid journey, and disappointed and shocked by what she had heard from Mrs. Markham of the judge's will, Josey was nearer giving way to a hearty cry than she had been before in a long time. It had been far better to have staid where she was, and enjoyed the life she liked, than to have come here and subject herself to suspicion and slights from the people who did not know her. And then she was so cold, and chilly, and uncomfortable generally.

But when the fire was made she felt better, and drawing an easy chair close to it assumed her usual indolent and lounging attitude. Twice Axie, who seemed to be excited, passed the door, once when she was taking the hot water to Rossie's room, and again, later, after she had received an impression of the strangers against whom she had mentally declared war. This time Josephine called her. She had heard an unusual stir above, and from Mrs. Markham's protracted absence, and Axie's evident haste, suspected that the bombshell she had thrown had taken effect, especially if, as she believed, Rosamond was particularly interested in Everard.

"Woman," she said, as the black face glanced in, "what is your name?"

"Axie, ma'am," was the crisp reply, and Josephine continued: "Oh, yes, I have heard my husband speak of you. I am very sorry he is not here to set matters right. What is the matter up stairs? Is any one suddenly ill?"

Axie was bristling with resentment toward this woman, who called Everard her husband so coolly, and in whom she would not believe till she had her master's word of confirmation. Still, she must not be insolent, that was against her creed; but she answered with great dignity, "I tole you Miss Hastin's was sick when you fust come. Her throat be very sore, an' her head mighty bad; so, you'll scuse me, now," and with a kind of suppressed snort Axie departed, jingling her keys and tossing her blue-turbaned head high in the air.

Josephine knew perfectly well how she was regarded in the house, and, irritated and chagrined, decided at once upon her policy. She should be very amiable and sweet, of course, but firm in asserting her rights. She was Everard's wife, and she could prove it, and it was natural that she should come to what she supposed was his home and hers. It was not her fault that she had made the mistake. The wrong was on his side, and she should stay there until he came, unless they turned her from the door, which she hardly thought they would do.

Just then Mrs. Markham appeared, apologizing for her long absence, and saying that though Miss Hastings was, of course, surprised at what she had heard, she did not discredit it, and would telegraph at once for Mr. Forrest.

"Meantime," she continued, "she wishes you to remain here till he comes, and has given orders to have you made comfortable. I believe there is a fire in your room, if you wish to go to it before dinner. Miss Hastings is too ill to see you herself."

"Thanks; she is very kind. I would like to go to my room, and to have one of my trunks sent up. Agnes will show you which one,—the small leather box," Josephine said, with a dignified bow, as she rose from her chair.

Calling Aunt Axie, Mrs. Markham bade her conduct the lady to her room, where a bright wood fire was blazing, and which looked very cheerful and pleasant; for, as it was Everard's room, where he always slept when he spent a night at the Forrest House, Rosamond had taken great pains to keep it nice, and had transferred to it several articles of furniture from the other rooms. Here Josey's spirits began to rise, and it was in quite a comfortable state of mind that she dressed herself for dinner, in a gown of soft cashmere, with just a little white at her throat and wrists. As it was only her mother for whom she mourned, she had decided that she might wear a jet necklace, which heightened the effect of her dress, if indeed it needed anything more to improve it than the beautiful face and wealth of golden hair. Even Mrs. Markham drew an involuntary breath as this vision of loveliness and grace came into the room, apologizing for being tardy, and inquiring so sweetly for Miss Hastings, who, she hoped, was no worse.

Her policy was to be a sweet as well as a firm one, and before dinner was over even Mrs. Markham began to waver a little in her first opinion, and wonder why Everard should have kept secret his marriage with this brilliant, fascinating woman, who seemed so much of a lady, and who evidently was as well born as himself, at least on the maternal side, for Josey took care to say that her mother knew Mrs. Forrest when she was a girl, and was present at her wedding in Boston, but that, owing to adverse circumstances, they saw nothing of each other after the marriage.

"Papa was unfortunate and died, and we moved into the country, where, for a time, mamma had a hard struggle to keep up, and at last took a few boarders in order to live," she said; and her blue eyes were very tender and pathetic as she told what in one sense was the truth, though a truth widely different from the impression she meant to convey.

Once Agnes, whose face was very white, gave her such a look of sorrowful entreaty that Mrs. Markham observed and wondered at it, just as she wondered at the great difference between the sisters, and could only account for it on the supposition that Agnes' mother was a very different woman from the second Mrs. Fleming, who had been a friend of Mrs. Forrest, and a guest at her wedding! Miss Belknap was, of course, brought into the conversation, and Josephine was sorry to hear that she was not at home.

"I depended upon her to vouch for my respectability. She knows me so well," she said, explaining that Beatrice had been for some time an inmate of her mother's house in Holburton, and that she had liked her so

much, and then, more bewildered than ever, Mrs. Markham went over
half-way to the enemy, and longed for the mystery to be explained.

The next day, which was Saturday, it rained with a steady pour, and
Josephine kept her room, after having expressed a wish to see Miss
Hastings, if possible; but when this request was made known to Rossie by
Mrs. Markham, she exclaimed:

"No, no,—not her; not Joe Fleming! I could not bear it till Mr. Everard
comes."

She was thinking of her hair and the letter, and the persistence with
which Joe Fleming had demanded money from Everard, and it made no
difference with her that Mrs. Markham represented the woman as pretty,
and lady-like, and sweet. She could not see her, and a message to the effect
that she was too weak and sick to talk with strangers was taken to
Josephine, who hoped Miss Hastings was not going to be seriously ill, and
offered the services of her sister, who had the faculty of quieting the most
nervous persons and putting them to sleep. But Rossie declined Agnes too,
and lay with her face to the wall, scarcely moving, and never speaking
unless she was spoken to. And Josephine lounged in her own room, and
had her lunch brought up by Axie, to whom she tried to be gracious. But
Axie was not easily won. She did not believe in Mrs. J. E. Forrest, and
looked upon her presence there as an affront to herself and an insult to
Rossie, and when about two o'clock the Rothsay Star was brought into the
house by her husband, John, who was in a state of great excitement over
the marriage notice, which had been pointed out to him, she wrung from
Lois the fact that she had carried a note to the editor, and had been paid a
quarter for it by the lady up stairs. She put the paper away where it could
not be found if Rossie chanced to ask for it.

But she could not keep it from the world as represented by Rothsay,
for it was already the theme of every tongue. The editor had read the note
which Josephine sent him before Lois left the office, and had questioned
her as to who sent her with it. Lois had answered him:

"De young lady what comed from de train wid four big trunks and
bandbox."

"And where is she now?" he asked, and Lois replied: "Up sta'rs in
Mas'r Everard's room."

This last was proof conclusive of the validity of the marriage, which
the editor naturally concluded was a hasty affair of Everard's college days,
when he had the reputation of being rather wild and fast, and so he
published the notice and in another column called attention to it, as the
last great excitement.

Of course there was much wondering, and surmising, and guessing,
and in spite of the rain the ladies who lived near each other got together
and talked it up, and believed or discredited it according to their several
natures. Mrs. Dr. Rider, a chubby, good-natured, inquisitive woman,
declared her intention of knowing the facts before she slept. Her husband
attended Rosamond, and she had a sirup which was just the medicine for a
sore throat and influenza, such as Rossie was suffering from, and she
would take it to her, and perhaps learn the truth of the story of Everard's
marriage.

Accordingly, about four o'clock that afternoon, Mrs. Dr. Rider's little covered phaeton turned into the Forrest avenue, and was seen from the window by Josephine, who, tired and ennuyeed, was looking out into the rain.

That the phaeton held a lady she saw, and as the lady could only be coming there she resolved at once to put herself in the way of some possible communication with the outer world. Glancing at herself in the mirror she saw that she was looking well, although a little paler than her wont, but this would make her more interesting in the character she meant to assume, that of an angelic martyr. As the day was chilly, a soft white wrap of some kind would not be out of place, and would add to the effect.

So she snatched up a fleecy shawl of Berlin wool, and throwing it around her shoulders, took with her a book, and hurrying down to the reception-room, had just time to seat herself gracefully and becomingly, when the door opened and Mrs. Dr. Rider came in.

Aunt Axie, who was a little deaf, was in the kitchen busy with her dinner, while Lois was in the barn, hunting for eggs, and so no one heard the bell, which Mrs. Rider pulled twice, and then, presuming upon her long acquaintance with the house, opened the door and walked into the reception-room, where she stopped for an instant, startled by the picture of the pretty blonde in black, with the white shawl, and the golden hair rippling back from the beautiful face.

Here was a stroke of what Mrs. Rider esteemed luck. She had stumbled at once upon the very person she had come to inquire about, and as she was not one to lose any time, she shook the rain-drops from her waterproof, and drawing near to the fire, turned to the lady in the easy-chair, and said:

"I beg your pardon for my very unceremonious entrance. I rang twice, and then ventured to come in, it was raining so hard."

Josephine admitted that it was raining hard, and remarked that she expected to find it warmer in Southern Ohio than in Eastern New York, but she believed it was colder, and with a shiver she drew her shawl around her shoulders, shook back her hair, and lifted her blue eyes to Mrs. Rider, who responded:

"You came from the East, then?"

"Yes, madam, from Holburton. That is, I am from there just now, but it's only two weeks since I returned from Europe, where I have been for a long time."

Here there was a solution in part of the mystery. This wife had been in Europe, and that was why the secret had been kept so long, and little Mrs. Dr. Rider flushed with eager excitement and pleasurable curiosity as she said:

"From Europe! You must be tired with your long journey. Have you ever been in Rothsay before? From your having come from the East I suppose you must be a relative of Mrs. Forrest, who was born in Boston?"

Josephine knew she did not suppose any such thing, and that in all probability she had seen the notice in the Star, and had come to spy out the land, but it was not her policy to parade her story unsolicited; so she merely replied that she was not a relative of Mrs. Forrest's, though her mamma and that lady had been friends in their girlhood. To have been a friend of the late Mrs. Forrest stamped a person as somebody, and Mrs. Rider began at once to espouse the cause of this woman, to whom she said:

"I hope you will excuse me if I seem forward in what I am about to say. I am Mrs. Rider, wife of the family physician, and a friend of Everard, and when I saw that notice of his marriage in the Star I could hardly credit it, though I know such things have been before; but four years is such a long time to keep an affair of that kind a secret. May I ask if it is true, and if you are the wife?"

"It is true, and I am his wife, or I should not be here," Josey said, very quietly.

"Yes, certainly not, of course," Mrs. Rider replied, hardly knowing what she was saying, and wishing that the fair blonde whose eyes were looking so steadily into the fire would say something more, but she didn't.

She was waiting for her visitor to question her, which she presently did, for she could never leave the matter in this way, so she said:

"You will pardon me, Mrs. Forrest, but knowing a little makes me want to know more. It seems so strange that Everard should have been a married man for more than four years and we never suspect it. It must have been a private marriage."

"Ye-es, in one sense," Josephine said, with the air of one who is having something wrung from him unwillingly. "A great many people saw us married, for it was in a drama,—a play,—but none of them knew it was meant to be real and binding, except Everard and myself and the clergyman, who was a genuine clergyman. We knew and intended it, of course, or it would not have been valid. We were engaged, and did it on the impulse of the moment, thinking no harm. Nor was there, except that we were both so young, and Everard not through college. We told mother and sister, but no one else, and as the villagers did not know of our intention to be married, or that Dr. Matthewson was a clergyman, they never suspected the truth, and the secret was to be kept until Everard was graduated, and after that——"

She spoke very slowly now, and drew long breaths, as if every word she uttered were a stab to her heart.

"After that I hoped to get out of my false position, but there was some fear of Judge Forrest, which kept Everard silent, waiting for an opportunity to tell him, for I was not rich, you know, and he might be angry; so I waited patiently, and his father died, and I went to Europe, and thus the years have gone."

The blue eyes, in which the tears were shining, more from steadily gazing into the fire than from emotion of any kind, were lifted to Mrs. Rider, who was greatly affected, and then said:

"Yes, I see; but when the judge died there was nothing in the way of acknowledging the marriage. I am surprised and disappointed in Everard that he should treat you thus."

Mrs. Rider's sympathy was all with the injured wife, who seemed so patient and uncomplaining, and who replied:

"He had good reasons, no doubt. His father disinherited him, I believe, and that may have had its effect; but I do not wish it talked about until Everard comes. It is very awkward for me that he is absent. I expected to meet him. I must come, of course; there was no other way, for mamma recently died, and the old home was broken up. I must come to my husband."

She kept asserting it as if in apology for her being there, and her voice trembled, and her whole air was one of such injured innocence that Mrs. Rider resolved within herself to stand by her in the face of all Rothsay, if necessary. Mrs. Rider was a very motherly little woman, and her heart went out at once to this girl, whose blue eyes and black dress appealed so strongly to her sympathies. She liked Everard, too, and did not mean to be disloyal to him, if she could help it, but she should stand by the wife; and she was so anxious to get away and talk up the wonderful news with her acquaintances that she forgot entirely the sirup she had brought for Rossie's throat, and would have forgotten to inquire after Rossie herself if Aunt Axie had not accidentally put her head in the door and given vent to a grunt of surprise and disapprobation when she saw her in close conversation with Josephine, and, with her knowledge of the lady's character for gossip, foresaw the result.

"Oh, Miss Rider, is you here?" she said, advancing into the room; "and does Miss Markham know it? I'll fotch her directly, 'cause Miss Ros'mon's too sick to see yer."

"Never mind, Axie," Mrs. Rider said, rising and beginning to adjust her waterproof. "I drove up to inquire after Rossie, and have spent more time than I intended talking with Mrs. Forrest," and she nodded toward Josephine, who also arose and acknowledged the nod and name with a gracious bow.

She saw the impression she had made on her visitor, who took her hand at parting, and said:

"You will probably remain in Rothsay now, and I shall hope to see a great deal of you."

Again Josephine bowed assentingly to Mrs. Rider, who at last left the room, followed by Axie, whose face was like a thunder-cloud as she almost slammed the door in the lady's face in her anxiety to be rid of her.

CHAPTER XXXII

WHAT THE PEOPLE SAID AND DID

Before bed-time half the people in Rothsay knew of the marriage, and that Mrs. Dr. Rider had seen and talked with the lady, who was reported as very beautiful, and young, and stylish, and cultivated, and traveled, and a

Bostonian, whose family had been on the most intimate terms with the Bigelows. She was also a friend of Bee Belknap, who had spent a summer with her, and probably knew of the marriage, which was a sort of escapade gotten up on the spur of the moment, and kept a secret at first because Everard was not through college, and feared his father's displeasure. But why it was not made public after the judge's death was a question which even the wise ones could not answer; and so the wonder and excitement increased.

The next morning, which was Sunday, dawned clear and bright. The rain was over, and at the usual hour the Rothsayites betook themselves to their accustomed place of worship. Trinity church was full that morning, for though the people hardly expected Mrs. J. E. Forrest herself, they did expect Mrs. Markham, and hoped to hear something more from her. But Mrs. Markham was not there, and the large, square pew which the Forrests had occupied for many years, and which was far up the middle aisle, was empty until the reading of the Psalms commenced, when there was heard outside the sound of rapidly approaching wheels, which stopped before the door, and a moment after there entered a graceful figure clothed in black, with the prettiest little Paris bonnet perched on the golden hair, the long crape vail thrown back, disclosing the fair, blonde face, which was a little flushed, while the blue eyes had in them a timid, bashful expression as they glanced quickly round in quest of the sexton, who, having fulfilled his duties at the bell, had gone to the organ loft, for he was blower as well as bell-ringer, and left to others the task of seating strangers. But Josey did not have to wait long, for four men,—two young, one middle-aged, and one white-haired and old,—simultaneously left their pews and made a movement toward her, the youngest reaching her first and asking if she would have a seat.

"Yes, thank you. Please show me Judge Forrest's pew," was the reply, and every head was turned as her long skirts went trailing up the aisle, and the air was filled with the costly and delicate perfume she carried with her, and which was fresh from Pinaud's.

What a long time she remained upon her knees, and how devout she was after she had arisen, and how clearly and sweetly she sang the "Gloria," and how wonderfully her overskirt was looped, and how jauntily her jacket fitted her, with such a pretty stand-up collar, and how white her neck was above it, and how beautiful the wavy hair under the lovely bonnet. All these details, and more, were noted by every woman in church who could get a view of her, while even the clergyman, good and conscientious man as he was, found it difficult to keep his eyes from straying too often to that crimson-cushioned pew and the black-robed figure whose responses were so audible and clear, and who seemed the very incarnation of piety and innocence. He had heard of Mrs. J. E. Forrest, and he guessed who the stranger was, and when service was over he came down to speak to her. Mrs. Rider, however, was there before him, and was shaking hands with the lady, whom she presented to the rector, and to his wife, and to several others who sat near, and who involuntarily moved in that direction.

And Josephine received them with a modesty of demeanor which won their sympathy, if not their hearts, at once. Not the slightest allusion did they make to her husband, but she spoke of him herself, naturally and easily. She had hoped to find him at home when she came and have him present her to his friends, but unexpected business had called him away, she believed. However, he would soon return, as Miss Hastings had telegraphed for him, and then she should not feel so much alone.

How very gentle and gracious she was, answering all questions with great modesty, and without seeming to volunteer any direct remarks, adroitly managing to drop a good many scraps of information with regard to herself and her past life, all of course highly advantageous to herself. Of Everard she said very little, but when she did speak of him it was always as "My husband, Mr. Forrest."

She should certainly expect him on the morrow, she said, and then she should not feel so much like a stranger, possibly an impostor, and she laughed a little musical laugh, and her blue eyes sparkled so brightly and her lips curled so prettily that every heart was won, and the whole bevy of ladies followed her to the carriage telling her they should call and see her very soon, stood watching her as she drove away, and talked together of her and her recreant husband, in whom there must be something wrong, or he would long ago have acknowledged this peerless woman as his wife. And so the talk increased and every conceivable story was set afloat, and poor Everard stood at rather a low ebb in public opinion, when the six o'clock train came in the next day and left him standing upon the platform, bewildered and confounded with the words which greeted him as he left the car, and which gave him the first intimation of what he was to expect. The editor of the Rothsay Star was standing there, and hitting Everard upon the shoulder, exclaimed:

"Hallo, Forrest. A nice trick you've been playing upon us,—married all this time, and not let us know."

"Married! What do you mean?" And Everard turned white to his lips, while his friend replied:

"What do I mean? Why, I mean that your wife is up at Forrest House, and thunder to pay generally."

CHAPTER XXXIII

EVERARD FACES IT

When Everard was interrupted in his interview with Rosamond, his first feeling was one of regret, for he had made up his mind to tell her everything. He had held her in his arms for one blissful moment, and pressed his lips to her forehead, and the memory of that would help him to bear the wretchedness of all the after life. But before he could begin his story, Lawyer Russell came in, and the opportunity was lost. He could, however, write, and he fully meant to do so, and after his arrival at Dighton he began two or three letters, which he tore in pieces, for he found it harder than he had expected to confess that he had a wife to the girl he had kissed so passionately, and who, he felt certain, loved him in return. He had seen it in her eyes, which knew no deception, and in the blushes on her cheek, and his greatest pain came from the knowledge that she, too, must suffer through him. And so he put off the writing day after day, and employed his leisure moments in hunting up the laws of Indiana on divorce, and felt surprised to find how comparatively easy it was for those whom Heaven had joined together to be put asunder by the courts of man. Desertion, failure to support, uncongeniality, were all valid reasons for breaking the bonds of matrimony; and from reading and dwelling so much upon it he came at last to consider it seriously as something which in his case was excusable. Whatever Rossie might think of it he should be happier to know the tie was broken, even if the whole world disapproved; and he at last deliberately made up his mind to free himself from the hated marriage, which grew tenfold more hateful to him when there came to his knowledge a fact which threw light at once upon some things he had never been able to understand in Dr. Matthewson.

He was sitting one evening in the room devoted mostly to the use of gentlemen at the hotel where he was stopping, and listening in a careless kind of way to the conversation of two men, one an inmate of the house, and the other a traveler just arrived from western New York. For a time the talk flowed on indifferent topics, and drifted at last to Clarence, where it seemed that both men had once lived, and about which the Dighton man was asking some questions.

"By the way," he said, "whatever became of that Matthewson, he called himself, though his real name when I first knew him was Hastings. You know the Methodist Church got pretty well bitten with him. He was always the tallest kind of a rascal. I knew him well."

Everard was interested now, and while seeming to read the paper he held in his hands, did not lose a word of all which followed next.

"Matthewson? Oh, yes, I know," the Clarence man replied. "You mean the fellow who was so miraculously converted at a camp-meeting, and then took to preaching, though a bigger hypocrite never lived. I don't know where he is now. He dabbled in medicine after he left Clarence, and got "Doctor" hitched to his name, and has been gambling through the country ever since. The last I heard of him somebody wrote to Clarence asking if he had a right to marry a couple, by which I infer that he has been doing a little ministerial duty by way of diversion."

"I should hardly think a marriage performed by him valid, though I dare say it would hold in court," the Dighton man, who was a lawyer, replied; adding, after a moment, "Matthewson is the name of his aunt, which he took at her death, together with a few thousands she left him. His real name is John Hastings. I knew him when he was a boy, and he was the most vindictive, unprincipled person I ever met, and his father was not much better, though both could be smooth as oil, and ingratiate themselves into most anybody's favor. He had a girl in tow some two or three years ago, I was told; a very handsome filly, but fast as the Old Nick himself, if, indeed, she was not worse than that."

Here the conversation was brought to a close, and Everard went to his room, where for a time he sat, stunned and powerless to move. Like a flash of lightning it came upon him just who Dr. Matthewson was, and his mind went back to that night when, with a rash boy's impetuosity, he had raised his hand against the mature man who, while smarting under the blows, had sworn to be revenged. And he had kept his word, and Everard could understand now why he had seemed so willing and even anxious that there should be a perfect understanding of the matter so as to make the marriage valid.

"Curse him!" Everard said to himself. "He meant to ruin me. He could not have known what Josey was, but he knew it was not a fitting match for me, and no time or way for me to marry, if it were; but that was his revenge. I remember he asked me if I did not fear the man whom I had punished, and said people like him did not take cowhidings meekly; and he is Rossie's half-brother; but if I can help it, she shall never know how he has injured me, the rascal. I'll have a divorce now, at all hazards, even though it may do me no good, so far as Rossie is concerned. I'll see that lawyer to-morrow and tell him the whole story."

But before the morrow came, Everard received Mrs. Markham's telegram, which startled him so much that he forgot everything in his haste to return home and see if aught had befallen Rosamond. It had something to do with her he was sure, but no thought that it had to do with Josephine entered his mind until he stepped from the car and heard that she was at the Forrest House. For an instant his brain reeled, and he felt and acted like a drunken man, as he went to claim his traveling-bag. Then, without a word to any one, he walked rapidly away in the darkness, with a face as white as the few snow-flakes which were just beginning to fall, and a feeling like death in his heart as he thought of Rossie left alone to confront Joe Fleming as his wife. And yet it did not seem very strange to him that Josephine was there. It was rather as if he had expected it, just as the murderer expects the day when his sin will find him out. Everard's sin had found him out, and as he sped along the highway, half running in his haste to know the worst, he was almost glad that the thing he had dreaded so long had come at last, and to himself he said:

"I'll face it like a man, whatever the result may be."

From the windows of Rossie's room a faint light was shining, but it told him nothing of the sick girl lying there, so nervous and excited that bright fever spots burned on her cheeks, and her hands and feet were like lumps of ice as she waited and listened for him, hearing him the moment he struck the gravel-walk beneath her window, for he purposely turned aside from the front piazza, choosing to enter the house in the rear, lest he should first encounter the woman, who, like Rossie, was waiting and watching for him, and feeling herself grow hot and cold alternately as she wondered what he would say. Like Rossie, she was sure he would come on that train, and had made herself as attractive as possible in her black cashmere and jet, with the white shawl around her shoulders, and her golden hair falling on her neck in heavy masses of curls. And then, with a French novel in her hand, she sat down to wait for the first sound of the carriage which was to bring him, for she did not dream of his walking that cold, wet night, and was not on the alert to see the tall figure which came so swiftly through the darkness, skulking like a thief behind the shrubbery till it reached the rear door, where it entered, and stood face to face with old Aunt Axie, who in her surprise almost dropped the bowl of gruel she had been preparing for Rosamond. She did spill it, she set it down so quickly, and putting both her hands on Everard's shoulders she exclaimed:

"Oh, Mars'r Everard, praise de Lord you am come at last! I couldn't b'ar it much longer, with Miss Rossie sick up sta'rs, and that woman below swashin' round wid her long-tailed gowns, an' her yaller ha'r hangin' down her back, and sayin' she is your wife. She isn't your wife, Mas'r Everard,—she isn't?" and Axie looked earnestly at the young man, who would have given more than half his life to have been able to say, "No, she is not."

But he could not do that, and his voice shook as he replied:

"Yes, Aunt Axie, she is my wife."

Axie did not cry out or say a word at first, but her black face quivered and her eyes filled with tears, as she took a rapid mental survey of the case as it stood now. Everard's wife must of course be upheld for the credit of the family, and, though the old negress knew there was something wrong, it was not for her to inquire or to let others do so either; and when at last she spoke, she said:

"If she's your wife, then I shall stan' by her."

He did not thank her or seem to care whether she stood by his wife or not, for his next question was:

"You said Rosamond was sick. What is the matter?"

"Sore throat and bad cold fust, and then your wife comed an' took us by surprise, an' Miss Rossie fainted cl'ar away, and has been as white, an' still, an' slimpsy as a rag ever since."

Something like a groan escaped from Everard's lips, as he said:

"Tell Miss Rossie I am here, and ask if I can see her,—at once, before I meet anybody else."

"Yes, I'll tell her," Axie said, as she hurried to the room, where, to her great surprise, she found her young mistress in her flannel dressing-gown and shawl, sitting in her easy-chair, with her head resting upon pillows scarcely whiter than her face, save where the red spots of fever burned so brightly.

In spite of Mrs. Markham's remonstrance Rossie had insisted upon getting up and being partly dressed.

"I must see Everard," she said. "You can't understand, and I can't explain, but he will come to me, and I must see him alone.

"Yes. Tell him to come up; I am ready for him," she said to Aunt Axie.

And Everard advanced, with a sinking heart, and knocked at Rossie's door just as a black-robed figure, with a white wool shawl wrapped around it, started to come up the stairs.

CHAPTER XXXIV

EVERARD AND ROSSIE

The voice which said "Come in" did not sound like Rossie's at all, nor did the little girl sitting in the chair look much like the Rossie he had last seen, flushed with health and happiness, and the light of a great joy shining in the eyes which now turned so eagerly toward him as he came in. On the stairs outside there was the rustling of skirts, and he heard it, and involuntarily slid the bolt of the door, and then swiftly crossed to where Rossie's face was upturned to his with a smile of welcome, and Rossie's hands were both outstretched to him as she said:

"Oh, Mr. Everard, I am glad you have come; we have wanted you so much."

He had thought she would meet him with coldness and scorn for his weakness and duplicity, and he was prepared for that, but not for this; and forgetting himself utterly for the moment, he took the offered hands and held them tightly in his own, until she released them from him and motioned him to a seat opposite her, where he could look into her face, which, now that he saw it more closely, had on it such a grieved, disappointed expression that he cried out:

"Kill me, Rossie, if you will! but don't look at me that way, for I cannot bear it. I know what I've done and what I am, better than you do."

Here he paused, and Rossie said:

"I am sorry, Everard, that you did not tell me long ago, when it first happened. Four years and more, she says. I've been thinking it over, and it must have been that time you came home when your mother died and you were so sick afterward. You were married then."

How quietly and naturally she spoke the words "married then," as if it was nothing to her that he was married then or now, but the hot blood flamed up for a moment in her face and then left it whiter than before, as Everard replied:

"Yes, if that can be called a marriage which was a mere farce, and has brought nothing but bitter humiliation to me, and been the cause of my ruin. I wish that day had been blotted from my existence."

"Hush, Everard," Rossie said. "You must not talk that way, and your wife here in the house waiting for you. I have not seen her yet, but they tell me she is very beautiful."

"Yes, with that cursed beauty which lures men, or rather fools, to their destruction; and I was a fool!" Everard answered, bitterly,—"an idiot, who thought myself in love. Don't call her my wife, Rossie. She has never been that; never will be. But I did not come here to abuse her. I came to tell you the whole truth at last, as I ought to have told it years ago, when my mother was on her death-bed. I tried to tell her, but I could not. I made a beginning by showing her Josephine's picture, which she did not like. The face was pretty, she said, but not the face of a true, refined woman, but rather of one who wore dollar jewelry," and here Everard laughed sarcastically as he went on; "then I showed the picture to Bee, who said she looked as if she might wear cotton lace. But you, Rossie, said the hardest thing of all, and decided me finally not to tell, for I had almost made up my mind to make you my confidante."

"I, Everard? I decided you? You must be mistaken. When was it, Everard?" Rossie exclaimed, her eyes growing very large and bright in her excitement.

"Do you remember I once showed you a picture of a young girl?" Everard said. "You were watering flowers in the garden; and you said she was very beautiful, but suggested that the jewelry, of which there was a superfluity on her neck and arms, might be a sham, and said she looked like a sham, too. How could I tell you after that, that she was my wife? I couldn't, and I kept it to myself; and mother died, and I went crazy, and you cut off your hair and sold it to pay what you believed to be a gambling debt, and you wrote to Joe Fleming, and I did not open my lips to undeceive you.

"I will have my say out," he continued, fiercely, as Rossie put up her hands to stop him; "I deserve a good cudgeling, and I'll give it to myself, for no one knows as well as I do just what a sneaking coward I have been all these years, when you have been believing in me and keeping me from going to the——. No, I won't swear; at least before you, who have been my good angel ever since you knew enough to chide me for my faults. Oh, Rossie! what would I give to be put back to those old days when I was comparatively innocent, and you, in your cape sun-bonnet and long-sleeved aprons, were the dearest, sweetest little girl in all the world, just as you are now. I will say it, though I am killing you, I know, and I am almost wicked enough not to care, for I would rather there were no Rossie in this world than to know she lived to hate and despise me."

"No, Everard, never that, never!" and Rossie again stretched toward him her pale little hands, which he seized and held while he told her rapidly the whole story of his marriage, beginning at the time he first saw Josey Fleming and went to board with her mother.

One item, however, he withheld. He did not tell her that it was her half-brother who had married him, nor did he give the name of the clergyman. He would spare her all pain in that direction, if possible, and let her think as well as she could of the brother she could scarcely remember, and who, she believed, must be dead, or he would ere this have manifested some interest in her.

Of Josephine he spoke very plainly, and though he did not exaggerate her faults, he showed conclusively, in what he said, that his love for her had long since died out, and he went on from one fact to another so rapidly that Rossie felt stunned and bewildered and begged him to stop. But he would not. She must hear him through, he said, and at the close of his story she looked so white and tired that he bent over her in alarm, chafing her cold hands and asking what he could do for her.

"Nothing but to leave me now," she said. "I have heard so much and borne so much that none of it seems real. There's a buzzing in my head, and I believe I'm going to faint again, or die. How could you do all this, and I trusted you so?—and, oh, Everard, where are you? It grows so dark and black, and I'm so sick and faint," and with a sobbing, hysterical cry, Rossie involuntarily let her tired, aching head fall upon the arm which held it so gladly, and which fain would have kept it there forever.

Rossie did not faint quite away, as she had done when the news of Everard's marriage reached her, but she lay still and helpless in Everard's arms until she felt his hot kisses upon her forehead, and that roused her at once. He had no right to kiss her, she no right to suffer it, and she drew herself away from him to the safe shelter of her pillows, as she said, with her old childish manner:

"Everard, you must not kiss me like that. It is too late. Such things are over between us now."

She seemed to accept the fact that he loved her, and though the love was hopeless, and, turn which way she would, there was no brightness in the future, the knowledge of what might have been was in one sense very sweet to her, and the face which Everard took between his hands and looked earnestly into, while his lips quivered and his eyes were full of tears, seemed to him like the face of an angel.

"Heaven pity me, Rossie," he said. "Heaven pity us both for this which lies between us." There was a knock outside the door and a voice Rossie had never heard before, said:

"Miss Hastings, if my husband is with you, tell him his wife will be glad to see him when he can tear himself away. I have waited an hour, and surely I may claim my own now."

There was an unmistakable coarseness of meaning in the words which brought the hot blood to Rossie's cheeks, but Everard was pale as death, as, with a muttered execration, he stepped back from Rossie, who said:

"Yes, go, Everard. She is right. Her claim is first. Say I am sorry I kept you. Go, and when I have thought it all out I'll send for you, but don't come till I do."

She motioned him to leave her, and with the look of one going to the rack, he obeyed, and unbolting the door, went out, shutting it quickly behind him, and thus giving the woman outside no chance for more than a glance at the white-faced little girl, of whose personal appearance no impression could be formed.

CHAPTER XXXV

MR. AND MRS. J. E. FORREST

It had been Josephine's intention to try and make peace with her husband, if possible, in the hope of winning him back to at least an outward semblance of harmony. And to do this she relied much on her beauty, which she knew had not diminished in the least since those summer days in Holburton, when he had likened her to every beautiful thing in the universe. She knew she was more attractive now than then, for she had studied to acquire an air of refinement and high-breeding which greatly enhanced her charms, and when she saw herself in the long mirror, with her toilet complete, and the made-up expression of sweetness and graciousness on her face, she felt almost sure he could not withstand her.

She had heard from Lois that Everard was in the house, and as the moments went by and he did not come, the sweetness left her face, and there was a glitter in her blue eyes, as she walked impatiently up and down her chamber, listening for his footsteps.

At last, as she grew more and more impatient, she went down to the dining-room, thinking to find him there; but he was still with Axie in the kitchen, and so she waited until she heard his step as he went rapidly up the stairs.

Swiftly and noiselessly she glided into the hall and followed, but was only in time to see the shutting of the door of Rossie's room and hear the sliding of the bolt, while her quick ear caught the sound of Rossie's voice as she welcomed Everard. For a moment Josephine stood shaking with rage, and feeling an inclination to kick at the closed door, and demand an entrance. But she hardly dared do that, and so she waited, and strained her ear to catch the conversation carried on so rapidly, but in so low a tone and so far from her that she could not hear it all, or even half. But she knew Everard was telling the story of the marriage, and as he grew more earnest his voice naturally rose higher, until she could hear what he said, but not Rossie's replies. Involuntarily clenching her fists, and biting her lips until the blood came through in one place, she listened still more intently and knew there was no hope for her, and felt sure that the only feeling she could now inspire in her husband's heart was one of hatred and disgust.

At last, when she could endure the suspense no longer, she knocked upon the door and claimed "her own" and got it, for her husband, whom she had not seen for more than two years, stood face to face with her, a tall, well-developed man, with a will and a purpose in his brown eyes, and a firm-set expression about his mouth which made him a very different person from the boy-lover whom she had swayed at her pleasure.

Everard was a thorough gentleman, and it was not in his nature to be otherwise than courteous to any woman, and he bowed to Josephine with as much politeness and deference as if it had been Bee Belknap standing there so dignified and self-possessed, and with an air of assurance and worldly wisdom such as he had never seen in Josephine Fleming. For a moment he looked at her in surprise, but there was no sign of welcome in his face, no token of admiration for the visible improvement in her. He had an artist's eye, and noticed that her dress was black, and that it became her admirably, and that the delicate white shawl was so knotted and arranged as to heighten the effect of the picture; but he knew the woman so well that nothing she could do or wear could move him now. When she saw that she must speak first, she laughed a little, spiteful laugh, and said:

"Have you nothing to say to me after two years' separation, or have you exhausted yourself with her?" nodding toward Rossie's door.

That roused him, and he answered her:

"Yes, much to say, and some things to explain and apologize for, but not here. I will go with you to your room. They tell me you are occupying my old quarters."

He tried to speak naturally, and Josephine's heart beat faster as she thought that possibly he might be won to an outward seeming of friendship after all, and it would be better for her every way. So, when the privacy of her chamber was reached, and there was no danger of interruption, she affected the loving wife, and laying her hands on Everard's arm, said, coaxingly and prettily:

"Don't be so cold and hard, Everard, as if you were sorry I came. I had nowhere else to go, and I'm no more to blame for being your wife than you are for being my husband, and I certainly have just cause to complain of you for having kept me so long in ignorance of your father's death. Why did you do it? But I need not ask why," she continued, as she saw the frown on his face, and guessed he was not to be coaxed; "the reason is in the apartment you have just quitted."

Josephine got no further, for Everard interrupted her and sternly bade her stop.

"So long as you censure me for having kept my father's death a secret from you I am bound to listen, for I deserve it; but when you assail Rosamond Hastings you have gone too far. I do not wish to quarrel with you, Josey, but we may as well understand each other first as last. You had a right to come here, thinking it was still my home, and I am justly punished for my deceit, for which no one can hate me as I hate myself. If I had been candid and frank from the first, it would have saved me a great deal of trouble and self-abasement. You heard of my father's death——"

"Yes, but no thanks are due you for the information. Mr. Everts, whom I met in Dresden, told me of it. At first I did not believe him, for I had credited you with being a man of honor, but he convinced me of the fact, and in my anger I started home at once, and came here, to find that girl the mistress of the house, and, they tell me, your father's heir. Is that true?"

"I've nothing but what I earn," he said, "but I think I have proved conclusively that I can support you, whatever may come to me, and I expect to do so still, but it must be apart from myself. I wish that distinctly understood, as it will save further discussion. You could not be happy with me; I should be miserable with you after knowing what I do, and seeing what I have seen."

Here she turned fiercely upon him, and with flashing eyes and dilated nostrils demanded what he meant.

"I will tell you when I reach it," he replied; "but first, let me go over the ground from the beginning——"

"No need of that," she replied, angrily. "You went over the ground with her,—that girl whom I hate with deadly hatred. I heard you. I was outside the door."

"Listening!" Everard said, contemptuously. "A worthy employment, to which no lady would stoop."

"Who said I was a lady?" she retorted, stung by his manner and the tone of his voice, and forgetting herself entirely in her wrath. "Don't you suppose I know that it was because I was not a lady according to your creed that your father objected to me and that you have sickened of me. A poor, unknown butcher's daughter is not a fit match for you; and I was just that. You thought you married the daughter of Roxie Fleming, who kept a boarding-house, and so you did, and something more. You married the daughter of the man who used to deliver meat at your grandfather's door in Boston, and of the woman who for years cooked in your mother's family. I knew this when you first came to us, and laughed in my sleeve, for I know how proud you are of family blood and birth, and I can boast of blood, too, but it is the blood of beasts, in which my father dealt, not the blue-veined kind, which shows itself in hypocrisy and the deliberate deception of years. I told your father, when I met him at Commencement, that my mother was present at his wedding, and she was. She made the jellies and ices, and stood with the other servants to see the ceremony. Wouldn't your lady mother turn over in her coffin if she could know just whom her boy married?"

Was she a woman, or a demon? Everard wondered, as he replied:

"If possible, I would rather not bring my mother into the conversation, but since you will have it so, I must tell you that she did know who you were."

"How! did you tell your mother of the marriage, and have you kept that from me, too?" Josephine asked, and he replied:

"I did not tell her of the marriage, although I tried to, and made a beginning by showing her your picture, and telling her your name and that of your mother, whom she at once identified as the Roxie who had lived in her father's family so long."

"And of course my fine lady objected to such stock," Josephine said, with a sneer in her voice.

"Josephine," and Everard spoke more sternly than he had ever spoken to her in his life, "say what you like to me, but don't mention my mother in that tone or spirit again. She did not despise you for your birth. No true woman would do that. She said that innate refinement or delicacy of feeling would always assert itself, and raise one above the lowest and humblest of positions. Almost her last words to me were of you, in whom she knew I was interested, for I had confessed as much.

"'If she is so good, and womanly, and true, her birth is of no consequence—none whatever,' she said. So you see she laid less stress upon it than do you, who know better than she did whether you are good, and womanly and true."

Here Josephine began to cry, but Everard did not heed her tears, and went on:

"There is in this country no degradation in honest labor; it is the character, the actions, which tell; and were you what I believed you to be when in my madness I consented to that foolish farce, I would not care though your origin were the lowest which can be conceived."

Here Josephine stopped crying, and demanded, sharply:

"What am I, pray? What do you know of me?—you, who have scarcely seen me half a dozen times since I became your wife."

"I know more than you suppose,—have seen more than you guess," he replied; "but let me begin with the morning I left you in Holburton, four years ago last June, and come down to the present time."

When he hinted that he knew more of her life than she supposed, there instantly flashed into Josephine's mind the memory of all the love affairs she had been concerned in, and the improprieties of which she had been guilty, and she wondered if it were possible that Everard could know of them, too. But it was not, and, assuming a calmness she was far from feeling, she said:

"Go on, I am all attention."

Very rapidly, Everard went over with the events of his life as connected with her up to the time of his father's death and his own disinheritance, and here he paused a moment, while Josephine said:

"And so it was through me you lost your money. I am very sorry, and I must say I think it mean in that girl to keep it, knowing as she does how it came to her."

"You misjudge her," Everard said, quickly. "You know nothing of her, or how she rebelled against it and tried to give it back to me. But she cannot do it while she is under age, and I would not take it if she could. I made her believe it at last, and then counseled with Miss Belknap as to my future course——"

"Miss Belknap, indeed!" Josephine exclaimed, indignantly. "Don't talk to me of Miss Belknap, the tricky, deceitful thing, to come into our house, knowing all the time who I was, and yet pretending such entire ignorance of everything. How I hate her, and you, too, for sending her there as a spy upon my actions."

"You are mistaken," Everard said. "Bee was no tale-bearer, and no spy upon your actions. Neither was she sent to you, for I did not know she was there till she wrote me to that effect. She had the best of motives in going to your mother's house. She wished to see you for herself, and,—pardon me, Josey, if I speak very plainly,—she wished to find all the good there was in you, so as to know better how to befriend you, should you need it."

"Which, thank Heaven, I don't, so she had her trouble for her pains," was Josephine's rejoinder, of which Everard took no notice, but simply went on:

"Beatrice has been your best friend from the moment she first heard of you, and after father's death she advised me to go straight to you and tell you the whole truth, and offer you a home such as I could make for you myself,—in short, offer you poverty and protection as my acknowledged wife."

"Strange you did not follow her advice, with your high notions of morality," Josephine said, with a sneer; and he replied:

"I started to do it in good faith, and went as far as Albany without a thought that I should not do it, but there I began to waver, for I saw you, myself unseen and my presence unsuspected, so that you acted and spoke your feelings without restraint.

"Perhaps you can recall a concert or opera which you attended with Doctor Matthewson as your escort, and perhaps, though that is not so likely, you may remember the man who seemed to be asleep in the seat behind the one you took when you entered the car, talking and laughing so loudly that you drew to yourself the attention of all the passengers, and especially the young man, who listened with feelings which can be better imagined than described, while his wife made light of him, and allowed attentions and liberties such as no pure-minded woman would for a moment have suffered from any man, and much less from one of Dr. Matthewson's character. I hardly know what restrained me from knocking him down and publicly denouncing you, but shame and disgust kept me silent, while words and glances which made my blood boil passed between you two until you were tired out and laid you head on his arm as readily as you would have rested it on mine had I sat in his place. And there I left you asleep, and I have never looked upon your face since until to-night, when I found you at Miss Hastings' door. After that scene in the car I could not think of offering to share my poverty with you. We were better apart, and I made a vow that never for an hour would I live with you as my wife. The thing is impossible; but because I dreaded the notoriety of an open rupture, and the talk and scandal sure to follow an admission of the marriage, I kept quiet, trusting to chance to work it out for me as it has done at last. And now that the worst has come, I am ready to abide by it and am willing to bear the blame myself, if that will help you any. The people in Rothsay will undoubtedly believe you the injured party, and I shall let them do so. I shall say nothing to your detriment except that it is impossible for us to live together. I shall support you just as I have done, but I greatly prefer that it should be in Holburton, rather than in Rothsay. It is the only favor I ask, that you do not remain here."

"And one I shall not grant," was Josephine's quick reply. "I like Rothsay, so far as I have seen it, and here I shall stay. Do you think that I will go back to Holburton, and bear all the malicious gossip of that gossipy hole? Never! I'll die first! You accuse me of being fond of Dr. Matthewson, and so I am, and I like him far better than I ever liked you, for he is a gentleman, while you are a knave and a hypocrite, and that girl across the hall is as bad as you are;—I hate her,—I hate you both!"

She was standing close to him now, her face livid with rage, while the blue of her eyes seemed to have faded into a dull white, as she gave vent to her real feelings. But Everard did not answer her, and as the dinner-bell just then rang for the third time, she added sneeringly, "If you are through with your abuse I'll end the interview by asking you to take me down to dinner. No? You do not wish for any dinner? Very well, I can go alone, so I wish you good evening, advising you not to fast too long. It is not good for you. Possibly you may find some cracker and tea in Miss Hastings' room, with which to refresh the inner man."

And sweeping him a mocking courtesy she started to leave the room, but at the door she met her sister, and stopped a moment while she said:

"Ah, Agnes, here is your brother, who, I hope, will be better pleased to see you than he was to see me. If I remember rightly you were always his favorite. Au revoir," and kissing the tips of her fingers to Everard, she left the room, and he heard her warbling snatches of some old love song as she ran lightly down the stairs to the dining-room, where dinner had waited nearly an hour, and where Aunt Axie stood with her face blacker than its wont, giving off little angry snorts as she removed one after another the covers of the dishes, and pronounced the contents spoiled.

"Whar's Mars'r Everard? Isn't he comin'?" Aunt Axie asked, as Josephine showed signs of commencing her dinner alone, Mrs. Markham, who ate by rule and on time, having had tea and cold chicken, and gone.

"Mr. Forrest has lost his appetite and is not coming," Josephine replied, with the utmost indifference, and as Agnes just then appeared, the sisters began their dinner alone.

But few words had passed between Agnes and Everard. She had taken his hand in hers and held it there while she looked searchingly in his face, and said:

"I didn't want to come, but she would have it so, and I thought you knew and had sent for her. Maybe I can persuade her to go back."

"No, Aggie, let her do as she likes,—I deserve it all. But don't feel badly, Aggie. I am glad to see you, at any rate, and I feel better because you are here; and now go to the dinner, which has waited so long."

Agnes was not deceived in the least, and her heart was very heavy as she went down to the dining-room and took her seat by her sister, who affected to be so gay and happy, and who tried to soften old Axie by praising everything immoderately.

But Axie was not deceived, either. She knew it was not all well between the young couple, and as soon as she had sent in the dessert, she started up stairs in quest of her boy, finding him in the chamber where his mother had died, and kneeling by the bed in such an abandonment of grief that, without waiting to consider whether she was wanted or not, she went softly to his side, and laying her hard old hands pityingly on his bowed head, spoke to him lovingly and soothingly, just as she used to speak to him when he was a little boy, and sat in her broad lap to be comforted.

"Thar, thar, honey; what is it that has happened you? Suffin dreffle, or you wouldn't be kneelin' here in de cold an' dark, wid only yer mother's sperrit for company. What is it, chile? Can't you tell old Axie? Is it her that's a vexin' you so? Oh, Mars'r Everard, how could you do it? Tell old Axie, won't you?"

And he did tell her how the marriage occurred, and when, and that it was this which had caused the trouble between him and his father. He said nothing against Josephine, except that he had lived to see and regret his mistake, and that it was impossible for him to live with her as his wife. And Axie took his side at once, and replied:

"In course you can't, honey, I seen that the fust thing. She hain't like you, nor Miss Beatrice, nor Miss Rossie. She's pretty, with them eyes and long winkers, an' she's kind of teterin' an' soft; but can't cheat dis chile. 'Tain't the real stuff like your mother was. Sposin' I go and paint my face all over with whitenin'. I ain't white for all dat. Thar's nobody but ole black nigger under de whitewash, for bless your soul, de thick lips and de wool will show, an' it's just de same with no 'count white folks. But don't you worry, I'll stan' by you. Course you can't live with her. I'll make a fire an' fetch you some supper, an' you'll feel better in de mornin',—see if you don't."

But Everard asked to be left alone, that he might think it out and decide what to do. He could not go to bed, and so he sat the entire night before the fire in the room where his mother had died, and where his father had denounced him so angrily, and where Rosamond had come to him and asked to be his wife. How vividly that last scene came up before him, and he could almost see the little girl standing there again, just as she stood that day, which seemed to him years and years ago. And but for that fatal misstep that little girl, grown to sweet womanhood, now might have been his. Turn which way he would, there was no help, no hope; and the future loomed up before him dark and cheerless, with always this burden upon him, this bar to the happiness which might have been his had he only waited for it. Surely, if his sin was great, his punishment was greater, and when at the last the gray morning looked in at the windows of his room, it found him white, and haggard, and worn, with no definite plan as to his future course, except the firm resolve that whatever his life might be, it would be passed apart from Josephine.

CHAPTER XXXVI

ROSAMOND'S DECISION

Rosamond had sent word to Everard that she would see him after breakfast, and he went to her at once, finding her sitting up just as she was the previous night, but much paler, and more worn-looking, as if she had not slept in months. But the smile with which she greeted him was as sweet and cordial as ever, and in the eyes which she fixed so steadily upon him he saw neither hatred nor disgust, but an expression of unutterable sorrow and pity for him, and for herself, too, as well. Rossie was not one to conceal her feelings. She was too much a child, too frank and ingenuous for that, and there was a great and bitter pain in her heart which she could not hide. Everard had never said in words that he loved her, but she had accepted it as a fact, and when her dream was so rudely dispelled she could no more conceal her disappointment than she could hide the ravages of sickness so visible upon her face.

"I've been thinking it all over," she began, as he sat down beside her, "and though my opinion may not be worth much, I hope you will consider it, at least, and give it some thought before deciding not to adopt it."

He guessed what was coming, and nerved himself to keep quiet while she went on:

"Everard, she is your wife. You cannot undo that, except in one way, and that you must not take, for it is wicked and wrong. You loved her once. You say you were quite as much to blame for the marriage as she, and you know you have been wrong in keeping it a secret so long. She has just cause for complaint, and I want you to try to love her again. You must support her, and it will be so much better, and save so much talk and gossip if you live in the same house with her,—in this house, your rightful home."

"Never, Rossie!" he exclaimed, vehemently, "never can I make her really my wife, feeling as I do. It would be a sin, and a mockery, and I shall not do it. You say I loved her once; perhaps I did, though it seems to me now like a child's fancy for some forbidden dainty, which, if obtained, cloys on the stomach and sickens one ever after. No, Rossie, you talk in vain when you ask me to live with Josephine as my wife, or even live with her at all. The same roof cannot shelter us both. Support her I shall, but live with her, never! and I am prepared for all the people will say against me. If I have your respect and sympathy I can defy the world, though the future looks very dreary to me."

His voice trembled as he spoke, and he leaned back in his chair as if he, too, were faint and sick, while Rossie continued:

"Then, if you will not live with her under any circumstances, this is my next best plan. Forrest House is her natural home, and she must stay here, whatever you may do."

"Here, Rossie! Here with you! Are you crazy?" Everard exclaimed, and Rosamond replied:

"I am going away. I have thought it all over, and talked with Mrs. Markham. She has a friend in St. Louis who is wanting a governess for her three children, and she is going to write to-day and propose me, and if the lady consents, I,—I am going away."

Rossie finished the sentence with a long drawn breath, which sounded like a sob, for this going away from all she loved best was as hard for her as for Everard, who felt suddenly as if every ray of sunlight had been stricken from his life. With Rossie gone the world would be dark indeed, and for a few moments he used all his powers of eloquence to dissuade her from the plan, but she was quite resolved, and he understood it at last, and answered her:

"Perhaps you are right; but Heaven pity me when you are gone!"

For a moment Rosamond was silent, and then she said, in her usual frank way:

"Yes, Everard, I understand, or I think I do, and it would be foolish in me to pretend not to know,—to believe,—I mean," and the bright color began to mount to Rossie's cheeks as she went on: "I mean that I believe you do care for me some,—that if I were dead you would remember me longer than any one else. I guess you like me a little, don't you, Everard?"

It was the child Rossie,—the little girl of his boyhood,—who spoke with all her old simple-heartedness of manner, but the face which looked up at the young man was not the face of a child, for there was written on it all a woman's first tenderness and love, and the dark eyes were full of tears, and the parted lips quivered even after she ceased to speak, and sat looking at him as fearlessly and as little abashed as she had looked at him when she asked to be his wife. And how could he answer that question so innocently put? "You do like me a little, don't you, Everard?" How, but to stoop and kiss the quivering lips which kissed him back again unhesitatingly, but when he sought to wind his arms around her, and hold her closely to him, she motioned him away, and said: "No, Everard, you might kiss me once, and I might kiss you back, as we would do if either of us were dying, and it was our farewell to each other, as this is. I can never kiss you again, never; nor you me, nor say anything like what we have been saying. Remember that, Everard. The might have been is past, and when we meet, as we sometimes may, it will be on the old footing, as guardian and ward, or brother and sister, if you like that better. And now listen, while I finish telling you what my wishes are with regard to the future."

Rosamond's was the stronger spirit then, and she compelled him to sit quietly by and hear her while she planned the future for him. Josephine was to live at Forrest House, and to receive a certain amount of income over and above the support which he would give her. But to this last he stoutly objected. Not one dollar of Rossie's money should ever find its way to her, he said. He could support her with his profession, and if Rossie did not choose to use what was rightly her own it would simply accumulate on her hands, without doing good to any one.

So Rossie gave that project up, but insisted that she should vacate the house as soon as she was able, and leave Josephine in possession, and Everard was commissioned to tell her so, and to say that she must excuse Miss Hastings from seeing her until she was stronger, and that she must feel perfectly at home, and free to ask for whatever she liked.

At first Josie listened incredulously to Everard; it seemed so improbable that Rossie would deliberately abandon her handsome home, and give it up to her. But he succeeded in making her understand it at last, taking great care to let her know that she was to have nothing from the Forrest estate except the rent of the house; that for everything else she was dependent upon him, who could give her a comfortable support, but allow nothing like luxury or extravagance.

To this Josephine assented, and was gracious enough to say that it was very kind and generous in Miss Hastings, and to express a wish that she might see her and thank her in person. But to this Everard gave no encouragement. Miss Hastings was very weak, he said, and had already been too much excited, and needed perfect quiet for the present. Of course, so long as she remained there she would be mistress of the house, and Josephine her guest. For himself, he should return to his old quarters in town, and only come to the house when it was necessary to do so on business. If Josephine was needing money, he had fifty dollars which he could give her now, and more would be forthcoming when that was gone.

Nothing could have been more formal than this interview between the husband and wife, and after it was over Josephine sat down to write to Mrs. Arnold in Europe, while Everard went boldly out to face the world waiting so eagerly for him.

CHAPTER XXXVII

MATTERS ARE ADJUSTED

If Josephine had not known herself to be worse even than Everard had charged her with being, she might not have submitted so quietly to the line of conduct he proposed to pursue toward her, but the consciousness of misdeeds, known only to herself, made her manageable, and willing to accept the conditions offered her. Had Rosamond been allowed to give her a part of her income she would have taken it as something due to her, but as that was forbidden she was well satisfied with the house and its surroundings, and the support her husband could give her. To return to Holburton, after having announced publicly that she was going to her husband, would have been a terrible mortification, and something which she declared to herself she would never have done, and so she resolved to make the most of the situation in Rothsay. To stand well with the people in town was her great object now, and to that end every art and grace of which she was capable was brought into requisition, and so well did she play her part that a few of the short-sighted ones, with Mrs. Dr. Rider at their head, espoused her cause and looked askance at Everard, who kept his own counsel, with the single exception of Lawyer Russell, to whom he told his story, and who assumed such an air of reserve and dignity that not even his most intimate friends dared approach him on the subject which was interesting every one so much.

Everard knew that he was an object of suspicion and gossip, but cared little or nothing for it, so absorbed was he in his own trouble, and in watching the progress of affairs at the Forrest House, where Josephine was to all intents and purposes the mistress, issuing her orders and expressing her opinions and wishes with far more freedom than Rossie had ever done. She, too, was very reticent with regard to her husband, and when Mrs. Dr. Rider asked in a roundabout way what was the matter, she replied, in a trembling voice:

"Oh, I don't know, except he grew tired of me during the years we were separated; but please don't talk to me about it, or let any one else, for I cannot speak of it,—it makes me so sick."

She did act as if she were going to faint, and Mrs. Rider opened the window and let in the cool air, and told Josephine to lean on her till she was better, and then reported the particulars of her interview so graphically and well that after a day or so everybody had heard that poor Mrs. Forrest, when asked as to the cause of the estrangement between herself and husband, had at once gone into hysterics and fainted dead away. Of course the curious ones were more curious than ever, and tried old Axie next, but she was wholly non-committal, and bade them mind their business and let their betters alone.

Rosamond was now the last hope, but she had nothing to say whatever, except that under the circumstances she felt that Mrs. Forrest at least ought to live at her husband's old home, and that arrangements to that effect had been made. As for herself, it had been her intention to teach for a long time, and as Mrs. Markham declared her competent, she was going to try it, and leave the place to Mrs. Forrest. Nothing could be learned from Rossie, who was too great a favorite with everyone to become a subject of gossip; and whatever might be the cause of the trouble between Everard and Josey, her spotless, innocent life was too well known for any censure to fall on her, and Josephine could not have reached her by so much as a breath of calumny, had she chosen to try, which she did not. With her quick intuition she understood at once how immensely popular Rossie was, and resolving to be friends with her, if possible, she waited anxiously for a personal interview, which was accorded her at last, and the two met in Rossie's room, where, in her character as invalid, Rossie sat in her easy-chair, with her beautiful hair brushed back from her pure, pale face, and her great, black eyes unusually brilliant with excitement and expectation.

Josephine, too, had been almost as nervous with regard to this interview as Rosamond herself, and had spent an hour over her toilet, which was perfect in all its details, from the arrangement of her hair to her little high-heeled slippers with the fanciful rosettes.

Rosamond was prepared for something very pretty, but not as beautiful as the woman who came half hesitatingly, half eagerly, into the room, and stood before her with such a bright, winning smile upon her lovely face that it was hard to believe there was guile or artfulness there. Rising to her feet Rossie offered her hand to her visitor, who took it and pressed it to her lips, while she said something about the great happiness it was to see one of whom she had heard so much.

"Why, I used actually to be half jealous of the Rossie Everard was always talking about," she said, referring to the past as easily and naturally as if no cloud had ever darkened her horizon, or come between her and the Everard who had talked so much of Rossie.

When Josephine first entered the room Rossie was very pale, but at this allusion to herself and Everard there came a flush to her cheeks and a light to her eye which made Josephine change her mind with regard to her personal appearance.

"Nobody can ever call her a beauty," she had said to herself at first, but as the interview progressed, and Rossie grew interested and earnest, Josephine looked wonderingly at her glowing face and large black eyes, which flashed and shone like stars, and almost bewildered and confused her with their brightness, and the way they had of looking straight at her, as if to read her inmost thoughts.

It was impossible to suspect Rossie of acting or saying anything she did not mean, for her face was like a clear, faithful mirror, and after a little Josephine began to grow ill at ease in her presence. The bright black eyes troubled her a little when fixed so earnestly upon her, and she found herself wondering if they could penetrate her inmost thoughts, and see just what she was. It was a singular effect which Rossie had upon this woman, whose character was one web of falsehoods and deceit, and who, in the presence of so much purity and innocence, and apparent trust in everybody, was conscious of some new impulse within her, prompting her to a better and sincerer life. Wondering how much Rossie knew of her antecedents, she suddenly burst out with:

"Miss Hastings, or Rossie,—I so much wish you'd let me call you by the name I have heard so often. I want to tell you at once how I have hated myself for taking that money, the price of your lovely hair, and letting you believe I was a dreadful gambler, seeking Everard's ruin."

She had her hand on the "lovely hair," and was passing her white fingers through it and letting it fall in curling masses about Rossie's neck and shoulders, as she went on:

"It was such a funny mistake you made with regard to me, and it was wrong in me to take the money. I would not do it now; but we were so poor, and I needed it so much, and Everard could not get it. Has he told you all about those times, I wonder, when we were first married, and he did love me a little."

"He has told me a good deal," was Rossie's straightforward answer; and sitting down upon a stool in front of her Josey assumed the attitude and manner of a child as she went on to speak of the past, and to beg Rossie to think as leniently of her as possible.

"Men are not always correct judges of women's actions," she said, "and I do not think Everard understands me at all. Our marriage in that hasty manner was unwise, but if I erred I surely have paid the severest penalty. Such things fall more heavily upon women than upon men, and I dare say you think better of Everard this moment than you do of me."

Rossie could not say she didn't, for there was something in Josephine's manner which she did not like. It seemed to be all acting, and to one who never acted a part, it was very distasteful. But she tried to evade the direct question by answering: "I have known Everard so long that I must of course think better of him than of a stranger. He has been so kind to me;" then, wishing to turn the conversation into a channel where she felt she should be safer, she plunged at once into her plan of leaving the house to Josephine, saying that she had never thought it right for her to have it, and speaking of the judge's last illness, when she was certain he repented of what he had done.

At first Josephine made a very pretty show of protesting against it.

"It is your own home," she said, "and though I appreciate your great kindness, I cannot feel that it is right to take it from you."

"But I thought you understood that it was quite a settled thing that I am to go away, as I have always intended doing. Everard told you so. Surely he explained it to you," Rossie said, in some surprise.

Josephine did not quite know how to deal with a nature like Rossie's, but she guessed that for once it would be necessary for her to say very nearly what she thought, and so for a few moments the two talked together earnestly and soberly of the future, when Rossie would be gone and Josephine left in charge.

"You will only be taking what is yours a little in advance," Rossie said, "for when I am of age I shall deed it back to Everard; and then, on the principle that what is a man's is also his wife's, it will be yours, and I hope that long before that it will be well with you and Everard; that the misunderstanding between you will be cleared up; that he will do right, and if,—if,—you are conscious of any defect in your character which annoys him, you will overcome it and try to be what he would like his wife to be, for you might be so happy with him, if only you loved each other."

The great black eyes were full of tears, and Rossie's face twitched painfully as she compelled herself to make this effort in Everard's behalf. But it was lost on Josephine, who, thoroughly deceitful and treacherous herself, could not believe that this young girl really meant what she said; it was a piece of acting to cover her real feeling, but she affected to be touched, and wiped her own eyes, and said despondingly that the time was past, she feared, the opportunity lost for her to regain her husband. He did not care for her any longer; his love was given to another, and she looked straight at Rossie, who neither spoke nor made a sign that she heard or understood, but she looked so very white and tired that Josephine arose to go, after thanking her again for her kindness and generosity, and assuring her that everything about the house should be kept just as she left it, and that in case she changed her mind after trying the life of a governess, and wished to return, she must do so without any reference to her convenience or pleasure.

And so the interview ended, and Josephine went back to her room and Agnes, to whom she said that she had found Miss Hastings rather pretty, and that she was on the whole a nice little body, and had acted very well about the house, "though," she added:

"I consider it quite as much mine as hers. That old man was crazy, or he would never have left everything to her, and he tried afterward to take it back, it seems, and right the wrong he had done. She told me all about it, and how his eyes followed her, and shut and opened as she talked to him. It made me so nervous to think of those eyes; I believe they will haunt me forever. And Everard never told me that, but let me believe his father died just as angry with him as ever. I tell you, Agnes, I am beginning to hate that man quite as much as he hates me, and if I were sure of as comfortable a living and as good a position elsewhere as he can give me here, I'd sue for a divorce to-morrow, and get it, too, and then,—'away, away, to my love who is over the sea.'"

She sang the last words in a light, flippant tone, and then sat down to write to Dr. Matthewson, whose last letter, received before she left Europe, was still unanswered.

Three weeks after this interview Rosamond left Rothsay for St. Louis, where she was to be governess to Mrs. Andrews' children on a salary of three hundred dollars a year. Everard and Josephine both went to the depot to see her off, the one driving down in the carriage with her, and making a great show of regret and sorrow, the other walking over from his office, and maintaining the utmost reserve and apparent indifference, as if the parting were nothing to him; but at the last, when he stood with Rossie's hand in his, there came a look of anguish into his eyes, and his lips were deathly white as he said good-by, and knew that all which made life bearable to him was leaving him, forever.

CHAPTER XXXVIII

"WAITING AND WATCHING FOR ME"

It was the first of January when Rossie left Rothsay for St. Louis, and three weeks from that day a wild storm was sweeping over the hills of Vermont, and great clouds of sleet and snow went drifting down into the open grave in Bronson church-yard, toward which a little group of mourners was slowly wending its way. Neither Florida skies nor Florida air had availed to restore life and health to poor wasted, worn-out Mollie Morton, although at first she seemed much better, and Trix and Bunchie, in their childish way, thanked God, who was making their mamma well, while the Rev. Theodore, in Boston, felt something like new hope within him at the cheerful letters Mollie wrote of what Florida was doing for her. But the improvement was only temporary, and neither orange blossoms or southern sunshine could hold the spirit which longed so to be free, and which welcomed death without a shadow of fear.

"I have had much to make me happy," Mollie said to Beatrice, one day, when that faithful friend sat by her holding the tired head upon her bosom, and gently smoothing the once black hair, which now was more than three-fourths gray, though Mollie was only thirty-one. "Two lovely children, and the kindest, best husband in the world,—the man I loved and wanted so much, and who I think, likes me, and will miss me some when I am gone forever."

This she said, looking straight at Beatrice, whose face was very pale as she stooped to kiss the white forehead and answered:

"I am sure he will miss you, and so shall I, for I have learned to love you so much, and shall be so sorry when you are gone."

"Truly, truly, will you be sorry when I am dead? I hardly thought anybody would be that but father and mother, and the children," Mollie said, while the lips quivered and the great tears rolled down her cheeks as she continued: "We are alone now, for the last time it may be, and I want to say to you what has been in my heart to say, and what I must say before I die. When I was up in that dreary back room in New York, so sick, and forlorn, and poor, and you came to me, bright, and gay, and beautiful, I did not like it at all, and for a time I felt hard toward you and angry at Theodore, who, I knew, must see the difference between me,—faded, and plain, and sickly, and old before my time, and you, the woman he loved first,—fresh, and young, and full of life, and health, and beauty. How you did seem to fill the dingy room with brightness and beauty, and what a contrast you were to me; and Theodore saw it, too, when he came in and found you there. But if there was a regret in his heart,—a sigh for what ought to have been, he never let it appear, but after you were gone, and only the delicate perfume of your garments lingered in the room, he came and sat by me and held my thin, hard hands, so unlike your soft white ones, and tried by his manner to make me believe he was not sorry, and when I could stand it no longer, and said to him: 'I am not much like her, Theo, am I?' he guessed what was in my mind, and answered me so cheerily, 'No, Mollie, not a bit like her. And how can you be, when your lives have been so different; hers all sunshine, and yours full of care, and toil, and pain. But you have borne it bravely, Mollie; better, I think, than Bee would have done.' He called you Bee to me for the first time, and there was something in his voice, as he spoke the name, which told me how dear you had been to him once, if, indeed, you were not then. But he was so good, and kind, and tender toward me that I felt the jealousy giving way, though there was a little hardness left toward you, and that night after Theo was sleeping beside me I prayed and prayed that God would take it away, and He did, and I came at last to know you as you are, the dearest, noblest, most unselfish woman the world ever saw."

"No, no, you must not say that. I am not good or unselfish; you don't know me," Bee cried, thinking remorsefully of the times when she had ridiculed the brown alpaca dress and the woman who wore it, and how often she had tired of her society, in which she really found no pleasure, such as she might have found elsewhere.

But she could not wound her by telling her this. She could only protest that she was not all Mrs. Morton believed her to be. But Mollie would not listen.

"You must be good," she said, "or you would never have left your beautiful home and your friends and attached yourself to me, who am only a drag upon you. But sometime in the future you will be rewarded; and, forgive me, Miss Belknap, if I speak out plain, now, like one who stands close down to the river of death, and, looking back, can see what probably will be. I do not know how you feel toward Theo, but of this I am sure, he has never taken another into the place you once filled, and at a suitable time after I am gone he will repeat the words he said to you years ago, and if he does, don't send him away a second time. He is nearer to your standard now than he was then. He is growing all the time in the estimation of his fellow-men. They are going to make him a D. D., and the parish of which he is pastor is one of the best and most highly cultivated in Boston. And you will go there, I hope, and be a mother to my children, and bring them up like you, for that will please Theo better than my homely ways. Trix is like you now, and Bunchie will learn, though she is slower to imitate. You will be happy with Theo,—and I am glad for him and the children; but you will not let them forget me quite, but will tell them sometimes of their mother, who loved them so much. I hoped to see Theo once more before I died, but something tells me he will not be here in time; that when he comes I shall be dead. So you will ask him to forget the many times I worried and fretted him with my petty cares and troubles. Tell him that Mollie puts her arms around his neck and lays her poor head, which will never ache again, against his good, kind heart, and so bids him good-by, and goes away alone into the brightness beyond, for it is all bright and peaceful; and just over the river I am crossing I seem to see the distant towers of 'Jerusalem the Golden' gleaming in the heavenly sunshine, which lies so warm upon the everlasting hills. And my babies are there waiting and watching for me. Sing, can't you, 'Will some one be at the beautiful gate, waiting and watching for me?'"

There was too heavy a sorrow in Beatrice's heart, and her voice was too full of tears for her to sing to the dying woman, who clung so closely to her. But what she could not do, little Trixey did for her. She had entered the room unobserved, followed by Bunchie, whose hands were full of the sweet wild-flowers they had gathered and brought to their mother, who was past caring for such things now. The yellow jessamine and wild honeysuckle lay unheeded upon her pillow, but at the sound of her children's voices a spasm of intense pain passed for a moment over her face, and was succeeded by a smile of peace as she whispered again: "Somebody sing of the beautiful gate," and instantly Trixey's clear voice rang through the room, mingled with little Bunchie's lisping, broken notes, as she, too, struck in and sang:

> "Will any one be at the beautiful gate,
> Waiting and watching for me?"

Dear little ones, they did not know their mother was dying; but Beatrice did, and her tears fell like rain upon the pinched, white face pillowed on her arm, as she kissed the quivering lips, which whispered softly:

"Darling Trix and Bunchie,—God bless them!—and tell Theo Mollie will be at the beautiful gate, waiting and watching for him, and for you all,—waiting and watching as they now wait and watch for me over there, the shining ones, crowding on the shore, and some are there to whom I first told the story of Jesus in the far-off heathen land. Tell Theo they are there, and many whom he led to the Saviour. It is no delusion, as some have thought. I see them, I see into Heaven, and it is so near; it lies right side by side with this world, only a step between."

Her mind was wandering a little, for her words became indistinct, until her voice ceased altogether, and Beatrice watched her as the last great struggle went on and the soul parted from the body, which was occasionally convulsed with pain, as if it were hard to sever the tie which bound together the mortal and immortal.

At last, just as the beautiful southern sunset flooded the river and the fields beyond with golden and rosy hues, and the fresh evening breeze came stealing into the room, laden with the perfume of the orange and lemon blossoms it had kissed on its way, Mollie Morton passed from the world where she had known so much care to the life immortal, where the shining ones were waiting and watching for her.

And far down the coast, threading in and out among the little islands and streams, came the boat which bore the Rev. Theodore Morton to the wife he hoped to find alive. Bee's summons had found him busy with his people, with whom he was deservedly popular, and who bade him God-speed, and followed him with prayers for his own safety, and, if possible, the recovery of his wife, whom they had never seen. But this last was not to be, and when about noon the boat came up to its accustomed landing-place, and Bee stood on the wharf to meet him, he knew by one glance at her face that he had come too late. Everything which love could devise was done for the dead, on whose white face the husband's tears fell fast when he first looked upon it, feeling, it may be, an inner consciousness of remorse as he remembered that all his heart had not been given to her. But he had been kind, and tender, and considerate, and he folded her children in his arms, and felt that in all the world there was nothing so dear to him as his motherless little ones.

The next day they left Florida for the bleak hills of Vermont, where the wintry winds and drifting snow seemed to howl a wild requiem for the dead woman, whose body rested one night in the old home where the white-haired father and mother wept so piteously over it, and even Aunt Nancy forgot to care for the tracks upon her clean kitchen floor, as the villagers came in with words of condolence and sympathy. Beatrice was with the mourners who stood by the grave that wild January day when Mollie Morton was buried, and she gave the message from the dead to the husband, who wept like a child when he saw his wife laid away under the blinding snow, which, ere the close of the day, covered the grave in one great mountain drift.

Both Everard and Rossie had written to Beatrice telling her of Josephine's arrival at the Forrest House, and, with a feeling that she was needed in Rothsay, she started for home the day after Mollie's funeral.

CHAPTER XXXIX

HOW THE TIDE EBBED AND FLOWED
IN ROTHSAY

Josephine had resolved to be popular at any cost, and make for herself a party, and so good use had she made of her time and opportunities that when Beatrice arrived the weaker ones, who, with Mrs. Rider at their head, had from the first espoused her cause, were gradually gaining in numbers; while the better class of people, Everard's friends, were beginning to think more kindly of the lady of the Forrest House, where an entire new state of things and code of laws had been inaugurated. Axie had, of course, vacated immediately after Rossie's departure, and Josephine had been wise enough not to ask her to remain. She knew the old negress was strongly prejudiced against her, and was glad when she departed, bag and bundle, for the little house she had purchased in town, where she could be near "her boy," and wash and mend his clothes, and fight for him when necessary, as it sometimes was, for people could not easily understand his indifference to the beautiful creature who was conducting herself so sweetly and modestly, and whom women ran to the windows to see when she drove by in the pretty phaeton which, through Rossie's influence, she had managed to get from Everard, or rather, from the Forrest estate. It is true the horse did not suit her. It was too old and slow, and not at all like the spirited animal she used to drive with Captain Sparks at her side in Holburton, but it was an heir-loom, as she called it, laughingly, raised from a stock of horses which had been in the family for years, and was so steady that Mr. Forrest was perfectly willing to trust her with it; and each day she drove around the town, showing herself everywhere, bowing to everybody high and low, and because she had heard that Miss Belknap used to do so, taking to drive the sick and infirm among the poor and needy, to whom she was all kindness and sympathy. With this class, however, she did not stand as well as with the grade above them. It would almost seem as if they were gifted with a special insight, and read her character aright; and though they accepted what she offered them, they did not believe in her, and privately among themselves declared she was not a lady born,—or a fitting wife for Everard.

Agnes never appeared with her in public, and was seldom seen at the house when people called. "She was very shy and timid, and shrank from meeting strangers," Josephine said, to the few who felt that they must ask for her, and who accepted the excuse and left Agnes free to become in Rothsay what she had been in Holburton, a mere household drudge, literally doing all the work for the colored woman whom Josephine employed and called her cook, but who was wholly incompetent as well as indisposed to work. So the whole care devolved on Agnes, who took up her burden without a word of protest, and worked from morning till night, while Josephine lounged in her own room, where she had her meals more than half the time, or drove through the town in her phaeton, managing always to pass the office where Everard toiled early and late, in order that he might have the means to support her without touching a dollar of Rossie's fortune.

As yet Josephine's demands upon him were not very great. Old Axie had been a provident housekeeper, and Josephine found a profusion of everything necessary for the table. Her wardrobe did not need replenishing, and she could not venture upon inviting company so soon, consequently she was rather moderate in her demands for money; but Everard knew the time would come when all he had would scarcely satisfy her, and for that time he worked, silently, doggedly, rarely speaking to any one outside his business unless they spoke to him, and never offering a word of explanation with regard to the estrangement, which was becoming more and more a matter of wonder and comment,—as people saw only sweetness and graciousness in Josey, and knew nothing of her other side.

Such was the state of affairs when Beatrice came home, very unexpectedly to the Rothsayites, who wondered what she would think of matters at the Forrest House. Josephine had spoken frequently of Miss Belknap, who, she said, was for a few weeks an inmate of her mother's family, and whom she admired greatly. Josey was the first to call upon Beatrice; and throwing herself upon her neck, burst into tears, saying:

"Oh, Miss Belknap, I am so glad you have come to be my friend and sister, and I need one so much. I wish I had told you the truth when you were in Holburton, but Everard was afraid of having it known, and now he is so cold and distant and I,—am,—so unhappy. You will be my friend and help me. You were always so kind to me, and I liked you so much."

Beatrice shook her off as gently as possible, and answered that she should certainly try to do right, and asked after Agnes, and how her visitor liked Rothsay, and if Rosamond had written to her, and gradually drew the conversation away from dangerous ground, and did it in such a manner that Josephine felt that she had more to fear from Bee Belknap than from all the world besides. And she had, for Bee's opinion was worth more than that of any twenty people in Rothsay; and when it was known that there was little or no intercourse between Elm Park and the Forrest House, that the two ladies were polite to each other and nothing more, that Beatrice never expressed herself with regard to Mrs. Forrest or mentioned her in any way, but was on the same friendly terms with Everard as ever, and when, as a crowning act, she made a little dinner party from which Josephine was omitted, the people who had been loudest in Josey's praises began to whisper together that there must be something wrong, and gradually a cloud not larger than a man's hand began to show itself on the horizon. But small as it was, Josephine discovered its rising, and fought it with all her power, even going so far as to insinuate that jealousy and disappointment were the causes of Miss Belknap's coolness toward her. But this fell powerless and dead, and Josey could no more injure Beatrice than she could turn the channel of the river from its natural course. For a time, however, Josephine held her ground with a few, but when early in June the new hotel on the river road was filled with people from the South, many of them gay, reckless young men, ready for any excitement, she began to show her real nature, and her assumed modesty and reticence slipped from her like a garment unfitted to the wearer. How she managed it no one could guess, but in less than two weeks she knew every young man stopping at the Belknap House, as it was named in honor of Beatrice, and in less than three weeks she had taken them all to drive with her, and Forrest House was no longer lonely for want of company, for the doors stood open till midnight, and young men lounged on the steps and in the parlors, and came to lunch and dinner, and the rooms were filled with cigar-smoke, and Bacchanalian songs were sung by the half-tipsy young men, and toasts were drank to their fair hostess, whom they dubbed "Golden Hair," and called an angel to her face, and at her back, among themselves, a brick, and even "the old girl," so little did they respect or really care for her.

And Josephine was quite happy again, and content. It suited her better to be fast than to play the part of a quiet, discreet woman, and so long as she did not overstep the bounds of decency, or greatly outrage the rules of propriety, she argued that it was no one's business what she did or how much attention she received. As Axie had predicted, the real color was showing through the whitewash, and people began to understand the reason why Everard was becoming so grave, and reserved, and even old in his appearance, with a look upon his face such as no ordinary trouble could ever have written there.

And so the summer waned and autumn came and went, and then Josephine, who, while affecting to be so merry and gay, writhed under the slights so often put upon her, discovered that she needed a change of air, and decided that a winter in Florida was necessary to her health and happiness, and applied to Everard for the means with which to carry out her plan. At first Everard objected to the Florida trip as something much more expensive than he felt able to meet, but his consent was finally given, and one morning in December the clerk at the St. James Hotel, in Jacksonville, wrote upon his books "Mrs. J. E. Forrest and maid, and Miss Agnes Fleming, Rothsay, Ohio," while a week later there was entered upon another page, "Dr. John Matthewson, New York City," and two weeks later still "Mrs. Andrews and family, and Miss Rosamond Hastings, St. Louis, Mo."

CHAPTER XL

DR. MATTHEWSON'S GAME

The St. James was full that season, and when Mrs. J. E. Forrest arrived she found every room occupied, and was compelled to take lodgings at a house across the Park, where guests from the hotel were sometimes accommodated with rooms, and where, in addition to her own parlor and bedroom, she found a large square chamber, which she asked the mistress of the house to reserve for a few days, as she was expecting an old friend of her husband's, and would like to have him near her, inasmuch as Mr. Forrest was not able to come with her on account of his business. Later in the season he might join her, but now he was too busy. She laid great stress upon having a husband, and she was so gracious, and affable, and pretty, that her landlady, Mrs. Morris, was charmed at once, and indorsed the beautiful woman who attracted so much attention in the street, and who at the hotel took everything by storm. She had laid aside her mourning, and blossomed out in a most exquisite suit of navy-blue silk and velvet, which, although made in Paris more than a year before, was still a little in advance of the Florida fashions, and was admired by every lady in the hotel, and patterns of the pocket, and cuffs, and overskirt were mentally taken and experimented upon in the ladies' rooms, where the grace, and beauty, and probable antecedents of the stranger were freely discussed.

Nobody had ever heard of Mrs. J. E. Forrest, and few had heard of Rothsay, but there were some people at the St. James, this winter, who remembered Miss Belknap and Mrs. Morton, and when it was known that Mrs. Forrest was their friend the matter was settled, and Josephine became the belle and beauty of the place. Young men stationed themselves near the door through which she came in to the hall to look at her as she passed, but if she was conscious of their homage she made no sign, and never seemed to know how much attention she was attracting. One or two ladies spoke to her at last as she stopped for a while in the parlor, and so her acquaintance began, and Miss Belknap was brought to the surface, and Mr. Forrest was talked about, and a little hacking cough was produced, by way of showing what had sent this dainty, delicate creature away from her husband, with no other guardianship than that of her sister. But Agnes' presence was sufficient to save appearances. She was much older, and so quiet and reserved, and even shy, that the ladies made no advances to her, and after a little scarcely noticed her as she sat apart from them, waiting patiently till her brilliant sister was ready to go home. Josephine was expecting a gentleman friend, whom she had known ever since she was a young girl, she said, the fourth day after her arrival, and the ladies were glad, as it would be so much pleasanter for her in her husband's absence; and so matters were made easy for the coming of Dr. Matthewson, who, since parting from Josephine in Dresden, more than a year before, had visited nearly every city of note in Europe, sometimes meeting with success in his profession as gambler and sometimes not, sometimes living like a millionaire and sometimes like a beggar. The millionaire life suited him the best, but how to secure it as a permanency, or even to secure a comfortable living which required neither exertion nor self-denial, was something which puzzled him sorely, until he received a letter from Josephine, which inspired him at once with fresh courage and hope. The letter, which was written from the Forrest House, was a long time in reaching him, and found him at last in Moscow, where his genius of bad luck was in the ascendant, and he had fallen into the toils of a set of sharpers, who were using him for their own base purposes. Handsome in face and form, winning in his manner, and perfectly familiar with nearly every language spoken on the Continent, he was very useful to them by way of bringing under their influence strangers who visited the city, and they kept a hold upon him which he could not well shake off.

When he received Josephine's letter telling him where she was, and the disposition Judge Forrest had made of his property, and Rosamond's determination not to use more of it than was absolutely necessary, but to restore it to Everard when she came of age, he made up his mind to leave Moscow at all hazards, and, crossing the sea, seek out the sister in whom he suddenly found himself greatly interested. And to this end fortune favored him at last by sending in his way a German Jew,—Van Schoisner,—between whom and himself there sprang up a friendship which finally resulted in the Jew's loaning him money enough to escape from the city which had been in one sense a prison to him. Van Schoisner was his compagnon-du-voyage, and as both were gamblers, they made straight for Vienna, where Matthewson's luck came back to him, and he won so rapidly and largely that Van Schoisner, who was tinged with German superstition, regarded him as one whom the god of the gaming-table especially favored, and clung to him and made much of him, and when a malarial fever attacked him took him to his brother's, a Dr. Van Schoisner, who kept what he called a private maison de sante, in an obscure Austrian town, half-way between Vienna and Lintz.

And here Dr. Matthewson paid the penalty of his dissipated life in a fit of sickness which lasted for months, and left him weak and feeble as a child. During all this time he did not hear from Josephine, whose letters never reached him, and he knew nothing of her until he reached New York, when he wrote at once to her at Rothsay, asking very particularly for Rosamond, and announcing his intention of visiting the Forrest House, if agreeable to the inmates.

To this letter Josephine replied immediately, telling him not on any account to come to Rothsay, but to join her in Florida about the middle of December, when she would tell him everything which had happened to her since their last meeting in Dresden. In a postscript she added:

"Miss Hastings is not here, and has not been since last January. She is somebody's governess, I believe."

And it was this postscript which interested the doctor more than the whole of Josephine's letter. If Rosamond were not in Rothsay, then where was she, and how should he find her? for find her he must, and play the role of the loving brother, which role would be all the more effective, he thought, because of the air of invalidism there was about him now, and which sat well upon him. He really was weak from his recent illness, but he affected more languor than he felt, and seemed quite tired and exhausted when he reached the house where Josephine was stopping, and where his room was in readiness for him; and Josephine cooed and fluttered about him, and was glad to see him, and so anxious that he should have every possible attention.

And Dr. Matthewson enjoyed it all to the full, and was never tired of hearing of the Forrest House, or of asking questions about Rosamond, of whom Josey at last affected to be jealous.

And so the days went on until the first week in January, when one morning, as the doctor and Josephine sat together on the long piazza of the hotel, a carriage from the boat arrived, laden with trunks, and children, and two ladies, one middle-aged, and apparently the mother of the children, the other, young, graceful, and pretty, even in her soiled traveling dress of dark gray serge. As she threw back her vail and descended from the carriage Josephine started suddenly, and exclaimed:

"Rosamond Hastings, for all the world! What brought her here?"

"Who? Where? Do you mean that girl with the blue vail and gray dress, and,—by Jove, those magnificent eyes?" Dr. Matthewson said, as Rosamond turned her face in the direction where he was sitting, and glanced rapidly at the groups of people upon the piazza, without, however, seeing any one distinctly.

"Yes, that's Rosamond," Josey replied, with a feeling of annoyance at the arrival of one who might work her so much harm. "I'll see her at once, and make that matter right," she thought, and trusting to Rossie's good nature and her ingenuity, she resumed her conversation with the doctor, who seemed unusually silent and absent-minded, and after a little excused himself, saying he was not feeling quite well, and believed he'd take a sail on the river, and see if the fresh air would not revive him.

Usually Josephine had been his companion in his sails on the river, but he did not ask her to go with him now. He preferred to be alone, and with a gracious bow he walked away, not so much to try the river air as to think over and perfect his plans for the future.

"By George!" he said to himself, "this is what I call luck. Here I've been wondering how I should find the girl, and behold, she has dropped suddenly upon me, and if I play my cards well the game is mine, and her money too, or my name is not Matthewson, ne Hastings, ne villain of the first water."

CHAPTER XLI

HOW THE GAME WAS PLAYED

Rosamond's life as a governess had been a very happy one, but still there was always present with her a consciousness of pain and loss,—a keen regret and intense longing for the "might have been," and a great pity for Everard, whose lot she knew was so much harder to bear than her own; for with him the burden was growing heavier, and the chain ever lengthening, which bound him to his fate. He had written to her frequently during the past year, friendly, brotherly letters, such as Josephine might have read without just cause of complaint. But he had given way once, and in a moment when his sky was very dark, had poured out his soul in passionate, burning words, telling how dreary life was to him without her, and asking if she could not bring herself to think that the divorce he could so easily get was valid, and would free him from the hateful tie which bound him?

And Rosamond had answered him, "Only God can free you from the bond," and had said he must never write like that to her again if he wished her to answer him; and so the last hope was crushed, and Everard took up his load once more and tried to bear it more manfully, and by a closer attention to his practice to forget the bliss which might have been his had he not rashly thrown the chance away. Rossie had said to him in her letter, "Pray, Everard, as I do; pray often, that you may learn to think of me as only your sister, the little Rossie who amused you and whom you liked to tease."

But Everard did not pray. On the contrary, he was in a most resentful and rebellious frame of mind, and blamed the Providence which had permitted him to go so far astray. It was well enough for women to pray, and those who had never been tried and tempted as he had been, but for himself, he saw no justice in God's dealings with him, and he could not ask to be content with what he loathed from his very soul, he wrote in reply to Rossie, who, while he grew harder and more reckless, was rapidly developing into a character sweeter and lovelier than anything Everard had known. And the new life and principle within her showed itself upon her face, which was like the face of Murillo's sweetest Madonna, where the earthly love blends so harmoniously with the divine, and gives a glorious and saintly expression to the lovely countenance. But Rossie's health had suffered from this constant sense of pain and loss. The bright color was gone from her cheeks save as it came and went with fatigue or excitement, and there was about her a frail, delicate look, wholly unlike the child Rossie, who used to be so full of life and vigor in the old happy days at the Forrest House. Still, she complained of nothing except that she was always tired, but this was, in Mrs. Andrews' mind, a sufficiently alarming symptom, and it was as much on Rossie's account as on her own that she planned the trip to Florida, where she hoped the warm sunlight would bring strength again to the girl whom she loved almost as a daughter.

And so they were at the St. James, where Mrs. Andrews found several acquaintances, but Rossie saw no one whom she knew, and as she had a severe headache she kept her room, and did not appear until the second day, when she dressed herself and went down to join Mrs. Andrews on the piazza, where the guests usually congregated in the morning. There was a crowd of them there now, and Mrs. Andrews, who was very popular and entertaining, was already the center of a group of friends, with whom she was talking, when Rosamond appeared, and made her way towards her. Everybody turned to look after her, and none more eagerly than Dr. Matthewson, who stood leaning against the railing, and waiting for Josephine to join him. He had watched for Rossie all the preceding day, after her arrival, and felt greatly disappointed at her non-appearance, but he knew she was there, his half-sister, and the heiress to hundreds of thousands, and, as he believed, of a nature which he could mold as he would clay, if he could only know just what her tastes were, and adapt himself to them. As yet he had been quite non-committal, only devoting himself to Josephine, and talking very little with any one, so that he could, if necessary, become a saint or a sinner, and not seem inconsistent. Probably he would have to be a saint, he thought; and when at last Rossie appeared, and passed so near to him that he might have touched her, he was quite sure of it. Girls with the expression in their faces which hers wore didn't believe in slang and profanity, and the many vices to which he was addicted, and of which Josephine made so light. Rossie was pure and innocent, and must never suspect the black catalogue of sins at which he sometimes dared not look. How fair and lovely she was, with that sweet modesty of demeanor which never could have been feigned for the occasion; and how eagerly the doctor watched her as she joined Mrs. Andrews, and was introduced to the ladies around her.

"Good morning. A penny for your thoughts," was cooed in his ear, and turning, he met Josephine's blue eyes uplifted to him, and Josephine herself stood there in her very prettiest white wrapper, with an oleander blossom in her golden hair.

She, too, had watched anxiously for Rosamond, whom she meant to secure before any mischief could be done, and she saw her now at once in the distance, and saw the doctor was looking in that direction, too, and knew, before she asked him, of what he was thinking. But a slight frown darkened her face at his frank reply:

"I am thinking how very pretty and attractive Miss Hastings is. You must manage to introduce me as soon as possible, or I shall introduce myself."

Just then Rossie turned her face fully toward her, and their eyes met in recognition. There was a violent start on Rossie's part, and the blood flamed into her cheeks for an instant and then left them ashy pale, as she saw the woman for whom she could not have much respect smiling so brightly upon her, and advancing to meet her as quickly and gladly as if they were the greatest friends.

"Oh, Miss Hastings!" she said, in her most flute-like tones, "this is a surprise. I am so glad to see you. When did you come?"

Rossie explained when she had come and with whom, and after a few brief remarks on the town and the climate, made as if she would return to Mrs. Andrews; but now was Josephine's opportunity or never, and still holding Rossie's hand, which she had not relinquished, she said:

"Come with me a moment, please; there are so many things I want to say. Suppose we take a little turn on the piazza," and leading Rossie around the corner of the hotel to a seat where no one was sitting, she plunged at once into the subject uppermost in her mind.

"Miss Hastings," she said, "you alone of all the people here know just how I am living with Everard, or, rather, not living with him. It was not necessary for me to explain everything, and for aught they know to the contrary, I have the most devoted of husbands, who may join me any day. You, of course, can undeceive them if you like, but——"

"Mrs. Forrest," Rossie exclaimed, "I have no wish to injure you. If I am asked straightforward questions I must tell the truth; otherwise I have nothing to say of your life at home, or of anything in the past pertaining to you and Everard."

"Thank you so much. I knew I could trust you," Josephine said, feeling immensely relieved. "And now come, let me present you to a friend whom I used to know in Holburton, and met afterward in Dresden. He is here for his health, and is so kind to Aggie and me. You must come to my room and see Agnes. She never stops a moment here after she has had her meals."

She talked rapidly and excitedly, and laid her hand on Rossie's arm, as if to lead her to Dr. Matthewson, who forestalled the intention by suddenly appearing before them. He was more impatient to speak to Rosamond than Josephine was to have him, and joined them for that very purpose. Never in his life had he seemed more at his ease or appeared to better advantage, and there was something very winning and gracious in his manner as he bowed to Miss Hastings, and hoped she found herself well in the delicious Florida air.

"You do not look very strong," he said. "I hope a few days of this sunshine will do you much good." He was very kind and considerate, and bade her be seated again while he talked with her a few moments on indifferent topics. Then, consulting his watch, he said to Josephine: "Mrs. Forrest, don't you think we should have that game of croquet before the day gets hotter? You see they are beginning to occupy the grounds already," and he nodded toward the opposite side of the park, where a group of young ladies and gentlemen were knocking about the balls preparatory to a game. "To-morrow we shall ask you to join us," he said to Rossie, "but as a physician, I advise you to rest to-day after your long journey. Coming suddenly into this climate is apt to debilitate if one is not careful. Good morning, Miss Hastings," and with a graceful wave of his hand he walked away with Josephine, leaving Rosamond to look after and admire his splendid physique and manly form, and to think what a pleasant, gentlemanly person he was, with such a melodious voice.

Already he was beginning to affect and influence her thoughts, and she sat and watched him as he walked very slowly toward the croquet-ground, where, instead of joining in the game, he sat down at some little distance and continued his conversation with Josephine, whose cheeks were flushed and who seemed unusually excited.

The doctor's first remark to her as they left the hotel had been:

"Well, Joe, did you fix it all right with her?"

"Fix what?" Josephine asked, knowing perfectly well what he meant, but being determined that he should explain.

"Why, have you hired her not to go back on you, and tell that you are a grass widow instead of a loving wife, whose husband is pining in her absence?"

The elegant doctor could be very coarse and unfeeling when he talked with Josephine, whom he understood so well, and who replied:

"If you mean will she hold her tongue about my affairs, she will, and she does not know that you are the 'priest all shaven and shorn, who married the youth all tattered and torn to the maiden all forlorn.' I did not think it necessary to tell her that. Possibly, though, she may have heard your name from Everard; I do not know how that may be. I only told her that I knew you in Holburton, and that I met you again in Dresden."

"Yes;"—the doctor smoothed his mustache thoughtfully a moment, and then added: "I say, Joe, don't be in such a hurry to get to the croquet. I want to talk with you. I've turned a new leaf. I've reformed. That time I was so sick in Austria, I repented. I did, upon my soul, and said a bit of a prayer,—and I believe I'll join the church again; but first I'll confess to you, who I know will be as lenient toward me as any one. I suppose you think you know just what and who I am, but you are mistaken. I am a hypocrite, a rascal, a gambler, and have broken every Commandment, I do believe, except 'thou shalt not kill,' and under great provocation I might do that, perhaps; and, added to all this, I am Rossie Hastings' half-brother."

"Rossie Hastings' brother! Do you mean you are Rosamond's brother? and did you know it when you first came to Holburton, and why isn't your name Hastings, then?" Josephine asked, excitedly, and he replied, in the most quiet and composed manner:

"One question at a time, my dear. I am her brother, and my name was Hastings once,—John Matthewson Hastings. I took the Matthewson and dropped the Hastings to please a relative, who left me a few thousands at her death. I did know Rossie was my sister when I first met Everard Forrest in Holburton, and to that knowledge you owe your present exalted position as his wife."

She turned her eyes inquiringly upon him, and he continued:

"I told you I was going to make a clean breast of my sins, and I am, so far as your business is concerned. I hated Everard and the whole Forrest race, and that was my revenge!"

"Hated Everard! For what? Had you seen him before you met him in Holburton?" Josephine said; and he replied:

"Yes, I had seen him, and I carried the marks of our meeting for weeks and weeks on my forehead, and the remembrance of it in my heart always. I had a stepmother,—a weak young thing whom I hated from the first, for no special reason that I now recall, except that she was a stepmother and I thought I must hate her; and I did, and worried her life almost out of her;

and when a baby sister was born I hated that, because it was hers, and because it would naturally share in my father's property, which was not large. The new mother was luxurious in her tastes, and spent a great deal, and that made trouble between her and my father, who, though a very elegant man in public, was the very Old Nick at home, and led his young wife such a life that even I pitied her sometimes, and did not wonder that she left him at last, and took refuge with her intimate friend, Mrs. Forrest, Everard's mother. Not long after she left home my father died, and I was made very angry because of some money he left to Rossie, which I thought ought to be mine, inasmuch as it came to him from my mother. So I persecuted my mother-in-law, who, I believe, was more afraid of me than of the old Harry himself. I went to the Forrest House and demanded first to see her, and then to see my sister, pretending I was going to take her away. The boy Everard was at home, had just come in from riding, and he ordered me from the house, and when I refused to go the stripling attacked me with his whip, and laid the blows on well, too, especially the one on my face, the mark of which I carried so long. I swore I'd have revenge on him, and I kept my word, though at one time I gave up the idea entirely. That was at the camp-meeting, where a lot of them converted me, or thought they did, and for a spell I felt differently, and got a license to preach, and tried to be good; but the seed was sown on stony ground and came to nothing, and I took seven spirits worse than the first, and backslid and quit the ministry, and went to studying physic, and was called doctor, and roamed the world over, sometimes with plenty of money, sometimes with none, and drifted at last to Holburton, where you asked me to be the priest in the play, and marry you to Everard Forrest. You probably do not remember how closely I questioned you about the young man. I wished to be certain with regard to his identity, and I was after talking with him about his home in Rothsay. He told me of Rossie, and boasted of the whipping he had given her brother, whose vengeance he did not fear. He was young. His father was rich, and proud as Lucifer, and would hardly think a princess good enough to marry his only son, much less you, the daughter of his landlady.

"Something told me I could not do Everard a worse turn than to tie him fast in matrimony. You were not his stamp; not the one to hold him long; he would repent the act sooner or later, while his father would make life a burden to him when he came to know it. So I was particular to leave nothing undone which would make the marriage valid, and when you were man and wife I felt perfectly happy, until,—I began to get interested in you myself, and then I sometimes wished my tongue had been cut out, for I'll be hanged if I don't admire you more than any woman I ever saw, notwithstanding that I know you like a book."

"Spare your compliments and keep to your story, and tell me why you have made no effort to see Rossie all these years," Josephine said, coldly; and he replied, "Reason enough. I was not particularly interested in her then, and did not think an acquaintance with her would pay; but later she has come before me in the character of an heiress, which makes her a very different creature; you see, don't you?"

"Yes, I see. Your sudden interest in her is wholly mercenary. Suppose I should betray you? Are you not afraid of it?" Josephine asked, and in her blue eyes there was a look which the doctor did not quite like; but he affected not to see it, and replied, "Afraid? No, because telling is a game two can play at as well as one. You cannot afford to quarrel with me, Joe."

The man's face was exceedingly insolent and disagreeable in its expression for a moment, while he glanced sidewise at his companion, who made no sign that she heard him, but seemed wholly intent upon the game, which was now growing very exciting. But when the expression changed, and he continued in his most winning tone:

"No, we must stick to each other, and whatever good comes to me I'll share religiously with you;" she began faintly to comprehend him, and turning her eyes upon him, said:

"Well, to return to first principles, Rossie is interesting to you now because she has money; but she will not use it even for herself."

"No!"—and the doctor mused thoughtfully a moment; then he said: "I like the girl's appearance, upon my soul I do! She is a pretty little filly, and if I'd met her years ago she might have made a man of me, but it is too late now; I am sold to Satan, body and soul, and must do his bidding. How much is she worth, do you think?"

"The Forrest estate is variously estimated from two hundred to five hundred thousand. I should say, perhaps, two hundred and fifty," Josephine replied, and the doctor continued:

"And she will not touch the principal on account of some queer notions she has of giving it back to Forrest when she is twenty-one?"

"No, she will not touch the principal, nor more of the interest than is absolutely necessary," Josephine said, and for a few moments the doctor was silent and seemed to be intently thinking.

When he spoke again he said:

"You say she is pious, or pretends to be, and if she does it is genuine; there is no deceit in that face. I'd trust it with my soul, if necessary. I tell you I like the girl. She is just the one to keep men from losing faith in everything good. I'll wager now that Forrest is in love with her, and that's one reason he does not take any more stock in you. Is he?" and the doctor looked steadily at Josephine, who turned very pale as he thus probed her so closely.

So far as affection was concerned she had none for her husband, but it hurt her pride cruelly to know that with all her beauty and grace she could not influence him one whit, or turn him from the girl she was sure he loved as he had never loved her. She generally told the truth to Dr. Matthewson, who had some subtle power to find it out if she did not, and now, though sorely against her will, she answered:

"Yes, he worships the ground she treads upon."

"Then, why in thunder doesn't he get a divorce from you and marry her? That surely would be an easy thing to do under the circumstances," was the doctor's next remark.

"That is more than I can guess, unless he is too proud to endure the notoriety of such a procedure. Certainly it is no consideration for me which deters him," Josephine said; adding suddenly, as she glanced up the street: "There she comes now. You'd better declare yourself at once."

But the doctor knew his own plans best with regard to Rosamond, who was coming toward the croquet-ground with two of her pupils, Clara and Eva Andrews. She did not see the doctor and Josephine until she was close upon them, and then simply bowing to them, she passed on and was soon out of sight.

That night, as she was about preparing for bed, a thick heavy envelope was brought to her room, directed in a hand she did not recognize. Breaking the seal and glancing at the signature, she read with a thrill of wonder and perplexity the name, "John Matthewson, ne Hastings," while just above it were the words, "Your affectionate brother."

"My brother," she repeated. "What does it mean?" and for a moment she felt as if she were going to faint with the rush of emotions which swept suddenly over her.

Of her brother, personally, she remembered nothing. She only knew that she had one; that in some way he annoyed and worried her mother; that he was not highly esteemed by the Forrests, and that he was probably dead. Latterly, however, since she had gone out into the world alone to care for herself, she had often thought of him, and how delightful it would be to have a brother who was good, and kind, and true, and who would care for her as brothers sometimes care for their sisters. Occasionally, too, she had amused herself with fancying how he would look if he were alive, and how he would treat her. But she had never dreamed of any one as handsome, and polished, and elegant as Dr. Matthewson, who signed himself her brother, and had filled three or four sheets of paper with what he had to say. Very eagerly she singled out the first sheet and began:

"Dear Sister Rossie:—You will pardon me for not addressing you as Miss Hastings, or even Rosamond, when I tell you I am your brother, and have always thought of you as Rossie, the little girl who, I suppose, does not remember me, and who, perhaps, has not been taught to think of me very pleasantly. But, Rossie, I am a changed man, or I would not present myself to you, a pure, innocent girl, and ask for sympathy and love. I do not believe you care to hear all the events of my life in detail, and so I shall not narrate them, but of a few things I must speak, in order that we may rightly understand each other. And first, your mother. I was a spoiled, wayward boy of sixteen when she came to us, and I was prejudiced against her by an aunt of mine, who, I think now, wanted my father herself. A stepmother was to me the worst of all evils, and I thought it was manly to tease and worry her, while I blush to say my father also treated her so shamefully that at last she fled from him, as you know, and took refuge at the Forrest House, where she finally died.

"I was there once to see her, and as you may not have heard the particulars of that visit, and I wish to keep back nothing you ought to know, I will tell you about it."

Then followed a pretty truthful account of the encounter with Everard, the cowhiding, and the vow of revenge, after which the doctor spoke of his subsequent career, his change of name, his sudden conversion at a camp-meeting, his life as a clergyman in Clarence, his back-sliding, and lapse into his former evil ways, his few months' study as a physician, his first trip to Europe, and at last his sojourn for the summer in Holburton, where he met Everard Forrest again, and was asked by Josephine to take the part of priest in the play called "Mock Marriage."

"Then it was," he wrote, "that the devil entered into me and whispered, 'Now is your hour for revenge on the stripling who dared lay his hand on you.' From all I could learn of the Forrests, or rather, of the judge, I guessed that he would rebel hotly against a penniless bride in Miss Fleming's social position, and that nothing could be more disastrous for Everard than such a marriage; and yet I aided and abetted it, and took care that it should be altogether binding, and so gained my mean revenge, for which I have been sorry a thousand times,—yes, more than that; and if I could undo the work of that night I would do it gladly. But I cannot, and others suffer the consequences. You see I am not ignorant of the manner in which Mr. and Mrs. Forrest live, and I am sorry for them both, and am laying bare my heart to you that you may know exactly the kind of brother you have found; and that, however bad he may have been, he is a different man now, or he would never intrude himself upon you.

"On my first interview with Everard in Holburton, I managed to get him to speak of you, and I half resolved to seek you and claim you as my own. But a sense of unworthiness kept me back. I was not a fitting guardian for a girl like you, and so I still kept silence, and after a time went to Europe again, where I remained until quite recently, and where, by a long and dangerous illness, I was brought to a realization of my sins, and resolved to lead a new life. Naturally, one of the first and strongest desires of my new life was to find you. Mrs. Forrest, who wrote to me occasionally, had told me that you had left the Forrest House, of which you were the lawful heir; and as my health required a warm climate, I came first to Florida, after my return to America, intending, in the spring, to spare no pains to find you. The rest you know.

"And now, Rossie, will you take me for a brother? If so, please leave a line at the office, telling me where I can see you and when, and in all the world there will be no one so happy as your affectionate brother,

"John Matthewson, ne Hastings."

Rossie was not as strong as when she was a child, and any over-fatigue or unusual excitement was sure to be followed by a nervous headache, which sometimes lasted two or three days; and as she read this letter she felt a cold, clammy sweat breaking out in the palms of her hands, while a cutting pain in her head warned her that her old enemy, neuralgia, was threatening an attack. That she believed every word of the letter need hardly be said, for hers was a nature to believe everything, and it made her very happy to know that the brother who heretofore had been to her only a myth, was found at last, and such a brother, too. Then the question arose as to how Everard would receive this man who had purposely done him so great a wrong. Would he forgive him for her sake, and believe in his repentance? She should write to him the next day and tell him all about it, and her heart throbbed with a new and keen delight at the thought of some one to care for her, some one to lean upon and advise her and help her with that dreadful Forrest estate. And then her busy little brain plunged into the future, and began to wonder where they should live and how, for that she should live with her brother she did not for a moment doubt. Her place was with him, and she should try so hard to make him happy, and keep him in the new way wherein he was beginning to walk. In this state of mind it was impossible to sleep, and when at last morning came it found her wakeful and unrefreshed, with dark rings about her eyes, and so severe a pain in her temples and the back of her neck that to go down to breakfast was impossible. She had barely strength to dress herself and lie down upon the couch, where Mrs. Andrews found her, after having waited some time for her appearance.

Very rapidly and briefly Rosamond told her the good news, which Mrs. Andrews accepted readily. She had heard before that Miss Hastings had a brother, if he were not dead, and having met the doctor the previous day and been much prepossessed with him, as strangers always were, she rejoiced with her young friend, but advised her to wait until her head was better before she risked the excitement of an interview. But this Rossie could not do. She should never be better till she had seen her brother, she said, and a message was accordingly sent him to the effect that Rossie would see him in her room whenever he chose to come.

The doctor did not wait a moment, and was soon at Rossie's side, bending over her, and telling her not to allow herself to be agitated in the least, but to lie quietly upon her pillow and let him do most of the talking.

In all the world there was hardly a more accomplished and fascinating hypocrite than Dr. Matthewson, and so well did he use his powers and art that if Rossie had had any distrust of him or his sincerity it would have been entirely swept away during the half hour he spent with her, now talking of himself as he used to be with great regret, and of himself as he was now with great humility; now telling how glad he was to find his little sister, and then complimenting her in a way which could not fail to be gratifying to any woman. Then he spoke of her health, and was sorry to find her so frail and delicate, and asked her many questions about herself, while he held her hand and felt her pulse professionally. "Had she ever thought her heart at all diseased, or that her lungs were affected?" he asked; adding, quickly, as he saw the sudden start she gave:

"Oh, don't be frightened, and conclude you have either consumption or heart disease. I only asked because some members of our family far back died with a heart difficulty, and if I remember right your mother had consumption. But we must not let you have either of them. You do not seem to have a great amount of vitality. Are you never stronger than now, and do these headaches occur very often?"

He had her hand in one of his, and with the other was stroking her head and hair, while she answered that nothing ailed her except the headache to which she had been subject all her life, and a predisposition to sore throat whenever she took cold.

"Ah, yes, I see," and the doctor looked very wise. "Bronchial trouble, no doubt, aggravated by our dreadful American climate. Excuse me, mignonne, if I confess to being more than half a European. I have lived abroad so much that I greatly prefer being there, and know the climate is better for me. Some day not far distant we must go there together, you and I, and I'll take such care of you that people will hardly know you when you come back. I'll have some color in these white cheeks, though I don't believe I could improve the eyes."

It was the great desire of Rossie's life to go to Europe some day, and she assented to all her brother said, and wrote to Everard immediately after her interview with the doctor, and told him of her brother, and what a good, noble man he had become.

Then, as carefully and gently as possible, she spoke of the wrong he had done to Everard, and for which he was so very sorry.

"I do not suppose you can ever like him as I do," she wrote, "but I hope you will try to be friends with him for my sake."

Accompanying this letter was one from the doctor himself, couched in the most conciliatory terms, full of regret for the past and strong in good intentions for the future.

"I shall be so glad to be friends with you for Rossie's sake, if for no other," he wrote in conclusion. "She holds you in higher esteem than any living being; so let her plead for me; and when we meet, as we sometimes must, or Rossie be very unhappy, let it be at least with the semblance of friendship."

Everard's first impulse on receiving these letters was to go to Florida at once and wrest Rossie from the fangs of the wolf, as he stigmatized the doctor, in whom he had no faith.

"I cannot forgive him," he said. "I will not, though he were ten times her brother; and I distrust him, too, notwithstanding his protestations of reform."

But he could not write this to Rossie. He said to her in his letter that if her brother was all she represented him to be, he was glad for her sake that she had found him, and that he hoped always to be friendly with her friends and those that were kind to her.

"But if he were the archangel himself," he added, "I should find it hard to forgive him for having removed from my grasp what I miss more and more every day of my life, and long for with an intensity which masters my reason and drives me almost to despair. But whatever I may feel toward him, Rossie, I shall treat him well for your sake, and if you can find any comfort in his society, take it, and be as happy as you can."

To Dr. Matthewson he wrote in a different strain. He did not believe in the man, and though he made an effort to be civil he showed his distrust and aversion in every line. If the doctor had repented, he was glad of it, but wished the repentance had come in time to have saved him from a life-long trouble. A boy's cowhiding was a small matter for a man to avenge so terribly, he said, and then added:

"It is no news to me that you are John Hastings, Rossie's half-brother. I knew that long ago, but kept it to myself, as I did not wish Rossie to know how much of my unhappiness I owed to her half-brother. Wholly truthful and innocent, she thinks others are the same, and if you tell her you are a saint she will believe it implicitly until some act of your own proves the contrary. She is very happy in your society, and I shall do nothing to make her less so, but don't ask me to indorse you cordially, as if nothing had ever happened. The thing is impossible. If we meet I shall treat you well for Rossie's sake, and shall not seek to injure you so long as you are kind and true to her, but if you harm a hair of Rossie's head, or bring her to any sorrow, as sure as there is a heaven above us, I'll pursue you to the ends of the earth to be even with you."

There was an amused smile on Dr. Matthewson's face as he read this letter, which showed him so plainly what Everard's opinion of him was. A meaning smile, too, it was, and one which his enemy would hardly have cared to see.

"So ho! the young man threatens me," he said to himself. "I am glad he has shown his hand, though it was foolish in him to do so, and proves that he is not well up in fencing. I wonder what he wrote to Rossie; and if she will show me the letter."

Rossie could not show it to him, but when next they met in her room, she said to him:

"I have heard from Everard, and he says that he is glad I am so happy with you, and he will be friendly with you always, and I do so hope you will like each other. Have you, too, heard from him?"

The doctor laughed a low, musical laugh, and drawing his sister to him, said:

"You cannot dissemble worth a cent. Don't you suppose I know that Everard's letter to you was not all you hoped it to be. He finds it hard to forgive me for having deprived him of something which his maturer manhood tells him is sweeter, more precious, and far more to be desired than the object of his boyish passion. And I cannot blame him. I am as sorry as he, in a different way, of course, and you——"

He did not finish the sentence, for Rossie broke away from him, and burying her face in the cushions of the couch on which they were sitting, burst into an uncontrollable fit of weeping.

"Don't," she said, as he made an effort to soothe her. "Don't speak to me, please. I must have it out now. I have kept it back so long. Oh, I wish I had died when I was a little girl, and before I grew to be a woman, with a woman's love, which I must fight all my life, and never know a moment of absolute rest and quiet. Oh, why did you do it? Why did you separate me from my love? for he is mine, and I am his. I was everything to him; he was everything to me. Oh, Everard, just this once I will say out what I feel. I love you,—I love you; and I cannot help it. I know it is wicked, and try to put it away. I bury it out of my sight; I trample on it; I stamp upon it; I think I have the mastery over it, and on the slightest provocation it springs into life more vigorous than ever, and I cannot conquer it."

She had said all she had to say, but she kept on sobbing piteously, like one in mortal pain; and, hardhearted, and utterly unprincipled, and selfish as he was, Dr. Matthewson could not be wholly indifferent to a grief such as he had never witnessed but once, and that was years ago; but she who wept before him then was a fair-haired German girl asking reparation for the ruin he had wrought. He had laughed at her, and telling her she would make a splendid queen of tragedy, had bidden her go upon the stage and achieve her fortune, then come to him, and perhaps he would make terms with her. But Rossie was a different creature. She knew nothing of such girls as Yula Van Eisner. She was Rossie, heiress of the Forrest property,— and he walked up and down the room several times, and blew his nose vigorously, and made a feint of wiping his eyes with his perfumed handkerchief, and then came and stood by her, and putting his hand on her bowed head, said to her:

"Don't, Rossie, give way like this, or you will drive me mad, knowing, as I do, that I have in one sense caused your sorrow. If I could undo it, I would, but I cannot. There is, however, a way out of it. Have you ever thought how easily he might get a divorce, which would make him free?"

"He would not be free;" and, lifting up her head, Rossie flashed her bright black eyes upon him indignantly. "The Bible would not recognize him as free, neither would I, and you must not speak of such a thing to me."

"Then I will not," he answered, still more soothingly; "but Rossie, it is folly to give way like this, though for this once I am glad you did. For now I understand better the cause of these pale cheeks and irregular pulse, and am sure you need entire change of air and scene, such as you can only find in Europe, where we are going in the spring. Think of a summer in Switzerland among the glorious Alps. I know every rock, and chasm, and winding path there, and shall be so happy in seeing you enjoy them."

He was speaking very kindly to her now, and she gradually grew calm, and listened while he talked of Europe and what they should see there, for he quite decided that they would go in the spring, and as nothing in the way of travel could suit Rossie better, she told Mrs. Andrews the next day of the plan and wrote of it to Everard, ignoring altogether his right as her guardian to be consulted. But Everard did not resent it, though for a time he felt half tempted to say that she should not go, for a strong presentiment of evil swept over him with such force as to keep him awake the entire night. But with the morning his nervous fears subsided, and he could see no reasonable objection to Rossie's going for the summer to Europe with her brother, whose perfect knowledge of the manners, and customs, and language of the different countries must make him a very pleasant traveling companion.

Rossie had written that she should go directly from Florida to New York, and so Everard wrote her his farewell letter, and sent her a draft for five hundred dollars, which he said she might need, as she would not care to be altogether dependent upon her brother. Rossie's first impulse was to return the draft, but Dr. Matthewson advised her to keep it and not wound Everard by returning it to him.

So Rossie kept it, or rather, gave it to her brother, and sent a letter of thanks to Everard and another to Bee, telling her of her intended journey, and bidding her good-by.

With that subtle and mysterious foresight with which women seem to be gifted, and for which there is no explanation, Beatrice anticipated danger at once, though in what form she could not define. She only knew that she wished Rossie was not going away alone with Dr. Matthewson, but she kept her fears from Everard, and wrote to Rossie that she should be in New York to see her off. And when Rossie stood at last on the deck of the Oceanic, Bee was there and Everard, too, taking his last look at the face which would haunt him in the years to come, as the faces of the dead haunt us when we feel that by some act of ours interposed in time we might have saved the life dearer than our own. Beatrice had said to him:

"I am going to New York to see Rossie. Will you go with me?" and without a moment's reflection he went, and spent one blissful day with her, a day never to be forgotten, when he drove with her in the Park, and watched the constantly changing expression of her sweet face, which had grown so pale and thin that he was more than half reconciled to let her go, hoping much from the sea air and the new life she would lead. To the doctor he was polite and courteous, and an ordinary observer might have thought them the best of friends, so that Rossie was satisfied, and would have been quite happy if she could have forgotten the distance which would so soon intervene between them.

On the whole Beatrice was favorably impressed with Dr. Matthewson, who was so kind to Rossie and so thoughtful for her that she dismissed her fears, and half wished she, too, were going with them. She said as much to Rossie when they stood upon the deck waiting for the order to be given for all visitors to leave.

"Oh, I'd give the world if you were," Rossie cried. "I should not feel as I do,—afraid, somehow, as if I was never to return,—never to see you again, or Everard."

She was holding his hand in both hers as she spoke, and in that moment of farewell she forgot everything except the presentiment that she was going from him forever; that their parting was final; and her tears fell like rain as she bent over and kissed his hand, and said:

"Good-by, Everard, good-by, and if it should be forever, you'll never forget me, will you?" These were her parting words, which, in the after time, he said over and over again, with a bitterer, heavier pain than that he felt when with Bee he stood upon the Jersey shore, and watched the Oceanic sailing down the bay.

And so Rossie passed from their sight, and the next they heard from her she had reached Liverpool, but was greatly fatigued with the voyage, during which she had been sick most of the time. It was only a few lines she wrote to Everard, to tell him she was safe.

"When I am stronger," she said, "I will send you and Beatrice a long letter, and tell you everything. Now I can only sit by my window and look out upon the busy streets of Liverpool and St. George's Hall right opposite, and occasionally there comes over me a feeling of something like homesickness when I remember how far I am from America and the friends who never seemed half so dear to me as now, when I am so widely separated from them."

The next he heard from Rossie she was in London, delightfully located in lodgings near Regent's Park, and playing keep house, while her brother was the best and kindest man in the world, and she was very happy. Then they went to Switzerland, and Rossie's letters were full of the enthusiastic delight she felt with everything around her. Of her health she seldom spoke, and when she did, it was not altogether satisfactory. Sometimes she was so tired that she had kept her room for two or three days, and again a headache, or sore throat, or cold, had confined her to the house for nearly a week; but she was very happy among the Alps, and wished that Beatrice and Everard were there with her to enjoy what she was enjoying. As the summer advanced, however, her letters were not so frequent, and the doctor sometimes wrote for her, saying she was not feeling well, and had made him her amanuensis. They were not to be alarmed, he said; it was only a slight heart difficulty, induced by the mountain air, which often affected tourists in that way. He should take her to Southern France early in the autumn, and then to Italy as the season advanced, and should not return to America till spring.

When Everard read this letter there came over him again a great horror of some impending evil threatening Rossie, and do what he might he could not shake it off. He thought of it by day and dreamed of it by night, and could he have found any good excuse for doing so, he would have started for Europe, and kept near the girl, who, it seemed to him, was in some imminent peril, though of what nature he could not guess.

Some time in November a letter came from Dr. Matthewson, dated at Nice, where he said they had been for two or three weeks, and where, as he expressed it, "I hope our dear invalid is improving. Switzerland was not the place for her, and she seemed to grow weaker every day she staid there, so I hastened back to Paris, and then came here, where she seems very happy, but is weak as an infant. She complains of nothing but weariness, and cannot get rested. Of course I have the best medical advice for her, and everything is done which can be to arrest the disease and give her some strength. The physicians have forbidden her reading or writing, even short letters, and I must do it for her for the present. I hope that neither you nor Miss Belknap will be needlessly distressed, for I assure you there is no immediate danger, and with proper care, such as she has now, she will, I think, be quite able to return to America in the spring. She is calling to me now from her chair by the window, and says. 'Tell them not to be troubled about me; that I walked too much in Switzerland and am not rested yet, but am so happy here in beautiful Nice, looking out upon the blue Mediterranean.'"

After this letter Rossie never wrote again, and though Everard and Beatrice wrote frequently to her, asking her to send them a line, if nothing more, Dr. Matthewson always replied, "She is forbidden to write even so much as her name;" and so the fall and winter crept on, and Rossie was first in Venice, then in Florence, and then in Rome. And then Dr. Matthewson wrote one day to Everard, saying that Rossie did not know of this letter, neither did he wish her to know, as it would only trouble her and retard her recovery, but to be brief, he found himself straitened for money just now, physicians charged so abominably in Europe, and on account of Rossie's illness their expenses were, of course, much heavier than they would otherwise have been, and if Everard would make an advance for Rossie of a few thousand dollars, he should be very glad. He was intending to leave Rome early in the spring, and go to Germany to a famous cure, where the prices were very high.

Double the amount of money asked for was placed at the doctor's disposal, and when that night Everard went to Elm Park to call upon Beatrice, he said, in reply to her inquiries for news from Rossie: "We shall never see her again."

CHAPTER XLII

ALAS, POOR ROSSIE!

It had been a long, dreary year to Everard, and when the anniversary came round of the day when Rossie sailed, it seemed to him that he had lived in that year more than a hundred lives. And yet, in a business point of view he had been very prosperous, and money was beginning to be more plenty with him than formerly, though he could not lay by much, for Josephine made heavy demands upon him. When she left Florida she did not return to Rothsay, where she knew she was looked upon with distrust by the better class. It was a dull, poky hole, she said, and she should enjoy herself better traveling, so she traveled from place to place during the summer and autumn, and in the winter went again to Florida,—but early in the spring she came back to the Forrest House, where she lived very quietly, and seemed to shun rather than court society. She, too, knew of Rossie's failing health, for she heard often from the doctor, and she expressed so much anxiety for her to Beatrice and Everard, hinting that they did not know the worst, that their fears were increased, and suspense was growing intolerable, when, at last, one morning in May, the mail brought to Everard the American Register from Paris, directed in a hand he had never seen before.

Evidently it was sent from the office, and probably had in it the whereabouts of some of his friends who were traveling in Europe, and who occasionally forwarded him a paper when they left one place for another. Mr. Evarts was still abroad, and Everard ran his eye over the list of names registered in different places to see if his was there, for that the paper had anything to do with Rossie he never dreamed. Indeed, she was not in his mind, except as she was always there, in a general way, and so the shock was all the greater and more terrible when he came suddenly upon a little obituary notice, and read, with wildly-throbbing heart, and eyes which felt as if they were starting from their sockets, so great was the pressure of blood upon his brain:

"Died, on the evening of April th, in Haelder-Strauchsen, Austria, of consumption and heart disease, Miss Rosamond Hastings, of Rothsay, Ohio, U. S. A., aged nineteen years and ten months. Seldom has death snatched any one more lovely in person and character than this fair young girl, who, in a strange land, far from home, passed peacefully and willingly to the home above, and whose last words to her weeping brother were: 'Don't cry for me, and tell them at home not to be sorry either. Heaven is as near me here in Austria as it would be in America, and I am so glad to go.'"

Everard could read no more, and throwing the paper from him he buried his face in his hands, and for a few moments gave way to such grief as men seldom feel, and never experience but once in a life-time. He did not weep; his pain was too great for tears; neither did any word escape his livid lips, but his frame shook as with an ague chill, and occasionally a long drawn, moaning sob told how much he suffered, while great drops of sweat gathered thickly upon his face, and in the palms of his hands. No other blow could have smitten him so heavily as he was smitten now. It is true he had felt a great dread lest Rossie should die, but underlying that was always the hope that she would come back again. But all that was ended now, the little ray of sunlight on his horizon had set in gloom, and the night lay dark and heavy around him, with no rift in the black clouds, no light in the future. Rossie was dead, in all her freshness and youthful beauty; Rossie, who had been to him a constant source of pleasure and joy, since he first took her in his arms, a tiny little girl, and kissed her pretty mouth in spite of her remonstrance, "Big boys like oo mustn't tiss nittle dirls like me."

He had kissed her many times since as his sister, and twice with all the intensity of a lover's burning passion, and once she had kissed him back, and he knew just where her lips had touched him, and fancied he felt their pressure again, and the perfume of her breath upon his cheek. But, alas, she was dead, and the Austrian skies were bending above her grave in that far-off town with the strange-sounding German name, which he had not stopped to pronounce.

"What was the name?" he asked himself, speaking for the first time since he read the fatal news, and reaching mechanically for the paper lying open at his feet.

But his eyes were blood-shot and dim, and it took him some time to spell out, letter by letter, the name Haelder-Strauchsen, and to wonder where and what manner of place it was where Rossie died, and if she were lying under the flowers and soft green turf she loved so much in life, and if he should ever see her grave.

"Yes, please Heaven!" he said, "I'll find it some day, and whisper to my darling sleeping there of the love it will be no sin to speak of then. I'll tell her how with her life my sun of hope went down, never to rise again."

Then, glancing once more at the paper, he read a second time "Died, April th," and tried to recall what he was doing on that day, the darkest and saddest which had ever dawned for him. Making allowance for the difference in time between Austria and Ohio, it was little past midday with him when it was evening over there where Rosamond was dying, and with a shudder he remembered how he was occupied then. Josephine had written him a note, asking him to come to the Forrest House as soon after lunch as possible, as she wished particularly to see him. As he walked up the avenue to the house, he had looked around sadly and regretfully at the different objects which had once been so familiar to him, and all of which had been so intimately associated with Rossie. It was a lovely April day, and beds of hyacinths and crocuses were in full bloom, and the daffodils and double narcissuses were showing their heads on the borders near the door. These had been Rossie's special care, and he had seen her so often working among them, trowel in hand, with her high-necked, long-sleeved apron on, that he found himself half-looking for her now.

But Rossie was not there; Rossie was dying far away over the sea; and only Josephine met him in the hall, civilly and haughtily, as had been her manner of late, and taking him into the reception-room where Rossie used to come to him and vex him so with her long dress and new airs of womanhood, told him she had an invitation to visit a friend who lived in Indianapolis, and who had invited her to spend the entire summer with her, and she wished to know if he could furnish her with money for the necessary outfit, and should she shut up the house again and let Agnes go to Holburton, or should she keep it open and leave Agnes in charge.

He told her she could have the money, and said that if Agnes wished to go to Holburton they might as well shut up the house for the summer; and then he left her and walked rapidly down the avenue, thinking of the girl whose presence seemed to fill the place so completely that once, when a bush near the carriage road rustled suddenly as a rabbit darted away, he stopped, half expecting to see a figure in white sun-bonnet and high-necked apron spring out at him just as Rossie used sometimes to do when she was a little child and he a well-grown boy. And she was dying then, when he was thinking so much of her, and she seemed to be so near him. "Dying then and dead now," he said, to himself, just as a step was heard outside, and Lawyer Russell came in, stopping short in alarm at the white, haggard face which Everard lifted to him.

"What is it, my boy? Are you sick? What has happened? Tell me," he asked; and motioning to the paper on the floor, Everard answered sadly, "Rossie is dead."

"Rossie dead! No, no, Ned, it can't be true," Mr. Russell said, and picking up the paper he read the paragraph indicated by Everard, while a tear moistened his eyelids and rolled down his cheeks.

The old man had been very fond of Rossie, and for a few moments he walked up and down the little back office with his hands behind him and his head bent down, then stopping suddenly he gave vent to the exclamation "By George!" uttered in such a tone that Everard looked up quickly and inquiringly, and said:

"What is it? What's the matter?"

"Ned, my boy, look here. This may not be the time nor place to speak of such a thing, but hanged if I can help it," the lawyer replied, coming close to Everard and continuing, "I take it that you considered Rosamond Hastings to have been the lawful devisee to your father's estate."

"I know she was," Everard said; and the lawyer went on in a choking voice:

"Poor little girl! She rebelled against it hotly, and would have deeded it to you if she had lived to come of age,—there's nothing surer than that. But you say she's dead, and she not twenty yet till June, and don't you see, in spite of fate, the estate goes to her brother, who is her heir-at-law, and that's what I call hard on you. I know nothing of the man except what you have told me, but if the half of that is true, he is a scamp, and will run through the property in a quarter of the time it took to make it. Maybe, though, he has some kind of honor about him, and if Rossie knew she was going to die, you may be sure she put in a plea for you, and perhaps he will divide; that's the best you can hope for. So we won't despair till we hear from the brother. There's another mail from the north to-night. A letter may come by that. It ought to have been here with the paper. It's a bad business all round,—very bad. Rossie dead; poor Rossie, the nicest girl and most sensible that ever was born, and the property gone to thunder!"

The old man was a good deal moved, and began again to walk the floor, while Everard laid his head upon the table in a half stupefied condition. Not that he then cared especially what became of his father's money, though the thought that it would go to the man he hated most cordially was a fresh shock to his nerves, but it was nothing to losing Rossie. That was a grief which it seemed to him he could not bear. Certainly he could not bear it alone. He must tell it to some one who would not, like Lawyer Russell, talk to him of money; and when it began to grow dark, so that no one could see how white and worn he was, he arose and walked slowly up to Elm Park, sure of finding a ready and hearty sympathy there.

"Oh, Everard, what is it?" Beatrice asked, when she first met him and saw his white, haggard face.

He answered her as he had answered Mr. Russell, "Rossie is dead," and then seated himself again in the chair from which he had arisen when she came in. Beatrice's tears were falling like rain, but Everard's eyes were as dry as if he had never thought to weep, and there was such a fearful expression of anguish on his face that Beatrice went up to him, and laying her hand on his head, said, pityingly:

"Oh, Everard, don't look like that. You frighten me. Cry, can't you, just as I do? Tears would do you good."

"Cry?" he repeated. "How can I cry with this band like red-hot iron around my heart, forcing it up to my throat. I shall never cry again, or laugh, never. Bee, I know you think me foolish and wicked, too, perhaps; half the world would think it, and say I had no right to love Rossie as I do, and perhaps I have not; but the dearest, sweetest memory of my life is the memory of what she was to me. I know she could never be mine. I gave that up long ago, and still the world was pleasanter to me because she was in it. Oh, Rossie, my darling, how can I live on and know that you are dead?"

Then Beatrice did not attempt to comfort him, for she knew she could not, but she sat by him in silence until he arose and went away, saying to her at parting, and as if he had not told her before, "Rossie is dead."

CHAPTER XLIII

THE LETTERS

The next day's mail brought four foreign letters to Rothsay,—one for Everard, one for Beatrice, one for Josephine, and one for Lawyer Russell. They were all mailed in Vienna, within two days of each other, and the one addressed to Everard was as follows:

"Vienna, April —, ——.

"Mr. Everard Forrest:—Dear Sir—I hardly know why I write to you first, unless it is because I know that what I have to say will hurt you most; you, who I think loved my darling Rossie. You have perhaps received the American Register which I ordered to be sent you from the office in Paris when I forwarded the notice, and so you know why I write to you now. I have written to you from time to time of Rossie's failing health, but never told you as bad as it was, for I did not wish to alarm you unnecessarily, and kept hoping that change of scene might bring the improvement I so greatly desired. But nothing helped her, though she never complained of anything but fatigue. 'So tired,' was all she ever said of herself, and she seemed like some sweet flower fading gradually.

"At Haelder-Strauchsen, a little town among the Austrian hills, I found she was not able to go on as I wished to do, to Vienna, and so we staid there, where she had the best of care. Neither of us thought the end so near until the last day, when she failed rapidly, and talked of you and Miss Belknap, and told me to tell you how much she loved you both, and that you were not to be sorry she was dead, for she was only going home, and Heaven was as near Austria as it was to America. She was so beautiful in her coffin, with a smile of peace upon her face, as if she were resting at last. The people literally covered her with flowers, and strangers' tears fell fast over her coffin as we laid her in the grave.

"I shall come to America soon, and will tell you all you wish to know with regard to her sickness and death, and the many things she said of you, and your kindness to her. I have a lock of her hair for you and Miss Belknap, which I will bring with me.

"And now good-by, and may Heaven pity us both and make us better men for having had our Rossie even for so short a time.

"Truly, John Matthewson."

His letter to Beatrice was in substance much the same as the one to Everard. There were a few more details of Rossie's illness, and a few more words which she said at the last of her friends in America.

Josephine's letter no one saw, and if they had few in Rothsay could have made it out, for it was written in German, which Josephine could readily understand. One or two sentences, however, deserve a place in our story, and must accordingly be given. After indulging in a good deal of sentimentalism with regard to Rossie's death, he added:

"But as every cloud has its silver lining, so has this dark pall which has overshadowed me so heavily. I can now offer you wealth as well as love, and this I dare say you will not object to. So, if you are not already at Indianapolis, go there at once, and perhaps I will join you there after I have paid my respects to Mr. Forrest."

To Lawyer Russell he wrote as follows:

"*Vienna, April —, ——.*

"*Mr. Thomas Russel:—Dear Sir—I have communicated to Mr. Forrest the sad news of my sister's death, and need not enter into the particulars with you, who will hear them from him. I write to you as the family lawyer, on another subject of which I cannot now speak to Mr. Forrest, lest he should misconstrue my motive, and think me anxious and premature in what I am about to say. As a lawyer of large experience you have undoubtedly already thought of the fortune willed to Rossie by Judge Forrest, and of which she died lawfully possessed, and you have probably thought what disposition would now be made of it. You know, of course, that Rossie always protested it was not hers rightfully, and that she should give it back to Everard as soon as she reached her majority. I, however, who am her lawful heir, do not see things as she did, and am not disposed to throw away the good the gods provide. Still I am disposed to be generous and make over to Everard at once a portion of the property. As you must know more about the estate than any one except Everard himself, I wish you would be hunting up the matter, and getting into shape some statement or estimate of the value of the property, so there may be no unnecessary delay when I come to Rothsay, as I shall do at once. I have in New York a friend who is a shrewd, honest lawyer, and I may bring him with me, not because I think there will be any trouble or opposition to my claim, but just to expedite matters and get them settled as soon as possible.*

"*Hoping that you fully understand and appreciate my motives, and that I shall find in you a friend and adviser, I am, yours truly,*

"*John Matthewson.*"

The old lawyer read this twice; then, with his hands under his coat-tails and his glasses on the top of his head, walked up and down his room, muttering to himself:

"Just what I told Ned,—the man is a scoundrel, and he will, with all his fine talk of generosity, bring a New York lawyer here to see to it, as if he wouldn't have fair play and get every cent his due, though I'll be blamed if I wouldn't take advantage of any quirk or loop-hole to crawl out of, if there was one, which there isn't. As Rossie's brother he is her heir, of course, and the whole thing goes to him, for I'll bet my head Ned will never take a dollar. Poor boy, as if he hadn't trouble enough with the loss of the girl, without this new thing to bother."

And if ever a man stood in need of sympathy it was Everard, who seemed completely crushed, and who looked so white and changed that even his best friends forbore speaking to him of Rossie, though they talked much of her among themselves, and many tears were shed for the young girl who had been so great a favorite, and whose grave was so far away. That Everard loved her with more than a brother's love was conceded now by all, and no one thought to blame him for it, but pitied him in his sorrow, which he did not try to conceal. When Lawyer Russell took the doctor's letter to him, and asked what he thought of it, he evinced no surprise or dissatisfaction.

"That's all right," he said, "he is her heir, and he shall have every dollar,—remember, every dollar. I would not take it from her, I will not have it from him; and you must do the business for me. I give it into your hands. I cannot confer with him; I should forget myself sometime, and fly at his throat. I will give you all the papers pertaining to the estate. I have kept the matter perfectly straight, so there will be no trouble in finding just how much he is worth. Now mind, don't you ever dare to think I will have a penny of the money, for I will not, so help me Heaven! till Rossie rises from her grave to give it to me. Then you may talk to me, and not till then."

This was Everard's decision, which both Mr. Russell and Beatrice approved, though both mourned bitterly over the fate which gave Judge Forrest's hoarded stores into the hands of one as unprincipled as Dr. Matthewson, whose arrival was anxiously looked for.

CHAPTER XLIV

THE NEW HEIR

He stepped from the car one June afternoon, elegantly habited in the latest Parisian style of coat, and vest, and hat, with a band of crape around the latter, and a grieved look on his handsome face, as if he were thinking of the dear little girl, dead so far away, and whose fortune he had come to take. With him was a sharp, shrewd-looking man, with round, bright eyes, which saw everything at a glance, and a decidedly foreign accent. To him the doctor always spoke in German, and in this language the two talked together for a few moments after alighting upon the platform in Rothsay.

Evidently they were not expected, for no one was there to meet them, but the doctor inquired for the best hotel, and making his way thither registered his own name and that of his friend, "Walter Klyne, Esq., New York City." Then, engaging two of the best rooms in the house, and ordering dinner at seven o'clock, he started out to reconnoiter, going first to Everard's office and greatly astonishing the young man, who did not know that he had yet landed in New York. It might be thought, perhaps, that the sight of him, with his band of crape upon his hat, and the peculiar air of sadness he managed to infuse into his voice and manner, would awaken in Everard a feeling of sympathy and kindness for one in whose sorrow he had so large a part, but it produced just the contrary effect, and though he went forward with offered hand to meet him, there swept over him a sensation of distrust, and aversion, and dread,—a feeling of horror for which he could not account, any more than he could explain the sudden chill which crept through his veins, as if Rossie's cold, dead hands were touching his, and Rossie's white, still face pressed against his own.

Dr. Matthewson was very polite and very much afraid of wounding Everard's feelings. He was sorry not to find Mr. Russell there, he said, as he wished to talk a little about business, and would like to go over the Forrest House, which he believed was shut up.

Everard gave him the keys, and added, hurriedly:

"You will have no trouble whatever, as I have no intention to dispute your right to the property. It was lawfully Rossie's, and, therefore, yours now."

It was the first time Rossie had been mentioned, and Everard felt as if his heart were bursting as he pronounced the name, while the doctor's lip quivered, and he shut his eyes tight to keep the tears back.

"Thanks," he said, as he took the offered keys. "We will speak of business by and by, when I can trust myself to tell you more fully what your sister's wishes were. Now, I only wish to see the house where she used to live. I will return the keys on my way back to the hotel. I wish you good evening, sir."

He lifted his hat courteously, and walked away with his friend, while Everard watched him for a moment with that same icy chill about his heart and the feeling as if from the darkness and silence of her far-off grave Rossie were beckoning to him and trying to warn him of danger.

Meantime the two gentlemen went rapidly along the streets of Rothsay, where, as strangers, they were stared at by the people, who watched them until they turned into the avenue leading to the Forrest House.

"A splendid inheritance! I quite envy you, old boy," Walter Klyne said, as they ascended the broad steps and stood upon the piazza.

"Yes, it will do very well for a country house, but it will take a mint of money to fix it up as I'd like to have it," was the doctor's reply, as he fitted the key to the lock and entered the wide, old-fashioned hall, already beginning to grow dim with the shadows of the late afternoon. "It's deuced cold, and damp, and ghost-like in here; don't you think so?" the doctor said, shivering a little as he hurried on through room after room, hardly seeing them at all, until he came to one, the door of which was open as well as the blind opposite, so that a flood of sunlight streamed through the window and fell across the floor.

"This is a jolly room; let's go in here," Klyne said, entering himself, and looking curiously around, while the doctor stood by the threshold, wiping from his face great drops of sweat, and starting at every sound, as if he fancied the place full of something harmful. "Why, Doc, what ails you? You are white as a sheet. What's the matter?" Klyne asked, and the doctor replied:

"Nothing, only this was her room; Rossie's, you know. I am sure of it; she described it to me so often, and I feel as if she was here with us; I do, upon my soul. That's her chair, where she used to sit, and these must be her books, and that's her bed where she used to sleep. Let's go away; it's like a graveyard to me."

He seemed so excited that his friend looked at him curiously, wondering if the glass of wine taken just before they left the hotel had affected his brain, or if it really was true that his grief for his sister was augmented by the sight of her old home, and the objects which had once made a part of her life.

"It's not like John Matthewson to love any one like that. There's a kink somewhere," he thought, as he left the room and followed on through one apartment after another, until the whole had been gone through, and they went out into the open air, where the doctor seemed to be more at his ease. Taking off his hat and wiping his forehead, where the perspiration was standing, he said:

"This is a confounded hot night after all, or I am no judge of the weather, and this place in particular seems hotter than Tophet. I say, Walt, do you believe in ghosts, or haunted houses, or any of that sort of nonsense?"

"Of course not. Why do you ask?" Walter Klyne said; and the doctor replied:

"Because I was just nervous enough to fancy that the whole Forrest race, Rossie and all, were after me as I went over the lonesome old hut. Maybe they don't like the idea of my being the heir, and that has brought them from their graves; but I feel better now, and I think we will be going, or the dinner will be cold."

Early next morning the doctor interviewed Lawyer Russell, and at the close of the conference the doctor knew that as Rossie's heir he was entitled to several hundred thousand dollars, some in lands and houses, some in bonds and mortgages, some in railroad shares and some in ready cash. The amount, so far exceeding what he had expected, surprised and delighted him, and inclined him to be very generously disposed toward Everard, with whom he had one long talk. He had taken all the necessary steps to prove that Rossie died at Haelder-Strauchsen, Austria, on the evening of April th; he had sworn to that effect before the lawful authority; and he was accepted by the public as the heir, though under protest, for there was no one in Rothsay who did not think it was a shame for Everard to be so defrauded of what ought always to have been his. This feeling the doctor perfectly understood, and it strengthened his resolution to be very generous toward the young man, to whom he offered half of the entire estate.

"Perhaps I ought to give you the whole," he said, "but hanged if I can quite bring myself to that. You see, when a poor chap like me gets a little money it is mighty hard to give it up."

"But I thought you had unlimited means in Europe," Everard said; and without the slightest change of countenance the doctor replied:

"I did have something there, though not so much as Rossie supposed. I deceived her purposely, thinking she would feel easier if she believed me very rich. But unluckily the firm failed where most of my money was deposited, so that I am much poorer now than when I went from America more than a year ago."

He seemed to be in earnest, and insisted that Everard should take half the property, until the latter stopped him by saying decidedly:

"Your talk is all in vain, for I shall never take a dollar of that money. It would prove a curse to me if I did. I do not want it, I will not have it, and I only ask that I hear no more on the subject." So saying he rose suddenly from his chair and left the room. The interview was ended; the doctor had discharged his duty; and it was not his fault that he was a richer man by more than two hundred thousand dollars than he expected to be. On the whole, he felt quite satisfied with matters as they were, and would not quarrel with the good luck which had made him so rich that he need never again feel a moment's anxiety.

He had nothing more to do but to enjoy himself, and let others do so too, for that was part of his creed. Naturally generous and free, he was always ready to share his fortune with others, and he made up his mind at once to be very popular in Rothsay, and to begin by liberal gifts to every public and charitable object, as that was sure to win him favor. Walter Klyne, who served no purpose whatever, was retained, nominally as legal adviser, but really because under his smooth, placid exterior the doctor carried a coward's heart, and did not like to be alone at the Forrest House, where he soon took up his quarters. There was an odor of aristocracy about the place which he liked, for it reminded him of some of the palaces in Europe which he had coveted, envying the possessor, and fancying how happy he should be were he the lord and owner. He was lord and owner now, with an income of more money than he had ever had at any one time in his life. He had men-servants and maid-servants, and fast horses, and carriages, and hunting-dogs, and choice cigars by the hundreds, and rare wines, which he drank as freely as water. He ordered several costly pictures from Munich and Dresden, with statuary from Florence, and filled the halls and grounds with the latter, and fitted up a gallery for the former, and set up to be a connoisseur and critic general of fine art, and gained considerable reputation in that line, and was spoken of as a highly cultivated and generous man, of whom Rothsay would have been glad if his coming there had not been brought about by the death of the sweet young girl, whose memory was so fresh and green in the minds of her friends. He had the most expensive pew in church, and was present every Sunday morning, and joined reverently in the service, though his preference, he frankly said, was for the plain Methodist chapel; and he made no secret that he had once been a Methodist clergyman, and said he should return to that body were it not that Rossie loved the church as a child loves its mother, and for her sake he should be a churchman, and instruct himself in all its usages and doctrines. So the Episcopalians claimed him, and made much of him, and took his gifts thankfully, and rejoiced that at last the Forrest money, which the judge had held so tightly, was being distributed among them in so liberal a manner. Could they have had their choice they would rather have seen Everard in his father's house. Dr. Matthewson was genial and pleasant, and very generous, but in some sense he was an interloper, while Everard was to the manor born; the purple was his by birth; the blue blood of Forrest and Bigelow was in his veins, and the people sympathized with and pitied him more than he ever dreamed.

It was a very lonely life which he led that summer after Rossie's death; and with the exception of Beatrice he seldom talked with any one, except upon business. He could not mingle with his old friends and seem as he used to do, with that sad memory constantly in his heart; that grave always yawning before him, where he had buried his darling. A thought of Rossie was always with him; not as he saw her last, standing on the deck and waving him her farewell, with tears swimming in her eyes, and a look upon her face whose meaning he could readily interpret, but as she was when a little girl sporting on the terrace behind the house, or romping on the grounds, with the white sun-bonnet hanging down her back, the strings chewed into a hard knot, her hair blowing about her face, and her starry eyes brightening when he joined her with his raillery and teasing jokes.

Sometimes in the stillness of the night he almost fancied that he heard again the quick tread of the busy feet which had run so willingly for him, and always when his grief was at its height, and his heart aching the worst, he felt that pale, thin hands were beckoning him from out the darkness of the grave, beckoning him to come, as if the spirit could not rest until it was joined by his. Once, when the impression was very strong upon him, and it almost seemed as if the dead hands touched his and were leading him away, he said, aloud:

"Rossie, are you here? Is there something you want me to do, and are you trying to tell me? I'd go to the ends of the earth at your slightest bidding."

But to this appeal no answer came from the far-off grave across the sea, though the hands still seemed beckoning with a never-tiring persistence which moved and troubled him greatly. Had he been at all tainted with spiritualism as it exists in modern times, he might perhaps have sought through mediums to know what his love would tell him, but he was free from superstitions of all kind, except this one, that Rossie was calling to him, and that ere long it would be granted him to join her in the world beyond. And to this end he tried to make himself ready, praying earnestly as he never prayed before that God would lead him to himself in any path he chose, so that it conducted him at last to Heaven, where Rossie was. Well he knew that if he would find that rest, all sinful affections must be overcome, and he be made humble and submissive as a little child. At first, however, it was very hard to be submissive and humble, and harder still not to hate the man who had blasted his whole life, and who seemed to be riding triumphantly in the high and pleasant roads of success. But gradually the hardness began to give way as the new life within him became clearer and brighter, and though he could not bring himself to like the doctor or find pleasure in his society, he could endure his presence, and no longer crossed the street to avoid meeting him if he saw him coming in the distance, and that was about all the progress he could make with him. He distrusted and disliked him, and never on any occasion went near the Forrest House, which, as the summer advanced, the doctor filled with his friends from New York, men of his own class, who were as unlike Everard as he was unlike his former self when he rebelled hotly against his fate and blamed the Almighty for having dealt so hardly with him. He did not feel that way now, and every Sunday found him an occupant of his father's old pew, where Rossie used to sit, and where he now knelt and prayed earnestly for grace to bear whatever might be in store for him, feeling, it is true, that nothing worse could happen to him than had already happened,—the loss of Rossie and the loss of his estate.

From Josephine he seldom heard. She was still in Indianapolis with her friends, but she did not write him often, and never asked for money.

He had sent her a Rothsay paper which had in it a column and a half of matter concerning the disposition of the Forrest property, and the new proprietor, but she had made no comment. That she could not live at the Forrest House he knew, and that she would not return to Rothsay he devoutly hoped, and so he grew more quiet and contented each day, though there was ever with him a sense of bitter pain and a constant thought of the grave across the sea where Rossie was buried.

And so the summer waned, and September came and went, and one morning in October a bombshell was thrown into Rothsay which made Everard stagger for a moment from the suddenness of its coming; then he rallied, and his first sensation was one of intense relief, such as the prisoner feels when told that ere long he will be free again to go and come as he likes.

It came first in the form of an article published in the Rothsay Star, and which was as follows:

"Divorce in High Life.—We learn from a friend residing in Indianapolis that there is a divorce suit pending between two parties well known in Rothsay. The gentleman, in fact, is still a resident here, but the lady is at present in Indianapolis, where she went last May with the intention of getting the divorce."

Everard read this article twice before fully comprehending its meaning. Then, when he knew he was one of the parties meant, that it was the Forrest name which must be mixed with the affair, his first feeling was one of shame and mortification, notwithstanding that he had once contemplated doing just what Josephine was doing for him. But his next feeling was one of intense relief that at last he would be free from the burden which had borne so heavily upon him. He went with the notice to

Beatrice, who, although she disapproved of divorces as a rule, looked upon this as an exceptional case, and was glad for him. Of course all Rothsay talked, and gossiped, and wondered, but asked no questions of Everard, who, outwardly, was just the same, and came and went as if nothing had happened or was likely to happen.

Dr. Matthewson seemed as much surprised as any one, but offered no opinion whatever on the subject, and after a few days he went to New York with his inseparable friend and adviser, Walter Klyne. Four weeks later a notice was sent to Everard to the effect that a divorce from him had been granted to his former wife, who chose to take her maiden name, and was again Josephine Fleming; also, that he, too, was divorced, with a right to marry again, if he chose.

From that time onward Everard was a changed man. It is true that Rossie was always in his mind, and he never for a moment forgot the pain and loss, which it seemed to him grew greater every day, but the consciousness that Josephine had no claim upon him made him in one way very happy, and he felt freer from care and anxiety than he had done since that fatal night when he made the mistake of his life. That Josephine would marry again he was confident, and it did not need Beatrice's hint, cautiously given, to awake in his mind a suspicion as to who the man would be; and still it was a shock when it came to him early in the spring that the Forrest House was to have a mistress, and that its last occupant was coming back with a right to rule and reign and spend his father's money as she chose.

CHAPTER XLV

THE NEW REIGN AT THE FORREST HOUSE

Doctor Matthewson had spent most of the winter in New York, but of Josephine's whereabouts little was known. She had been in New York, and Holburton, and Boston, where she was the guest of Mrs. Arnold, with whom she had been abroad, and whose good opinion she had succeeded in retaining by telling her a part only of the truth, and doing it in such a manner that she appeared to be the party to be pitied rather than Everard. Mrs. Arnold was not a person who looked very deeply into matters, she chose rather to take them as they seemed, and Josephine had been very faithful to her and her interest while they were abroad; and though she was shocked and surprised when she first heard the story of the marriage, Josephine told it so well for herself as to make it appear that she had not been greatly in fault, and the lady believed her more sinned against than sinning, and invited her to her own home in Boston, where she was stopping somewhere about the middle of March, when word came to the man in charge of the Forrest House that the doctor, who had already been gone two months and more, would remain away still longer, and that when he returned Mrs. Matthewson would accompany him. Who Mrs. Matthewson was the letter did not state, but Beatrice readily guessed, and was not at all surprised when, a week later, she received a letter from Mr. Morton, who was still in Boston, and who wrote that he had been asked to officiate at the marriage of Miss Josephine Fleming with Dr. John Matthewson, said marriage to take place at the house of one of his parishioners, Mrs. Arnold, April th, at eleven o'clock, A. M.

What Everard thought or felt when he heard the news he kept to himself, but the townspeople unanimously disapproved of the match, and arrayed themselves against the bride elect and decided that she should be made to feel the weight of their disapprobation, and know that they resented her marriage and coming back there to live as an insult to Everard and an affront to themselves. Nor were they at all mollified by the arrival of cards inviting them to the wedding. There were in all a dozen invitations sent to as many families in Rothsay, and Beatrice had a letter from Josephine, in which she tried to make everything seem fair and right with regard to the divorce and marriage, and hoped Miss Belknap would be friendly with her when she came back to Rothsay.

"For myself," she added, "I would rather not go where Everard is, and where his friends can hardly wish to see me. But the doctor is inexorable, and insists upon living at Rothsay a portion of the year at least. He likes the Forrest House, he says, and would not sell it for the world. It suits him for a summer residence, and we shall be there some time in June. He is very kind, and I trust that after the stormy life I have led there is a bright future in store for me, which, I assure you, I shall appreciate, and if I can atone for whatever has been wrong and questionable in the past I certainly shall do so."

And to do Josephine justice, she did mean to retrieve her character if possible, and be at least a true wife to the man who had chosen her, knowing perfectly well what she was and how little to be trusted. There was about Josephine a most powerful fascination for Dr. Matthewson, who thought her the most beautiful and attractive woman he had ever seen. And the doctor liked beautiful and attractive things; they suited his luxurious tastes, and Josephine was just the one to adorn the kind of home he was now able to have. She would be equal to any emergency, and he would enjoy the attentions she was sure to receive at the different watering-places and hotels, where he meant to take her. If any of her admirers should become too demonstrative he could easily rid himself of them and bring his wife under subjection, for he meant to be her master, and to do exactly as he pleased in everything, and he made a beginning by refusing to sell the Forrest House, as she wished him to do. For Josephine was determined not to go back to Rothsay, and at first made it a condition in marrying the doctor that he should dispose of the place, or at least not require her to live there even for a few weeks. She had no wish to meet Everard, or to come in contact with his friends, who were sure to slight her now. But the doctor was resolved upon making the house into a kind of palace, where he could enjoy himself after his own ideas, and as he had not the slightest consideration for the wishes or feelings of others, he laughed at Josephine's scruples, which he called whims, and carried his point with regard to the Forrest House, and the evening of the th of April there appeared in the Boston papers the following notice:

"Married, this morning at ten o'clock, by the Rev. Theodore Morton, Dr. John Matthewson to Miss Josephine Fleming."

Washington and New York were the cities where the happy pair spent their honeymoon, and it was not until the middle of June that they took possession of their Rothsay house, which had undergone quite a transformation. All through the months of April and May carpenters from Cincinnati had been there, following out the plan which the doctor had forwarded to them with the most minute instructions. Bay-windows were sent out here, and hanging balconies there, and pretty little sunny nooks for plants were cut through the solid mason-work; rooms were thrown together, trees were removed to admit more light and give finer views, until the stately, old-fashioned house assumed the appearance of a modern and rather graceful structure, which the Rothsayites, and even Beatrice herself, thought greatly improved. Every room was refurnished and changed in some way except Rossie's,—which was left untouched. Not an article of furniture was changed or moved from its place. Some of Rossie's books were on the shelf where she left them; a work-box was on the table, and in the closet one or two half-worn dresses hung, a prey to any moth or insect which chose to fasten upon them. But the rest of the house was beautiful, and fresh, and new, and ready for the bride, who came one afternoon in June, and was met at the station by the coachman, with the new carriage and high-stepping horses, which pawed the ground and arched their glossy necks as the long train swept by.

There was no one there to meet the bride, for the marriage was very unpopular in town, and every door was virtually closed against the lady who, for once in her life, looked pale and tired, as she took her seat in the carriage, and leaning back wearily, said, to the doctor:

"Please take the straightest road home, for I am tired to death."

But if the doctor heard her he did not heed her request. He had no feelings of shame or twinges of conscience. He wished the people to see his splendid turnout, and they drove through Main street, past all the shops and offices, where the men and boys stared at them, and a few made a show of recognizing the courteous lifting of the doctor's hat, and the patronizing wave of his hand.

Josephine was closely vailed, and pretended not to see the ladies who were on the street, and who did not turn their heads as the elegant carriage went by. But Josey knew that they saw her, and felt that her worst fears were to be realized; and when, at a sudden turn in the road, they came upon Beatrice, whose cool little nod seemed more an insult than a recognition, her cup of humiliation was full, and there were tears of mortification and anger in her eyes, and her headache was not feigned when at last they drew up before the house, where a strange woman was waiting to greet them. This was Mrs. Rogers, the housekeeper, imported for that purpose from Cincinnati, as were the other servants. These, however, had all heard the antecedents of their new master and mistress very freely discussed, and the result was that a mutiny was already in progress, for, as the girl who held the post of scullion said, "she had lost one cha-rac-ter by living with folks who wasn't fust cut, and she didn't care to lose another." Still, the wages were good, and all decided to stay a while, and see what the lady who had two husbands living and had once been a servant herself (such was the story as they had it) was like. So they came to meet her, and thought her very handsome and stylish, and a fit occupant of the beautiful rooms of which she was mistress, and for which she did not seem to care, for she never stopped to look at them, but went directly to her own apartments, which she did have the grace to say were pretty.

"Yes, it is all very nice," she said to the doctor, "but I am frightfully tired, and nervous, too, I think. This last hot day's ride has just upset me. I believe I'll have a cup of tea brought to my room, and not go down to dinner, if you'll excuse me."

"You won't do any such thing," was the doctor's reply. "You'll put on one of your swell-dresses, and go down to dinner with me. I wish the servants to see you at your best, and somebody may call this evening."

"Somebody call!" Josephine retorted, with intense bitterness in her voice. "Don't flatter yourself that any one whom I care for will call to-night, or ever, while I remain in Rothsay."

"Why, what do you mean?" the doctor asked, and she replied:

"I mean that as Everard Forrest's divorced wife, married to another man, I am to be tabooed in this town. Didn't you notice how the ladies we passed on the street pretended to be looking another way so as not to see me. They did not wish to recognize me even with a nod, and you surely noticed the insulting bow which Miss Belknap gave me. There was not a particle of cordiality in it. I knew it would be so, and that was why I was so opposed to coming here. I wish I had remained firm to my first resolution."

She was more than half crying with anger and vexation, but the doctor only laughed at what he termed her groundless fears. Supposing she was a divorced woman, with her first husband living in the same town, what did that matter? He knew of many such instances, and if the people in Rothsay were disposed to slight him at first, he should live it down, for money could accomplish everything.

But Josephine was not to be soothed by his words, and bade him mind his business and leave her to herself. It was the first ebullition of temper she had shown toward him; so he received it good-humoredly, and touched her playfully under her chin, and had his way in everything, and took down to dinner a most beautiful and elegantly-dressed woman, who looked as if made for just the place she was occupying at the head of that handsomely appointed table.

No one called either that evening, or the next, or the next, and when Sunday came she was really sick with mortification and disappointment, and the doctor went to church without her, and met only cold words from those to whom he tried to talk after service was over. Nobody mentioned his wife, although he spoke of her himself, and said that she was sick, and asked Mrs. Rider to tell her husband to call in the afternoon and see her. Even that ruse failed, for there was no solicitude expressed for the lady's health, no inquiry as to what ailed her, and the doctor drove home in his handsome carriage, feeling that after all Josephine might be right, and that the people were determined to show their disapprobation. But he meant to live it down, and not let the good fortune he had so coveted turn to ashes on his hands. But living it down was not so easy as he had supposed, and as day after day went by, and no one came to see his grandeur, or paid the least attention to him, his spirits began to flag, and he half-suspected that he had made a mistake in bringing his wife to Rothsay, where the Forrest star was evidently in the ascendant.

Once he decided to fill the house with young men from New York and Cincinnati, but when he thought of Josey he gave that up, for his love, or rather passion, for her was strong enough to make him wish to keep her smiles and blandishments for himself; and so the New York guests were given up, and he spent his time driving his fast horses through the country during the morning, and in the afternoon lounging, and smoking, and reading, and looking over his handsome house until his elaborate dinner, which was served at half-past six, and notice of which was given to the portion of the town nearest him by the loud bell which he caused to be rung as a signal to himself and wife that dinner was ready. The doctor was very particular and exacting on every point of table etiquette, and required as much form, and ceremony, and attention, as if a multitude of guests sat daily at his board, instead of himself and Josephine, who was always elegantly dressed in silks, and laces, and diamonds, and looked a very queen as she took her seat at the head of her table with a languor which was not feigned, for in her heart she was tired and sick to death of the grand, lonely life she led. Nobody came near her, and when by chance she met any of her old acquaintances they were too much hurried to do more than bow to her; while even the tradespeople lacked that deference of manner which she felt was her due. The doctor seldom asked her to join him in his drives, and as she did not care to go out alone and face the disapproving public, she spent her time mostly in her room reading French novels and eating candy and bonbons, with which she was always supplied.

Everard she had never met face to face, though she had seen him in the distance from her window, and watched him as he went by with a strange feeling at her heart which wrung a few hot, bitter tears from her, as she remembered the summer years ago when her boy-lover was all the world to her, and the life before her seemed so fair and bright. Not that she really wanted Everard back, but she wanted something; she missed something in her life which she longed for intensely, and at last made up her mind that it was Agnes, the despised sister, who was in Holburton, earning her own living as housekeeper for Captain Sparks.

When they first returned to the Forrest House, Dr. Matthewson had signified to her his wish that Agnes should remain where she was. She would hardly be ornamental in his household, he said. He liked only beautiful objects around him, and Agnes was not beautiful. She would be an ugly blot upon the picture, and he did not want her, though he was willing to supply her with money, if necessary. But Agnes did not wish for his money. She could take care of herself, and was happier in Holburton than she could be elsewhere. But as the summer went by, the longing in Josephine's heart for the companionship of some woman grew so strong that she ventured at last to write, begging her sister to come, and telling how lonely she was without her.

"I have been hard and selfish, and wicked, I know," she wrote, "but, Aggie, I am far from being happy, and I want you here with me so much that I am sure you will come. I believe I am sick or nervous, or both, and the sight of your dear old face will do me good."

Josephine did not tell her husband of this letter, lest he should forbid her sending it. She was beginning to be a good deal afraid of him, but she thought she knew him well enough to feel sure that if Agnes were once in the house he would make no open opposition to it, and she was willing to bear a good deal in private for the sake of having her sister with her again. So she wrote her letter, and as the day was fine, took it to the post-office herself, in order to insure its safety.

CHAPTER XLVI

THE LETTER FROM AUSTRIA

There had been some trouble with the clerks in the post-office at Rothsay, and two new ones had just been appointed, and one of these had entered upon his duties only the day before. As he came from Dayton, and was a stranger in town, he knew very few people by sight, and was altogether ignorant of the name and antecedents of the beautiful lady, who, after depositing her letter, asked if there was any mail for the Forrest House. Half-bewildered with her beauty and the bright smile she flashed upon him, the clerk started and blushed, and catching only the name Forrest, looked in Everard's box, where lay a letter not yet called for, as Everard had left town early that morning for a drive into the country, where he had some business with a client. It was a soiled-looking letter, with a foreign post-mark upon it, and had either been mislaid a long time after it had been written, or detained upon the road, for it was worn upon the edges, and had evidently been much crumpled with frequent handling. It was directed to J. Everard Forrest, Esq., Rothsay, Ohio, U. S. A., and in a corner, the two words, "Please forward" were written, as if the writer were in haste and thought thus to expedite matters.

Very mechanically, and even indifferently, Josephine took it in her hand, and glancing at the name saw the clerk had made a mistake and given her what belonged to another. But she saw, too, something else, which turned her white as ashes, and riveted her for a moment to the spot with a feeling that she was either dying or mad, or both. Surely, she knew that writing. She had seen it times enough not to be mistaken. And she had thought the hand which penned it dead long ago, and laid away under the grass and flowers of Austria. "Rossie," she tried to say, but her white lips would not move, and there was about them a strange prickling sensation which frightened her more than the numbness of her body.

"I must get into the air where I can breathe," she thought, and with a desperate effort she dragged herself to the street, taking the letter with her, and grasping it with a firm grip as if fearful of losing it, when in fact she had forgotten that she had it at all, until the air blowing on her face revived her somewhat and brought her back to a consciousness of what she was doing.

Then her first impulse was to return the letter to Everard's box, and she turned to go back when she saw her husband entering the office, and that decided her. She would not let him see the letter, for if there were a great wrong somewhere, he knew it and had contrived it, and the cold sweat broke out from every pore as she began dimly to conjecture the nature of the wrong, and to shudder at its enormity. She was feeling stronger now, and fearful lest her husband should overtake her she hurried across the common toward home, where she went at once to her room, and, locking the door, sat down to read that letter from the dead. She had made up her mind to do that during her rapid walk. She must know its contents, and so she broke the seal and began to read. And as she read she felt the blood curdle in her veins; there was a humming in her ears; a thick feeling in her tongue, and a kind of consciousness that she was somebody else, whose business for the rest of her life was to keep the letter and its contents a secret from the world. But where should she hide it that no one could ever find it, for nobody must see it? Safety, honor, everything dear to her depended upon that. Not even her husband must look upon it or know that it was written; and where should she put it that he would not find it, for he took the liberty to look through her private drawers and boxes just when it pleased him to do so? She could not put the letter in a box or keep it about her person, and she dared not destroy it, though she made the attempt and lighted the gas in which to burn it to ashes. But as she held it to the blaze something seemed to grasp her hand and draw it back. And when she shook off the sensation of fear which had seized her, and again attempted the destruction of the note, the same effect was produced, and an icy chill crept over her as if it were a dead hand clutching hers and holding it fast.

"I can't destroy it; I dare not!" she whispered; "and what if somebody should find it? What if he should? He told me once that he had been guilty of every sin but murder, and under strong provocation he might be led to do even that;" and a shudder of fear ran through her frame as she cast about in her own mind for a safe hiding-place for the letter which affected her so strangely. Suddenly it came to her that she could loosen a few tacks in the carpet, just where the lace curtains covered the floor in a corner of the bay window, and pushing the letter out of sight, drive the tacks in again, and so the secret would be safe, for a time at least. To do her justice, for once in her life conscience was prompting her to the only right course left her to pursue,—give the letter to Everard and abide the consequences. But she could not make up her mind to do this, knowing that utter poverty and disgrace would be the result, and she had learned by this time that poverty with Dr. Matthewson would be a far different thing from poverty with Everard.

To hide the letter under the carpet was the work of a moment, and, unlocking the door, she was going for a hammer, with which to drive the tacks, when she heard her husband's voice in the hall below, and knew that he was coming. He must not know that she held his guilty secret, lest he should murder her, as in her nervousness she felt that he might do, and so she retraced her steps to the couch, where she lay half fainting, and as white as marble, when the doctor entered the room and asked her what was the matter.

She did not know, she said; she had been down to the village and walked rather fast, and was very warm, and had drank freely of ice-water, which made her feel as if her head were bursting. She should probably feel better soon.

But she did not get better, and she lay all that day and the next upon the couch, and seemed so strange and nervous that her husband called in Dr. Rider, who, after a few questions, the drift of which she understood, and to which she gave false replies for the purpose of misleading him, assigned a cause for her ailments, and then went away. Thus deceived, and on the whole rather pleased than otherwise, Dr. Matthewson was disposed to be very attentive and indulgent to his wife, with whom he sat a good portion of each day, humoring all her whims and trying to quiet her restless, nervous state of mind.

"You act as if you were afraid of me, Josey," he said once, when he sat down beside her and put his arm around her with something of the old lover-like fondness. "You tremble like a leaf if I touch you, and shrink away from me. What is it? What has come between us? You may as well tell, for I am sure to find it out if there is anything."

She knew that, and it seemed to her as if his eyes were following hers to the bay window and seeing the letter hidden under the carpet. She must say something by way of an excuse, and with her ready tact she answered him: "I am keeping something from you. I have written Aggie to come to me. I was so lonesome and sick, and wanted her so much. You are not angry, are you?"

Her great blue eyes were swimming with genuine tears, for she was a little afraid of what her husband might say to the liberty she had taken without his permission. Fortunately, he was in one of his most genial moods. Dr. Rider had said to him privately that in her present nervous condition Josephine must not be crossed; and he answered laughingly that he was not angry, but on the contrary, very glad Aggie was coming, as he believed her a capital nurse; and "Josey," he added, "you need building up. You are growing as thin as a shad and white as a sheet, and that I don't like. I thought you would never fade and fall off like Bee Belknap. I met her this morning, and she positively begins to look like an old maid. I hear she is to be married soon," and he shot a keen, quick glance at his wife, into whose pale cheeks the hot blood rushed at once, and whose voice was not quite steady as she asked:

"Married,—to whom? Not Everard?"

"No-o," the doctor answered, contemptuously, annoyed at Josephine's manner. "I hope she has more sense than to marry that milksop, who has grown to be more like a Methodist parson than anything else. You called him a milksop yourself, once," he continued, as he saw the flash in Josephine's eyes, "and you must not blame me for taking my cue from you, who know him better than I do. I believe, on my soul, you half feared he was going to marry, and were sorry for it. He is nothing to you. A woman cannot have two husbands; that's bigamy."

The doctor was growing irritable, and Josephine knew it, but she could not forbear answering him tartly:

"There are worse crimes than bigamy,—a great deal,—and they are none the less worse because the world does not know of them."

"What do you mean?" he asked, sharply, and Josephine replied:

"Nothing in particular; only you told me once that you had broken every commandment except the one 'Thou shalt do no murder,' and that you might break that under strong provocation. Of course there are sins at your door not generally known. Suppose some one should be instrumental in bringing them or the worst of them to light?"

"Then I might break the only commandment you say I have not broken," he answered, and in the eyes bent so searchingly on Josephine's face there was an evil, threatening look, before which she quailed.

She must never let him know of the letter hidden under the carpet, and watched by her so carefully. Every day she went to the spot to make sure it was there, and every day she read it again until she knew it by heart, and had no need to read it except to see if she had not by some chance made a mistake and read it wrong. But she had not; the proof was there, of crime, and guilt, and sin, such as made her terribly afraid of the man who fondled and caressed her now more than he had done in weeks, and who at last welcomed Agnes, when she came, even more warmly than she did herself, though in not quite so demonstrative a manner.

Agnes had gone straight to her sister's room, which Josephine had not left since the day she took the foreign letter from the office and hid it under the carpet. She had become a monomaniac on the subject of that letter, and dared not leave lest some one should find it, but sat all day in her easy-chair, which had been drawn into the bay window, and stood directly over her secret. And there she sat when Agnes came in, and then, as if all her remaining nerves had given way, she threw her arms around her neck and sobbing out, "Oh, Aggie, I am glad you have come; I could not have borne it much longer," fainted entirely away.

CHAPTER XLVII

AGNES FINDS THE LETTER

If there was one thing more than another which Agnes detested, it was carpet-bugs; those little black pests which, within a few years, have crept into the houses in certain sections of the country, carrying with them ruin to whatever they fasten upon, and dismay and wretchedness to those who will persist in hunting for them. Among the latter class was Agnes, who, from the moment the cry of carpet-bugs was raised in Holburton, had spent half her time upon her hands and knees, searching for them on the edges of the carpets, and the rest of her time hunting them in bundles, and boxes, and drawers. They seemed to owe her a special spite, for they had eaten her woolen shawl, and her furs, and her best delaine dress, and life was becoming a burden to her, when she received Josephine's letter, begging her to come at once to the Forrest House.

Always ready at a kind word to forgive her sister for any amount of unkindness, Agnes decided at once to go, feeling that it would be some comfort to escape from the dreadful bugs. She did not think they had yet reached Rothsay; but she meant to make it her first business to hunt for them, and equipped herself with all the ingredients named in the category for their extirpation. Persian powder, red pepper, Scotch snuff, cut tobacco, Paris green, hellebore, and even Prussic acid formed a portion of her luggage when she reached the Forrest House, and found her sister so ill and weak that for a time she had no thought for carpet-bugs, and had there been an army there they would have reveled in perfect security for all of her interference. But after a few days, when Josephine seemed better and was sleeping quietly, the desire for research and battle came upon her again, incited by the softness of the velvet carpet in her sister's room, which she thought furnished such a rich field for the marauders. As it happened, the bay window was the point at which she commenced operations, as it was farthest from Josephine's bed.

"They have been here, too," was her whispered exclamation as she caught sight of the familiar sign, the carpet loosened from the floor; and eager in her search she turned the carpet back farther and farther until she saw the corner of the letter just protruding in sight. To draw it out and glance at the name upon it, "J. Everard Forrest," was the work of a moment, and then she wondered how it came there, and if it were some old thing received by Everard years ago, and left lying about as something of no interest to him or anybody. It looked old and worn, and as if it had been read many times. Surely there could be no harm in her glancing at the contents just to see if it were of any value.

Thus reasoning, Agnes opened the letter, saw the signature and the date, and then with lightning rapidity read the whole, and Josephine's secret was hers no longer, for Agnes had it, and the effect on her at first was almost as great as it had been on Josephine. That a great wrong had been committed she was certain, just as she was certain that the letter was being withheld from its rightful owner. But by whom? That was the question she asked herself during the moment she sat motionless upon the floor, unable to move, or scarcely think clearly, in her bewildered state of mind. She did not quite believe it was Josephine, and if not, then it must be Dr. Matthewson, and he, if the letter were true, was capable of anything wicked and bad; and there came over her a great fear of him just as it had crept over Josephine when she first knew his sin. Agnes must not let him know what she had found, and, believing Josephine innocent, she must not disturb her, and add to her nervousness. Everard, she had heard, was out of town for a little vacation, which he usually took at that season, and Miss Belknap was therefore the only person in whom she could safely confide.

"She will know just what to do," Agnes thought, and, hiding the letter in her pocket, she arranged the carpet and curtains very carefully, put the easy-chair in its place, and was at her sewing by the window when Josephine awoke, after a sleep of nearly two hours' duration.

She was feeling better, and was disposed to be very kind and indulgent toward Agnes, who, she saw, was looking tired and pale.

"Why, Agnes," she said, "you are almost as white as I am. What is the matter? You have been shut up too closely with me. You have not been out since you came, and you are so accustomed to the air and exercise. Suppose you go for a walk. I am sure it will do you good." Now was Agnes' opportunity, and saying that she thought a walk would do her good, she hurried from the room, and was soon on her way towards Elm Park.

Beatrice was going to be married, and notwithstanding what Dr. Matthewson had said of her faded looks, she had never been so beautiful and sweetly attractive in her fresh girlhood as she was now at twenty-nine, with the great happiness shining in her face and showing itself in every action. Poor, nervous Mollie was not forgotten, for her memory lived in her lovely children, Trix and little Bunchie; but Theodore had felt it right to claim at last his early love, who was not ashamed to confess how dear he was to her and how glad she was to be his wife and the mother of his children.

The wedding, which was to be very private, was to take place the th of September, now only two weeks in the distance, and Beatrice was exceedingly busy with her preparations,—so busy that she had not found time to call upon Agnes, as she intended to do when she heard of her arrival at the Forrest House. She had always liked Agnes, and was glad when her maid came to her room saying that she was in the parlor waiting to see her.

"Ask her to come up here," she said, and in a moment Agnes was with her, seeming so agitated and excited that Beatrice guessed at once that something was wrong, and asked what was the matter.

It was not in Agnes' nature to keep one in suspense, and she answered by putting the letter into Beatrice's hand and saying:

"I found it under the carpet, and because I dared not show it to him,— the doctor, I mean,—who I am sure put it there, I brought it to you. Read it quick, and then we must act together; but never let him know I had a hand in it; he would kill me if he did; there's murder in his nature, or he never could have done this."

Agnes was speaking to ears which did not hear what she was saying, for Bee had taken the letter, postmarked at "Wien," and addressed in a handwriting she knew so well, and the very sight of which made her heart throb with pain as she remembered the dear little girl whom she believed to be dead in the far-away foreign town. But when she glanced at the date, a vague terror seized her and held her fast while she read the letter, which I give to the reader:

"Haelder-Strauchsen, Austria,
   June 10th, 18 —.

"Dear Everard:—Are you dead? Is everybody dead in America, that I am forgotten,—deserted,—and left here alone in this dreadful place? Not dreadful because they are unkind to me, for they are not. Only they say that I am mad, and treat me as such, and I always have an attendant watching what I do, and I cannot get away, though I have tried so many times. Where my brother is I do not know; he left me here more than a year ago, to go to Vienna for a day or two, he said, and I have never seen him since or heard from him; and the head of the house,—Dr. Van Schoisner, says that he is undoubtedly dead; and I might believe him, perhaps, if he did not insist that I am his niece, Myra Van Schoisner, and not Rosamond Hastings at all. He says she died last April, a year ago, and was buried by the river which I can see from my window, and that her brother, Dr. Matthewson, left soon after and has not returned.

"Oh, Everard, it is all so dreadful, and sometimes my head buzzes and feels so big that I am afraid I shall go crazy, as they say I am. I have written and written to you and Bee and Lawyer Russell, and even to my brother, hoping he might be living; but no answer has come, and now I do not think my letters ever left this Maison de Sante, as they call the institution, which stands several miles back from the Danube. Take the boat at Lintz, and get off at ——, and come quick, and get me away from here before I die. I wonder I have not died before this, it is so awful to be shut up and called somebody else, and hear only a foreign language, of which at first I could not understand a word, and they tried not to let me learn. Only the doctor speaks English, and a woman called Yulah Van Eisner, who came as attendant two months ago, and who has promised to get this letter off for me.

"I spoke brother's name to her,—Dr. Matthewson,—and she almost foamed at the mouth, and actually spit upon me because I was his sister; but I made her know I was good, made her listen to me; and she became my friend, and taught me to speak with her, and will help me to get away if she can. She says my brother is not dead; he is a villain, and wants my money; and that Myra Van Schoisner is in the grave where they say I am; and it's all horrible, and I am so sick and frightened, and so afraid I shall be mad if you don't come quick.

"Dear, dear Everard, come to your poor
"Rossie."

This was all Rossie had written, but a postscript had been added, in a cramped, uneducated hand, and broken English, to this effect:

"I open this paper to tell when comes come to Hotel Rother Krebs, in Lintz, where I is work zu hause, and wait for die Amerikaner. Asks for Yulah Van Eisner. I hates him much."

To say that Beatrice's nerves were shaken by this letter would be putting in very mild language just how she felt. With her usual quickness of perception, she saw and understood the diabolical plot which had been so long successful, and her first impulse was to rush through the streets of Rothsay, and, proclaiming the doctor's perfidy, have him arrested at once. Her next and soberer thought was to proceed in the matter more quietly and surely, and to this end she questioned Agnes minutely as to where and how she found the letter, and if she could throw any light upon the way in which it came there. But Agnes could not; she only knew she had found it, and that she believed Dr. Matthewson himself had by some foul method obtained possession of it and hidden it away for safe keeping, though why he had not destroyed it and so made its discovery impossible, neither she nor Beatrice could guess. Her sister, she said, was in a very strange, nervous state of mind, but she could not connect her with the crime in any way, for, unscrupulous as she might be, she would not dare make herself amenable to the law by being a party to her husband's guilt.

This was Agnes' view of the matter, and Beatrice coincided with her, but bade her to be very watchful at the Forrest House and see if any search was made for the missing letter, and by whom.

Beatrice's next interview was with Lawyer Russell, who, in his surprise, bounded from his chair half-way across the room as he exclaimed:

"Lord bless my soul, Rossie alive! Rossie not dead! but hid away in a private mad-house! It's the most hellish plot I ever heard of,—ever,—and it is State prison for him, the villain; but we must move cautiously, Miss Belknap, very cautiously, as we have the very Old Nick to deal with in that doctor. I'm glad the boy is gone just now, as it would have been like you to have blated it out to him, and then all creation couldn't have stopped him from throttling the wretch in the street and spoiling everything. This letter was written long ago, and there's no knowing what may have happened since to our little girl. She may be dead sure enough now, or, what is worse, mad in real earnest. So don't go to kicking up a row just yet, till we get more proof, and then we'll spring the trap so tight that he cannot get away. I'm honestly afraid, though, that he has done something worse with the little girl since he had this letter, which the Lord only knows how he got. He must have a key to Everard's drawer; but we'll fix him! and, Miss Belknap, I say, you or somebody must go to Europe and hunt up poor little Rossie. I'll be hanged if it don't make me cry to think of her shut up, and waiting and waiting for us to come. Go on your wedding trip. You and the parson will do better than Everard, whose name they have heard, and for whom they may be on the watch. Morton is new to them, and will excite no suspicion. This girl,—what's her name,—Yulah Van Eisner, must be found first, of course, if she is not already put out of the way, and with her help you'll fetch her, poor little girl. You ought to go right away, and we'll say nothing to Everard till you've found her. Suspense and then disappointment would kill him outright. And he must not go; that hound would track him sure, and everything be spoiled. You must do it, and you can, better than anybody else."

Beatrice felt that she could too, and had rapidly concocted in her mind a denouement both startling and novel, and highly satisfactory. But there was one difficulty to be surmounted. Theodore's people might not be willing for him to be gone so long, and in that case she said:

"I'll postpone the wedding and go alone."

But this was not necessary, for, in response to the long letter which went that night to Boston, there came a telegram, "I can go!" and then all Bee's thoughts were turned to the work she had on hand, and she grew so restless and nervous and impatient for the day when she could start that people noted and commented upon her changed looks and manner, wondering greatly what ailed her, and if her heart were not in the marriage.

Everard was in Rothsay now, and with her every evening, talking always of Rossie, whose grave he bade her be sure and find, and bring him something from it, if only a blade of grass. Once he startled her by saying he had half made up his mind to join her party, and go with her, so great was his desire to see where Rossie was buried. But Bee turned upon him so fiercely, declaring that she preferred going alone with Theo, that he abandoned the plan altogether, and felt a little hurt at the vehemence with which his company had been rejected.

The wedding was very quiet and small, and the bride very absent-minded and non-committal in her answers to their inquiries as to where she was going, and how long she expected to be gone. But whatever they might have thought of her, the bridegroom was perfectly satisfied, and seemed supremely happy as he bade his friends good-by, and followed his impatient wife into the car which was to take them to New York, and the ship, which, on the th of September, sailed away for Europe, where they hoped to find poor Rossie.

Agnes was at the wedding, and, with the exception of Lawyer Russell, was the only one who had the slightest suspicion of the reason which had taken the newly-wedded pair so suddenly to Europe. But Agnes was safe as the grave, though often at her wits' end to know what to make of her sister, who grew worse instead of better, and who sometimes talked and acted as if she had lost her reason. She had missed the letter from its hiding-place, and gone nearly wild in her excitement and anxiety as to who had found it. But as her husband's manner was unchanged, except as he fretted at her continued illness, she gradually grew more quiet, though there was constantly with her a presentiment of some great evil which was to be brought about by means of the lost letter.

CHAPTER XLVIII

LA MAISON DE SANTE

Just where it was situated, how far from Vienna, how far from Lintz, or how far from the Danube, does not matter to the reader, who needs only to know that there was such a place, embowered in trees, and flowers, and shrubs, and seeming to the casual passer-by like a second little Eden, where one had nothing to do but to enjoy the brightness of the Austrian skies, and the beauty of the premises around. But every door was barred, and every window had a net-work of iron in front of it, through which white, haggard faces looked wistfully, and strange, wild laughs, mingled sometimes with cries of rage, were heard to issue at all hours of the day. Frequently the inmates of that house, or those who were on the "good list," walked in the beautiful grounds, but never walked alone. An attendant was always with them, watchful, vigilant, without, however, seeming to be so; for the rule of the house was kindness, whenever it would answer, and as much freedom as was compatible with safety. Except in extreme cases, where the patient was poor and obscure, it was not a cruelly conducted household which Baron or Doctor Van Schoisner had in charge; but in all the world there was not, perhaps, a more avaricious, grasping man than the baron, who would have sold his soul for thirty pieces of silver, and for forty almost have consented to a murder. If, for purposes of their own, people wished to incarcerate their friends, and paid him well for it, their secret was safe with him, and the victim was insane as long as he lived, if necessary. But there his wickedness ceased, and his patients were generally made as happy and comfortable as it was possible to make them. He, alone, held the secrets of his employers. Not a whisper of the truth ever escaped his lips, and to his attendants everybody was crazy, and must be watched and treated as such, no matter what were their pretensions to the contrary; so when poor little Rossie awoke one morning to find herself deserted, she became at once a lunatic. All liberty of action was gone; even her name was taken from her, and she was told that the Rosamond Hastings who she professed to be, was dead, and lying under the grass where the wild violets were growing, while she was Myra, the niece of the baron, who had come to the house the same night with the beautiful American girl who was so sick, and who had died in a few days. No wonder if for a time her brain reeled, and she was in danger of being in reality insane.

Poor little Rossie had enjoyed much and suffered much since the day when we last saw her, waving a farewell to her friends from the deck of the steamer which bore her away. Her brother had been uniformly kind and affectionate to her, but many things had arisen to shake her confidence in him, and to make her think it possible that he was not the honorable, upright man he professed to be. Then, as the year wore on, and they got farther and farther from home, her letters were unanswered, and there began to steal over her a longing for America which she could not conceal, and which took all the color from her face and roundness from her form, until at last she was really sick with hope deferred and an anxiety to know why none of her letters were answered.

At Florence she was very ill of a fever contracted in Rome, and from the effects of which she did not recover, although she was able at last to go on toward Vienna, their ultimate destination. At Salzburg they halted for a few days, and there her brother brought to her a stranger, whom he introduced as a friend and old acquaintance, Dr. Van Schoisner, to whom he said he owed his life, and who had a kind of Sanitarium for people diseased in body and mind, upon the river Danube. Van Schoisner, who spoke English very well, was exceedingly kind and tender in his manner toward Rossie, whom he questioned so closely, and in such a peculiar way, that she first was annoyed, and then confused and bewildered, and finally contradicted herself two or three times in her statements with regard to her recent illness, and when he asked how she would like to go to his beautiful place on the river and stay a few weeks while he treated her, she shrank away from him, and bursting into tears said she would not like it at all,—that she did not need to be treated, as there was nothing the matter with her but homesickness, and only America could cure that.

Van Schoisner laughed, and stroked her hair, and said he would soon have her all right, and then went to her brother, between whom and himself there was a long conference, during which both sold themselves, body and soul, to the evil one, and were pledged to do his work.

"If she would only abandon that nonsense of hers about giving her fortune to that Forrest, as soon as she comes of age, and would share it with me, I wouldn't do it, for, by Jove, I've a kind of liking for the girl," Dr. Matthewson said, as there came a little prick of conscience, and a drawing back from the thing he proposed to do, which was nothing more or less than burying Rossie alive inside a mad-house, where, so long as the price was paid, she would be as really dead to the world as if the grass were growing over her, and where the chances were that she would either die a speedy death, or, with her temperament, become a hopeless lunatic.

Money he must have, and as he believed in neither God nor the devil, he had no scruples as to how he got it, only he would a little rather not murder one outright to get it. Every argument which he could think of had been brought to bear upon Rossie, with a view to inducing here to keep the fortune willed her, but she had stood firm as a rock in her decision to make the whole over to Everard as soon as she came of age, and so he had recourse to the horrid scheme of which we have hinted.

He knew Van Schoisner well, and knew that he was the man for any deed, however dark,—provided there was money in it, with little chance of detection; and he sent for him to meet them at Salzburg to confer on important business. So Van Schoisner went and found what the business was, and talked to Rossie about her head, and brain, and cerebellum, until she lost her wits and said she hadn't any cerebellum, and never had. She was homesick, and that was all. This, of course, was proof conclusive of a diseased state of mind. A girl who hadn't any cerebellum, and who persisted in throwing away hundreds of thousands of dollars, must be insane and dealt with accordingly. So the bargain was made, and Rossie's fate was sealed. And then arose the question of the friends at home. What should be said to them to quiet all suspicion?

"She must be dead, of course," Van Schoisner said. "Nothing easier than that. A notice in the paper; a letter containing particulars; crape on your hat; a tear in your eye, and the thing is accomplished."

"Yes," returned the doctor, "but suppose that chap who is in love with her takes it into his head to come spooning after her grave, and inquires about her death, and wants to see the very room, and all that,—and it would be like him to do it,—what then?"

Van Schoisner rubbed his forehead thoughtfully a moment, and then said:

"That's the hardest part to manage, but I think I can do it, only give me time. I have a niece in the country a few miles from here, very sick with consumption,—in the last stages, and poor, too, with no friends but myself. I pay her board where she is, and visit her sometimes. She was born in London, her father was an Englishman; so she speaks English perfectly, and might be your sister. I have talked of taking her to Haelder-Strauchsen, and will do so at once, though the journey will shorten her life. But that will not matter, as she must die soon. Once at Haelder-Strauchsen she is your sister, and your sister is my niece. The attendants never ask questions nor talk. Do you comprehend?"

Dr. Matthewson thought he did, but left the matter wholly to his ally, who had, if possible, drank deeper from the cup of iniquity than himself.

As the result of this conversation there was brought to the hotel a few days later a white-faced, fair-haired girl, in whose great blue eyes and about whose mouth and nose death was plainly written. They called her Myra, and said she was Van Schoisner's niece, whom he was taking to his home for better care than she could have in the country. No one attended her. Her uncle could do all that was necessary, he said, and he seemed very kind to her, and staid by her constantly upon the boat when at last they started for home, accompanied by Dr. Matthewson and Rossie, who was greatly interested in the sick girl. It was night when they reached the landing where they were to stop, and from the windows of the close carriage Rossie saw nothing of the country through which they passed for a few miles, but was conscious at last that they were entering spacious grounds, and stopping before a large, square building, with two wings on either side.

The room assigned her was in one of the wings on the third floor, as was Myra's also. It was very prettily furnished, and the windows looked out upon the grounds, but there was stretched before them a gauzy net-work of iron, which Rossie noticed at once, and asked for the reason. Then her brother explained to her the real character of the house, but said that as they were transient visitors it would not affect them in the least, and all she had to do was to rest and get as well as possible, so they might go on to Vienna.

And Rossie tried to rest and enjoy the beautiful place, but the occasional sight of some of the patients walking in the distance, the strange sounds, like human cries, which reached her in the night when everything was still, and, more than all, a great languor and desire to sleep which she could not shake off, wore upon her so fast that in a few days she was seriously ill again, and lost all consciousness of time or what was passing around her. How long she remained in this condition she never knew; only this, that she awoke one morning to find Van Schoisner with her, apparently watching her as she slept, and administering some powerful stimulants. He was very kind, indeed, and told her Dr. Matthewson had been obliged to go to Vienna on business, which might detain him a few days, but he would soon be back, and she was to be as happy and quiet as possible till his return. Her next question was for the sick girl, who, he said, had died a week ago, and then he bade her try to sleep again, as perfect rest was what she needed most.

"And I went to sleep," Rossie said, afterward, when telling Beatrice of that awful time when she was kept a prisoner at Haelder-Strauchsen, with no hope of escape. "I went to sleep and slept so heavily and long that it must have been days before I awoke, and when I did, my head ached so hard, and everything seemed so confused, and I could not understand a word the woman said, for she spoke only German, which I never could make out. I tried to make her know that I wanted my brother, but she shook her head and put her finger to her lips, and finally went out and locked the door after her. Then I got up and went to the window, and leaned my head against the bars, and cried for home, and you, and Everard, till I felt so sick and dizzy that I went back to bed, and lay there till Van Schoisner came and told me nothing had been heard from Dr. Matthewson since he left the Sanitarium, two weeks before.

"'I certainly expected him to return,' he said, 'and am afraid some evil has befallen him. I have written to the hotel where he intended to stop, and they have not seen him.'

"He called him Dr. Matthewson all the time, as formal-like as if he had not been my brother, and once he called me Myra, and when I said he was mistaken, for I was Rossie Hastings, he smiled kind of pityingly, and said:

"'Poor little girl, be anything you like to yourself. To me you are Myra. Rossie died just across the hall, and is buried in such a pretty spot.'

"I thought he was crazy, and felt afraid of him, but had no suspicion then of the real state of things. That came gradually, as days and weeks went by and I heard nothing from my brother, and seldom saw any one but the doctor and the attendant, Margotte, who never talked with me except by signs, so I had no opportunity to learn the language, which I greatly desired to do, in order to make myself understood, and convince her that I was not Myra, and was not mad, as I knew she believed me to be.

"Oh, it was so horrible that time, and my head got so confused, and I used to pray constantly 'God keep me from going really mad!' and he did, though I was very near it. At first they would not let me have paper or ink to write to you with, but I begged so hard on my knees, clinging to that man's feet, that he consented at last, and I wrote to you, and Everard, and

Lawyer Russell, and my brother, too, though I did not know where he was, and Margotte took the letters, which I know now were never sent, but were burned to ashes, for Yulah told me so,—good, kind Yulah, who came to me like an angel from Heaven.

"Margotte was sick, and Yulah took her place. She had been there once as a patient, mad herself, from some great wrong done to her by one she loved and trusted. Her baby had died there, and been buried in the grounds, and she was attached to the place, and after her cure, staid from choice, and was nurse and attendant both, and the most faithful and vigilant of them all, and the one the doctor trusted the most. So he put me in her charge, and the moment I saw her sweet, sad face, and looked into her eyes, which seemed always ready to run over with tears, I loved her, and put my tired head in her lap, and cried like a child.

"'Qu'avez vous, petite Myra?' she said, and then I knew she spoke French, and my heart gave a great bound, for I knew I could talk with her a little, and I mustered all my knowledge of the language and told her I was not Myra at all; I was Rosamond Hastings, from America; shut up, detained there unlawfully, for what reason I did not know; that I had written and written home and nobody had answered me, and the doctor said my brother, who came with me, was dead, but I did not believe it; and a great deal more, to which she listened patiently, as one might listen to the meaningless prattle of a child.

"But when I mentioned brother's name, she sprang to her feet and shaking me off asked fiercely, 'votre frère, comment s'appelle-t-il?' I told her again, 'Dr. Matthewson; Dr. John Matthewson, from America,' and for a few moments she acted as if she were perfectly insane, and glaring at me with her terrible eyes, she spit upon me and demanded, 'You are sure you are his sister? You are nothing else to him, though that is bad enough?'

"I made her believe at last, and then she asked me so many questions that before I knew it I had told her all about the Forrest House, and the will, and Everard, and everything, she all the time looking straight at me with her great bright eyes, which seemed to be reading me to see if I were telling the truth.

"'I see, I see, I understand. Poor child, God sent me here to be your friend, and I will!' she said, when I had finished; and then she broke out angrily against my brother, whom she called a villain, a murderer, a rascal, and said he had done her a terrible wrong, which she had sworn to avenge, and she saw a way by which she could keep her word.

"'I go to America myself, but what your friends shall know,' she said, and to my great delight she spoke to me now in English, but whispered very low. 'It is better they not to know I can talk in your tongue, and they not suspect; and I must be very strict, watch you very much is my order, because you dangerous, you try to kill yourself, he say, and I never let you from my sight. But I fix 'em. I cheat. I have my revenge much. You will see what I do.'"

This was in part the story told afterwards to Beatrice by Rossie, who did not then know that Yulah Van Eisner was the girl who had once pleaded so piteously for justice at the hands of Dr. Matthewson, and been by him spurned with contempt, which had turned her love into bitter hatred. She saw no reason to discredit Rossie's story, and understood readily why she had been immured in a living tomb, and guessed that to her friends at home she was supposed to be dead, and that the knavish brother had the inheritance. She did not, however, communicate all her suspicions to her charge, as she did not wish to wound her unnecessarily, but she meant to get her away, and set herself steadily to that object. Through her influence writing materials were again furnished to Rossie, who, acting upon Yulah's advice, wrote two letters to Everard, one of which went into Von Schoisner's hands and was burned as usual, while the other was secreted about Yulah's person and found its way to America, but not until some time had elapsed, and Yulah had given up her situation to Margotte, with the understanding, however, that there was always a place for her in the Maison de Sante, either as attendant or nurse, when she chose to return.

CHAPTER XLIX

THE ESCAPE

There were not as many visitors as usual that season in Lintz, and those who did come were mostly English or French, who did not spend their money as freely as the Americans were accustomed to do, so that it was a matter of rejoicing to the master of the Rother Krebs when one afternoon in October the stage brought from the station two passengers whom, with his quick eye, he set down as Americans, and bustled out to meet them, deciding that they were people who would not stand for a few thalers more or less. Beatrice was very tired, for they had not stopped at all since landing in Liverpool, but had crossed at once to the Continent, and traveled day and night until they reached Lintz, where Yulah was waiting for them. She had sought and obtained the situation as chambermaid in the hotel, and, like the master, had watched impatiently for Americans, though from a very different reason. And when her Americans came, she knew them as if by instinct, taking Mr. Morton, however, for Everard, and feeling greatly disappointed when she learned that it was a Mr. and Mrs. Morton, who were occupying No. —, the great room in the house where princes had dined and slept. Still, something told her that Beatrice was the lady she was looking for, and when the latter retired to her room after dinner she found a sad-faced woman pretending to be busy with something about the washstand, though everything seemed in its place. Suddenly she faced about, and the eyes of the two women met and looked into each other with an eager, questioning gaze.

"You are Yulah," Beatrice said, in German, and the girl answered with a cry of joy, "Yes, and you are the Lady Beatrice she talks so much about, and he is not Mr. Everard."

"No, my husband, Mr. Morton. We were married just before we sailed. Where is she? When did you see her last, and how soon can we have her? Will they let her go without any trouble, and what are we to do?"

Beatrice asked her questions so rapidly as to confuse and bewilder the girl, who shook her head, and answered in English:

"You ask so many, I don't know quite all. But I go to-morrow and tell her, and see how we can do best. He will never let her go, there is too much money in her. That doctor pay big sums. We must take her, that's all, and be so careful. You stay here till I come or send some word: not to-morrow, but next day, perhaps. I not talk more now. I be at my duties."

She left the room then, and Beatrice saw no more of her until the day but one following, when about dark she came into the room, flushed and excited, and evidently a little shaken out of her usual quiet, composed manner. She had been to Haelder-Strauchsen; she had seen Rossie, but had not told her of her friends' arrival.

"I did not dare," she said, "she's so weak and sick, no heart, no courage, but stands by the window all the day, looking to the west, and whispering, sometimes, 'Oh, Everard, why do you not come, and I waiting so long?' But we'll get her sure. God fixed it for us, and he,—the doctor, I mean,—is awful with something they think is cholera, and all is fright and confusion, for the nurses is afraid and leaving, and Miss Rossie's attendant is glad to have me take her place. So I am going back to-morrow, and you must go with me and stay in the town a mile away, until I send or bring you word what you do next. You are not afraid of cholera? Americans mostly is."

Bee was mortally afraid of it, but she would have faced death itself for the sake of recovering Rossie, and it was arranged that they should take the boat the next day for the little town near the Maison de Sante, where Yulah told them there was a comfortable inn, where they could remain in quiet as long as they liked. Travelers, especially Americans, often stopped there, she said, and their being there would awaken no suspicion. Accordingly, the next afternoon found them occupants of a pleasant chamber in the inn, with an outlook to the river and another to the road which led out to La Maison de Sante. Yulah had come with them on the boat as a second-class passenger, and had held no communication whatever with them, lest suspicion might in some way be aroused; and immediately after landing had taken the road to the Sanitarium, while Beatrice tried in vain to keep composed and quiet, and await the turn of events. That she should actually see Rossie that night she could not realize, and when about dark a note was brought her by a little boy, her limbs trembled so violently, and she felt so faint and giddy, as to be scarcely able to read it.

The note was as follows:

"Have a big carriage at the south gate, one little ways off, at eleven to-night. Get Michel Fahen,—he my friend; this his little boy; he keep the carriages."

That seemed to bring Rossie very near, and Bee's face was white as ashes as she questioned the boy, who said Michael Fahen was his father, and rented carriages to people, and if she liked he would bring him to the room. Michel was a powerfully-built man, who looked as if he could keep a whole army at bay by the sheer strength of his fists, and when told what was wanted of him, or rather that he was to wait with them near the south gate of the Maison de Sante at eleven that night, shot at them a keen, quick glance of intelligence and comprehension which made Beatrice sick with fear, lest, after all, they should fail. But his words and manner were reassuring. He could guess what they wanted, and he was the man to do it. He did not believe in the place; there were many there who ought to be out. Yes, he'd help her; he'd drive them to Vienna, if necessary; he knew the south gate, in the rear of the house, opening on a lonesome and unfrequented road.

"And I shall succeed," he said. "Michel Fahen never fails; arms strong, horses fleet, and Yulah cunning as the very ——."

His confidence in himself inspired them with confidence in him, and at the time appointed they were in his carriage, and entering the narrow road which lay to the rear of the Maison de Sante, and more than a quarter of a mile distant. That portion of the grounds was filled with trees and shrubbery, and was not often used either for convenience or pleasure by the inmates of the house, the chimneys of which were by daylight just perceptible through the tall, thick trees.

Bee could see nothing in the darkness except the occasional glimmer of a light moving from point to point, as she sat, half-fainting with nervous fear and impatience, while the clock in the tower told first the hour of eleven, and then the quarter, and then the half, and then,—surely there was a footstep in the direction of the gate, and a voice she recognized as Yulah's called softly, "Michel, Michel, are you there? Help me lift her; she is dead, or fainted, and I've brought her all the way."

"Can one of you hold my horses?" Michel asked, and in an instant Beatrice was at their heads, patting, and caressing, and talking to them in the language all brutes recognize, whether in English or German, while Mr. Morton and Michel were at the gate, which was high and locked, and over which they lifted bodily a figure which lay perfectly motionless in the arms of Michel, who bore it to the carriage, and laid it down gently, but not until Beatrice, with a woman's forethought, had made sure who it was.

She had risked too much to be disappointed now, and bidding Michel wait a moment, she struck a match with which she had prepared herself, and holding it close to the inanimate form in his arms, saw the face she knew, but so white, and worn, and still, with the long, curling lashes lasting on the pallid cheeks, where tears and suffering had left their traces in dark, purplish rings, that with a gasping cry she said: "Oh, Theo, it's Rossie, but dead; I am sure she is dead."

"Now, Michel, drive for your life!" Yulah exclaimed, as she sprang to the box beside him, after having seen Rossie carefully lifted into the carriage, where she lay supported mostly by Mr. Morton, though her head was in Beatrice's lap, and Beatrice's hands were busy unfastening the waterproof hood, and her tears were flowing like rain on the face which, even in the darkness, looked ghostly white and corpse-like.

The manner of escape had been as follows: The doctor had died that afternoon, and as his disease had undoubtedly been cholera in its most malignant form, great consternation had prevailed in the building among the employees, some of whom had left, and most of whom kept as far as possible from the wing where he had died, and where Rossie's room was situated. Yulah alone was fearless, and came and went as usual, in her capacity of attendant in place of Margotte, who had fled to the town. To prevent contagion, it was thought best to bury the body at midnight, with as little ceremony as possible, and thus everything was in confusion, of which Yulah took advantage. She was very popular in the house, and when she asked permission to go out for the evening and take one of the nurses with her, it was readily granted her, with the injunction that she should wait until her patient was asleep, or at least quiet for the night. To this she readily assented, saying that she would lock her in the room so as to prevent the possibility of her venturing into the hall while the body was being removed. This arranged, her next business was to prepare Rossie, who had recently sunk into a state of despondency amounting almost to insanity itself, and who spent most of her time sitting or standing by the window, with her face toward the setting sun, and such a hopeless, weary expression upon it as was very touching to see. She was standing thus, although it was already too dark to see more than the lights in the distant town, when Yulah came hurriedly in, and, bolting the door, went up to her and said, in broken English:

"Cheer up, petite, joy and glad at last. They are come; they here for you!"

"Not Everard! Oh, has he come?" and a low cry broke from Rossie's quivering lips.

But Yulah stifled it at once by putting her hand over her mouth, and saying:

"Careful, much careful. They must not hear. I fix it for you, and you be still and listen."

Very rapidly she told her that Mrs. Morton and her husband, whom she called anything but Morton, were at the inn waiting for them, and detailed her plan of escape, to which Rossie listened in a kind of apathetic way, which showed that she did not clearly comprehend what was meant, or who was waiting for her. Certainly she never thought of Beatrice, but she understood that all she had to do was to obey orders, and taking the seat which Yulah bade her take, she sat as immovable as a stone, with her great, black eyes following every movement of her nurse, who, alarmed at last at their expression and the rigid attitude of the figure, which scarcely seemed to breathe, tried to rouse her to something like sense and feeling, but all in vain.

One idea and one alone had possession of Rossie. If she would escape she must be still, and she sometimes held her breath lest she should be heard by the men, who, at the far end of the long hall, were passing in and out of the room where the dead body lay. No one came near No. —, or paid

251

any attention when, about half-past ten, two female figures emerged from the door,—one wrapped in a blue waterproof, with the hood drawn closely over the face; the other unmistakably Yulah, who, locking the door behind her and putting the key in her pocket, hurried with her companion down the two long flights of stairs, and through a back, winding piazza, to the rear of the house, where the door she had unfastened an hour before stood partly open, and through which she went, dragging her companion after her. It was literally dragging until the safety of the thick shrubbery was reached, when Rossie gave out and sank down at Yulah's feet unconscious, and fainted entirely away. To add to Yulah's alarm, there was a sound of footsteps near. Somebody was in the wood besides herself, and she waited breathlessly until the sound ceased in the distance, as the person or persons, for there seemed to be two, hurried on. Then, taking Rossie in her arms, she made what progress she could, groping through the dark and underbrush, as she dared not keep to the path. But the gate was reached at last, and with Michel's strong hands to help, Rossie was lifted over it and into the carriage, which was driven rapidly in the direction of the nearest railway station.

CHAPTER L

GOING HOME

Three weeks after the events recorded in the last chapter, the City of Berlin came slowly up the New York harbor, and of all the eager, expectant faces in the crowd of people upon the deck, none was happier or more eager than that of Beatrice, who, now that her work was accomplished, and Rossie safe in her possession, had given herself up to the pleasures of her honeymoon, and been the merriest, happiest, most loving of brides, during all the voyage, except when she looked at the white-faced girl who lay in her berth so quietly, or sat so still in her chair on deck, looking out upon the sea with eyes which did not seem to see anything or take note of what was passing.

The flight from Haelder-Strauchsen to the nearest railroad had been accomplished in safety, and there they waited a few hours for the arrival of the train, which was to take them away from the scene of so much danger. And here it was that Beatrice suggested to Yulah that she go with them to America, either as Rossie's maid or her own.

"I mean to do it all the time, then I see what come to he,—the villain,— and I take much care my poor little one, who so tired and scared in her head, but who come right sure when the boy Everard is near," Yulah said, as she stroked the thin, hot hands, folded so helplessly across Rossie's breast.

Very rapidly she communicated her intention to Michel, telling him at the same time the full particulars of Rossie's incarceration in the Maison de Sante, and bidding him repeat it in Haelder-Strauchsen, if there was a great stir on account of the abduction. Mr. Morton had paid his bills at the inn, and said that he should not return, as he was going to a point higher up the river, so no suspicions could be awakened there of anything wrong until the alarm was given at the house. And this, in all human probability, would not be till late the next morning, when, as Yulah failed to appear, inquiries might be made, and the door of No. — be forced open, and by that time the fugitives would be miles and miles away, speeding on toward the west, and Michel Fahen would be smoking his pipe very unconcernedly at the door of his kitchen, knowing nothing whatever of any escaped lunatic, or of Yulah Van Eisner's whereabouts; knowing nothing, except that he carried some English-talking people to a railroad station, and was rewarded for it by many, many thalers. So, of whatever commotion or excitement there was, Mr. and Mrs. Morton were ignorant, and kept rapidly on their way until the continent was crossed, and they felt safe in the seclusion of crowded London. Here they rested in lodgings a few days, and called the best medical advice for Rossie, who, since recovering from the dead faint in which she had been more than an hour, had been just on the border land, where her reason seemed hesitating whether to go or stay. When it first came to her in the carriage who it was bending so lovingly over her, she had burst into a wild fit of weeping, which frightened them more than the faint had done. Her first words, when she did speak, were:

"Everard, where are you? hold my hand in yours and I shall not be afraid."

At a sign from his wife, Mr. Morton took Rossie's hand in his and held it, while Bee whispered to her, "Don't talk now, darling. It is all right. We are going home."

How much Rossie realized of that rapid journey, which was continued day and night, they could not guess, for she never spoke again or showed any sign that she understood what was passing around her, except to answer their questions in monosyllables and smile so sweetly and trustfully in their faces when they told her, as they often did, that she was safe, until London was reached, and they laid her in the clean, sweet bed in the large, airy room in quiet Kensington, where they had taken lodgings.

For several days they staid in London, and then took passage for home in the City of Berlin, where everything was done to make the voyage comfortable and easy for Rossie, who talked but little, and who, when she did speak, always asked, "How long before I shall see Everard?"

It was only the Maison de Sante and the incidents connected with it which had any power to excite or even interest her. With regard to everything else, except Everard, she was silent and indifferent, asking no questions, and even taking Beatrice's marriage as a matter of course, and never offering a comment upon it. But when at last America was in sight and they were coming up the harbor, she roused from her apathy and went up on deck with the others, and sat in her chair, with a bright flush on her cheeks and a sparkle in her eyes which made them as bright as stars. She was looking for Everard, and trying to make him out in the group of men waiting on the distant wharf for the boat.

"I must tell her," Bee thought; and sitting down beside her, she said: "Darling, I know you expect Everard to meet you, but he is not here. He did not even know we were going for you, and we would not tell him for fear we might fail, and then he would feel worse than ever. But he is in Rothsay, and will be so glad to get his dear little girl once more. Don't cry," she added, as the great tears gathered in Rossie's eyes and rolled down her cheeks. "We meant it for the best, and you shall see him soon, very soon. We will go on to-night, if you think you can bear it. Are you strong enough?"

"Yes, go on,—quick,—fast, just as we came through Europe. I want to see Everard," Rossie whispered, and so they went on that night in the express which left for Pittsburg, from which city a telegram was forwarded to Lawyer Russell, to the effect that Mr. and Mrs. Morton would be in Rothsay on the late train.

CHAPTER LI

BREAKING THE NEWS AT
THE FORREST HOUSE

A wild storm was sweeping over Southern Ohio that November night, and nowhere was it wilder or more violent than in Rothsay, where the rain fell in torrents, and ere it reached the ground was taken up by the wind and driven in blinding sheets through the deserted streets. But wild as the storm was in the village, it seemed wilder still in the vicinity of the Forrest House, which fairly shook on its solid foundations with the force of the tempest. Tree after tree was blown down, shrubs were uprooted, and the fanciful summer-house which the doctor had erected on the spot where Rossie used to tend and water her geraniums and fuchsias, went crashing down, a heap of ruins, while within, in the most costly and elegant chamber, a fiercer storm was raging between a soul trying to free itself from its prison walls of clay and the body which struggled so hard to retain it.

Josephine had not improved, as at one time it was thought she might. The secret which she held and the loss of the letter had worn upon her terribly, and the constant dread of some impending evil had produced a kind of brain fever, and for days her life had been in imminent danger, and the doctor had staid by her constantly, marveling at the strangeness of her talk, and wondering sometimes if it were possible that she could have become possessed of the secret which at times filled even him with horror and a haunting fear of what might come upon him should his guilt be known. But Josephine could have no knowledge of his crime. Van Schoisner was safe as the grave so long as the money was paid, as it would continue to be, for he had set aside a certain amount, the interest of which went regularly to Haelder-Strauchsen, and would go so long as Rossie lived. This, in all human probability, would not be long, for Von Schoisner wrote of her failing health, and told how bewildered she was growing in her mind. Should she become hopelessly insane, he would be almost as safe as if she were dead, the doctor thought, and he always waited with fierce impatience for news from Austria, when he knew that it was due. Von Schoisner's last letter had reported her as very weak, with growing symptoms of imbecility, and though the villainous man did feel a pang of remorse when he remembered the sunny-faced girl who had so loved and trusted him, he knew he had gone too far to think of retracing his steps. There was nothing left but to go on, and as his life at the Forrest House had not proved a success he had made up his mind to sell it and go to Europe to live permanently as soon as Josephine was better. He could hide himself there from justice, should it attempt to overtake him, and he waited anxiously for any signs of amendment in his wife.

She did seem better that stormy night, when even he quailed a little and felt nervous as he listened to the roaring wind, which, he fancied, had in it the sound of human sobbing. She had slept for more than an hour, and when she awoke she was quiet, and more rational than she had been for days. But there was a look of death about her mouth and nose, and her eyes were unnaturally bright as they fixed themselves on Agnes, who sat watching her.

The doctor had taken advantage of her sleep to steal away for a while, and in the dining-room was trying to stifle his conscience with the fumes of tobacco and the brandy, of which he drank largely and often. Thus Agnes was left alone with her sister, whose first question, asked in a whisper, was:

"Where is he,—the doctor, I mean?"

"Gone to rest," was the reply, and Josephine continued:

"Yes, let him rest while he can. It will soon be over, and then a dungeon for him, and darkness, and blankness, and utter forgetfulness for me; Aggie, that's all a fable about a hereafter,—a rag of mythology which recent science has torn in shreds. We do not go somewhere when we die; we perish like the brutes."

"Oh, no, no! God forbid!" and falling on her knees, with her hands clasped together, Agnes murmured words of prayer for the soul so deluded and deceived.

"Hush, Agnes," Josephine said, almost fiercely. "There's more important work on hand just now than praying for one who does not want your prayers, for even if there be a hereafter, it's now too late for me, and I care no more for it than a stone. I cannot feel, and it's no use to try. If there is a hell, which I don't believe, I shall go there; if there is not, then I am all right, and the sooner I am like the clods the better; but I must do one good act. Agnes, do you think Everard would come here to-night if he knew I was dying,—for I am; I feel it, and I must tell him something, which will perhaps make him think more kindly of me than he does now. Can you manage it for me?"

"No, no," Agnes exclaimed. "He would not come here to-night of all others, because——"

She checked herself suddenly, and then added:

"Listen to the rain and the wind; did you ever hear such a storm?"

"Yes, I hear," Josephine replied, excitedly. "It was sent for me, and I am going out on its wings, but it seems dreary to go in such a way. Oh, Aggie, if there should be a hereafter,—but there is not. We all do sleep,— sleep. But Everard, Everard,—I must see him, or maybe you would tell him when I am dead. Lock the door, Aggie; then come close to me and swear,— swear that you will tell him,—that Rossie——Oh, Agnes, I am so afraid of him,—the doctor, that I dare not say it!" and on the white face there was a look of terror such as Agnes had never seen before.

There could be no doubt in her mind as to what her sister meant, and regardless of consequences, she bent down and whispered:

"I know,—I understand. Rossie is not dead. She is alive and coming home."

"How do you know? Have you seen the letter?" Josephine almost shrieked, and Agnes replied:

"Yes, I found it under the carpet long ago, just after I came here, but I did not suppose that you had ever seen it."

"I had; I did; I put it there," Josephine said, gasping out the story of her having taken it from the office, and the hiding it afterward. "And you found it? Where is it now?" she asked, and Agnes replied:

"I gave it to Miss Belknap, and she——"

Agnes did not finish, for Josephine started upright in bed, exclaiming:

"I see; I know. She went suddenly to Europe,—to find Rossie; tell me the truth. Has she found her, and is she coming home, and what will it be for him?"

Agnes knew that by him Dr. Matthewson was meant, and she replied unhesitatingly:

"State prison for him and poverty for you."

"Yes, I know. Poverty, disgrace, State prison for life, and how soon? Tell me how soon? He might have time to fly, for I,—I,—he is not good, but I'd rather he did not go to prison. He is my husband, you know. How soon? Tell me truly."

"To-night,—now,—the train is due and overdue. I do not believe he can get away. I think he is watched. Lawyer Russell knows,—not Everard yet; and Mr. and Mrs. Morton are coming to-night with Rossie," Agnes said, rapidly; and the next moment a wild shriek rang through the house, which Dr. Matthewson heard above the storm, and he came reeling up the stairs from his brandy and cigars, but was sobered at once when he found his wife in the most horrible fit he had ever witnessed.

When it was over, and she became conscious again, it was pitiable to see how hard she tried to speak and warn him of his danger, but could not, for the power of utterance was gone, and she only gave forth inarticulate sounds which he could not comprehend any more than he could understand what had affected her so strangely. It was in vain that he appealed to Agnes, who was whiter if possible than her sister, and trembling from head to foot. She was sworn to secrecy,—and if she had inadvertently said to Josephine things which she ought not, she must keep silence before the doctor, and bear the glance of the eyes which looked so imploringly at her, and seemed about to leap from their sockets when she shook her head in token that she could not tell. There were flecks of blood and foam about the pallid lips, and drops of sweat upon the face and hands, the latter of which beat the air hopelessly as the dying woman tried to speak. At last, when they had no more power to move, they dropped helplessly upon the bed, and the white, haggard face grew whiter and more haggard as she lay with ears strained to catch the sound for which she listened so intently, and which came at last in a shrill, prolonged whistle, which was distinctly heard in the pauses of the abating storm, as the train so long delayed swept through the town. Then, summoning all her remaining strength for one last great effort, Josephine raised her arm in the air, and motioning to the door, said to her husband in a voice which was to sound in his ears through many years to come:

"Doomed,—doomed,—fl——"

She could not finish and say "fly," as she wished to do, for the word died away in a low, gurgling moan; the white foam poured again from lips and nose, and when the convulsions ceased and the distorted features resumed their natural look, the soul had gone to meet its God.

CHAPTER LII

BREAKING THE NEWS TO EVERARD

It was an hour behind the usual time when the train from the north stopped for a moment at Rothsay, and four people, or rather three, stepped out into the storm, and hurried to the shelter of the carriage waiting for them. The fourth, whose face was carefully hidden from sight, was carried in the strong arms of Yulah, and held like a child until Beatrice's house was reached, where it was taken at once to the room which Rossie used to occupy, when visiting at Elm Park. Rossie was very tired and very weak, both in body and mind, but had not seemed at all excited during the journey from New York until Rothsay was reached, and she was in the carriage riding along the old familiar road she had once thought she should never see again. Then she roused from her apathy, and sitting upright looked eagerly out through the driving rain toward the Forrest House, which lay to their right, and seemed to blaze with lights, as the startled servants moved rapidly from room to room,—for it was just then that the soul had taken wing and was on its flight to the world untried.

"Look, look!" she said, "so many lights in the old home, as if to welcome me back. Is Everard there waiting for me?"

"No, Rossie," Beatrice said. "We are not going there to-night. I thought it best to bring you home with me until you have seen Everard."

There was a little sigh of disappointment, and then Rossie laid her head on Yulah's arm, and did not speak again until she was on the soft bed in the blue room at Elm Park, where, when Bee asked her how she felt, she whispered: "So happy and glad, because I shall see him in the morning; send for him very early."

And when the morning came a message was dispatched to Everard to the effect that Mr. and Mrs. Morton had returned and wished to see him immediately. But another message had found its way to the office before this one, for knots of crape were streaming in the November wind from every door-knob at the Forrest House, and the village bell was tolling in token that some soul had gone to the God who gave it.

In his office Everard sat listening to the bell, every stroke of which thrilled him with a sensation of something like dread, as if that knell of death were in some way connected with himself. Who was it dead that day that the bell should clamor so long, and would it never strike the age, he asked himself, just as the door opened and Lawyer Russell came in, flurried and excited, and red and white by turns as he shook the rain-drops from his overcoat, for the storm, though greatly abated, was not over yet.

"Who is dead? Do you know?" Everard asked, and Mr. Russell replied:

"Yes, Ned; it will be a great shock to you,—an infernal shock,—though of course you were all over any hankering after her; but it's that Matthewson woman. She died last night, and there's about forty yards of crape flying from the doors up there, and the doctor, they say, is actually taking on to kill, and blubbering like a calf; but we'll fix him. You'll see; he's watched; there's a po——oh, Lord! what have I said, or come near saying?"

And in his disgust at himself for having nearly let out the secret before the time, the lawyer retreated into the adjoining room, leaving Everard alone to meet what had been a terrible shock to him, for though he had heard at different times from Agnes of Josephine's illness, he had never believed her dangerous; and now she was dead; the woman he once fancied that he loved. There were great drops of sweat about his mouth and under his hair, and his lips quivered nervously while, human as he was, there came over him with a rush the thought that now indeed he was free in a way which even Rossie would have recognized had she been alive. But Rossie, too, was dead; his freedom had come too late.

"Everybody is dead," he whispered, sadly, while hot tears sprang to his eyes and rolled down his cheeks,—tears, not for the woman at the Forrest House, for whom the bell kept steadily tolling, but for the dear little girl dead, as he believed, so far away, but who, in reality, was so very near, and even then asking when he would come.

"Soon, darling, soon," Beatrice said, for she had sent a note to Everard, and the messenger was at his office door and in the room before Everard was aware of his presence.

"Mrs. Morton at home!" he exclaimed, as he took the note from the servant's hand.

"Dear Everard," Beatrice wrote, "we came home last night on the late train, and I am so anxious to see you, and have so much to tell. Don't delay a minute, but come at once.

Yours, Bee."

She had something to tell him of Rossie, of course, and in an instant he was in the street, speeding along toward Elm Park, and glancing but once in the direction of the Forrest House, where every blind was closed, and where, through the leafless trees, he could see the flapping of the yards of crape which Lawyer Russell had said were streaming from the doors. For an instant a cold shudder went over him as if he had seen a corpse, but that soon passed away, and when Elm Park was reached he was in such a fever of excitement that the sweat-drops stood like rain upon his face, which, nevertheless, was very pale, as he greeted Beatrice, and asked:

"Did you hear anything of her? Did you find her grave, or see any one who was with her at the last?"

Beatrice had planned everything thus far with great coolness and nerve. She had kept Rossie quiet, and made her very sweet and attractive in one of her own dainty, white wrappers, and arranged her beautiful hair, which had been kept short at the Maison de Sante, but which was now growing in soft, curling rings, giving to her small, white face a singularly young expression, so that she might easily have passed for a child of fourteen as she reclined upon the pillows, a smile upon her lips, and an eager, expectant look in her large, bright eyes, turning constantly to the door at every sound which met her ear. At last she heard the well-remembered voice in the hall below and the step upon the stairs, for Bee had after all lost her self-control, and in answer to Everard's rapid questions, had said: "We did hear news of Rossie, and, oh, Everard, don't let anything astonish or startle you, but go up stairs to the blue room, Rossie's old room, you know."

He did not wait to hear more, but darted up the stairs, expecting, not to find his darling there alive, but dead, perhaps, and thus brought back to him, for Bee was capable of anything; so he sped on his way, and entered the room where the fire burned so brightly in the grate, and flowers were everywhere, while through the window came a sudden gleam of sunlight, which fell directly on the couch where lay, not a dead, but a living Rossie, with a halo of gladness on her face, and in her beautiful eyes, which met him as he came so swiftly into the room, pausing suddenly with a cry, half of terror, half of joy, as he saw the little girl among the pillows raise herself upright and stretch her arms towards him, while she called so clearly and sweetly: "Oh, Everard, I am home again, and you may kiss me once."

There was a sudden movement of his hand to his head as if the blow had struck him there, and then he staggered rather than walked toward the white-robed figure, which sprang into his arms and nestled there like a frightened bird which has been torn from its nest and suddenly finds itself safe in its shelter again. For an instant Everard recoiled from the embrace as if it were a phantom he held, but only for an instant, for there was nothing phantom-like in the warm flesh and blood trembling in his arms; nothing corpse-like in the soft hands caressing his face, or in the eyes meeting his so fondly. It was Rossie herself come back to him from the grave where he had thought her buried, and the shock was at first so overpowering that he could not utter a word; he could only look at her with wildly staring eyes, and face which quivered all over with strong emotions, while his heart beat so loudly that every throb was audible to himself and Rossie, who, as he did not speak, lifted her head from his shoulder and said, "What is it, Everard? Are you not glad to have me home again?"

That broke the spell, and brought a shower of kisses upon her face and lips, while he murmured words of fondness and love, and poured forth question after question, until Rossie grew bewildered and confused, and whispered faintly: "I don't know; I don't understand; I am very tired; ask Beatrice, she knows; she did it; let me lie down again."

He saw how pale and weary she looked, and placed her among the pillows, but held her hands in his, while he turned to Beatrice, who had been standing just outside the door, and who now came forward.

"Not here; Rossie is too tired. She cannot bear it," she said, as he asked her what it meant, and where she had found his darling.

Then, drawing him into the adjoining room, she told him very rapidly all the steps which had led to Rossie's release from the mad-house, which had been intended as her living tomb. And as he listened to the story, Everard grew more and more enraged, until he seemed like some wild animal roused to the highest pitch of fury; and seizing his hat, was about rushing from the room, when Beatrice detained him; and, locking the door to prevent his egress, said to him: "I know what is in your mind. You wish to arrest the doctor at once, but there is no haste at present. Everything has been attended to for you. Ever since Lawyer Russell heard from me that Rossie was alive, the Forrest House has been under close espionage, and escape for the doctor made impossible. Last night, in all that storm, officers were on guard, so that he could not get away if he had received a hint of what has been done."

"Yes, I know; but now,—now,—why not seize him now? Why wait any longer, when I long to tear him limb from limb?" Everard exclaimed, gnashing his teeth in his rage, and seeming to Beatrice like a tiger doing battle for its young.

"Because," she answered, and she spoke softly now, "we must hold his sorrow sacred. We must let him bury his dead. Surely you know that Josephine died last night?"

"Yes, yes, but I'd forgotten it in my excitement," he gasped, and his face was whiter, if possible, than before. "You are right; we must not molest him now, but have a double watch,—yes, treble, if necessary. He must not escape."

There was terrible vengeance in Everard's flashing eyes as he paced up and down the room. Dr. Matthewson, though he were ten times Rossie's brother, had nothing to hope from him; but for the sake of the dead woman lying in such state at the Forrest House, he must keep quiet and bide his time. So, after another interview with Rossie, whose weak state he began to understand more plainly, he left her, and schooled himself to go quietly back to his office and transact his business as if he were not treading the borders of a mine which would explode when he bade it do so. At his request, the number of officers was doubled, and every possible precaution taken lest the victim should escape, which he did not seem likely to do, for he made a great show of his grief, and sat all day by the side of his dead wife, seeing no one but Agnes and those who had the funeral in charge. Thus, he did not even know of Beatrice's sudden return, which took the people so by surprise, and was the theme of wonder and comment second only to the grand funeral for which such great preparations were making, and which was to take place the third day after the death.

CHAPTER LIII

THE ARREST

At Elm Park the utmost secrecy was maintained with regard to Rossie, whose presence in the house was wholly unsuspected by any one except the few necessarily in the secret. The servants knew, of course, but they were trusty and silent as the grave, and almost as eager for the denouement as Yulah, herself, who had personal wrongs to be avenged, but who seldom spoke to any one lest she should betray what must be kept. Two or three times, after dark, she had stolen up to the Forrest House, which she examined minutely, while she shook her fist and muttered in execration of the man who, she heard, sat constantly by his wife, with his face buried in his hands, as if he really mourned for the woman whom he knew so much better than any one else. And to a certain extent his grief was genuine. Her beauty had dazzled and pleased him, and something in her selfish, treacherous nature had so answered to his own, that in a way she was necessary to him, and when she went from him so suddenly, he experienced a shock and sense of loss which struck him down as he had never before been stricken.

Agnes wished to have her sister taken to Holburton and buried by her mother. But Holburton was too democratic a town, and Roxie Fleming's bones far too plebeian for his wife to lie beside, and so he bought a vacant lot in Rothsay, and gave orders that no expense should be spared to make the funeral worthy of his money and position as the richest man in the county.

And now, at the close of the third day, the grand funeral was over,—and grand it certainly was, if a costly coffin, a profusion of flowers, twenty carriages, and a multitude of lookers-on, could make it so; but how much real grief there was, aside from what Agnes felt, was a matter of speculation to the people, who went in crowds to the Forrest House, which was filled from kitchen to parlor. And the doctor knew they were there, and felt a thrill of gratification at the honor paid him, though he sat with his head bent down, and never once looked up or seemed to notice any one. Even had he glanced about him at the sea of heads filling anterooms and halls, he would not have remarked the men, who, without any apparent intention, were always in the foreground, just where they could command a view of the chief mourner in the imposing procession which moved slowly to the cemetery, where all that was mortal of Josephine was buried from sight. At the grave the doctor's grief took a demonstrative form, and he stood with his face covered with his hands, while his body shook as if from suppressed sobs, and when a low cry escaped Agnes as the coffin box scraped the gravelly earth, he put out his arm toward her as if to comfort and reassure her; but she instinctively drew back, with a feeling of treachery in her heart, as if for the sake of the dead sister she ought to warn him of his danger, and give him a chance to escape, if it were possible, which she doubted; for, though she did not know just what the plan was, she knew how closely the house had been watched, and recognized in the crowd the men whom she had seen on the premises, and whose office she rightly conjectured. But she had sworn to keep the secret, and so her lips were sealed, and she never uttered a word as they drove back to the house, where she went directly to her room, and on her knees begged forgiveness if she were doing a wrong to the unsuspecting man, who, all unconscious of peril, went also to his own room to draw what consolation he could from the fumes of his best cigars and the poison of his brandies.

And so he was as surely doomed as if the manacles were already upon his hands, and the prison walls around him. In the hall below there was the sound of voices in low consultation, Everard's voice, and Lawyer Russell's, and the officers of justice, who had taken possession of the house and locked every door below to shut off all means of escape. In the kitchen the astonished and frightened servants were crowded together, asking each other what it meant and what was about to happen, but not one of them dared to move after the officers commanded that they keep quiet, whatever might occur. Then, up the stairs came the two strange men, with Everard and Mr. Russell following close behind, and on through the hall to the door of the doctor's room. It was a little ajar, and he heard their footsteps, and half rose to meet them as they stepped across the threshold. But when he saw Everard's white, set face, and saw how excited Lawyer Russell seemed, there flashed over him an inkling of the truth, and when the foremost of the officers advanced toward him, and laying his hand on his arm, arrested him for perjury, he felt sure that the desperate game he had been playing had ended in disgrace and defeat. But he was too proud to manifest any emotion whatever. If his revolver had been in his pocket, where he usually carried it, he would have used it unhesitatingly, but it was not. He had no means of defense, and in as natural a tone of voice as he could command, he asked what they meant, and on what ground the arrest was made; how had he perjured himself, and when?

"When you swore that Rossie was dead, and knew that it was false, and that she was incarcerated in a mad-house where you put her, you villain! Rossie is not dead; she is here in town,—at Elm Park, and all your infernal rascality is known," Everard burst out, for he could restrain himself no longer, and he felt a thrill of triumph when he saw how white the doctor grew, and how for a moment he tottered as if he would fall.

He did not attempt to get away; he merely said:

"Rossie here? Rossie alive? Take me to her. I must see her. Gentlemen, there is some mistake, which can be cleared up if only I can see her. I beg of you, take me to her."

But his request was not granted. He was a prisoner, and all resistance was vain. Cold and pallid, and seemingly indifferent, he did just what they bade him do, and went with them down the stairs and out of the house he was never to enter again. On the piazza outside they encountered a strange woman, who threw herself directly in the prisoner's way, and shrieked into his ear:

"It bees you, Dr. Matthewson. I knows you, sure, and I has the revenge. I finds her there in Haelder-Strauchsen, and sends the letter here to him, (pointing to Everard), and the lady, Madame Morton. She comes and I gets her away, and you into the conciergerie,—ha, ha! What does you think now of the tragic queen?" and she snapped her fingers in his face, which was deadly white, and livid in spots as he recoiled from her, exclaiming:

"Yulah! betrayed by you!"

"Yes, me. I swore it. I's glad to be revenge," she cried, and was going on with more abuse when the officer stopped her, and hurried the doctor away to a place of safety, where a close guard was placed over him, and he was left alone with his wretched thoughts.

It did not take long for the news to spread over the town, for secrecy was no longer necessary, and never had there been such wild excitement in Rothsay. That Rossie Hastings had been alive all this time, and buried in a mad-house, while her brother enjoyed her property, seemed almost incredible, but there could be no doubt of it, for old Axie had seen her, and talked with her face to face, and in their fury a mob, preceded by the old negress, assembled in the streets, and surrounding the building where the doctor was confined, demanded the prisoner, that they might wreak vengeance on him then and there.

Order was, however, soon restored, and the wretched man was left in quiet to think over his wicked past, and to dread the future, which he knew had no hope for him. His sin had found him out, and though he had not conscience enough to be much troubled with remorse, his pride and self-love were cruelly wounded, and he writhed in the anguish of bitter mortification and rage.

CHAPTER LIV

TELLING THE TRUTH TO ROSSIE

Rossie had asked, on her voyage home, who lived at the Forrest House, and had been simply told that Josephine was there still, but no mention had been made of the unnatural marriage lest it should excite her too much. Now, however, it was desirable that she should know the truth, in part, at least, for her testimony would be necessary when the trial came on. So Everard told it to her a few days after the arrest, when she seemed stronger than usual, and able to bear it.

She had been steadily improving since Rothsay was reached, though she talked but little, and was most of the time so absorbed in thought that she did not always hear when spoken to, or answer if she did. She heard, however, when Everard came, and recognized his step the moment he touched the piazza, and her pale face would light up with sudden joy and her large eyes glow like coals of fire; but since their first interview she had not suffered him to kiss her, or even to hold her hands in his as he sat and talked to her. Josephine living was a bar between them still, and Everard guessed as much, and told her at last that Josephine had died on the very night of her return to Rothsay. She was sitting in her easy-chair, with her head resting upon a pillow, and her little white, thin hands held tightly on her lap, as if afraid of the masculine fingers beating restlessly upon the arm of her chair. But when she heard of Josephine's death, her hands involuntarily unlocked and crept toward the restless fingers, which caught and held them fast while Everard went on very slowly and cautiously to tell her the rest of the story,—the part which involved her brother, whose name he had not before mentioned to her. At first she listened breathlessly, with parted lips and wide-open eyes, which almost frightened him with their expression of wonder, and surprise, and incredulity.

"Everard,—Everard!" she gasped, "you are not telling me the truth? Say you are not. I would almost rather have died in that dreadful place than know my brother did this. Surely it is not true?"

"Yes, true in every particular," Everard replied, softening now as much as possible what he had still to tell of the man whose trial would come on very soon, and for whom there was no escape.

"Couldn't you save him, Everard, if you should try? Couldn't I do something?" she asked.

"No, Rossie," he answered. "You could not save him, and ought not if you could. Men like him must be punished,—must answer for their misdeeds, else there is no such thing as justice or protection for any one. You are not angry with me, Rossie?" he continued, as she drew her hand from his and leaned back in her chair.

"No, not angry; only it is all so very horrible, and brings the buzzing back, and the confusion, and I hardly know who I am, or who you are, or what it's all about, only you must go away. I can't hear any more," she said, wearily; and after that there were days and weeks when she lay in bed, and scarcely moved or noticed any one, except Everard, whom she welcomed with her sweetest smile, saying to him always the same thing:

"I have been thinking and thinking, and praying and praying, and I suppose it is right, but oh! I am so sorry."

Everard knew that her mind was dwelling upon the miserable man, who, when told of her condition and that the trial was to be delayed till she was able to give her testimony, had said:

"No need of that. I don't want Rossie dragged into the court to swear against me. I know more than she does; nothing can save me. I shall not put in a defense;" and he did not.

Coldly, proudly, and apparently unmoved, he sat in the criminal's seat and listened to his trial, and saw the looks of horror and execration cast at him, and saw Yulah's face, like the face of a fiend, sneering exultingly at him, and heard at last his sentence of imprisonment with the utmost composure; and no one who saw him on his way to his new home would have dreamed of the fate which awaited him. Only once did he show what he felt, and that was when the prison dress was brought for him to put on. He had been very fastidious with regard to his personal appearance, and he flinched a little and turned pale for an instant, then rallying quickly he tried to smile and affect some pleasantry with regard to the unsightly garb which transformed him at once from an elegant man of fashion into a branded felon, with no mark of distinction between him and his daily companions.

CHAPTER LV

CONCLUSION

After the trial was over, and the doctor safely lodged in prison to serve out his length of time, Rothsay gradually grew quiet and ceased to talk of the startling events which had thrown the town into such commotion. They were getting accustomed to the fact that Rossie was alive and with them again. She had appeared in the streets with Beatrice two or three times, and many of her old friends had been admitted to see her, but she was still very weak in body and mind, and was kept as quiet as possible. Beatrice had made a short visit with her husband to Boston, but had returned again to her own home, bringing Trix and Bunchie with her, hoping the effect on Rossie might be good. And it was, for from the moment the children came and turned the orderly house upside down with their play and prattle, she began to improve and seem much like the Rossie of old, except that her face and figure were thinner and there were no roses on her cheeks, and there was always a tired look in her eyes and about her mouth. Of her brother she never spoke, nor of Josephine either; neither had she ever been near the Forrest House, which, without her knowledge, had gradually been undergoing a transformation, preparatory to the time when she should be equal to visit it. Both Everard and Beatrice, with Aunt Axie to assist them, had been busy as bees, removing from the house every article of furniture which either the doctor or Josephine had bought, and replacing it with the old, familiar things of Rossie's childhood.

When the doctor refurnished the house he had ordered all the rubbish, as he called it, to be stored away in the attics and unused rooms, where it had lain untouched save as dust and cobwebs had accumulated on it, and thus it was comparatively easy for the rooms to assume their natural appearance, except so far as they had been changed by new windows and doors, and partitions thrown down to make them more commodious. Could Axie have had her way, she would have put everything back as it was, and not have left a vestige of the past, but Everard had the good sense to see that the changes were such as both he and Rossie would like when accustomed to them. He put himself with Rossie, for he knew he should live there with her, although nothing definite was settled by word of mouth. He had a plan which he meant to carry out, and when the house was restored to itself, and the same old carpets were on the floor, and the same old pictures on the wall, and the chairs in his father's room standing just as they stood that day when Rossie came to him so fearlessly and asked to be his wife, he went to her and said she was to ride with him that morning, as there was something he wished to show her. She assented readily, and was soon beside him in Beatrice's phaeton, driving toward the Forrest House grounds, into which he suddenly turned.

"Oh, Everard," she cried, as her cheek flushed scarlet, "where are you going? Not there? I cannot bear it yet. It will bring the buzzing back, and all the uncertainty. Don't go, please. It's like a haunted place."

But Everard was firm, and quieted her as well as he could, and pointed out Aunt Axie standing in the door just as she used to stand waiting for her young mistress, and John farther on in the stable-yard, and even the old dogs barking in the early sunshine, and running to meet them as they came up. It did not seem strange nor haunted now, and Rossie made no resistance when Everard lifted her from the phaeton and carried her into the house, which seemed so restful and home-like that she felt all her old morbid feelings and fears dropping from her, and flitted from room to room like some joyous bird, until she came to the judge's chamber, where she paused a moment on the threshold, while there flashed upon her a remembrance of that day which seemed so long ago, when she had entertained it so fearlessly, and done that for which she always blushed when she recalled it. Passing his arm around her Everard drew her into the room, and closing the door made her sit down beside him, while he said, "Rossie, you surely have not forgotten a scene which took place here more than six years ago, when a miserable, sorely-tried young man sat here a beggar, with a secret on his mind far worse and harder to bear than prospective poverty. And while he sat thinking of the future, and shrinking from it with a dread of which you cannot conceive, there came to him a little sweet-faced girl, who, in her desire to comfort him and give back what she believed to be his, asked to be his wife, without a thought of shame. No, Rossie, don't try to get away from me, for you cannot. I shall keep you now, forever," he continued, as Rossie tried to free herself from the arm which only held her closer, as Everard went on: "In one sense that time seems to me ages and ages ago, so much has happened since, while in another it seems but yesterday, so distinctly do I recall every incident and detail, even to the dress and apron you wore, and the expression of your face as it changed from perfect unconsciousness to a sense of what you had done. You came to me a child, but you left me a woman, whom I do believe I would even then have taken to my heart but for the bar between us. That bar is now removed, and Rossie, my darling, I have brought you here to the old home, and into the very room, to answer the question you asked me then, that is, if you are still of the same mind. Are you, Rossie? Do you still wish to be my wife?"

He had her face between his two hands, and was looking into her eyes, which filled with tears as she said to him: "Oh, Everard, yes, yes. I have wished it so much when it was wicked to do so, and now that it is not, I wish it still; only I am afraid I must not, for there is such a horrible fear before me all the time which I cannot shake off. Day and night it haunts me, that I am not all right in my brain. I saw so much and suffered so much that I can't put things together quite straight, and my head buzzes at times, and I do not remember, and am even troubled to know just who I am and what has happened. Oh, do you think, do you suppose I am going to be a,——a,——" She hesitated, and her lips quivered pitifully as she finally pronounced the dreadful word,—"fool."

Everard's laugh was something pleasant and good to hear, it was so long and loud.

"Fool, Rossie. No. You are only tired out and must have the perfect rest which you can find alone with me," he said, and he covered her face with kisses. "And were you ten times a fool, I want you just the same. And you are mine, my own precious little Rossie who will be my wife very soon. There is no need for delay, I want you and you need me, and Beatrice ought to go to her husband, which she will not do while she thinks you need her care. So it will be within two weeks at the farthest. You need no preparation, just to come home,—though we will go away farther South for a while, where the season is earlier and where the roses will soon come back to these pale cheeks and vigor to the poor, tired brain."

Rossie let him arrange it all as he pleased, and the wedding took place two weeks from that day in Beatrice's drawing-room, without parade or show, for both bride and groom had suffered too much to care for publicity now; but both were perfectly happy, and Rossie's face was sweet and beautiful as are the faces of Murillo's Madonnas, as she lifted it for her husband's first kiss, and heard him say, "My wife at last, thank God."

There was a trip southward as far as the mountains of Tennessee, where, in a lovely, secluded spot Rossie gained so rapidly both in body and mind, that the second week in May was fixed upon for their return to the

Forrest House, where Aunt Axie again reigned supreme, and where Agnes had found a haven of rest at last. Beatrice, who had gone with Trix and Bunchie to Boston, had offered Agnes a home with her as nursery governess to the children, but Rossie had said to her first, "If you can, Aggie, I wish you would live with me. It will make me happier to have you at the Forrest House," and so Agnes went to the Forrest House, and was there to meet the newly-married couple, when they came back one lovely afternoon in May to take possession of their old house, amid the pealing of bells and the rejoicings of the people, who had assembled in crowds upon the lawn in front of the house, where Everard's most intimate acquaintances had arranged a grand picnic, to which all who were his friends and wished to do him honor were publicly invited. It would seem as if everybody was his friend or Rossie's, for the whole town was out, filling the grounds, which were beautifully decorated, while over the gateway a lovely arch of flowers was erected with the inscription on it, "Welcome to the rightful heirs."

And so, amid the ringing of bells and the huzzas of the crowd, and strains of sweet music as the Rothsay band played a merry strain, Everard and Rossie drove up the avenue and passed into the house where they had known so much joy and sorrow both, and which hereafter was to be to them an abode of perfect peace and happiness.

There was a dance upon the lawn that night, after the hundreds of lamps and lanterns were lighted, and people came from afar to see the sight, which equaled the outdoor fetes of the Champs d'Elyesees, and were continued until the village clock chimed twelve, when, with hearty handshakes and three cheers for Mr. and Mrs. Forrest, the crowd departed to their respective homes, and peace and quiet reigned again at the Forrest House.

And now, there is little more to tell of the characters with whom my readers have grown familiar.

Dr. Morton is still in Boston, and perfectly happy with Beatrice, who is the best of wives and step-mothers, idolized by husband and little ones, and greatly honored by the people, notwithstanding that she sometimes startles them with her independent way of acting and thinking.

Yulah is at the Forrest House in the capacity of waiting-maid, and no one looking at her usually placid German face would dream of the terrible expression it can assume if but the slightest allusion is made to the wretched man who in his felon's cell drags out his miserable days, with no hope of the future, and nothing but horror and remorse in his retrospect of the past. Once or twice he has written to Rossie, asking her forgiveness, and begging her to use her influence to shorten his term of imprisonment. But Rossie is powerless there, and can only weep over her fallen brother, whose punishment she knows is just, and who is but reaping what he sowed so bountifully.

In course of time Everard heard from Michel Fahen of the excitement caused by Rossie's escape, of the means taken at first to trace her, and of the indignation of the people, and the invectives heaped upon Van Schoisner when Michel told, as he was finally compelled to do, what he knew of Rossie's unjust detention as a lunatic. It is more than six months now since Rossie came home a bride, and in that time no cloud, however small, has darkened her domestic horizon or brought a shadow to her face. The house has been refurnished from garret to cellar, and is seldom without guests, both from city and country, while the village people are never tired of taking their friends to see the beautiful grounds, of which they are so proud, and to call upon the fair young matron, on whom the duties of wifehood sit so prettily, and who is as sweet and innocent as in the days when she wore her white sun-bonnet, and was known as Little Rossie Hastings.

THE END